No Price Too High

No P

Warp Marine Corps, Book Two
By C.J. Carella

Published by Fey Dreams Productions, LLC

Cover by: SelfPubBookCovers.com/VISIONS

Books by C.J. Carella

Warp Marine Corps
Decisively Engaged
No Price Too High

Crow and Crew
Acts of Piracy (Forthcoming)

New Olympus Saga:
Armageddon Girl
Doomsday Duet
Apocalypse Dance
The Ragnarok Alternative
The Many-Worlds Odyssey (Forthcoming)

New Olympus Tales:
The Armageddon Girl Companion
Face-Off: Revenge (Forthcoming)

Beyonder Wars:
Bad Vibes (Short Story)
Shadowfall: Las Vegas
Dante's Demons

Contents

"Legionnaires, you became soldiers in order to die, and I'm taking you to a place where you can die!"

- General Francois De Negrier

"The most noble fate a man can endure is to place his own mortal body between his loved home and the war's desolation."

- Robert A. Heinlein

"Our arrows will blot out the sun!"
"Then we will fight in the shade."

- Exchange of words before the battle of Thermopylae, 480 B.C.E.

Prologue: A Hasty Defense

Star System Melendez, Year 163 AFC

BATTLE STATIONS. THIS IS NOT A DRILL.

Rear Admiral (Upper Half) Horacio Elba was halfway down the corridor leading to the Tactical Flag Command Center before the all-hands alert had fully filtered down to his brain; the keening sound of the General Quarters alarm hammered his eardrums and finished waking him up. He'd been sleeping in his uniform ever since the war began, like every other officer in CRURON 56. They'd been on full alert for two months, and their worst fears had finally come true. The aliens were coming.

"Warp emergence, forty light-minutes," the Space Watch Officer announced as Elba walked into the TFCC. The specialist hesitated for a second before delivering the rest of the bad news. "Sir, we've evaluated the energy signatures of the opforce. Given the number of hulls detected entering the system, this has to be the entire Lhan Arkh Upper Quadrant Fleet."

Despair is a sin.

The thought did little to comfort Admiral Elba as he glanced at the holotank display, where the sensor data that had taken the better part of an hour to reach his fleet was being assembled into icons representing the enemy ship classes. Three dreadnoughts. Five battleships. Nine battlecruisers. Twenty destroyers and twenty-five frigates. This was a main thrust into human space, and all he had to oppose it was a pitiful fifteen-ship formation.

His squadron consisted of the *City*-class battlecruiser *USS Charlotte*, six antiquated *President*-class light cruisers, and eight escorts, evenly split between frigates and destroyers. Until a few months ago, this sector, centered around Star System Melendez, had been considered 'safe;' his ships were there to prevent piracy and to keep an eye on the Butterflies and Lizards, the two Starfarer nations with warp lines leading into the system. Both polities had been relatively friendly, but good fences – and decent-sized fleets – made for the best neighbors. The Days of Infamy had changed everything. Several human outposts inside Butterfly and Lizard territories had been attacked and destroyed by angry mobs covertly supported by the Lampreys. The fact those massacres had been allowed to happen turned those Starfarer nations into potential hostiles, and CRURON 56 was far too weak to protect the sector in the face of a serious attack from either of them.

The decision had been made to evacuate Melendez System before one of those notional neutrals switched sides or allowed the Lampreys to move through their territories. They'd hoped there would be enough time to save most of the civilians and merge CRURON 56 with other picket squadrons further down the warp-line.

The Lampreys' arrival meant that the aliens had bribed, bullied or otherwise persuaded one of the two neighboring Startfarers to allow a fleet to enter their territory. Admiral Elba's guess was it'd been the Lizards, who had skirmished with the US a few decades back and were known to hold a grudge. For all he knew, the scaly little bastards might have joined the anti-human coalition.

The admiral shook his head. None of that mattered at the moment. He had a system to defend.

There were twelve million people on Melendez-Four, the only inhabitable planet in the system. An additional million spacers who'd lived and worked on the star system's asteroid belt had been evacuated in the two months since the order was given. Removing the planet's inhabitants was taking far longer. Spacers knew how to travel light and move fast. Dirtsiders had no clue, most of them, anyway. Elba had spent ninety of his hundred-and-fifteen years inside some artificial vehicle or installation, always knowing that the hard vacuum of space was never further than a few dozen feet from where he slept. He understood how quickly things could go hell far better than those who spent their lives at the bottom of a planet's gravity well and took basic life support for granted.

To make matters worse, twenty percent of Melendez-Four's inhabitants, a little under half of those who had been born on the planet, could not endure warp space. Leaving them behind was a death sentence, but taking them into warp, even under full hibernation, would result in over seventy percent fatalities, and any survivors would become incurably insane. Abandoning two million Americans to the tender mercies of the Lampreys would haunt Elba and everyone in CRURON 56 for the rest of their lives.

Removing the nine and a half million who could be saved was proving to be difficult enough. Every freighter, passenger vessel, troop transport and logistical support ship in range had been mobilized and had spent two months ferrying refugees out of Melendez System. Their efforts had saved one million refugees from the planet proper in addition to the spacers. More ships were joining the effort, but it would take three more months to evacuate those that could and would flee.

Time had run out.

"Warp emergence! Ten light minutes from M-4. Same energy signatures."

That would be the enemy's next to last jump. The final warp emergence would put the Lamprey Fleet some ten to twenty light seconds away from Melendez-Four, which would give the enemy time to recover from warp transit and maneuver towards the target, three to five hours away at normal sub-light cruising speeds.

"All ships. Prepare for warp transit," Admiral Elba ordered. His cruiser squadron would emerge in geosynchronous orbit around Melendez-Four. Normally he would have tried to engage the enemy fleet as far out as possible to thin out its numbers, but given the disparity in firepower he decided to operate under the umbrella of the planet's defenses.

Melendez-Four had two orbital fortresses, four Planetary Defense Bases and a local defense fleet comprised of eight monitors, STL ships unable to warp but as heavily armed as a cruiser. Those installations would double CRURON 56's available firepower. If their combined forces inflicted enough losses on the Lampreys, the aliens might break off the attack and allow the evacuation to continue. The hideous ETs weren't known for their intestinal fortitude when it came to pitched battles; they preferred to rely on trickery and would attack only when victory was certain. From what he knew about Lamprey capabilities, his chances of achieving a stalemate were maybe one in three. Not exactly gambling odds, but it was the hand he'd been dealt, and he intended to play it as well he could.

He could order the squadron to run, of course. A simple change in warp coordinates, and his ships would be on their way to the Memphis System, nine warp-hours away. All civilian ships capable of warp transit had already fled, but the eleven million civilians still on the planet would be at the mercy of the Lampreys. The admiral shook his head minutely and let his orders stand.

Transition.

Elba found himself surrounded by the dead. Hundreds of solemn figures looked at him, and he found it difficult to meet their steady gazes, in no small part because he recognized every face he saw. They were the crew of the *Charlotte* and the other ships of CRURON 56. All of whom had been alive and well when the squadron had entered warp space. He was overwhelmed with the certainty those ghosts came from the near future. They were all going to die. And they were going to die at his hands.

Emergence.

It took a few seconds to recover. The admiral shook off the disconcerting vision – *They're only hallucinations*, he sternly told himself – and oversaw the preparations for the battle to come. The monitor squadron moved closer to support his ships and the cruiser squadron rearranged its formation to provide fire lanes for the STL ships and orbital fortresses. When the Lampreys began their slow and ponderous final approach, they would get a warm reception.

"Emergence! Half a light second away!"

"What? Are they insane?"

Lampreys – like all other Starfarer species – took far longer to recover from warp transit than humans. The enemy fleet had arrived at ideal combat range, and the crews of those ships would be incapacitated for as long as thirty seconds. Automated systems could only do so much – true artificial intelligence was not only frowned upon, but turned out to be even more vulnerable to warp space than biological sophonts. Usually the best a ship could do upon emergence was to fire a volley of missiles in the general direction of a target. And even capital ships didn't have enough launch tubes to make such a volley count for much.

These dreadnoughts and battleships were different.

Even as CRURON 56 and the planetary defenders began to fire on the invaders, Admiral Elba peered closely at the alien ships, now that they were close enough for a full sensor scan. Their outlines bulged with box launchers everywhere; they vomited a massive missile volley upon emergence, each ship unleashing as many salvos as a dozen normal ones. Traveling at 0.01 *c*, that swarm of ship-killers would reach the squadron in less than a minute.

"Divert all fire to point defense!" Elba ordered. Every ship and orbital platform stopped targeting the Viper ships and turned their guns against the unexpected onslaught. CRURON 56 could have handled an ordinary volley from an enemy fleet that size, three to four thousand missiles. Point defense emplacements on the *Charlotte* alone could destroy twenty missiles per second at the current range. The rest of his ships were somewhat less capable, but their combined fire would reduce four thousand 'vampires' to a mere handful that couldn't hope to inflict much damage.

Fifty thousand missiles were headed towards Melendez-Four and its defenders.

They did their best. Main and secondary guns shifted their aim and went into rapid-fire mode, risking their tubes and energy modules in a desperate bid for survival. Their laser and graviton charges were grossly overpowered for the job, but their accuracy was just as good as the lighter point-defense weapons. Every missile Elba's ships and the planetary defenses had at hand were hastily reprogrammed to intercept their counterparts and launched. For fifty seconds, starships, monitors, fortresses and planetary defense bases threw everything they had against the impossibly-massive barrage.

At T-minus-thirty seconds, nineteen thousand missiles were left. At T-minus-ten, as the swarm began to converge, presenting better targets, only two thousand remained.

Post-battle calculations estimated some seven hundred and fifty missiles struck CRURON 56 and the orbital defense units.

Charlotte heaved under multiple impacts. Her warp shields swallowed several missiles, but others – too many others – targeted her unprotected sectors, breaching her ordinary force fields and armored hull. Entire compartments were emptied into space or engulfed in plasma fires; the ship shook like a beast in pain. Elba slammed against the harness securing him to the command chair; the impact knocked the breath out of him. Lights flickered for a moment before stabilizing again. His imp dispassionately ran the fleet's damage reports as quickly as they were generated.

All the fortresses and monitors were gone; unprotected by warp shields, they'd been easy prey despite their heavy conventional defenses. Of the light ships, only one badly-damaged frigate remained. A light cruiser had been destroyed outright. The *Charlotte* and the rest of the survivors were all damaged but functional, for whatever that was worth. The admiral had some cracked ribs; two of the tactical center's specialists were down, one of them badly injured, but everyone else was fit for duty.

The Lampreys had plenty of time to recover from warp transit; they began advancing steadily as their beam weapons engaged the survivors of the overwhelming salvo.

Elba was faced with a simple choice: CRURON 56 could stand and die, inflicting negligible losses on the enemy, or it could flee.

No.

A third solution suggested itself.

"Attention all ships," he announced. "Cease fire. Divert all offensive power toward force field generation. Prepare for warp transit." Elba transmitted the coordinates directly to the squadron's warp navigators; they would be the only ones who would know with certainty what was about to happen. All of them understood the situation, and all of them acknowledged the orders without protest. He allowed himself a moment of pride in them. Twenty seconds went by as the enemy ships fired on the silent squadron. Most of the hits were absorbed by the ships' warp shields; the rest didn't inflict enough damage to stop Elba's plan.

"It's been an honor serving with y'all. Engage."

CRURON 56 performed the first warp ramming maneuver in known galactic history.

Five ships entered warp space. The lone frigate tried to follow and died in the attempt, preceding the rest of the squadron's demise by a brief instant.

Each vessel appeared in the path of a Lhan Arkh capital ship. With closure speeds in excess of three hundred kilometers per second and total surprise, there was no chance of avoiding a collision. The American cruisers' warp shields devoured huge chunks of the Lampreys' vessels as they ran into each other. That didn't save the attackers, however. The catastrophic explosions unleashed as each Lamprey warship was destroyed flowed over their shields and onto the unprotected sections of the American ships, consuming them in turn. The Lamprey dreadnoughts and one battleship were destroyed outright. Two others were crippled by near misses.

During his final foray into warp-space, Rear Admiral Elba saw the dead nod at him approvingly.

Earth, Sol System, 163 AFC

"The surviving Lhan Arkh's vessels withdrew without finishing their attack run on Melendez-Four, which still retained its planetary defense bases," Admiral DuPont said as he concluded the report. "There has been no additional enemy activity in the system since then. Given their losses, coupled with the ones sustained at the Battle of Paulus, the Lampreys have been neutralized for at least a year, possibly more. Most of their capital ships in this sector are gone, and their other fleets cannot be reassigned without risking attack from their neighbors. They haven't been quite reduced to a frigate navy, but it's close, and it will take them time to rebuild."

White House Chief of Staff Tyson Keller had always thought kamikaze tactics were for losers, in every sense of the word. CRURON 56 had made their sacrifice count, though. They had saved some ten million people, and given those left behind extra time to hide and hope the Lampreys didn't find them right away when they finally came back. Long-term, however, exchanging a cruiser squadron for three dreadnoughts and a battleship was not worth it. The ETs could replace those hulls and even their crews faster than the US could.

It also means we may or may not be losers, but we sure as hell are losing.

Even worse, the suicide run was the kind of trick that only worked that well once. The JCs figured that the easiest way to deal with warp-ramming was to keep some thrust power in reserve to perform radical maneuvers the moment a close warp emergence was detected, allowing the target to 'dodge' the kamikazes. The end result would be a loss of five to ten percent available power for the enemy, which would lower the chance to ram by over sixty percent, after which the wannabe suicide ship would be a sitting duck with a survival time measured in seconds.

All things considered, however, Tyson couldn't condemn the squadron commander's choice. Elba had sacrificed his command to save millions of civilians. They had lain down their lives between their people and the desolation of war. That's what it all came down to in the end.

"Thank you, Admiral. Keep us appraised."

President Albert P. Hewer terminated the conference call, leaving him alone with Keller in the new and improved Oval Office, located in the District of Nebraska, a patch of marginal farmland that had become the capital of the United Stars of America.

"We can speak freely," Hewer said to his second-hand man. "Just lowered the Cone of Silence." Both men were just old enough – they'd both celebrated their two hundredth birthdays a good while ago – to chuckle at the joke.

"Yes, sir, Mister *Presidente Vitalicio*, sir," Tyson said as he poured himself a drink.

"That gag got stale decades ago, Ty."

"I'll keep making it as long as you keep running for reelection."

"Just to keep me on my toes?"

"Just to remind you this wasn't supposed to be an Eternal Administration. The Puppies chose to help the US, not North Korea."

"You know how it goes. Just when I think I'm out, they pull me back in." Another joke only pre-Contact Ancients would get.

"Heh. You had to quote the worst *Godfather* movie of the bunch." Tyson shrugged. "I know all your excuses by heart, Al. 'Nobody else can do the job.' 'Look at the pack of idiots vying for the White House.' 'After this crisis is over, I'll retire – but, wait, here's another crisis.'"

"I almost quit after we settled the Risshah's hash. Then the Crabs tried to fill the void they left. And after they'd been taught their lesson, along came the Horde. The Gremlins, may they all burn in Hell. And so on and so forth. And now it's the Lampreys, Vipers and the Goddamn Galactic Imperium. You really want to switch horses in the middle of this shitstorm? We may lose the war before the next election anyhow. We don't do posthumous swearing-in ceremonies."

"You don't sound too optimistic," Tyson said. He'd been to the same briefings as the President, and he knew the situation wasn't just terrible, it was close to completely hopeless. But the one good thing about Al was that the man had no quit in him. To hear him spout defeatist crap was worrisome.

"We're stretched too thin," Hewer said. "We don't have the manpower and production capacity. A little under two billion of us, counting immigrants and probationary citizens and every living being that will salute the flag, plus two billion Pan-Asians and about two billion from everyone else, mostly from Africa. There're still less humans in the galaxy than before First Contact. Even with the longevity treatments helping things along. It's depressing."

"We're about due for a population explosion," Tyson pointed out. "People are finally figuring out the kinks of being able to live for centuries. Now, they save enough money to take twenty years off, raise a litter of kids, then go back to the grind. We're going to double in size in about a generation, and double every thirty years of so after that."

"But we don't have a generation. Each member of the Tripartite Galactic Alliance can outgun and out-produce us, let alone as a group. This time, we get to play Imperial Japan during the Second Big Mess; it doesn't matter how good we are if they can bury us in bodies. Or starships, in this case. Especially if they come up with new tricks for a change. Those missile ships are bad news. They play straight into their strengths. Ton by ton, a missile is more expensive than a starship; that volley they fired at those poor bastards at Melendez cost more than the fleet that launched them. They can afford the expense, though. It's just the kind of stunt we used to pull back when we were the industrial powerhouse of the world. Spend a million bucks to put a smart bomb through some poor dumb bastard's window. Except now we're the poor dumb bastards."

"So you're telling me we turned the US into a banana republic for nothing."

"Not a banana republic, an unofficial parliamentary monarchy. Temporarily. We've kept the trappings of a republic and I aim to see the republic restored after we're secure. Assuming we live that long. And no, I'm not surrendering. I just don't know if we can win this one."

"You never know, Al. Vegas odds were that the Snakes were going to eat our lunch, and we made them extinct. We've always been the underdog and we've done pretty well despite that."

"Not like this. Even with the Wyrms weighing in on our side, the numbers look terrible. And the Wyrms will quit on us as soon as things get tough. They know they can negotiate their way out of this. We can't. The Days of Infamy made it clear they don't want a few concessions from us, or even to reduce us to client status. They want us gone from the galaxy, root and branch."

"Then we need to get the Puppies on board."

"They have agreed to help out: lots of supplies, all 'sold' to us with insanely generous credit terms, and a few extra ships, some of them crewed by 'volunteers.' Figure an extra ten percent in firepower, twenty in logistics. Not enough. The House of Royals at the Doghouse is evenly divided, and the High King has decided to stay officially neutral, for now. He'll slip us as much aid as he can without provoking a declaration of war from the triple assholes, but that's about it. It won't make a difference."

"There is the Lexington Project. That's just about ready."

Even as he spoke, Tyson knew he was whistling in the dark. Lexington was a 'super-weapon' project that looked good enough to fast-track, but that didn't mean much. Ordinarily, he'd have considered it a waste of time and money: the resources spent in developing and fielding new weapon systems could have produced a lot more ordinary, tried-and-true ships, missiles and the logistics necessary to keep them running. Problem was, they couldn't match their enemies' production capacity no matter what. Their only hope was to try to come up with some innovation that would overcome the ETs' numerical and industrial superiority.

And who tried to do just that, historically? The Confederacy, with the CSS Virginia *and those suicide subs. The Germans in WW2, with all their* Wunderwaffe *collection. And what did all that inventiveness get them? A big steaming pile of nothing.*

Of course, he reminded himself, in those same wars the winners had also come with a few new toys of their own. Toys like the *USS Monitor*, or Fat Man and Little Boy. But the winning side had also fielded the most battalions and ships. If you went by past history, the US was screwed.

Guess we'll have to make our own history.

"Yep. Lexington is coming on line," Al said, sounding about as enthusiastic as Tyson felt. "Going to take at least a couple of years to fully implement. A year minimum for any kind of deployment, and those new gizmos will be crewed by newbies, with zero combat experience. As likely to get slaughtered as to make a difference. Same with all our other tricks. I don't know if we can produce enough new gadgets, not in time to turn the tide."

"So we buy some time."

"We will try. You heard what the JCS had to say. A few good ideas, but most of them are long shots. The biggest thing going for us is that the Tripartite Alliance isn't coordinating worth a damn. Each bunch is making its own push into our star systems, and the Imperium has been downright halfhearted so far. And the sad thing is, each separate push might be strong enough to steamroll us."

"We play the hand we were dealt, Al. We put it to the touch."

"To win or lose it all. Yeah, maybe I should use Montrose's Toast during the next State of the Union address. That'll cost the Eagle Party a dozen seats in the midterms. People are getting risk averse in their old age. Nobody wants to hear the 'lose it all' part. I sure don't."

"Buck up, Al."

The President looked him in the eye. "We're going down fighting, Ty. But I think we're going down." He shuddered, despair clearly written on his homely features. "Not that I'll let it show when I'm out in public. Never let them see you sweat. And who knows? Maybe the horse will learn how to sing."

Tyson shrugged. That would have to do; Al was getting punch-drunk with the steady stream of bad news coming from every direction, but he would fake it till he made it, and that should be enough for now. Tyson would keep doing his job, of course. There were a few surrender-monkeys in Congress that needed to go, for one. Luckily one of them was into child porn and most of the others had been feathering their nests for a good while. He'd had files on them for a little while and been waiting for the need to use them. Removing those assholes wouldn't even require any wet work. His people in the press would take them down in quick succession, and that would encourage the others not to obstruct the new war plans.

It was going to get ugly, both internally and externally. Wars to the knife were like that.

One

New Parris, Star System Musik, 164 AFC

Charlie Company, Battalion Landing Team, 101st Marine Expeditionary Unit, led the way towards the cauldron of battle.

"Dammit, where's Charlie-Three?" USWMC Captain Peter Fromm said, resisting the impulse to slam a gauntleted fist against a console in the command vehicle. The rest of the company was due to start moving forward in about thirty seconds, a bounding overwatch maneuver that required his weapons platoon (Third Platoon, a.k.a. Charlie-Three) to set up and provide cover for the advance.

Artillery from both sides was already in action; the dull roar of distant explosions was getting closer as the defending Vipers struck out at the three battalions trying to destroy their ground base and the American tubes 'prepared' the area by trying to smash all enemy strongpoints. Speed was vital when going on the offensive: staying still only made you a better target. And the overwatch platoon was behind schedule, holding up everyone else.

"Lieutenant O'Malley sent two squads forward to check for possible snipers," said First Lieutenant Hansen, Fromm's executive officer. "He's confirmed the position is clear and the platoon is deploying. Five more minutes, he says"

To wait would mean delaying the entire battalion's advance. O'Malley's timidity had already cost them ten minutes while he hunted for imaginary snipers. He'd probably caught some ghost sensor reflection and reacted with his typical over-cautiousness. Third Platoon's sergeant would make sure the weapons sections took their positions as quickly as possible, but they were running out of time.

The modified Land Assault Vehicle that served as the company's mobile command post enhanced Fromm's computer implants, enabling him to watch what was happening from multiple angles, from the godlike view afforded by recon drones to the personal helmet sensors of every soldier in his unit. A quick look showed him that the weapons platoon was just beginning to dismount from their vehicles and set up their heavy weapons. Five minutes was an optimistic estimate.

Fromm made a decision. "Send out the Hellcats and Charlie-Two," he ordered, placing icons on the tactical map. "Move Charlie-One over that ridge to the east, have their LAVs set hull-down to provide overwatch while Third gets its head out of its collective ass."

"Roger that." Hansen began to relay the orders while Fromm watched the unfolding situation and prepared for his next move.

Enemy shells were blasting the narrow mountain pass separating the 101st from its primary objective, a Viper Planetary Defense Base. The terrain being traversed by the battalion was a rocky desert plain broken by scattered mesas that rose up to two hundred feet in places. Sections of it were still smoking, indicating spots where defending units had been caught and destroyed by the artillery preparation that had preceded the attack. They were going to have to rush forward and hope the dug-in aliens had been neutralized by the rain of high explosive and plasma that had descended upon them. Intelligence estimated the pass was defended by a company of Viper Crèche Defense fighters (an alternative translation for the alien designation was 'Child Protective Services'). There would be some survivors even after the extended barrage and the longer they left them be, the more likely it was they would try to do something about the invading force.

Movement to contact against unknown and likely strongly-held enemy positions wasn't the kind of thing any commander wanted to do, because the butcher's bill was guaranteed to be high. But the remfies in charge had decided it needed to be done that way, and now it was time to do or die, with any questions to be saved for the after action report.

If things had gone according to their OPORD, Charlie-Three should have been providing cover for the rest of the company from the heights of one the mesas, hitting possible enemy positions with mortars while their missile and heavy gun sections took out anybody trying to engage the American forces. Their slow deployment meant First Platoon would take their place instead of joining in the advance.

The sixteen Hellcats that comprised Fourth Platoon rushed forward. The Mobile Infantry suits looked like mechanical headless felines: four-legged, nine feet long and no more than three feet high at the shoulder, or a foot lower when lying fully prone. Suit and wearer together weighted about two thousand pounds, but they exerted only slightly more pressure per square inch than a standing trooper in normal combat armor. Shields and armor nearly equal to a Land Assault Vehicle's, and enough weapon pods to rival a heavy weapon section completed the ensemble. The Hellcats could run at up to a hundred miles an hour, and their power packs allowed for thirty-six hours of sustained operations.

To Fromm's surprise, the mechanical kitties were performing as advertised. He'd spent the last eight months integrating Charlie-Four into his company, and he still didn't have a good feel for the powered armor systems – or a good feeling about them.

Heavily armed and armored battlesuits had entranced visionaries since long before First Contact. Reality kept disrupting those dreams, however. Once you added enough armor and weapons to justify their use, the artificial musculature necessary to move them at more than a walking speed, and the energy supply required to empower both, what you got was something too tall and bulky to be anything more than a better target. The more armor and shields you added, the better a target it became, until you ended up with a tank rather than anything even vaguely humanoid. After many failed prototypes, a team of designers had realized that, if a bipedal suit of armor wouldn't work in open field combat, maybe a different body plan would. Something like, say, a dog or a cat. The end result now led the way.

Second Platoon followed the Hellcats, five LAVs carrying its three rifle squads, command element and an area field generator that created an invisible umbrella with a three-hundred-yard radius. The troop carriers were long, angular vehicles with a topside bubble turret holding an assortment of support weapons and a boxy four-shot missile launcher on each side. They floated a foot or so off the ground, driven by gravity thrusters at a steady 150 k.p.h. Despite the protection afforded by their heavy force fields and sixty millimeters of carbyne-steel composite armor, any vehicle that stayed in the open for too long risked immediate destruction.

Enemy rockets and shells fell upon the two advancing platoons. Gatling air-defense lasers mounted on the vehicles' turrets went into action, exploding about half of the barrage mid-flight. The surviving munitions detonated against the area force field and went off harmlessly over the advancing vehicles as they pressed forward towards their objective, a clump of massive boulders a quarter of a klick away.

Two hundred and fifty meters – less than three football fields long – isn't a long way when you're dashing forward at over ninety miles an hour. It took Charlie-Two's vehicles and their picket line of Hellcats a little over six seconds to reach their rally point.

It took a lot less for two camouflaged Viper anti-tank teams to emerge from hiding and engage the Marines.

Camo blankets were thrown aside; their spoofing systems had made the Viper's dug-in positions look like a harmless pile of rocks, and they had survived the artillery barrage and evaded detection by the drones orbiting overhead. The closest unmasked position was a grav-gun emplacement; it swung towards one of the Hellcats, but its target caught the sudden movement and managed to shoot first. The MI trooper walked a long burst of 15mm AP rounds into the Viper position before it could line its shot, the plasma penetrators tearing gun and gunners to undistinguishable bits of plastic, metal and charred flesh.

The second team sprang into action a couple of seconds later, and whoever was watching that sector didn't react in time.

A cage launcher holding a quartet of hypervelocity missiles popped out from its concealed position like a jack-in-the-box and fired at Second Platoon's lead LAV. Four depleted uranium darts, propelled with enough acceleration to reach escape velocity in under two seconds, hit their target. The short range meant their speed at the point of impact was a mere five thousand meters per second, but that was enough. The attack had come from inside the area force field's perimeter, so only the vehicle's own shields protected it. They shed one of the missile hits and were overloaded in the process; its tough hull armor sent a second dart flying into the air, leaving a blazing contrail in its wake. The other two penetrated. The LAV spun in place before dropping inertly to the ground. Fromm's tactical display showed the troop carrier's status carat change color from green to red, switching a second later to black. The view from the drones showed the vehicle disappearing in a blossoming fireball. Sixteen men had been inside; their personnel carats all turned black at the same time.

The Vipers didn't live long enough to enjoy the success of their ambush. Less than a second after they fired, they were obliterated by a barrage of plasma and graviton blasts from First Platoon's LAVs. None of that mattered to the dead Marines, of course.

They pressed on. Once Charlie-Two and -Four were deployed defensively, the rest of the company moved forward, except for Third Platoon, which was finally ready for action and had the range and visibility to provide overwatch from their current position while the rest of the company moved to its next objective. About time they were ready to do their damn jobs, Fromm thought bitterly. He'd commanded Charlie-Three during the siege of Kirosha's legations, a brutal extended battle which had shown him the quality of the troops in that unit. They could do better than that.

The Vipers' artillery barrage was intensifying, and they were using coordinated time-on-target shield busters, multi-stage munitions that unleashed half-mile-long plasma jets after an initial explosion meant to weaken or breach the area force fields protecting each platoon. Once the advance reached one of the taller mesas ahead, their bulk would obstruct most of the incoming. Only a few more seconds and they would be safe…

A trio of missiles went off overhead, their baleful discharges spearing through the shield and down towards their target – the company command vehicle. Fromm's universe flashed bright white before fading into darkness.

* * *

"Goddammit," Fromm said, leaning back on his chair when his imp stopped overloading his vision.

Field training exercises combined the realities of moving over actual terrain with extremely vivid sensory input piped directly into everyone's brains via their cybernetic implants. The grueling advance under fire that had ended with his notional demise had felt so close to the real thing that his body was still pumping adrenaline into his bloodstream. The sensory overload that simulated 'death' wasn't anywhere near as traumatic as being on the receiving end of actual high-energy ordnance, as Fromm could attest from all-too-personal experience, but it wasn't pleasant, either.

"Not fun at all," Lieutenant Hansen agreed, recovering from his own administrative murder.

Now that they were done for the rest of the exercise, their training vehicle grounded and showing up on any active unit's sensors as scattered flaming debris, they could watch the rest of the action while they waited for the FTX to be over. The enlisted personnel in the vehicles could slack off; the driver, gunner and comm specialists in the command vehicle leaned back on their seats and played video games or caught up on their emails or Facetergram feeds. Fromm didn't have that luxury; he kept watching the action. The diagrams and visual feeds cleared up as the computers dropped the simulated jamming and interference that had been part of the exercise. He now could see everything that was going on, unimpeded by the normal fog of war.

The loss of Charlie Actual had slowed the advance but not stopped it. One more LAV and three Hellcats had also been reduced to – virtual – wreckage by the artillery barrage. The battalion commander had ordered Charlie Company's survivors to hold their positions and provide cover while Bravo leapfrogged it and pressed forward.

The end result, three hours later, wasn't pretty: over thirty percent casualties, and no joy in taking the objective. The operation had ended in a disaster of historical proportions; Warp Marine units had only taken those casualty levels in a handful of military operations during their century and a half of existence.

Fromm tried not to take it personally, and failed. His company had been the tip of the spear, and it had taken unacceptable losses without achieving anything. There had been no opportunities where a dash of brilliance might have saved the day, the way they so often did in fiction. In reality you did your job and often failed because someone else fucked up, or due to simple bad luck.

He wanted to blame Lieutenant O'Malley but he couldn't. The delay in setting up and providing mortar fire had directly led to the destruction of a squad, but the artillery barrage that had decimated the rest of the company hadn't been his fault. When you maneuvered you were exposed to enemy fire. The MEU's artillery battery hadn't been able to suppress the enemy's. There would be plenty of blame to go around during the post-game analysis.

A big part of him was sick and tired of the training rotation he'd been stuck in for the better part of a year while the war went on. He'd lived through the start of the conflict and two 'minor conflicts' before that; some would think that he'd shed enough blood for God and Country and it was time to let others do their share. When he thought about it rationally, he shared the sentiment. He knew only too well how random chance could take you down no matter how well-trained, tough and motivated you were; this FTX was a case in point. But he still kept poring over briefings about the war, trying to guess where and when the 101st would be deployed. The choice of enemies in the field exercise was probably not an accident. Fromm wanted to get a piece of the Lampreys, but the Vipers would do.

Fighting was the only way he knew how to begin to pay his obligation to the Marines he'd led to their deaths, in Jasper-Five and Astarte-Three. Nothing would ever make up for those losses, but doing his part to make sure their sacrifices wouldn't be in vain was all he had left.

That, and laying down his own life.

* * *

A passing freighter dropped a load of emails from Earth later that evening. Fromm got two, one from Heather McClintock and one from his sister. He read Heather's first.

Fromm hadn't seen her since his last leave, six months ago. He'd hopped a ride on a troop transport headed for Sol System and met her in New Washington, where she'd been stuck behind a desk. The three days they'd spent together had been worth the combined eighteen hours of warp transit. Since then, they'd kept in touch with weekly or monthly emails, depending on how busy they were. Neither of them had a lot of spare time; their energy was focused on their respective careers.

Most people their age had to do that if they wanted to get ahead. In a world where your competition could have decades of experience over you, the only way to rise in the ranks was to work harder than the old farts were willing to. You wanted to make your mark before you were fifty, take twenty years off to raise a family, and then jump back into the grind for another three or four decades. The seventy- to ninety-year olds were the toughest competition. In the Corps, they tended to dominate the Major and Colonel ranks, and filled the talent pool from which general officers were selected. Or, at the enlisted level, they ruled the E-8 and E-9 roost. The ranks above were in the hands of hundred-year olds. Fromm didn't follow the Navy's inner workings, but he figured that their command ranks were filled by the same age brackets, except for the occasional maverick like Lisbeth Zhang, who'd gotten her first ship at the tender age of thirty-two – only lose it at Jasper-Five. Of course, the old bastards would blame Zhang's problems on her age and lack of experience, even though most anybody would have lost their command under those circumstances.

Fromm wondered what'd happened to the ballsy bubblehead officer as he opened Heather's message. He hadn't really followed up on her, but Heather had, and apparently Zhang had left the Navy and dropped off the face of the Earth. She deserved better than that, but a lot of people did. He set that aside and started reading. You could put anything from a full sensory display to mere video or sound clips in an email, but most people still preferred to use the written word to communicate.

All's well, Heather wrote. *Still on desk unit on Old Mother Earth, but that may change in the near future*. Which meant she'd be going out into the field again, probably as an 'illegal' intelligence officer. That usually wasn't as dangerous as being a ground-pounder, but it could have its moments, and if the shit hit the fan the spooks would have little or no support while in far-foreign space.

He could sympathize with being on one's own, surrounded by enemies.

Walking down the middle of the broad street, bullets flattening against his force field, the pressure of a multitude of hits making him stagger slightly as he moved on, the heavy grav-cannon vibrating against his body armor as he unleashed hell on the hundreds, on the thousands of screaming red-skinned aliens in the fancy uniforms of the Kirosha Royal Guard, their bodies torn apart by the relentless energy stream. He guided the beam towards the main target, the shield generator that must be destroyed before the enemy overwhelmed the Starfarer embassies and murdered everyone inside.

A brief flash of light was his only warning before a massive wave of force washed over him...

Fromm blinked. The memories of those frenzied minutes still came back once in a while, uninvited guests he hadn't quite learned how to get rid of. The dreams were bad; the urge to cringe or throw himself to the ground when hearing an unexpected loud noise was worse. The explosion had ripped off three of his limbs and very nearly killed him. There were wounds that even the best Starfarer tech couldn't repair, and the besieged compound had been running out of critical medical supplies when he'd become a casualty, so the best tech hadn't been available. He had lines of scar tissue at the points where his vat-grown limbs had been attached, courtesy of the emergency patchwork which was the best that Navy corpsmen using substandard methods and materials had managed to achieve. The Frankenstein's Monster-like marks did not affect his range of motion, and removing them would take time he couldn't afford to waste at the moment, so the scars remained, a constant reminder of how close he'd come to the end of the line.

He shook his head and read the rest of the email; whatever joy he'd been feeling at hearing from Heather was gone, replaced with a dull, bleak numbness. The flashbacks had a way of ruining his mood.

The rest of the email became just words on his field of vision, the warmth they usually stirred in him gone. Even the news that former Ambassador Llewellyn was getting his just desserts failed to cheer him up. Llewellyn, whose incompetence had helped precipitate the crisis that killed dozens of Americans at Jasper-Five, was currently serving a four-year sentence in Venus, assigned to the terraforming project there. Working on the second planet from the sun was nobody's idea of fun; the convicts would be trapped in small subterranean habitats, doing hard labor while surrounded by a lethal atmosphere with an average temperature in the hundreds of degrees even after fifty years of artificial cooling. With a war on, on the other hand, hard time in Venus might be considered a lucky break; convicts could be inducted into penal battalions and used as cannon fodder, but that was rarely done. Fromm doubted Llewellyn would count himself lucky; the fact that his family connections hadn't saved him from his fate also meant he'd been finally cut off from their support. The 'rat might even have to figure out how to work for a living after his sentence was over, assuming he didn't piss someone off and end up the victim of an 'unfortunate accident.' Those were easy to come by in Venus.

Other people's suffering, even when well-deserved, had never pleased him very much, and in his current mood the news mostly irritated him. He skimmed over Heather's parting words – she wasn't one for effusive endearments anyway – and went over the dutiful message from her sister. Lucinda Fromm-Bertucci and her husband ran a catering service for the rich and famous in Windsor. She hadn't had any contact with the military after doing her four years' Obligatory Service, spent largely in Logistics, and she acted as if her very survival had nothing to do with the efforts of men and women in uniform fighting and dying light years away from home. Her email didn't mention the war at all, except to note that business was down because there were 'hardly any receptions or parties being thrown in the city.' She concluded her email with a terse 'Take care.' That only deepened his dark mood.

Sometimes he wondered why he did any of this. Whether anything mattered at all. He remembered the day he'd chosen life in the Corps, when such things had mattered very much, but the memories seemed distant, like someone else's story.

Windsor, New Michigan, 153 AFC

"You can't be serious."

Peter Fromm shrugged and looked away from his friends, savoring the view from the high-rise where they were throwing the End of Ob-Serv party. The open balcony looked upon the lake where the city of Detroit and much of the original site of Windsor, Canada had once stood. His imp provided a pre-Contact image of the cityscape that the Snakes had burned into slag, creating a miles-wide crater that Lake St. Clair and the Detroit River had quickly filled. He didn't need video replays to remind him of the screaming and dying of its inhabitants. The restless ghosts of the dead still called out to him, a hundred and fifty years after the fact. The doomed people of Detroit-Windsor had left hundreds of hours of audiovisual records of their demise, and Fromm had watched most of them, obsessively going over the worst ones.

"Pete? Hello? Anybody home?"

He turned his gaze back to the inside of the luxury apartment where a bunch of other twenty-something Freebirds were cavorting; he'd missed something June or Brad had said. It'd be easy enough to have his imp play back the tape and find out what they'd told him, but he didn't bother. His friends would be happy to repeat themselves.

"Sorry," he said.

"You're not even drunk or stoned," June Gillespie said accusingly. "And you don't get to drop that bombshell and then ignore us. What's your excuse? We just got out and you're ready to go back in? After you almost got killed?"

A brief image flashed through his mind – the hulking shapes of Horde pirates, plasma rounds detonating uselessly on their heavy force fields as they advanced towards him and the rest of his squad. He repressed a shudder and turned it into a shrug.

"I'm staying in, that's all. It's a good deal, and I'll be going to college, same as you."

"New Annapolis," Brad said in the same tones he would have used for 'the Seventh Circle of Hell.' "How about NIT? What happened to the plan?"

"Now you sound like my father." Fromm's parents had been elated when the acceptance e-package from the Nebraska Institute of Technology had arrived. Getting a degree from the premiere school in the nation was a golden ticket, a stepping stone to wealth and glory. Brad and June had also been accepted; their plan had been to all go there once they were free and clear.

Had. Plans changed.

He'd thought about showing up to the party in his dress blues, but that wouldn't have gone over well. Telling his best friends that he had just signed for a full ten years in the Corps was turning out badly enough. Almost as badly as telling his family had been, earlier that day.

"Well, your old man is right, Pete. It's a waste, man. A total waste. We already did our time in uniform. Time to get on with real life. To have a life without being told when to sleep, wake up, eat, take a dump. Seriously. Did you enjoy that shit so much you're going back for a big heap of seconds? You did your duty. You even got to fight. Just what you get when you do your last two years in the freaking Corps. That thing at Galileo-Nine should have gotten all that hero crap out of your system."

The pirate was eight feet tall and almost as wide. He swung the heavy particle-beam projector and played the ongoing energy pulses like a hose. Two of Fromm's squaddies screamed briefly before their shields failed and they were torn apart. Fromm's Iwo cycled empty; he closed his eyes, unaware he'd been screaming as well until First Sergeant Bolton shook him and slammed him into a bulkhead, shutting him up. When he dared to look, he saw the massive alien's body sprawled three feet in front of him, smoke pouring from the exit wounds on his back.

Everybody in his squad but him was dead.

"You got 'im, Fromm," the NCO said. "Not bad for a Foxtrot-November, even if you punked out at the end. Now quit yer crying and get on your feet, Marine! We ain't done clearing out the station."

He blinked rapidly for a few seconds, slowly realizing he'd almost punched Brad. The sudden motion, which he'd arrested just in time, was completely lost on his friends.

"Take it easy, Brad," June broke in. The look in her face made it clear she knew Brad's badgering wasn't going to help matters. Her boyfriend ignored her, too angry to stop his tirade. Brad and Peter had grown up together, had been as close as brothers. Fromm could see his anger was mostly out of concern. But there was also an element of pique involved: Brad didn't like surprises, or changes of plans, and he took them personally.

"What's with your obsession with the Marines, for Christ's sake? At least in the Navy you can actually make a career."

"Brad!"

"All right, Junes. Sorry, Pete, but I just can't believe you're doing this. We're having this party to celebrate being done with the whole yes-sir, no-sir, three-bags-full-sir crap. Why are you doing this?"

Fromm looked back out and gestured towards the flat expanse that used to be Detroit. It took them a second to get it.

"Jesus. First Contact? Ancient history, Pete. You aren't a Golden Oldie. You didn't live through it. Might as well get upset about the Japanese killing General Custer."

"The ETs are still out there," Fromm said. "There's fighting going on right now, over at Xon System."

Brad sighed. "That's just a police action. A skirmish here or there, or a little conflict whenever someone's worked up the nerve to ask President Hewer if he's ever going to retire and he starts something to distract everyone. We killed off the Snakes over a century ago, man. It's over. The other Starfarers may push us around the edges, but they aren't going to risk an existential war with us."

"That's not what I hear."

"You're taking that Galactic Studies crap too seriously. It's scaremongering, plain and simple, to keep us on an eternal war footing."

"Not really, but never mind that," June said, always the voice of reason. "Okay, forget about Brad and his lack of knowledge about anything that doesn't involve nanotech…"

"Hey!"

"And I quote: 'the Japanese killing General Custer.' Give me a break."

"Didn't they? Or was it the Soviets? Something like that. Who cares?"

"Woogle it." June turned back to Fromm. "Yes, the other Starfarers pose a potential threat. But the fact is, we've got enough soldiers and spacers already. You could be an engineer, a designer, and accomplish a lot more using that brain of yours for something constructive. Why waste all that talent to become a killer?"

"I…" Fromm struggled for words. He didn't know how to explain the incident at Galileo-Nine, the terror he'd felt, and the way he'd set that terror aside and done what he'd had to. He couldn't just say that he'd never felt so alive as during those insane moments in the pirated mining complex. The memories haunted him, but the thought of never going back bothered him more.

I am a killer. He couldn't say that, though; they'd never understand.

And then there were the Detroit Archives. Ancient history, perhaps, but unlike Brad, Fromm felt certain history could easily repeat itself. Starfarer species weren't exterminated routinely, but it happened: three times in the last century and a half, as a matter of fact. Humans had been responsible for one of those extinctions and played a role in the second. To think it couldn't happen to the US, to Earth, was idiotic. Only an over-privileged kid could indulge in that sort of illusion, and not for long.

"Well?" June asked.

"It's what I want to do now," Fromm finally said. "Maybe in ten years I'll change my mind and do something else, but this is what I'm doing now."

Brad started to say something else again, but June shushed him.

"I hope you don't regret this," she said. "But I fear you will."

New Parris, Star System Musik, 164 AFC

"As you may have guessed, ladies and gentlemen, I've got our new marching orders," Fromm told the assembled company officers, platoon commanders and senior NCOs. The non-coms were the oldest people present, all veterans with no less than twenty years in the service, people who had been involved in at least one of the many wars, police actions or low intensity conflicts the USA could not seem to escape as it carved its own place in the galaxy. Charlie Company's commissioned officers ranged in age from their late twenties to early sixties; the older officers had found their niche and were unlikely to rise in rank but were damn good at their job. The dynamics of the Corps often led to senior officers commanding people old enough to be their fathers or grandfathers, resulting in numerous leadership challenges. Young Second Lieutenants were expected to lean heavily on their NCOs, but by the time they got their silver bar, they'd better had learned to do their own thinking, doubly so for those who made it to O-3 rank. Fromm's service record was decent enough that people respected him despite being on the young side.

"We will be deploying in twenty-one days," he continued. It'd been a month since the FTX, and while he wasn't a hundred percent satisfied with the company's progress, the higher-ups had decided they were ready to dance and he was willing to lead them.

"'bout fucken time," First Lieutenant Ivan Guerrero of Second Platoon muttered under his breath. One of the older breed, Charlie-Two's commander had been driving his people hard ever since the FTX; that platoon was the fittest unit under Fromm's command. Which meant it was going to get the toughest assignments. Guerrero knew that, and he was willing and able, full of gung-ho oorah attitude. Maybe to a fault.

"It is what it is. There hasn't been much need for ground-pounders since the war started," Fromm said, and nobody could argue the point. After the Days of Infamy had kicked off the conflict, the ensuing fighting had consisted solely of space actions, and most of those hadn't involved any Marine boarding parties. Warp insertions had been a most unwelcome surprise to other Starfarers in the early days of America's entry into the galactic community, but now just about every alien warship carried a large contingent of troops aboard, making warp raids insanely risky. On the other hand, being forced to carry large security contingents meant enemy ships had less space for weapons, shields and other important systems, so in a sense Marine Assault Ships served an important purpose even when they weren't used. In any case, the one-way teleportation trips had become as rare as massive paratroop operations back in pre-Contact days. Word was that a lot of Marine Assault Ships were being pulled off the line to be reconfigured, although nobody was sure into what.

Fromm agreed with Guerrero's sentiment, but he hadn't minded the quiet time, either. He'd spent the previous months making sure his company was as ready as it could be for the hard days ahead. And he knew only too well that there were going to be plenty of those. He'd been on the front lines during the Days of Infamy and come back from that deployment with three replacement limbs and a large selection of bad memories.

And a handful of good ones, mostly involving a certain female spook he hadn't seen in half a year, but that wasn't important now.

"So here's the deal," he continued. "The 101st Marine Expeditionary Unit has been assigned to the *USS Mattis* as part of Landing Squadron Three." A Landing Squadron consisted of three Marine assault ships like the *Mattis*, a four-frigate escort, and three logistics vessels. "All part of Expeditionary Strike Group Fourteen. We will sail off to reinforce Sixth Fleet at New Jakarta."

More nods, and several somber expressions. New Jakarta was a Pan-Asian colony and warp junction; its location made it a possible target for the Vipers. In theory, the system was shielded from direct invasion by the fact that all its warp lines led to neutral or friendly star systems, but Melendez System had been in a similar position, and the enemy had simply pushed through neutral space, daring the local Starfarers to make an issue out of it. So far, nobody had objected. Some, as in the case of the Lizards, had actually abandoned any pretense of neutrality and welcomed the Tripartite Alliance. Sixth Fleet, plus whatever forces the Greater Asian Co-Prosperity Sphere could put together, would make sure any attacks there were met head-on.

"We have a week to implement any changes and fix anything that needs fixing," Fromm said. He glanced at the company's senior NCO.

"We'll be ready, sir," First Sergeant Markus Goldberg said confidently. Privately, Goldberg still harbored doubts about Third Platoon's Lieutenant O'Malley. The officer's slow reaction time and tendency to rely too much on his sergeant had become apparent during the FTX. A counseling session had ended with multiple assurances things would change. Fromm had fought off the urge to meddle, and now he was worried he might have overcompensated and left the unit in the hands of a subpar commander.

"I know everyone will be ready," he said in a confident tone.

* * *

"Why don't we all take a breath?" Lance Corporal Russell 'Russet' Edwin said in what he thought was a reasonable tone. He was the only asshole without a drawn weapon and when you're outgunned, your best option is to be reasonable.

The hooker's crib was much too small to fit four people. A bed and a small dresser filled most of the space; the only other piece of furniture, a nightstand, was currently being wielded by the hooker in question, a plump and pretty girl by the name of Francesca, formerly from the People's Republic of Sicily, here on a guest worker's visa earning a living the old fashioned way. She was crouched on the bed, naked as the day she'd been born, ready to start swinging with her improvised club. Blood was dribbling from a cut on her lip, and the left side of her face was already beginning to bruise. Her eyes were bright with murderous rage.

Standing next to the bed was Russell's fellow Marine, PFC Hiram 'Nacle' Hamlin, a lanky kid straight from New Deseret, currently holding a set of brass knuckles that Russell had given him for Christmas. There was blood on the business end of the weapon, but Russell was certain none of it belonged to Francesca but rather to the other bleeder in the room, a fat Navy asshole who was half-propped against the opposite corner, his nose spurting red and glaring out of the one eye that hadn't been punched shut. His injuries wouldn't stop him from using the holdout beamer he was clutching in a trembling hand, though. The little pistol's power pack only had enough power for six shots, but each of them would cook twenty or thirty pounds of flesh and organs with a direct hit, or burn right through an arm or a leg. The bubblehead had been nerving himself to shoot Nacle, Francesca or likely both of them when Russell walked into the room and interrupted the ongoing drama.

Just seconds ago, he'd been enjoying the amorous attentions of another lady of the night, a sweet little thing from the Canary Islands whose name he couldn't recall at the moment. Shouted curses and the sounds of a scuffle next door wouldn't have drawn him away from what's-her-name, not usually, but he'd recognized Nacle's voice, and the cursing had gotten his attention. Nacle only cursed when the shit had well and truly hit the fan. So he'd rushed towards the noise and walked into this Charlie-Foxtrot.

The bubblehead turned his beamer on him. Three pounds of trigger pressure and Russell would be seeing Jesus or the guy downstairs, more likely the latter, or even more likely he'd be seeing nothing at all. It was times like these when Russell wished he could believe in something.

"Easy there," he told the Navy guy. "Chief Petty Officer Murphy, right?" He'd seen the bubblehead around, mostly in low-rent whorehouses like this one. Murphy had a bad rep; he was an asshole, the kind who liked to get rough with the girls, ignoring safe-words and house rules; he'd been banned from a lot of establishments in and around Pendleton as a result.

"Edison," Murphy said, or rather lisped; a thin spray of blood and spittle accompanied the name, and Russell caught a glimpse of jagged broken teeth. Nacle had been going to town on the fucker before the beamer came into play.

"That's me; Lance Corporal Edison," Russell said cheerfully, as if he'd run into the guy at a party.

"Your cock-sucker buddy just tried to kill me."

"She told you *never* to lay hands on her," Nacle said through clenched teeth. "She told you."

Shit. The kid was sweet on Francesca. He didn't play with whores all that much, and when he did he got all romantic on them. Stupid.

"Stow it, Nacle," Russell hissed at him before turning back to Murphy. "Hey, Murph. Let's be reasonable. There's been no real harm done…"

"No harm?"

The beamer wavered between Russell and Nacle.

"The med techs will fix your mouth, Murph. No fuss no muss. You just tripped and fell, that's all. That shit happens all the time. But you pull that trigger and it's all over, brah. For whoever you shoot, and for you."

"Fuck you!"

"Fuck me? Murph, you pull that trigger, you'll be fucking yourself."

The asshole was drunk, in pain and pissed off, so there was no telling what he was going to do. Russell waited, wondering if this was the way he was going to step out. The sad thing about all this wasn't that he'd been this close to death a bunch of times before, but that he'd been this close to death *in a whorehouse* a bunch of times before. This was supposed to be the kind of place you went to forget about all the close calls that happened when you were on duty. But Russell had always been a frugal shopper, and bad things often happened at discount brothels.

Nacle tensed up, about to do something stupid.

Stop! Russell texted him via his imp's tactical channel. The kid froze.

Out loud: "Whaddayasay, Murph? Can we work things out?"

Murphy looked like he was trying to think about it but finding it a bit of a chore. Concussion, maybe.

"Va fanculo!" Francesca screamed all of a sudden and threw the nightstand at the bubblehead.

If she'd tried that boneheaded move on a Marine, she would have gotten blasted, and everyone else as well. Murphy didn't have those killer instincts, though. He flinched and threw up his arms to protect his already battered face, and Nacle and Russell lunged at him before he could bring the weapon back into line.

The beamer went off, but Russell had already grabbed Murphy's hand at the wrist, and the charged-particle bolt made a hole in the ceiling. Nacle had the asshole pressed against the wall and was delivering a series of brutal underhand jabs, the brass knuckles making a wet smacking sound every time they hit flesh. Murphy whimpered, then screamed when Russell got enough leverage to break the man's wrist. The little pistol dropped to the floor. Francesca started to make a grab for it, but Russell kicked it under the bed before things went from bad to unsalvageable.

The Navy puke sagged down, barely conscious. "You fucking asshole," Russell said in a mild voice. "You pull a gun on me, you better have a plot saved up."

"He was hitting her," Nacle said, punching him one more time. Murphy went limp and they let him flop to the floor like a bag of meat. "She called me on my imp. I was kind of okay if all they did was have sex, you know? It's her job. But he didn't have to hit her."

"I know." Russell turned to Francesca, who was beginning to get the shakes. "Where's Ronnie?"

She shook her head. "Dunno."

Ronnie was the whorehouse's bouncer, a massive guy with heavy-worlder muscle enhancements. He must be drunk or stoned, or Murphy had paid him off to look the other way while he had his fun. Either way, he wasn't going to be much help.

"Grab his shit. All of it," Russell ordered Nacle while he knelt down and groped under the bed until he found the beamer.

"He pay you?" he asked Francesca while his buddy gathered the bubblehead's clothes and personal items.

"No."

"Okay. Put the stuff on the bed, Nacle." He rummaged around until he found a couple of credit sticks among Murphy's things, the kind of device you used to pay for stuff you didn't want showing up in your financial statements. Prostitution was technically illegal in New Parris, although nobody had ever been arrested for it unless there'd been another crime involved. Francesca's work card listed her as an 'entertainer.' Russell checked the credit sticks' balances and handed her one of them, about three hundred bucks' worth, three times her going rate for a full evening. "That should cover your time. This never happened, got it?"

She nodded. Russell wouldn't expect her to hold out if the cops leaned on her, but hopefully it wouldn't come to that.

"Give us the room. We need to take care of this."

"*Molto bene*." She hugged Nacle and whispered something in his ear before she threw a bathrobe on and left. Hopefully the guy would get a discount for his next date. Least he should get for almost getting their asses killed.

Russell considered his options. He could call Gonzo and a couple of other close friends, the ones who'd help you move a body, and make Chief Petty Officer Murphy disappear. He'd done it before, but never on New Parris. There was shit you could pull off on deployment in far foreign that just wouldn't fly at home, and the Marine Corps' main base was as close to home as it got. Too many cameras, too many people with their imps recording everything they saw. If the asshole went missing, there would be an investigation, and even though Murphy clearly didn't have many friends, the chances of their getting away with killing the bastard weren't great.

If it came down to it, he'd do what he had to, but there were alternatives.

* * *

"You shoulda wasted the fucker," Gonzo commented when Russell told the story over a card game a couple weeks later, on their last liberty before they sailed off on the *Mattis*.

"More trouble than it was worth. I took care of it."

"How?"

"Well, turns out Murph had a whole system going. He liked to beat on women; guess that was the only way he could get it up. He bribed the bouncer to look the other way and brought a couple doses of memory-wipe drugs and a full set of nano-meds to his dates. He'd have his fun, then heal up the girl and make sure she didn't remember anything. He'd been doing it for a while. So we used his own drugs on him, made sure his imp wasn't recording, which it wasn't, and when he woke up the next day he had no idea what'd happened to him, other than he was missing a bunch of teeth; the nano-meds he'd brought fixed his insides and the broken wrist, but not his mouth."

"That it? All he got was a beatdown he doesn't remember?" Gonzo said. "He pulled a gun on you and Nacle. That don't seem fair."

"No, that wasn't it. I figured that kind of hobby costs a lot more money than a Chief Petty Officer makes. I did a little digging that night and found out he'd been skimming supplies off his ship and selling them on the side to pay for his fun. He was at the Med Center trying to get new teeth fabbed when the MPs picked him up. He'll get a good fifty years' hard labor; some of those supplies were pretty important, the kind of stuff that gets people killed if they run out at the wrong time."

"What an asshole."

"Chances are he won't live through those fifty years. Couldn't happen to a nicer guy."

"How about the bouncer?"

"He's MIA. A lot of people weren't happy with him after it all came out, and nobody's going to miss him."

Everybody at the table nodded. The local cathouses enforced their own brand of justice, and they could play very rough. Ronnie's over-muscled body would never be found, and he was sure the bouncer hadn't gone gently into the night, either. Russell wouldn't be surprised if someone invested some money into making sure former CPO Murphy didn't make it out of prison in one piece. He wouldn't be surprised at all.

"Well, that's that, then," Gonzo said.

"Yeah. Nacle should be all right now."

"Well, he won't end up on the wrong end of a court martial, but that don't mean he'll be all right. He's sweet on that girl, isn't he?" Gonzo grinned; he was clearly planning to give the Mormon kid a hard time about it. Russell reminded himself to make sure things didn't go too far; he'd seen how Nacle reacted when he got his dander up.

"He's a romantic. He'll get over it. It's not like he was going to marry her and bring her to Mama and Papa over at New Deseret. It don't matter none anyways. We're off to kill us some ETs. That will cheer him up."

"True that."

Two

Earth, Sol System, 164 AFC

"Let's be blunt, Commander," the Marine Major said. "Your career in the Navy is ruined. You know that."

"Yes, sir," Lieutenant Commander Lisbeth Zhang agreed, trying not to squirm in her seat. The jarhead was simply stating the facts, but she didn't enjoy being reminded of them.

Even in wartime, you didn't go very far after losing a ship, let alone both vessels in the task unit you were commanding. If you did, you'd better go down with said ship. You most certainly weren't supposed to be the sole survivor of such a disaster. Whatever the circumstances, at first glance it looked as if she'd abandoned her command and left everyone in it to die, and too often a first glance was all you ever got. Her subsequent actions on Jasper-Five had not been enough to redeem herself in the merciless eyes of the Bureau of Navy Personnel. As far as BUPERS was concerned, Lisbeth had been tried and found wanting. She'd been cleared of any actual wrongdoing, but that didn't mean she was going to be in a starship bridge any time soon.

Lisbeth had spent the last few months on the beach, stranded on Earth while waiting for new orders. Nobody seemed to know what to do with her, or want to spend much thought on the matter. Even with the massive mobilization going on, there were more available officers than hulls, so she'd probably be stuck on some non-combat assignment when they finally decided to make her earn her munificent pay. It would be decades, if ever, before she went into the dark, and then it'd be somewhere in Logistics, probably as the XO of a supply scow, not anywhere near a combat vessel. If she spent a century doing her best, maybe that would change, or maybe not. A service ruled by near-immortals had a long memory, both institutional and personal.

"Your record shows a great deal of potential, however," the jarhead officer went on. "Among other things, you are a superb small-craft pilot. Aced all your shuttle qualifiers as a cadet, and your handling of that escape pod when it came apart over Jasper-Five was impressive."

"Thank you, sir," she said, suppressing a snort. Yeah, she could handle a shuttle. Which had as much to do with commanding a warship as her skills in hand to hand combat, or in basket weaving for that matter. She already regretted agreeing to this interview, but she'd been advised not to miss it by her few remaining friends in the service. Beggars couldn't be choosers.

"And you have a Warp Rating of 3," the major added. "The Corps is prepared to offer you a position in a new program. A black program, which limits what I can tell you about it, among other things because I don't need to know very much about it. You won't be briefed any further until after you accept the offer. Until you are at your new post, to be exact. You would transfer to the Corps, and the move would entail a loss in grade, but I'm told that you will pick up rank rather rapidly. The assignment will involve a remote deployment, mostly out of contact, for an undetermined length of time."

Lisbeth's eyes widened as the Marine officer spoke. The questions and the statement about her warp rating pointed towards something that had long been rejected as impossible. Could it be...? It was the only thing that fit. She fought to keep her face impassive as the leatherneck finished his spiel.

"Where do I sign up?" she said as soon as he was done.

Groom Base, Star System 3490, 164 AFC

USWMC Captain Lisbeth Zhang watched the screens as the transport ship made its final approach and waited to see if her guess had been more than a wild-eyed fantasy.

Fantasy or not, there she was, at the ass end of the galaxy, some gigabytes' worth of paperwork later, wearing her brand-new Marine uniform. She'd made Captain at last, although a Marine Captain was a mere O-3, three ranks below a Navy Captain and one rank below her previous pay grade. It sucked, but at least she had a career path of sorts ahead of her. The jarheads would value her ground combat experience a lot more than the Navy, that was for sure. And if she was right about this black project, she might be going into space combat a lot sooner than she'd ever hoped to.

The transport ship's viewing room was crowded; most of the passengers were volunteers who knew very little about their mission and who'd rushed to take a gander at their destination as soon as the ship emerged from warp. Lisbeth traded glances with her fellow recruits; her imp revealed the public details of their records, popping up in her field of vision when she focused on any of them. They were all officers. The Marines were mostly 75s – their Military Occupation Specialties were focused on shuttle piloting. There was also a smattering of former Navy personnel, all recent transfers to the Corps, all with high scores in small craft handling. Lisbeth was the only one who had commanded a warship, which made her feel all kinds of special. Not.

Everyone, Navy or gyrene, had a high warp rating. You needed a WR-2 to serve on the bridge of a starship or be launched from a warp catapult with a reasonable expectation you'd come out the other side. The indispensable and rather strange warp navigators, the men and women who actually willed a ship to come out the other end of a warp point, were rated at 3 or higher. A large percentage of WR-2s ended up in the Corps just so the jarheads could send them to their near-certain deaths, something she found incredibly wasteful. Okay, maybe it wasn't a near-certain death, but it wasn't exactly safe.

All the volunteers in the transport ship had the silver or gold spiral symbol on their profiles that denoted a WR-3 or -4. Even considering that over fifty percent of humanity was warp-rated, about five times the ratio of the next most FTL-adept species in the known galaxy, this group was pretty unusual.

Everyone in the transport had pointedly kept their thoughts about the project to themselves, but most of them must suspect the exact same thing she did. Just cross-checking their public records was enough. All her life, she'd grown up reading, watching movies and playing games involving a fighting platform that Starfarers didn't use, that everyone said just couldn't be effectively deployed in combat. But humans had been breaking all kinds of rules since First Contact. What was one more?

Star System 3490 didn't even rate a name and didn't look all that impressive on the data and viewing screens. It was a red dwarf, and a warp dead end, connected to a minor American colony by a single ley line. The closest thing to an inhabitable world in the system was a Mars-like planet with an unbreathably-thin atmosphere and average temperatures in the twenty-degree Fahrenheit range; its only saving graces were its near-Earth gravity and its Class Two microbiology, which had released some oxygen into the air, even if not in enough concentration to support humans.

Someone had been spending a lot of time and energy on the planet: there was a ground installation large enough to fit in a good ten, twenty-thousand people, and an orbital starship yard busily at work on a number of vessels Lisbeth quickly identified as assault ships, the troop carriers that could conduct shuttle and warp-catapult deployments and which, while officially Navy property, were largely manned by the Corps. Just the sort of ships the senior service might consider expendable enough to lend to this black project.

"Holy shit," one of her fellow Marines said, glancing at another part of the viewing screen.

Lisbeth had seen plenty of warp emergences before, even at this close range, mere kilometers away. The sight was no longer awe-inspiring, although it was never something you ever got fully used to. People described it as a shimmering glow followed by a display of colors not unlike the aurora borealis on Earth. The glowing colors had a depth to them, though; they inspired the feeling of peering into a vast chasm with no bottom in sight. Everyone felt a brief thrill of vertigo when looking into a warp breach; a few of the spectators in the viewing room wobbled on their feet.

Twelve tears in the fabric of space-time appeared at the same time, clustered closely together. Twelve tiny ships emerged from them. Her imp provided her with a size estimate: about the same length of a standard combat shuttle, but with a narrower profile. They weren't pretty. Lisbeth magnified the image, focusing on one of the vessels, and saw what looked like a capital ship's energy cannon with several graviton thrusters, warp generators and other systems welded all around it. Shimmering warp shields in the front and rear made it hard to pick up details. But the fact that it had warp shields was impressive enough. Nothing that size should be able to mount warp generators.

The squadron kept station with the transport ship for several seconds. Nobody spoke until they dropped back into warp and disappeared from sight.

"Warp fighters," another Marine officer said, wonder in her voice. "They fucking did it. Warp fighters!"

The common room erupted in cheers.

Lisbeth cheered along. She'd guessed right, and her life was never going to be the same.

* * *

The first briefing was thrilling and sobering at the same time.

"You're probably wondering why I've gathered you here," the brigadier general giving the toy-and-pony show said, drawing a few chuckles from the crowd. There were over two hundred of them in the auditorium, about one-third of them female, which made sense, since shuttlecraft pilot was one of the few combat career paths more or less open to women. The physical requirements weren't quite as harsh, and few females wanted to undergo the costly and painful muscle-and-bone treatments needed to lug a hundred pounds on your back for extended periods of time.

This particular Canine and Equestrian Theater presentation was unusually simple, without the holotank on the podium that meant a PowerGram™ presentation was at hand. In fact, it looked as if the general was going to speak without using any multimedia add-ons, which was somewhat unusual.

"My name is Dennis Singh, and I'm in charge of the Lexington Project. A long time ago, I used to be in the Air Force. Made it to bird colonel a few weeks before First Contact. After a century and a half, it turns out my old skill set has become useful again.

"You've seen them. Yes, they are warp-capable attack ships. And yes, we want you to fly them."

There was the beginning of a cheerful roar, but the general quickly put a stop to it.

"This is going to be no picnic, ladies and gentlemen. We are fielding a genuinely new weapon platform, the first since we developed warp shields and catapults, before most of you were born. As all of you know, Starfarer technology has been stable for thousands of years: ship designs that came out when we hairless monkeys were hunting mammoth with spears are still in service, with only a few tweaks here and there. Through Providence or random chance or what have you, humans have certain unique capabilities that have allowed us to develop new technological applications that no one else even considered, simply because no other known species can make use of them. Count your blessings: it is the only reason we're still here."

The enthusiasm of the crowd dimmed somewhat. Everyone knew that humanity's continued survival was as close to a miracle as you could get: without their species' tolerance to warp space, Earth would have been depopulated by the Lampreys when they came back to finish the job they'd started during First Contact. And that miracle hadn't been cheap, either. No matter what one's warp rating was, nobody enjoyed the experience of leaving standard four-dimensional reality and plunging into a place that nobody really knew much about, other than that it provided the only way to break the laws of relativity and move from one point to another faster than the speed of light. There were a myriad side effects: temporal distortions, hallucinations and extreme psychological stress were just the most common. And they got worse the more frequently you jumped, especially without adequate time to recover between transitions. Humans handled those side effects better than everyone else, but they still paid a price for the privilege of traversing astronomical distances in the blink of an eye.

A civilian starship's crew could expect to perform two or three warp jumps a week during routine operations. Military maneuvers required multiple transits, often separated by minutes instead of hours, with vastly increased risks. Even human crews took casualties after more than four or five jumps in a day.

They'd seen the warp fighter demonstration outside. The tiny ships had done two warp jumps in a matter of *seconds*. The implications of that feat began to sink in.

"Why are humans different from the rest of the inhabitants of the galaxy?" General Singh asked rhetorically. "To begin to address that question, I must go on a brief foray into Galactic history. We are not the first to have this distinction, just the only ones in recent history. As Fermi's Paradox suggests, many thousands of technologically-advanced species have risen in the billions of years since the formation of the Milky Way Galaxy. And as anyone who took Gal-Hist 101 knows, Starfaring species generally spend one to ten thousand years playing with starships and colonizing planets, after which they either Transcend or die out. What happens when you Transcend is unknown; the species or civilization in question simply goes somewhere else, leaving only well-policed ruins behind. Over millions of years, most of their records have been lost as well.

"From the fragments that remain, however, there are stories about 'warp-wizards,' species that could use warp-space in ways most others cannot. They tend to spread rapidly and dominate much of the galaxy before moving on or being destroyed. Which helps explain why so many Starfarers have a hair up their butts when it comes to us.

"Our ability to resist warp transit appears to be both biological and cultural. At some point in our evolution, humanity developed a mutation that enables our minds to cope with warp space. Our studies show that this mutation is directly related to the human brain's ability to enter a trance state. As it turns out, most sophonts are not capable of going into trances or similar altered states of consciousness, unless they are well and truly insane, as in nonfunctional, chewing on the walls insane. Which I suppose means you don't have to be crazy to travel into warp space, but it surely helps."

Some chuckling followed the comment, but it had a nervous edge.

"The cultural aspect is related to that biological trait. Humans have an over-developed ability to believe in things that cannot be proven to exist. Most of our cultures are more religious than just about every other Starfarer civilization, for example. Call it faith or delusion; we've got more of it than the rest. And it seems to help us endure exposure to warp space. We've been working to enhance that ability through chemical and psychological means. Our goal was to enable humans to endure multiple transits over a short time span."

That sounded dangerously close to brainwashing, Lisbeth thought. People took all kinds of stuff to make warp transitions easier, from common sedatives to mixtures of uppers and downers, some of them highly illegal. She wondered what kind of witches' brew was in store for the pilot candidates.

"The Lexington Project – named after the first US aircraft carrier, by the way – got started at the same time as the initiatives that gave us our spiffy warp shields and Marine assault catapults. Unlike those developments, it took us a long time to get any traction. The Navy gave up on the program, and the Corps picked up the ball, although with a tithe of the original budget. The initial hurdles were in engineering: miniaturizing warp generators so they would fit inside a small fighting platform took some work. Same with graviton thrusters powerful enough to let fighters keep up with capital ships. But most of those problems were solved a good fifty years ago. The hardware wasn't the main problem; the software, the human element, was. To be effective, a warp fighter pilot must be able to endure multiple jumps over a short period of time. Dozens of jumps an hour, to be exact."

Here we go, Lisbeth thought. She liked to listen to Warmetal music, especially the original German stuff, as her way to cope with warp transitions, but there weren't enough metal tunes in the universe for the kind of stuff the jarhead general was talking about.

Once you were inside warp space and the initial shock didn't cripple you mentally or physically, you could endure as long as thirty hours of exposure with only a slightly-increased chances of suffering adverse side effects. But each transition performed without at least a few hours to recover added cumulative strains on the crew and passengers. More than two of them within an hour was highly unadvisable.

If you jumped too many times in too short a time, very bad

things happened. The story of the cruiser *Merrimack* was the most-quoted case. A series of unfortunate events, involving pirates, a multi-system chase, and an ambush, forced the ship to conduct six warp jumps spread over a mere seventy minutes. On the seventh jump, only about thirty percent of the cruiser emerged on the other side – and a single crewmember, the navigator, who died shortly thereafter, stark raving mad the whole time. The rest, all thirty-two hundred of them, were listed as missing, presumed dead.

Death was the best fate you could hope for the missing crew. For all anyone knew, the Merrimacks were still trapped somewhere in warp space.

And that's what you've signed up for.

"We've learned a lot," General Singh went on. "It wasn't easy, or cheap. But we have made several breakthroughs and are finally moving from R&D to full implementation. We are putting the finishing touches on what will become the first space-capable Carrier Strike Group. You will be the last candidate class before we go on our first shakedown cruise. The project is being fast-tracked; I think you all can figure out why."

They all did. Anybody who could do math knew just how bad the odds against the USA were. The question was whether fast-tracking the Lexington Project would produce anything of use in time to change the outcome of the war.

Problem was, she was unlikely to find out the answer until it was too late to change her mind. Not that it mattered. As far as she was concerned, she'd been living on borrowed time ever since her XO sacrificed himself to save her life aboard the *USS Wildcat*. Death didn't scare her all that much.

Failure did.

* * *

Lisbeth had to use every ounce of willpower left in her to make sure her legs didn't wobble on her way out of the flight simulator room.

One big reason regular fighters had no place in space combat was simple: graviton engines had a relatively fixed performance, and they didn't scale down very well. A small ship couldn't go much faster than a big one, and shuttle-sized craft were actually much slower than a full-sized starship. The reactionless grav thrusters that propelled virtually all manned spacecraft had an effective top speed of one thousandth the speed of light. You could move that maximum up by a few tenths of a percent, but that was it. Alternative methods using reaction mass were just impractical for manned vessels. Missiles could reach ten times that speed through the use of magnetic or gravitonic catapults that imparted tremendous initial velocity, along with standard reaction rockets that accelerated them further and gravity or impeller thrusters for steering. Try that with a fighter and you'd be scraping its pilot out of the cockpit, not to mention that a return trip would be somewhat difficult, given that its reaction mass would be exhausted covering any normal engagement distance.

It'd taken some amazing engineering to provide the fighters with enough thrust to keep up with regular ships, but that didn't matter. A slower-than-light fighter was just too slow and small to survive space combat. With a warp drive, the equation changed radically, of course. Warp fighter combat was unlike anything pilots from pre-Contact day would recognize, except for the constant risk of death. Fighters emerged into normal space at a pre-determined speed and heading, usually matching or slightly exceeding the target's, fired a spread of weapons over five to ten seconds, and warped out of existence. During those brief seconds, it would be exposed to return fire, but its warp shields would protect eighty percent of its surface area. The very brief time to acquire and engage the unexpected target would make things very difficult for the defenders. Those warp systems were what make the fighters so deadly.

They were also the reason she was having trouble walking in a straight line.

The simulator couldn't quite replicate what you felt when you performed a warp jump. Instead, if messed with your sense of balance to produce a similar sense of disorientation. It was plenty to make even the simplest things difficult, and when you got that jolt every five seconds or so, things got funky.

She was getting used to it, which left her feeling proud and somewhat dismayed at the same time. After the first round of simulated combat, she'd puked her guts out, along with just about everyone else. They'd had their second flurry of washouts after that. The first one had happened when about half a dozen pilot candidates were deemed physically or psychologically unfit. Unfortunately, the fitness tests were classified, so those poor bastards had traveled all the way here only to be rejected and assigned other duties for the duration of the project. It wasn't scut work; the washouts would end up in other occupational specialties in support, maintenance and flight control. But they weren't going to be flying missions, and Lisbeth knew most of them would feel like losers; she certainly would have if she'd been in their shoes. All in all, they were down seventeen pilots from the original two hundred and twenty-three, and real warp endurance training hadn't even started yet.

"Best rollercoaster ever, isn't it?"

Lisbeth turned toward the speaker, who had just walked – well, staggered – out of another simulator.

"I'm getting used to it," she said. "This time I managed to keep breakfast down."

The fact that she'd skipped breakfast that morning had helped a lot, of course.

"Yeah, I guess I'm getting jaded, too," Lieutenant Fernando Verdi agreed. The Marine pilot was even more than a newbie than she was; he'd gotten roped into the project from the infantry, and any flying he'd ever done before had been while playing *Halo of Duty*'s aerial missions. He grinned at her. "Feel up for a second breakfast? I kinda went light on the first one."

"Yeah, me too. Let's go." Now that it was over she actually felt a little hungry, and her schedule was free until mid-morning.

A few minutes later, they were scarfing down some ersatz eggs and bacon while enjoying the view from the mess hall. Clear sapphire-alloy windows looked down on the largely-barren planet where Groom Base – informally known as 'Area 52 2.0' – was located. Bacteria living in a nearby lake and similar other bodies of water generated some oxygen; the combination of the two made it cheaper to general basic consumables for the base. The star system's location at the end of a single warp line deep inside American space made it ideal to build an anonymous, self-sustaining facility. With very few exceptions, everyone who arrived to Star System 3490 was there for the duration. That was one way to ensure word never got out until Project Lexington, a.k.a. the Flying Circus, was ready to show the ETs a thing or two.

You could send emails or vids out, but only after a team of censors and decryption specialists went over every scrap of data to ensure nothing indicating the nature of the posting made it through. And they got the usual infodump of news, mail and gossip from the rest of the country whenever an American ship arrived bringing supplies. Other than that, they were completely cut off. It would be a boring posting without all the training and tests.

"I looked at your service jacket," Fernando said after a few minutes of eating in companionable silence.

Lisbeth nodded. She'd have been surprised if he hadn't. Everyone checked everyone's public records and Facettergram profiles the second they lay eyes on each other. She knew, for example, that Fernando Verdi had been born in Memphis-Seven, was forty-three years old, had served in the Corps starting on his third year of Obligatory Service and had seen action on five occasions, earning a number of medals and commendations. He also liked to post cute kitty videos and play full-sensory MMOs in his spare time. With a little effort, she could find out what kind of porn he liked, but generally prying to that level was considered impolite.

"I mean, I did a little digging," he went on.

Her grin turned into a frown. That meant requesting access to her full personnel records, which should have resulted in her being notified someone was snooping around. Living in the Second Information Age meant anybody could take a close look at you, but not anonymously. If you peeped on somebody, your identity was revealed to the one you were peeping on. Turnabout was fair play when it came to personal information. At least, that was the theory. There were ways around it.

"I was just curious, okay? Not too many O-4s joined this program; we mostly got shuttle pilots. So I asked around, called in a few favors, unofficial-like."

"So you know the sordid truth. That I had my first command blown up right from under me," she said, not fighting to keep the anger and bitterness out of her voice. If he wanted to pick a fight, he'd get one.

Fernando's expression didn't show any contempt or hostility, though. "It would have happened to anyone, Zhang. The threat board was clear when you made your approach to Jasper-Five. Nobody could have seen that coming. And the stuff you pulled after surviving those mines, well, I think you'll fit in just fine in the Corps. And you have starship command experience. Guess where that'll take you."

"What do you mean?"

"They're refitting a whole bunch of assault ships for the Carrier Strike Group, plus a larger vessel, I think a cruiser although that's still classified, to serve as the flagship. If this takes off, they'll be building a lot more. And they'll need people to captain them. You being a former bubblehead and now a fighter pilot, that puts you on the fast track to command rank."

She had thought about it during her precious spare time, but had dismissed the idea as highly unlikely.

"The Navy will take over as soon as the program is successful," she said. And the Navy wasn't likely to forget her record.

"Maybe. I think the Corps may get to keep the fighters for a good while. For one, they're not just good for blowing starships to smithereens. They're going to be very useful for ground-attack missions, too. Close air support might make a comeback."

"We'll see."

The Navy clearly hadn't wanted anything to do with this program. She could guess the admirals were all asking for more battleships and dreadnoughts while bitching about every penny spent on this 'boondoggle.' But if it proved its worth, they'd be falling over themselves to take over.

None of that mattered though. She'd get to fly, one way or another.

Assuming she learned how to survive multiple warp exposures per minute. They were starting those next week.

Sometimes her job sucked.

Three

Associated Star Province Doklon, 164 AFC

Why does the job always *suck?*

Heather McClintock knew the answer to that, of course. Her previous assignment had sucked ass, but she'd handled it as best as could be expected. And her reward had been an even suckier job, which she'd handled yet again. And her reward for *that* was her current mission. The laughing faces of her parents and siblings mocked her during the seeming eternity of warp transition, ridiculing all the choices that had led her here.

Emergence.

The *USS Narwhal* (currently posing as the private freighter *Cordero*) arrived in the middle of the thick atmosphere of Doklon-Eight, a gas giant in the periphery of the local star system. The ship's physical speed had been close to zero upon emergence, and its military-grade shields held against the impact, but turbulence made it shake uncomfortably. The winds outside were in excess of four hundred miles an hour, and the *Narwhal*'s inertial compensators couldn't quite cancel them out. It was unpleasant but necessary: the massive bulk of Doklon-Eight would mask the energy signature of their jump from enemy sensor systems.

Being shaken inside a tin can after nineteen hours in warp was a perfect capper for the three-month long mission. The *Narwhal* had spent its days traveling from one ley line to another, making an oblique approach towards Imperium space while behaving like the freighter it appeared to be. She'd spent the whole trip surrounded by a team of SOCOM operators, nine-tenths male, two-thirds of which thought it was their sacred duty to pick her up. Granted, they'd mostly been polite enough to take no for an answer, but the whole thing had grown tedious rather quickly.

And now, after a final jump from neutral to enemy territory, the real fun was about to begin.

"Doing a slow orbit around this gas ball," Captain Douglas announced. They'd emerged on the far side of the planet, keeping the gas giant between the ship and Doklon-Three, their ultimate target. "As soon as we have eyes on the objective, we'll send out the insertion team and conduct our final approach."

Heather gritted her teeth. In less than half an hour, she and the rest of the insertion team would be warp-catapulted towards their final destination, the Satrap's Office on Doklon-Three. Most infantry warp jumps spanned no more than two light-seconds. This one would cover almost a light-*hour*. A miniscule distance for a starship, but pushing the limits of survivability for humans protected only by their armored suits.

All part of the job, she thought as she adjusted the clamshell breast-and-back plates covering her upper torso after checking that the twin power packs supplying her force fields and suit systems were both full. She wasn't as familiar with combat armor as a Marine or Special Ops trooper, but she'd had a very recent refresher course on Jasper-Five, courtesy of an endless horde or murderous natives. And now she'd be dropping into another hostile system, one populated by well-equipped locals led by actual Starfarers. This time, a moment's bad luck would result in almost-certain death.

Assuming she survived the warp drop in the first place, of course.

After she sealed her helmet, a network of artificial muscles and carbon-nanotube armored fibers slithered out of their housings in the clamshell chest-piece and covered her limbs with a flexible and damage-resistant webbing that allowed her to carry a hundred and twenty pounds of equipment with very little effort on her part. She checked her weapons – a stubby blaster carbine and a pistol, both firing 3mm bullets – and the far more important portable computer, a small armored briefcase containing enough processing power to serve as a battle fleet information center. Everything was in order.

A short walk through the narrow service corridors led her to the hidden hold where a warp catapult and the rest of the team awaited. Fourteen men and two women, SSEAL – Space, Sea, Air, Land – operators from the US Special Operations Command. Three of the men and both women had the heavy builds indicating extensive muscle-and-bone replacements, enhancements originally developed to allow humans to thrive in heavy-gravity environments but also useful to carry heavy loads and break stuff. Heather had undergone a light version of the procedure, which enabled her to bench press twice her body weight while still looking like a normal human being. The five operators had gone for the full version: they were grotesquely broad-shouldered and thick-limbed, quite capable of wrestling a gorilla and coming out on top, or of rending a normal human limb by limb. More importantly, they could easily carry three hundred pounds of equipment and spare ammo even if their combat suits malfunctioned. One of the women – Petty Officer Faye Deveraux

– had her helmet off; her delicate, freckled-skinned face looked absurdly tiny compared to the rest of her body. She caught sight of Heather and gave her a wink before lowering the featureless helm over her head.

Don't worry, superspy, the operator sent out via her imp. *We'll take good care of you.*

That's sweet, Faye, Heather sent back. *Just don't get in my way.*

Funny.

The rest of the short platoon mostly ignored her. They'd all worked with spooks before, but the two communities didn't care much for each other, and after rebuffing their advances, Heather had been classified as an ice queen who thought she was too good to fraternize with them. She was fine with that. They were all professionals, and they would all do their jobs to the best of their ability. They didn't have to be best friends.

Commander Ben Nalje walked over. The CO of the SSEAL platoon could have just as easily contacted her from the other side of the cargo hold, or anywhere else in the ship, but the physical approach was its own message to the sixteen-man group.

"Everything's nominal," he told her on a private channel. "Ship passives just finished a pre-insertion scan. The visuals are fifty-nine minutes old, but the op-force is right where it's supposed to be. No enemy starships in the system, just as expected. The next arrival isn't due for six weeks."

"Sounds good," she said, not sounding very reassured. They both knew this kind of operation could go sideways without warning, however. The tiniest bit of bad luck could turn months of training and preparation into chaotic and bloody failure. But that was part of the job.

"We've got this," Nalje added, all but exuding confidence.

"Prepare for warp insertion," the *Narwhal*'s skipper said over the all-hands channel.

The seventeen men and women stepped onto the circular platform that would catapult them through time and space. The insertion team and their attached CIA officer could have been robots, their features hidden behind gray-black full helmets. Their body language was relaxed as the operators positioned themselves around the platform, weapons held at the ready.

The countdown began. Heather took a series of breaths calculated to induce the proper state of mind. She closed her eyes in useless reflex; one could not avoid experiencing the reality of warp.

Transition.

Her own way of coping was to concentrate on the objective at hand. Heather went over all the data she would need when she came out the other side. As long as she did that, she could ignore the shadowy figures that surrounded her and the disturbing things they whispered to her.

The Star Province of Doklon was a minor Galactic Imperium domain, a primitive world still in the process of being absorbed and properly colonized. The local species, intelligent tool-using Class Two centauroids, had risen to the equivalent of the Late Bronze Age when the Imperium discovered them. Conquering the planet had followed standard Gal-Imp procedures: the Starfarers had picked a compatible government – in this case, a loose alliance of city-states – and provided it with enough technical aid to take over the world within a few decades. The new ruling classes now served at the pleasure of an appointed System Satrap and sent their children off-world to be educated in the ways of the Imperium, after which they'd come back with more in common with their new overlords than the illiterate masses they would spend centuries uplifting into their roles as good proletarian servants. As far as that sort of thing went, the conquest and assimilation process had been rather civilized. The total number of locals murdered, enslaved and otherwise brutalized in the process had been a mere ten percent or so of the total.

None of that was important to the mission, of course. What made Doklon-Three important was the presence of a Satrap's Office in the planet's capital. The administrative center had a full set of imperial systems on-site, their databanks holding exabytes of information the USA badly needed. Contact between the US and the Galactic Imperium had been minimal; the two Starfarer polities did not have a common border, and trade between them had been done through a long chain of middlemen. Most of the information America had about their newest foe was second-hand. This raid hoped to change that.

Kill you kill you killyoukillyoukillyou…

The gleeful voice echoing through her head sounded just like Uncle Bert. He'd never said those words to her in real life, but there'd always been something off about him, and her childhood suspicions had been confirmed after his suicide and the ensuing discovery of vast volumes of snuff porn he'd hid inside his implant for all those years – some of which he'd produced himself. Here in warp space, his ghostly presence promised her the same horrible fate of his other victims.

The job at hand. That was that mattered. She reviewed the data, ignoring the mad gibbering of the dead serial killer.

Doklon Province was on a far corner of the Imperium, and its primitive civilization and remoteness didn't warrant much in the way of defenses. The only modern facilities were in the Satrap's Office, and they were guarded by a squad of Imperium Legionnaires. There were also two regiments of sepoy infantry nearby, locals armed with laser rifles and light personal force fields. The success of the mission depended on the local troops' reaction time. The information they'd purchased in preparation for the raid suggested they'd be sluggish enough. If their intelligence was wrong, things would get hairy.

Emergence.

Seventeen men and women made the jump. Sixteen arrived.

"Fuck. Jürgen didn't make it."

Heather hadn't seen much of Spacer First Class Karl Jürgen during the trip. The taciturn operator had been a quiet professional who'd done his job as the platoon's heavy machine gunner as well as could be expected. And now he was lost, along with one of the platoon's three heavy weapons.

No time to ponder how that loss would affect the mission, let alone mourn the dead. The team had arrived in two groups. Heather and the eight operators on First Squad had emerged in a formal dining room: she recognized the layout from the virtual simulations they'd all trained in. The main difference between the training holograms and reality was that this room's furniture and elaborate decorations had been destroyed by the warp emergence.

Second Squad's landing point had been right inside the building's communications room, which contained the planet's only store of quantum-entangled transmission particles. QE telegrams were the only way to send instant messages across interstellar distances. The warp intrusion destroyed everything in the room and killed the night crew manning the QE-telegraph. That had been the most important part of the mission, since an Imperium fleet was stationed only forty warp-minutes away from the system. Now there was no way the locals could alert anybody of the raid until the next scheduled starship visit, six weeks away.

"Move out."

First Squad headed out towards the database core while Second Squad secured the Legionnaires' barracks and dealt with any on-duty sentries. Alarms were blaring out: their keening was beyond a human's hearing range, but their suit systems translated them into something they could perceive, just to add to the sense of urgency everyone already felt. Heather followed the team into a wide carpeted hallway, much wider than they would be in a human building, its walls decorated with elaborate native tapestries depicting heroic historical events. The raid had been timed to strike late at night, at the local equivalent of three a.m., when diurnal metabolisms were at their lowest ebb. They were halfway towards their objective before they ran into the first local.

The Doklon native wore a servant's livery, a simple purple-white-tunic with six sleeves or trousers. It came from around a corner, froze at the shocking sight, and was cut down by Petty Officer Deveraux. Her carbine fired a burst of subsonic rounds that struck the servant with a trio of barely-audible pops. Despite being almost as large as a Terran horse, the centaur dropped like a rock under the impacts: the 3mm slugs delivered a fast-acting neurotoxin, guaranteed to kill any Class Two species in the space of a heartbeat. The squad moved on while the unfortunate Doklonite kicked feebly a couple of times before expiring.

The Core Room was around a corner. The point man caught a couple more natives rushing towards its entrance and turned their graceful gallop into a crashing mess of tangling limbs with two center-of-mass bursts of poisoned bullets. Heather watched the killings from a vid-feed up on one corner of her field of vision as she moved up. She turned the corner in time to see one of the operators kicking down the door.

A lone Imperium civilian was inside, a member of the Taro species, bulky purple-skinned bipeds with a forest of twisting sensory cilia on their heads filling the role of ears, eyes and nose. The alien was sitting by his desk, apparently doing nothing, but Heather's imp caught a stream of information emanating from his cyber-implants, sending out instructions to wipe out the data cores in the room. He caught two bullets in the chest and one in the head for his troubles, but the systems were already self-destructing.

Unfortunately for the brave Imperial, Heather had come prepared for such an eventuality.

Even as the systems running the data cores began to comply with the now-dead ET's final command, Heather used her implants to hack into them. Access codes that had taken years and millions of dollars to acquire stopped the wipeout orders in their tracks before they could erase more than a fraction of a percent of the priceless data.

An Imperium Data Core contained all the information needed to run a major settlement and provide it with the equivalent of Earth's old Internet, as well as the contents of public libraries, databases and government files. And the confidential files of assorted government agencies. Not everything, only what the local Satrap would need to know, but that was more than enough to justify risking a special operations starship, a platoon of SSEALs and a CIA agent.

Heather pushed the corpse off the desk and placed the portable device on it, letting it do the rest of the work. Reams of data flowed into the little case at a transmission speed of hundreds of petabytes per second. The download would take three minutes.

And from the volume of energy fire coming from outside, that might be more time than they had.

She peeked through the visual feed of one of Second Squad's operators, Petty Officer Hernandez, who was busily laying down fire with his Squad Automatic Weapon. The SAW spat short bursts of 4mm plasma-tipped bullets that chewed through force fields and the flesh and bone beneath them: a squad of centaurs in deep blue uniforms went down, their bodies torn apart by multiple hits. There were more aliens behind those, but they quickly realized that rushing forward was suicide. They leaped behind cover and began to fire their lasers.

The sepoy weapons fired single laser pulses and could not unleash bursts or continuous beams. They were more than deadly enough to suppress any rebels on the primitive planet, but the SSEALs' personal force fields could handle multiple hits without going down; their return fire tore through walls and vehicles and found the shooters hunkering down behind them.

The Imperium hadn't wanted to equip the local levies too well, just in case they decided to turn their weapons on their new masters. The Doklon Imperial Levies were meant to be at a distinct disadvantage against Starfarer enemies. Which was exactly what they were facing now.

The squad of Imperial Legionnaires protecting the Satrap's Office had been asleep in their quarters when the raid began. Those soldiers would have been a much greater threat if they'd been ready to fight, but Second Squad had murdered them in their beds. All that remained were lightly armed and shielded natives.

Of course, quantity always beat quality if the quantity was large enough. Heather had learned that the hard way on Jasper-Five. A scan of the local military communication grid confirmed her worst fears: the two regiments stationed nearby were being hastily readied for action and moving with commendable speed. It wasn't common for garrison troops to be in such a hurry to stick their proverbial dicks into a not-so-proverbial meat grinder, but the

Levies were recruited from the planet's most warlike societies, young males whose entire sense of self-worth was based on showing courage in the face of death. Combine that courage with even second-rate equipment, not to mention the heavy weapons held at the battalion level, and the SSEAL Team's life expectancy could be measured in minutes – along with one jumped-up CIA intelligence officer.

Heather strapped the now-priceless portable computer to her chest place and checked the charge on her carbine. She was supposed to leave the fighting to the operators, but if the damn evac didn't show up in time, she might have to join in the fun, for whatever that was worth.

"First Squad, move to the courtyard," Commander Najle ordered, using the slightly-too-calm tone of a professional facing a near-desperate situation. "Second Squad, fall back into the building. It's considered sacred by the local Eets, so they probably won't blow it up. Move it!"

They ran through the deserted corridors as the staccato reports of supersonic plasma-tipped bullets and the whine-crackle of lasers thundered not too far away. The Satrap's Office building had been originally built as a temple complex for the local priest-kings, and it had a large central courtyard once used for ceremonial purposes. Fortunately for the SSEAL team, it was also just about the right size to accommodate an orbital shuttle. Warp drops were one-way trips; their ticket out would have to depend on conventional means.

Doklon-Three didn't have planetary defenses, being a backwater in a peaceful sector of the Imperium, but some of the sepoys' heavy weapons could take down a shuttle. Not easily – their targeting systems were deliberately primitive – but that wasn't the kind of thing you wanted to take chances on. Fortunately, the *USS Narwhal* was prepared to deal with the problem.

Just as Heather reached the courtyard, the dark magenta night skies of Doklon-Three glowed with dozens of new 'stars' as a barrage of missiles from the covert ops starship entered the planet's atmosphere. The sight made her shudder: the hapless people of Earth must have seen something very similar during First Contact, when death rained from the heavens.

The effect of this orbital bomb run was far less extreme. Except for those actually killed by it, she supposed.

The missiles targeted the signature emissions of any heavy weapon emplacements capable of threatening the shuttle. Since the ship didn't have the time or equipment to conduct detailed scans, at least some of the targets were civilian communication systems. Heather tracked the fire mission with her imp: twenty-three installations and vehicles were struck; the intelligence estimate was that there were no more than fifteen weapon systems capable of threatening an orbital shuttle. Fifty missiles struck, each delivering enough explosive force to turn a city block into a flaming crater. The ground shook under her feet; some of those explosions had been close. She tried not to think of the hundreds, likely thousands of soldiers and luckless civilians consumed by the expanding fireballs turning the night into hellish day.

War was death and mutilation, most of its victims guilty of nothing worse than doing their jobs or being at the wrong place at the wrong time. Heather hated war. But once she was in one, she intended to do her best to win. The only thing worse than a battle won was a battle lost. Some general had said that; she reminded herself to Woogle it later.

"Pelican One inbound for pickup. Hunker down, boys and girls. Danger close. Repeat, danger close."

Pelican One looked like an ordinary orbital cargo shuttle, the ubiquitous craft able to maneuver in and out an atmosphere and ferry passengers and as much cargo as it could fit inside its three-hundred-ton displacement. This particular stubby, ugly ship had hidden attachments for weapon and shield mounts that gave her almost as much protection and firepower as an assault shuttle. It lashed the area around the Satrap's Office with a storm of plasma and hypervelocity missile fire. The starship missile barrage that immolated the Doklonian heavy weapons had felt like a distant earthquake; the sharp impacts of the shuttle's weaponry were like thunderbolts. Windows shattered and flames rose up over the edges of the building, drowning out the natives' small arms fire.

First Squad reached the LZ a few seconds before the shuttle arrived. Everyone was there, but two operators were being carried in. Heather did a quick status check: their wounds were critical but the men would likely survive until they reached the *Narwhal* and its well-outfitted sick bay.

The platoon poured into the ship in hurried order and it lifted off before its cargo hatches were fully closed, regaling Heather with a first-hand look at the capital city. Whatever it'd looked like before the American raid was impossible to tell: everywhere she looked was filled with uncontrolled fires, overturned vehicles, and patches of darkness between the flames: one of the missiles must have hit the local power plant, causing a blackout, or maybe the locals themselves had turned the lights off.

Gunboat tourism. No fun for anybody involved.

She hoped the contents of her computer were worth all the carnage and chaos she'd helped inflict.

Four

Aboard the *USS Mattis*, 164 AFC

Heinlein-Five has fallen.

That wasn't what the news reports said, of course. The AP newsfeed merely asserted that 'heavy fighting against the Nasstah invaders continues throughout Heinlein System.' Problem was, none of the stories mentioned Fifth Fleet, which had been tasked to protect the system. You learned to read between the lines; if Fifth Fleet was still around, it would have been featured in the reports. Which meant it wasn't around anymore: destroyed or fled, it didn't make a difference for the system. Heinlein-Five wouldn't last very long without a fleet covering it. The planet wasn't heavily fortified: a handful of Planetary Defense Bases wouldn't hold off an armada that had eliminated or run off a major naval formation.

The commander of the 101st MEU had announced an impromptu meeting of all company and attachment commanders, fifteen minutes from now. Fromm would get the real story then. It was probably worse than he expected.

We are losing.

Heinlein-Five was a large US colony, and its fifteen million inhabitants made it one of the largest outer settlements of the country. Barely thirty percent of the US population had settled beyond Earth and a handful of core planets, despite all efforts to stimulate colonization. Most people preferred to stay home and be fat and comfortable in the great cities of Sol, Wolf 1061 and Drake. Those likely dead colonists were a huge loss to the country. And worse, a ley line connected Heinlein directly to an even larger system: Parthenon, with two habitable systems and a combined population of over thirty million, not to mention being a major warp nexus that led towards the heart of US space. If Parthenon fell, the Vipers could cut off half a dozen systems, to be taken at their leisure, and threaten Wolf 1061, one of the core worlds, with a population in the half-billion range and the second largest industrial base in the US. Lose that system and the war would be just about lost. And Earth itself was a mere thirty warp-minutes away from Wolf 1061.

Space war depended on defense in depth. You wanted to

control all the warp pathways leading to your core worlds, the planets containing the bulk of your population and economy. The best way to do that was to establish colonies or bases on all known connecting points, providing supplies and rallying points for your defensive fleets. Most Starfarers' central systems lay dozens of warp jumps away from their nearest neighbors, requiring attackers to overwhelm the defenses waiting for them every step of the way. To get to that point took centuries or even millennia of expansion, however. Earth had a bit over a century to spread out; it wouldn't take too many defeats before an enemy fleet could make it to Sol System.

Given all that, Fromm had a good idea where the *Mattis* and the rest of Sixth Fleet were heading. The only question was how bad things were going to get once they arrived.

The officers and NCOs in the briefing room all looked like attendees at the funeral of some beloved relative. Smiles were rare and seldom lasted more than a few seconds. Most people were sitting down quietly. Fromm nodded at Lieutenant Hansen and sat down next to him as the rest of Charlie Company's leaders arrived. They didn't have to wait long.

Colonel Marvin Brighton stepped up to the podium. He had been in the Corps for close to a century, and in charge of 101st MEU for a good twenty years, and in the months since joining the unit, Fromm had learned he was a practical, no-nonsense leader, concerned primarily with results; a fighter and doer with little interest in rising any further in the ranks.

"The stuff you've been hearing is partly true," he said. "The Vipers kicked us out of Heinlein System. Fifth Fleet gave them a hard time, but in the end it had to withdraw. They had no choice: if we lost the fleet, the Vipers would have had a straight shot to Parthenon. As it is, they lost a lot of ships, maybe more than we could afford. But forget about the rumors that the fleet was destroyed."

Fromm felt a surge of relief. Even a badly-mauled fleet was better than nothing.

"They are going to have to pull back to refit, however, so we are going to take their place. The GACS' full Space Defense Force is relieving us at New Jakarta so we can proceed. Our mission is simple: we must hold Parthenon against all attacks. As long as we have forces in the system, the Vipers cannot spread to the rest of American space; if it falls, our situation will become critical. Our orders are to hold at any cost."

Parthenon-Three was a 'full-goldie' planet with thirty million inhabitants spread around a couple dozen cities and a hundred towns and villages, protected by twenty-four heavily-armed Planetary Defense Bases as well as a ring of orbital fortresses and an impressive fleet of monitors. Parthenon-Four, on the other hand, was too cold and dry for human tastes. Only some two hundred thousand humans dwelled there, concentrated around four terraforming stations and a handful lesser facilities.

"The hundred-and-first and the rest of Landing Squadron Three will be deployed to Parthenon-Four to protect and assist the evacuation of all American personnel there. When that mission is complete, we will relocate to Parthenon-Three to supplement the local garrison."

Some of the Marine officers sneered at that. The local defense forces would be Army and National Guard formations, recruited mostly from non-warp capable humans born in-system. Their training wasn't bad, although most Corps officers would disagree, but their equipment would be largely outdated, and their logistics wouldn't be great. There just wasn't enough money for everyone, and most federal and state funds were allocated to the PDBs and space fortresses. If it came down to ground combat, the Corps would be expected to do most of the heavy lifting. However, the Marines just didn't have the manpower to defend an entire planet; Sixth Fleet could field about one division equivalent of ground troops, hardly enough to cover the twenty-four PDBs that were all that stood between Parthenon-Three's millions and a fiery death.

People often forgot that the Warp Marine Corps' combat forces only comprised some two hundred battalions and a handful of formed brigades and divisions, a little over four million troops all told, compared to fifty million Navy personnel and about thirty-five million in the other branches of the service, including the Guard, volunteer militias and so on. Marines could launch strikes and seize relatively-small patches of ground, but to hold or defend entire planets, you needed the Army.

Fromm discreetly used his imp to fill in the details while Colonel Brighton went on. The planet's defensive forces included six Army divisions (mechanized infantry for the most part), five National Guard divisions (mostly support), and ten militia brigades; the latter were volunteer weekend warriors, loosely-organized and poorly equipped. Over a hundred and eighty thousand troops, of which some twenty thousand would be actual fighting soldiers, the rest being in support roles.

Sixth Fleet was delivering ten MEUs to the system, about thirteen thousand Marines and five thousand Navy personnel, some ten thousand of whom would be expected to carry a gun, drive or operate a weapon system, and go kill the enemy, which would nearly double the combat strength of the local forces in actual firepower and mobility. To say nothing about the difference in experience: most of those planet-bound soldiers had never fired a shot in anger. How they would fare when a host of Viper dropships and landing pods came calling was anyone's guess. Still, Fromm thought the eye-rolling from his fellow officers wasn't smart: they were going to need the locals' help when the proverbial manure smacked against the rotating blades, and they should be thinking about how to improve their effectiveness rather than looking down on them.

It wouldn't be his problem, at least not at first. He would be busy in Parthenon-Four, which had four battalions in place, all regular Army, and those two thousand soldiers had plenty of combat experience fighting natives. Parthenon-Four had developed intelligent life, and the locals were primitive but fiercely hostile. They had managed to pick up some dangerous weapons in the seventy years since their First Contact, enough to make themselves a regular nuisance. A month didn't go by without some violent incident somewhere near the terraforming stations, and the evacuation would provide the locals with plenty of chances for mayhem.

There was no telling how soon it would be before the Viper invasion force arrived, but he and Charlie Company were unlikely to be bored before then.

Parthenon-Four, 165 AFC

"I hate the cold," PFC Hiram 'Nacle' Hamblin said.

"Better get used to it," Gonzo said. "Cold as balls, twenty-four seven, twice as cold come Christmas."

"It ain't that bad," Russell broke in, trying to smooth things over. Nacle was feeling a bit sensitive after the whole deal at the whorehouse, and Gonzo still hadn't figured out how far he could push before things got out of hand. "Average temp is only like fifteen degrees below Earth-normal."

"Yeah. A whole forty-five degrees. Frozen water on the ground eight months a year except 'round the equator. And big-ass Abominable Snowmen roaming everywhere, ready to bite your head off."

"I ain't scared of no ETs," Nacle said. "Just don't like the cold is all."

Funny how people were about things, Russell thought. The

cold wasn't going to kill anybody, unless they decided to strip naked and frolic around at night, when temps usually got within spitting distance of freezing even in the equator. Their field uniforms, let alone their full battle-rattle, were designed to trap enough body heat to make exposure unlikely unless they went far enough north to hit perma-zero temps and their batteries ran out, so freezing to death wasn't something to worry about.

The local critters, on the other hand, could kill you dead. The place, cold as it was, was teeming with hostile life along the warmer bits in the middle, including a species of intelligent tool users. The natives had some fancy scientific name but were commonly known as Big Furries. They were massive grey-and-white super-gorilla analogs, although the Woogle article claimed their innards were more like a dolphin or whale back on Old Earth. They were also smart enough to mine and work iron, and more recently some asshole had decided it'd be fun to sell them guns, so they were big tough monsters with guns.

All in all, this deployment was going to suck. The terraforming facilities had bars and whores, but word was their prices were high and they would soon close down as the evacuation got underway. They were going to end up spending their time chasing giant snow apes with nothing to do in between.

The combat shuttle lurched before the groundside grav-grapples took the boat and lowered it the rest of the way. The view from the sensor feed was nothing to write home about: vast expanses of dull-red forests, with patches of lighter orange-leafed trees here or there. No snow on the ground, at least, which made sense since they were on the tropics, such as they were. When he zoomed in on the trees, he saw they were covered in bristles or spines; they kind of reminded him of pines back home in New Illinois, where most the plants and animals were Earth imports. Not that he'd ever seen many trees growing up in the giant slum known as the Zoo.

Some sort of squirrel-monkey critters were leaping around the trees or gnawing at pinecones. Russel wondered if they were edible and if so, what they tasted like. Some of the tastiest critters he'd found were ETs. Sure, they often had the nutritional value of chewing tobacco, and sometimes it took a Marine's full nano-med suite to clear out the toxins in their juices, but they were tasty nonetheless.

The video feed blurred as the shuttle landed.

"Well, here we are."

Out they went, by the numbers, not as quickly or organized as if they were on assault mode, not when they were in their field grays and carrying their rucksacks, but not off by that much, either. It wasn't that cold, with a morning time temp of fifty-three-F. According to his imp, it was going to get up to the sixties by the afternoon. The only snow he could see was on top of some impressive mountains peeking over the horizon. Not too bad, for an ice planet. Although even an ice planet was bound to have nice spots, and only a moron would pick anywhere but those spots to live in.

The landing pad was a little bit off the main terraforming facility. As he walked down the ramp with the rest of Third Platoon, Russell saw three big gas cyclers looming ahead like artificial mountains, five hundred feet tall and nearly as wide, each designed to spew a mix of greenhouse gases meant to warm up the planet. Only one of them was working; a thick column of putrid-looking smoke rose from its top. Operations were winding down; the brass had decided holding Parthenon-Four wasn't worth the effort.

A loud detonation interrupted his sight-seeing. Russell didn't waste any time; he was down on the ground, his service pistol out, before his mind fully processed what had happened.

"Oh, no!" Nacle shouted, looking up from his own prone position. Russell took a peek through the private's imp just in time to see a second missile slam into a descending shuttle, smoke coming from the point where the first hit had penetrated its shield.

Fuck. That could have been us.

The second missile sparked a fire in the shuttle's rear cargo hold, but it looked like nothing vital had been destroyed, although any poor bastard in the way of the explosion would probably disagree. The shuttle spun in place and spat out a stream of laser and 25mm plasma-tipped rounds, searching for the rocket team. A moment later, a volley of guided artillery erupted from one of the Army positions surrounding the facility. Looked like at least some of the local GIs weren't asleep at the switch. A series of explosions went off in the distance: air bursts. He didn't need to see them to know what the effect of those blasts would be like: 200mm shells made a mess of anything they hit.

There were no more missile launches.

"Clear the area!" Staff Sergeant Dragunov shouted. "Move it, people!"

Off to Russell's left, Gunny Wendell took Lieutenant O'Malley firmly by the arm and helped him lead the way. The platoon's CO looked a bit dazed and confused; instead of hitting the ground like the rest of the troops, O'Malley had only gone down on one knee while he tried to figure out what was going on. The officer's sluggish reaction just confirmed his suspicions that the El-Tee didn't know what the fuck he was doing. Too bad; it made Russell miss the time when Captain Fromm had been in direct command of the platoon. The skipper was a damn good officer, even if he'd gotten a bunch of them killed at Jasper-Five.

The platoon cleared the landing zone fast as the damaged shuttle made its final descent. The grapples grabbed it and gently lowered it to the pad. By then everybody except the corpsmen and emergency techs was safely behind the blast shields that would keep the shuttle's possible destruction from spreading the damage.

The shuttle didn't blow up. There were a couple of WIAs inside, but the missiles had hit mostly supplies, and none of it had included explosive ordnance. They might be short some commo equipment, rations and blankies, but nobody had died.

Still, it was one hell of a way to start a deployment.

* * *

"What the *hell* is going on here?"

"No idea, sir. Locals have taken potshots at aircraft before, but never with SAMs."

Fromm's shuttle shuddered in mid-air as the pilots raised its force fields to maximum power. It'd been sheer luck that the hit on First Platoon's shuttle hadn't destroyed anything vital – or filled its passenger compartment with fire and death. His own transport was next in line, carrying him and the command element of Charlie Company.

"We're getting reports of similar attacks on other landing zones, sir," Lieutenant Hansen said. "Looks like four missile teams."

"Casualties?"

"Two other shuttles damaged. Twelve WIAs." Hansen paused for a second. "Two confirmed KIAs from Bravo."

Fromm shook his head in frustration. The Vipers had been busy. They'd either armed the natives or inserted a covert team – or teams – sometime before the Days of Infamy. Some equivalent of the US Green Berets was his guess, special forces operators specializing in training and outfitting native troops to conduct asymmetric warfare operations. Getting them past local security wouldn't have been easy, but Fromm had seen first-hand how devious the enemy could be. They'd managed to provide enough advanced weapons and support systems to wipe out two US corvettes at Jasper-Five, not to mention nearly annihilate the Starfarer legations on that planet. That had been the Lampreys' work, but the Vipers were just as sneaky.

They're trying to ensure we'll never have anything but war between us and any natives under our influence.

Relations with the so-called Big Furries had never been good. Some local ETs would engage in trading with human settlements, but only after they'd been taught that raiding didn't pay off. Most of their clans had rebuffed any attempts to deal with them. A handful of missionaries had been brutally murdered even after reprisals made it obvious that doing so was an elaborate method of suicide. Current policy was to avoid them, but a few greedy bastards had sold them guns in exchange for a variety of luxury goods. The Furries' favorite trade weapon had been a – very illegal – .60 caliber breech-loading single shot rifle, perfect for hunting or killing their fellow furries, but harmless against armored troops, although a few civilians who'd ended up on the receiving end of sniping attacks would disagree. No American smuggler would have been crazy enough to sell mil-spec weaponry to the natives, though. That had to be the work of the enemy.

And now we're going to have to conduct COIN ops, and find out the hard way what else they've got waiting for us.

Anything that slowed down the evacuation of Parthenon-Four and inflicted casualties would be a net gain for the Vipers. Likely more than enough to justify smuggling a few SF teams and their equipment.

We'll just have to wipe them out with as few losses as possible.

Unfortunately, the cheapest methods to achieve that goal were also the most brutal.

Five

Groom Base, Star System 3490, 164 AFC

"Drop initiated. Transition in ten, nine..."

Lisbeth Zhang glanced around the warp catapult. She and twenty-seven of her closest friends were crowding the big circular pad. Her flight suit felt rather inadequate for the trip she was about to undertake, a hundred-mile jump that would take no time at all in the physical universe but which would feel rather longer from her personal point of view.

She'd never understood how Marines did it, forgetting for a moment she was a member of the gun club now. Oh, they didn't do it often, and only a fraction of them were warp-drop certified, but doing it at all seemed insane. Lisbeth didn't mind traveling through warp when she had a spaceship wrapped around her, protecting her from the bizarre world outside four-dimensional reality. Back during her Obligatory Service term, she'd been rated as a level 3, good enough to perform FTL navigation. Not that she'd ever considered going for Warp Propulsion as a career. That was a restricted officer designation, not qualified for commanding vessels, in no small part because warp navigators soon became rather eccentric. She belatedly realized that fighter pilot might become a similar dead end, for the same reasons.

No sense worrying about that now. Contemplating the odds of surviving this warp drop was slightly more comforting. The chances of death, irreparable psychological damage or simply never returning to the real world were low, well under a hundredth of a percent for WR-2 ratings, and an order of magnitude lower for every higher level; things had improved a great deal from the early days of the new Marine Corps and the desperate boarding actions that had helped lead the US to victory against the Snakes. Back then, the odds of a negative outcome had been a shade under one percent. Not great betting odds when your life, sanity or very existence were on the line.

"...one."

Off to Neverland.

A short jump only took a few seconds of subjective time. Normally, she powered through them by blasting Warmetal right into her eardrums. This time, however, she went in cold; part of their training regimen involved not relying on the usual crutches – music or prayer or doing math in your head. The bloodless corpse of Lieutenant Omar Givens was waiting for her in the darkness, looking just as he had after sacrificing his life to save hers.

Guilt and terror washed over her – until she threw a mental switch, banishing all emotion and all but one thought, focused on a single word:

Stop.

Weeks of meditation, drugs and bizarre mental exercises turned the word into a spell of sorts. The ghost vanished without a trace, leaving her alone in the dark.

It worked! If freaking worked! She'd thought the whole warp prep program had been nothing but pseudo-mystical crap. Lisbeth and her fellow candidates had been conditioned into entering trance states nearly at will. Doing so inside warp had turned out to be shockingly easy. She spent the rest of the trip in quiet serenity, no ghosts or hallucinations anywhere.

Emergence.

Lisbeth staggered a couple of steps when her feet touched the ground and stumbled into another Marine, almost knocking both of them down.

"Sorry," she mumbled.

"No worries," the guy – Lieutenant Garcia; he was in her squadron – said. He shook his head. "Weird; I feel fine now. It usually takes longer."

"Yeah." Even trained Marines usually took a second or two to recover from a warp drop, but other than a moment's clumsiness, she was fine. Her mind was clear. Maybe the brainiacs in charge actually had a clue.

A moment after she had that thought, the screaming started.

People were backing away from something near the center of the pad. Lisbeth pushed her way past a couple of startled candidates and saw the brawl. One trainee had jumped another and was *biting* him despite the efforts of two other Marines trying to restrain him. He was tearing the poor bastard's throat open!

"Lar! Stop it!" one of the men shouted, doing his best to pull the man's head back from his victim. He had two inches and a good twenty pounds on the nutjob, but he wasn't making much progress. Another Marine stumbled back when he caught an elbow in the face. Blood spurted from a pressure cut over one eye; the blow had broken skin and probably bone as well.

The growling candidate ripped off a chunk of his victim's flesh. There wasn't the telltale burst of blood you got if the carotid had been torn open, but the madman was leaning over to take another bite and finish the job.

Lisbeth dove in before he got the chance.

She'd never gotten muscle-enhanced: her family didn't have the cash to spare, and if she needed a strong back, that was what ordinary spacers were for. So she'd learned to fight dirty to compensate for the mass and strength differential between her and the average dickhead. A quick jab to the throat distracted the berserker before he could chomp down on his victim a second time. The blow should have stunned him for at least a second; the kidney-punches the guy holding him from behind was delivering should have disabled him even more decisively, but the berserker didn't stop. He turned to Lisbeth, and she froze when she met his eyes. They were solid orbs of darkness: she felt in her heart that she was looking at the stuff of warp space.

The thing wearing the Marine's body like a costume dropped his victim and lunged at her, dragging the two men holding him as if they weighted nothing. He reached for Lisbeth's face, and she barely ducked away, sickly realizing that if he grabbed her he would rend her limb from limb.

Fernando Verdi shouted a Karate *kiai* and delivered a full-power sidekick into the monster's chest. Lisbeth heard ribs break under the impact. Fernando's well-braced blow knocked the man-who-wasn't backwards; he and the other two fell back in a tangle of flailing limbs. The Marine who'd called the berserker's name managed to put him in a half-Nelson, but the struggling figure kept twisting around, oblivious to the pain that should be immobilizing him.

Lisbeth kicked him in the balls with all her strength. There was a sickening squishing sound as her boot's steel toe connected with the pelvic bone, and she felt the impact rupture something, but the thing didn't stop. He was growling – no, he was speaking in some language she couldn't understand, and was turning his head to bite the Marine holding him; vertebrae cracked as he twisted his neck beyond a normal human's range of motion.

Lieutenant Garcia stepped up from the side, a standard-issue multi-tool held tightly in a white-knuckled grip, its cutting blade out. He grabbed the madman's hair with one hand and drove the tool right through his temple with the other.

"Jesus God," Garcia whispered as he twisted the little knife inside the monster's head. "God."

That did the trick. The maniac collapsed as more Marines dogpiled him. Corpsmen and a security team finally showed up – the whole thing had taken maybe ten seconds, although it'd felt like an eternity – just in time to save the Marine with the chewed-up neck and to declare the other guy dead.

People were cursing and milling about. Lisbeth mostly just stood there, watching the aftermath unfold with an eerie sense of detachment.

That wasn't someone going crazy. That poor bastard dragged something back from warp space.

Part of her knew those thoughts might be signs she was losing her own mind. But a bigger part was certain that she was right.

* * *

"They're canceling the tests until they figure out what went wrong," Fernando said as they tried to relax over drinks at the officers' club.

"Yeah." She'd gotten the same announcement he had. "Figured they would."

"They've put three hundred pilot-trainees through the same process already; over six thousand warp drops with hardly an incident," he went on. "They had a couple of psychotic breaks – both temporary; they're back on duty after being treated – but nothing like this."

She wanted to share her suspicions with him, but she was afraid he might think she was having a psychotic break.

"That was crazy," was all she added to the conversation.

He nodded. "Well, that's the dark side of trance states. It can lead to things like berserker rages, or the kind of thing people called spirit possession."

Maybe that's exactly what it was.

"Someone going stark raving mad out of six thousand warp drops isn't the worst odds, I suppose," she said. Except if they ever went out to fight, they'd be conducting dozens of jumps per sortie, and dozens of sorties per deployment. Six thousand divided by those numbers didn't look like such a tiny chance after all.

"Not the best, either," Fernando replied. "Hopefully they'll be able to figure out why things went sideways and make sure it doesn't happen again."

"Or they won't and they'll still send us out there," she said.

"What, you thinking about dropping out?"

A few people had asked to leave the program, and after some counseling to decide how serious they were about quitting, they'd been allowed out. They were now working alongside the washouts on other specialties. The new Marine Aviation branch needed logistics clerks, space traffic controllers and cockpit-wipers, too.

She shook her head. "Getting blown up into plasma or going batshit crazy or breaking your neck stepping out of the shower, we all got to go sometime." Even the longevity treatments didn't guarantee immortality. Actuarial studies based on other Starfarers' statistics predicted that sheer bad luck would kill you before you made it very far past the eight-century mark. No human had had the chance to live that long yet, of course, but plenty of geezers had kicked the bucket long before that. Lisbeth had seen enough death to know that your time could come at any moment.

Only one thing you could do about that. Live your life like it all could be over tomorrow.

Speaking of that… She finished her drink and grinned at him.

"How about we move this somewhere more private?"

He smiled back at her.

Later, as they drifted off to sleep in her compartment's bed, she felt able to share the truth with him.

"I looked into the guy's eyes, Nando. They weren't normal. I think there was something inside of him, some *thing* he picked up in warp space."

A soft snore was her only answer. Figures.

Already regretting the thankfully unheard outburst, Lisbeth curled up next to him and closed her eyes.

Cambridge, Ohio, 164 AFC

The drive between the Columbus Interplanetary Spaceport and the McClintock ancestral home took a little over half an hour. Nobody met her at the airport, which suited Heather fine. She didn't mind the alone time.

The Hertz rental whirred merrily down the interstate, a two-door Camaro Coupe. She'd picked it up as much for its bright red coat of paint as for its sporty electric engine, which allowed her to barrel down the self-drive lane at a good ninety mph; she passed dozens of autopilot cars along the way, their passengers watching movies, reading or surfing the web, except for a couple engaged in some back-seat loving. Heather could have easily engaged the Coupe's autopilot and done something other than driving, but that would have been less relaxing than pushing the car for all it was worth. If all she wanted was a short trip, she could have rented an aircar for an extra thirty bucks a day and gotten there in five minutes. Driving helped dispel the tension growing inside her as she got closer to home.

Well, her parents' home. And to some degree her siblings', since neither of them had left Earth or even Ohio. It wasn't her home, though. Not for a good long while.

I wish I'd gone to Parthenon instead.

Heather shook her head. The timing wouldn't have worked out. After making it back to Earth and finishing her debrief, she was between assignments and really had no excuse to avoid visiting her parents. She wasn't sure where her lords and masters would send her next, but it could well end up being the place where she earned a posthumous star at the CIA Memorial Wall in Langley. This Thanksgiving might be her last.

Her parents had sounded happy enough about the visit. Dad had offered to pick her up at the spaceport, but she'd talked him out of it. She needed the quiet drive to get ready for the family gathering. A copious amount of alcohol would help even more, but her family wouldn't approve, and they already had plenty of reasons to be disappointed in her, starting with her career choices.

She drove past the new Mosser Glass factory after she got off the exit. The company was the biggest employer in the region, and had kept growing steadily over the years, turning Cambridge into one of the wealthiest cities of the state. Her father had been the Mosser's chief executive for over forty years; he'd retired a few months before Heather officially joined the State Department after being unofficially inducted into the Central Intelligence Agency. Retirement wouldn't last very long, not with private pensions only lasting fifteen years and anti-aging treatments growing steadily in price the longer they kept you alive, but for the last seven years he'd been putzing around the house with nothing to do. Which hadn't improved things at home; her last visit, three years ago, had made that abundantly clear.

Well, at least Peggy and Donald will be there this time, along with their better halves. It'll be nice to see the kids, too.

That thought helped, a little. By the time she pulled up to the pre-Contact 'McMansion' and parked in front of the six-car garage, she felt a little better. Walking up to the kitchen door brought back several memories, good, bad and indifferent. She let herself in.

Mom was in the kitchen, subvocalizing something while she poured herself a glass of Pinot. Her Norwegian-immigrant servants – Heather didn't recognize either of them; her mother never kept the help around for very long – were busy at work. Mom was in their way, but they just stepped carefully around her.

The tall, platinum-blonde woman looked thirty-something, about the same as she had all of Heather's life. She smiled at her.

"There you are," her mother said. Her eyes weren't fully

focusing on anything in the real world. Heather's suspicion that she was split-screening was confirmed with a quick check of her mother's Facetergram profile, which included her current status: half of Mom's attention, if not more, was focused in a Regency Romance MMO. Bernice McClintock had always preferred to spend her time in assorted virtual realities. Legally, you couldn't be in full VR for longer than six hours a day; most people got around that limit by eschewing total sensory immersion and simply switching back and forth between the real world and whatever fantasy they preferred to live in.

"Hi, Mom."

The women exchanged a dutiful hug and pecks on their cheeks.

"You look healthy, at least," the McClintock matriarch said. "We were so worried when we heard you were caught up in that horrible thing out in the colonies."

Jasper-Five wasn't technically a colony but rather a free-associated system, but Heather saw no point in correcting her mother, who turned away for a moment and subvocalized something only her fellow gamers could hear. She poured herself a glass of what her mother was having and the two women made their way out the kitchen, past the still-empty dining room, and into the den where the rest of the family awaited.

The room was filled with a full hologram of today's game, the Jets versus the Vikings. Montana was up by three. Watching the massive shapes of the players reminded Heather of the muscle-enhanced SSEALs she'd recently worked with. She'd attended Jürgen's funeral, watched as they lowered a ballast-filled coffin into the ground in lieu of the corpse nobody would ever find. Warp space never gave back its victims.

"Heather?"

She blinked; Dad had paused the game and everyone had greeted her – and she'd somehow spaced out through all of it.

"Happy Thanksgiving," she said lamely.

"Great to see ya, Hetty." Peggy McClintock said; her welcoming smile was genuine enough. Heather's sister looked happy but also a little tired; she'd taken two decades off to raise her children, and she was only on her seventh year of motherhood. "Been too long."

"I know. How are things?" Peggy hadn't been home last time Heather came to visit; she and the husband and kids been on vacation in the wilds of mostly-uninhabited Great Britain.

"You know, the usual. Sometimes I think we should have podded the kids and went on with our lives."

"I know you're kidding," Peggy's not-so-better half said, moving to stand by his wife's side and shake Heather's hand. Howie Dupree was, much like Heather and Peggy's father, a big, broad-shouldered guy with the aggressive can-do attitude that had led both men to great things. In Howie's case, it'd helped him become Senior Vice President of Orbital Manufacturing. The job took him to Mosser's facilities in Low Earth Orbit and the Moon far more often than Peggy liked, not least because she suspected Howie was having an affair with someone during his frequent off-planet trips. Heather had heard the tearful story five years ago, the last time she made the mistake of spending some face time with her sister. They were still together, so Heather assumed they'd worked things out, one way or another.

Peggy beamed at her husband. "Of course I'm kidding. I wouldn't pod our kids. It's not natural."

Heather could agree with her on that much, at least. The current fashion among the well-to-do was to place their newborn babies in a sealed life-support pod and raise them via virtual-reality interface, ensuring that their little darlings weren't exposed to any actual dangers while they grew up in the strictly-controlled environment. Podding was expensive and controversial; the process had only been around for twenty years or so, and the first generation of pod-babies were just beginning to emerge from their virtual environment into the real world, with mixed results.

She shook her head at the thought of children growing up in a constant state of hibernation, never risking a skinned knee or elbow, their only inputs being what their parents chose for them, their only friends other pod children linked through a virtual network that strictly managed their interactions while their bodies rested comfortably in a fluid solution and nanobots ensured they remained in perfect health until they were finally decanted on their eighteenth birthday, when their parents no longer had the legal right to keep them inside the artificial wombs. That just couldn't be good for anybody.

"So how's life treating you at State?" Howie asked her.

"You know, it's pretty busy, what with a war going on and all."

"I know. We're working three shifts just to keep up with the military contracts. A bunch of our people got reactivated, too, so they're back in uniform and we're having a heck of a time trying to replace them. We're getting retirees coming back, but they want more money to interrupt their vacations from life. It's a big mess."

A soldier jumped into the trench; Heather barely deflected his bayonet thrust with her Iwo and countered with a kick to the balls and a brutal blow with the gun's butt that broke the alien's jaw and spun him to the ground, where a point-blank burst finished him off.

Heather forced herself to nod and smile politely. *You have no idea what a big mess looks like, Howie*, she didn't say out loud. The big guy, just like her father, had done his four Ob-Serv years on Earth, his only hardships consisting of sore feet and back during Basic and having to live under military discipline while taking college-level courses.

"Dad's thinking about coming out of retirement, too," Peggy added, gesturing towards the elder McClintock, who was hovering nearby and dividing his time between looking at his prodigal daughter and glancing at the frozen game, clearly wondering if it'd be rude to switch it back on.

"Good for him," Heather said, turning towards him. "Good for you, Dad."

He looked at her and shrugged. "Guess we all have to do our part for the war effort."

Yeah, because going back to work at a hundred and fifty grand a year plus bonuses is the same as venturing off-planet where you can get your ass shot off.

That wasn't entirely fair, of course. Without civilians producing the beans and bullets the armed forces needed, the war would be lost as surely as if nobody fought it. But it wasn't the same. She looked at her brother Donald, a near-clone of Howie and Dad, and his wife, currently working as a college professor and saving up for her turn at maternal leave. They all seemed as alien to her as the natives of Jasper-Five. More alien, perhaps: the Kirosha had understood what war meant. She downed the rest of her pinot, and got ready to go back for seconds. It was going to be a long holiday.

I should have gone to Parthenon.

Six

Parthenon-Four, 165 AFC

"Another column is on the move, sir."

Fromm's imp marked the hostile formation on the virtual map hovering on one side of his field of vision. He opened another display next to it; this one piped in the visual input from the recon drones orbiting the area, and it showed a few hundred armed natives. The war band was moving in loose order through the relatively open spaces between the massive old-growth trees that dominated the forest. The dense canopy that made satellites nearly useless did little to stop the swarm of insect-sized robots at his command from spying on the enemy.

The Big Furries on the vid-feed were armed with a mixture of trade rifles, medieval weapons and a handful of Viper lasers. They were large humanoids, covered in shaggy gray-white pelts, averaging seven feet in height and weighing over four hundred pounds; their body plan resembled a bear more than a hominid, and their hunched postures suggested they'd only recently become full bipeds. The marching warriors were clearly angry, if their body language was at all similar to humans; every once and again they stopped walking and howled at each other, working themselves into a good frenzy. They had good reasons for their rage: Fromm had condemned their people to death or exile. This particular clan had chosen death, just for the chance to take some of the hated invaders with them.

He'd done what he had to. His company's mortars and the Army artillery assets in his sector had laid out several carefully-targeted fire missions. In a few days, he had destroyed the crops and food stores of every Big Furry village within a week's walk of the Terraforming Center he'd been tasked to protect. Casualties among the tribesmen had been minimal, but now the locals had three stark choices: travel away from the human facilities to beg, borrow or steal food from untouched villages further out, starve, or march towards Fromm's forces, where they could be slaughtered in a series of set-piece engagements. Most of the natives had gone for the first option, and they were no longer Fromm's problem. The die-hards moving forward were.

He sent the grid coordinates to Lieutenant O'Malley, who was overseeing the mortar section personally. "Fire when ready."

"Aye-aye. Anti-pers on the way."

A few seconds later, the three 100mm mortars from Charlie Company's weapons platoon began their fire mission. The self-propelled anti-personnel bomblets took longer than they would have in a simple ballistic trajectory, but they maneuvered through the forest quickly enough, detonating over the Furries and showering them with a lethal downpour of shrapnel. Dozens of locals fell, their greenish blood spattering everywhere. The survivors pressed on at a dead run. The mortars fired a second volley, a third, each set of air bursts scything down a tenth or more of the aliens.

The fourth and last volley struck the leaders of the band, who had foolishly clustered around a war banner of sorts, the skull of some great beast mounted on a pole and painted bright green. The mortar bombs tore the banner apart, not that there was anybody living to pick it up once the barrage was over. Of the three-hundred-strong war band, less than half remained, most of those wounded. Those hale enough to run away did so. The rest bled and called for their mothers or begged for water, as dying warriors had since the beginning of time. Fromm didn't need to hear their words as they writhed on the green-covered ground to know that. Alien or human, some things never changed.

"Check fire," Fromm ordered before the mortar section could exterminate the runners. It would waste ammo, and hopefully the remaining warriors would head home and spread the word that advancing towards American territory was nothing but suicide.

He could have slaughtered every village in range, but then the Viper operators would have simply contacted their neighbors further out, and they would have moved into the vacant territory and resumed hostilities. The Big Furries generally didn't fear death in battle. Now, however, the tribes would spend their time warring against each other for food and territory instead of hampering the evacuation process. The Vipers would find very few volunteers for their proxy war.

Not that he intended to give them a chance to try any new tricks.

* * *

"A little fresh air will do ya good, Nacle," Gonzo said in a cheerful tone.

Nacle shook his head and kept quiet.

"Come on, it ain't even all that cold outside."

"Ease up, Gonzo," Russell said. "We're unassing in five, so look sharp."

They'd been short of warm bodies – the local grunts weren't worth shit – so the Skipper had sent out most of Third Platoon out with the rest of the company, everyone except the mortar section, which was in the rear providing fire support and also keeping an eye on the Army arty to make sure they didn't fuck up. That meant that Russell and his fire team got to play infantryman, backing up the regular 0311s with their heavier weapons. Russell was cool with that, but both Gonzo and Nacle were a bit tense. They hadn't enjoyed their time at Jasper-Five, which had been a bit harder work than usual, and assaulting a fortified position manned by a mix of Viper operators and bloodthirsty natives wasn't going to be a lot of fun. But that was why they got paid the big bucks.

The LAV shuddered for a moment, its armored hull ringing like a giant bell under a massive impact that shifted its sixty-ton weight.

"Motherfuck!" Gonzo growled.

"Hypervelocity missile," Russell said. The troop carrier didn't stop, though, so the direct hit had knocked out the force field but hadn't penetrated the LAV's armor. If it had, spalling fragments would have turned at least some of the Marines inside into ground chuck, body armor and personal shields or not.

This wasn't going to be much fun at all.

The LAV stopped behind a rocky outcrop and lowered the rear exit ramp. Russell could hear the thunder of Charlie Company's mortars and local yokels' arty, pasting the enemy positions. They obviously hadn't suppressed the ETs enough to keep them from lobbing heavy ordnance against the Marines' vehicles, and it was going to get a lot worse, now that they were out in the open.

"Go, go, go!" shouted Staff Sergeant Dragunov The squad poured out of the assault vehicle, their imps drawing them virtual pathways to follow as they scrambled out into the snow-covered mountainside. Their objective was a fortress built around a cavern complex, a stone warren protected by area force fields and a number of Viper heavy weapons. Taking the place was going to be a bitch and a half.

Russell rushed to his designated spot while the LAV rose just high enough above the outcropping for its turret to engage the fortress. The crack of its 30mm grav cannon was loud enough to make his teeth vibrate as he reached a snow-capped boulder and knelt behind it. Gonzaga was right behind him, his ALS-43 at the ready. Nacle arrived a second later.

"Be careful," the Mormon said. "They got a firefly over there."

"Shit."

The floating mirror balls could fire dozens of laser beams every second; they weren't powerful enough to penetrate their personal force fields, not with one hit, but fireflies never hit you once. Their primary purpose was to shoot down artillery and mortar shells, but a grunt would do if they didn't have anything better to blast.

"Gonzo, try to take it out."

"Copy that."

The gunner lifted the ALS-43 over his head, using the weapon's sight system to aim it without exposing himself. It wasn't the best way to shoot the weapon, fancy sights or not, but it was a lot safer than poking your head up and eating a laser. He fired two bursts.

"Miss," he said.

"I'm going to pop a 20-mike-mike to get its attention. Try again when I do."

"Roger that."

Russell fired a 20mm self-propelled missile. The firefly tagged it before it'd risen more than fifty feet, which would have detonated its warhead and regaled the Marine fire team with a self-inflicted dose of hell – except Russell hadn't armed the missile before shooting it.

Gonzo fired another burst. Russell, watching through the weapon's sights, saw the tell-tale bloom of energy that meant at least one of the 15mm plasma rounds had found the pesky floating ball and taken care of it

"All right, let's move."

The world narrowed into a series of mad dashes for cover. The occasional laser crackled overhead, but most of the incoming was from the trade rifles some asshole smugglers had sold the natives. To make things worse, some of those rounds were plasma-tipped: the Vipers had contributed to the cause by handing out explosive bullets, just like the ones in Russell's Iwo, except four times bigger. A direct hit with one of those and that'd be all she wrote.

His fire team moved slowly forward, pausing only to send back some explosive love. Russell went through half of his 20mm loads. Most of the smart rounds ended up splattered against the enemy force fields, or blasted by other fireflies back behind their lines, but at least one of them hit something important, triggering a massive explosion less than a hundred yards away. He felt the shockwave from behind a big-ass rock he was using for cover; the

Vipers and their Furry pets must be hurting.

"Hold one," Russell said while he sent out a status report and checked for new instructions.

No new orders from higher; Lieutenant O'Malley usually let people alone, maybe a little too much. The objective was the same, and a quick check with his imp showed him the company was two-thirds of the way there. They'd taken a few casualties; no KIAs, but a couple of Hellcats had been disabled, and five grunts from Second Platoon were down with serious injuries. It'd been simple bad luck; they'd been caught by some ET with a heavy laser and the balls to keep the beam on target long enough to chew through force field and armor alike. A quick check of the tape showed the Viper gunner had paid the ultimate price for being a badass when he got a sheaf of mortar bombs dropped on his position. Now the bastard was comparing notes with Alien Jesus.

The surviving scalies had pulled back after that, letting the Furries hold the perimeter while they rallied deeper inside the cavern. Russell had only caught a few glimpses of the Vipers; they weren't pretty, eight-limbed and sort of like a snake and a spider had gotten drunk enough to make some babies. The enemy were down to one area force field, too, and had run out of swatters; Russell could tell because he was getting a full panoramic view of the battlefield, without the interruptions that meant a bunch of recon drones had been clawed out of the sky. From overhead, the fight didn't look like much, other than occasional explosions; just a bunch of grunts moving through narrow passes between rock outcroppings, trying not to slip on icy patches and only pausing long enough to shoot or lob grenades. He couldn't see very far into the cavern, other than a double handful of Big Furries with rifles. They would pop up behind cover to take a shot, duck back to reload, rinse and repeat. Even with the area force field, most of them had the sense not to fire from the same spot more than once. The lone exception ate a 20mm mini-missile that opened a hole in the force field and took his head clean off.

After a minute or two, Sergeant Dragunov sent new vectors to everyone, paths forward where most of the enemy fire couldn't bear. Russell passed the info along to the fire team and they started moving again. Time to crawl now. At least it looked like any mines or booby-traps the ETs had set up had been cleared up by the mortars. He saw a couple of places where chewed-up rocks marked the spot where a mine had been detonated before it could hit the advancing Marines. That was good news, as long as the mortar section hadn't missed any –

A sudden threat warning triggered reflexes developed over years of training and personal experience. Russell rolled off to one side as fast as humanly possible, away from the spot an enemy anti-personnel device had marked for destruction.

He was almost fast enough.

Technically, the explosion that smashed his body against the rocks like the hand of an angry god didn't come from a mine, but rather a single-shot rocket launcher. The weapon was fairly simple: a short-range missile mated to a motion-sensing low-power laser, dropped alongside a likely path. The ambush weapon had been hidden from view under a lightweight, extruded foam cover shaped to look like a random rock. It was simple, hard to detect, and its warhead was powerful enough to pulp a Marine even under full shields and body armor.

Overwhelming pain gave way to cold numbness, which scared Russell even more. Agony meant you were still alive; feeling nothing could mean your nanomeds had kicked in, or that you were on your way out.

"We got you." Gonzo's voice seemed to be coming from far away, but hearing it made all the difference in the world. He wasn't dead. He was still there. "We got you, buddy. Hang on."

He could see the sky, broken here and there by rocky outcroppings. Gonzo and Nacle were dragging him back. "Get a medic here right the fuck NOW!" Nacle was calling through his imp, and that scared Russell again, because the Mormon only swore when things were well and truly FUBAR.

Numbness everywhere. He couldn't move his arms, his legs. He tried to crane up his head to see the damage, but Gonzo gently pushed him back down.

"Just relax, Russet. It's all good. It's all good, man. Just hang on."

"Pull the other one," Russell said – or tried to. His throat was bone-dry, and the built-in water dispenser in his helmet wasn't working. None of his helmet systems were; all he had was his imp. That was all he needed, though.

A couple mental commands were all it took, and Russell was able to see through Gonzo's sensors. His buddy was looking down at a charred, mangled carcass, missing an arm and a leg. It took Russell a moment to accept the fact that was him, and another moment to swallow back the scream that tried to force its way past his parched lips.

"Shit. Stop squirming, Russet," Gonzo said. "You had to look, didn't you?"

Another wave of coldness washed over him. Either Gonzo had given him another dose of painkillers, or it was time to face the Reaper.

He went into the dark without knowing which.

* * *

"They've located all the exits, sir," Lieutenant Hansen said.

"All right. Have everyone hold in place or pull back out of the enemy's fields of fire," Fromm ordered while he mentally drafted a new fire mission. The Furry cavern complex had included several escape tunnels, but they were all accounted for now. He'd hoped to take some prisoners, but storming the caves would only result in more casualties, and in any case the Vipers rarely allowed themselves to be captured alive. His company already had one KIA and ten WIAs; no sense adding to the butcher bill.

The multi-platoon advance had achieved its objectives, forcing the enemy back and destroying all but one area force field. That would be enough for his purposes. The mortar section switched ammo types as he directed the assaultmen from Third Platoon to prepare to volley missiles. A few seconds later, he gave the ETs in the cave a final dose of hell.

A volley of light missiles battered the enemy energy barrier with plasma discharges, enough to disrupt it in time for four thermobaric mortar bomblets to reach the interior of the cave. The tunnels were filled with highly volatile chemicals in the space of a heartbeat, and ignited a moment later.

Fromm couldn't see inside the caverns, other than a grav-wave general layout of the underground complex. The view from outside was impressive enough, as a huge fireball erupted from the cavern's mouth like some ancient dragon's breath. All his troops were under cover, but they still were shaken up by the massive detonation. The entire mountainside crumbled onto the cavern's entrance, sealing it up.

Inside the caves… Well, it would have been mercifully quick, at least.

Most of the tunnels collapsed; the entire mountain shuddered as portions of its interior settled down. By the time it was over, there wasn't enough space inside the complex to fit anything larger than a mouse. It would serve as a fitting monument to the ETs who'd made their last stand there, and the Marines who'd ensured they died for their cause.

As he watched the smoky ruin and went over the casualty

reports, a part of him was refighting old battles. If he'd held back some of those especial munitions during the final fight at Jasper-Five, many Marines would still be alive. Instead, he'd had them broken down by fabbers to make more conventional shells, never expecting the primitives he was facing to ever bring area force fields into play.

It's not what you don't know that gets you killed. It's the things you think *you know.*

The Vipers had made it clear they wanted to take this system. And they were deploying their full bag of tricks to do so. He'd better make sure his own preconceptions didn't get him killed, along with everyone under him.

Groom Base, Star System 3490, 164 AFC

The Lockheed Martin SF-10 War Eagle – you could blame the name on a number of notable Auburn University alumni among the design team – didn't look pretty. It was a sixty-foot long cylinder with two bulbous warp generators at each end, with another bulge in the middle for its power plant and graviton thrusters. The tube of a 20-inch graviton cannon protruded under the frontal warp generator; the weapon ran down the entire length of the fighter and packed the punch of a battleship's main gun, although the onboard capacitors only allowed it to fire five times before the little ship went Winchester (out of ammo) and had to return to base to reload. A trio of medium lasers and a pair of plasma projectors that comprised the fighter's secondary armament were hardly visible on the spacecraft's surface.

It didn't look pretty at all, but it was the most beautiful thing in the universe.

Lisbeth Zhang watched the line of starfighters arranged neatly on the hangar bay below the viewing window. In less than two hours, she and ten other pilot trainees under a slightly more experienced squadron commander would undertake their first flight mission: to engage and destroy the antiquated and barely-functional battlecruiser *Bull Run*. She'd taken a little stroll onto the observation deck for one last look at Tenth Squadron: twelve War Eagles, ready for action. At the moment, those twelve fighters represented five percent of the entire Marine Aviation force. A whole two hundred and forty War Eagles had been built, and further production had been halted to prepare for deployment: the same fabbers that could make more fighters were now busy making spare parts for the ones already in service. As it was, going into battle with a single class of vessel was risky as hell. Normally you wanted at least two variants in service, so a single design flaw didn't ground the entire fleet. But needs must when the devil rides. That should be the motto of the Spacefighters. Needs must.

After she was done sightseeing, Lisbeth headed down to the Ready Room for final pre-flight briefings and prep.

Getting to this point had been no picnic.

She got there early, but there was already a line of pilots waiting to get their medicine, the latest concoction of drugs unofficially known as 'Mélange' or simply 'The Spice.' Lisbeth had Woogled the terms and discovered they referred to some pre-Contact sci-fi story that'd been long on mysticism and light on science, not to mention based on the idiotic belief that humans were the only intelligent species in the universe. Some idiots in R&D must be either super-geeks or very old geeks, probably both. Whatever.

Normally, the chemical cocktail would have been added to her nano-med pack, to be injected at the discretion of her imp's medical systems. Mélange usage followed its own rules, however, in no small part because each dose was carefully tailored to each pilot, down to their current physiological state. Before her experiences in the Lexington Project, she might have found the whole thing more than slightly ridiculous. Not anymore, though.

They'd lost two more people. One had merely never come back from warp space. The other had…

Lisbeth shuddered.

"You okay, ma'am?" a Lieutenant behind her asked.

"Yes, thank you," she said absently. She didn't want to explain. Lisbeth had been there and she still didn't fully believe it. It'd been over a month since the incident, but it felt like it'd just happened. That sense of immediacy was just one of the many things that were bothering her.

It was her turn. The med-tech ran a full scan of her vitals. A couple of minutes later, an ampoule of Spice was produced. She took the injection on her upper arm, feeling the coolness of the liquid solution as it spread through her body. Other than that, there was no apparent effect, but Lisbeth knew that wouldn't last. Sooner or later, something would happen.

The amazing thing was, only a handful of candidates had resigned from the program. The effects of Mélange and the visions they induced were disturbing, yes. But they were also fascinating. Maybe even addictive. She still had nightmares about what happened to Captain Brangan, but she hadn't considered leaving the program. Part of it was patriotism: the fighters were going to make a huge difference in the war, she was sure of it. But that wasn't the only reason.

Lisbeth relived Brangan's death while heading towards the locker room. They'd made yet another warp jump, and she'd done a quick headcount. She'd had just enough time to breathe a sigh of relief – everyone was accounted for – when Brangan had *dissolved* before her eyes. The poor guy hadn't had a chance to scream. His body, uniform, everything, had appeared to liquefy and twist into a swirling funnel shape for a fraction of a second before disappearing without a trace. Nothing had been left behind, not even a droplet of blood, a skin cell, nothing. It was as if he'd never existed.

She saw it happen again, this time in slow motion, and felt Brangan's mind, or maybe his soul, still alive and aware as he was dragged somewhere else, a level of existence beneath warp space, where something was waiting for him. Something bad. She saw all those things, several seconds worth of information, in the time between one step and the next, and she didn't even slow down or stumble. Her brain absorbed the information in no time at all, without affecting her outwardly.

All the candidates were required to report any hallucinations, fugue states, lost time episodes, and changes in mood or behavior. At first, she'd done so dutifully, but now she was maybe mentioning one out of three of those episodes, and she was certain the same was true of the other candidates. For one, there were so many that she'd spend all her time going over each and every event. For another, the bizarre visions had stopped happening in real time. She'd found herself experiencing minutes' worth of flashbacks or waking nightmares within the space of an eyeblink. They didn't affect her performance in any negative way. If anything, her reaction time, spatial awareness and coolness under fire were all improving.

She exchanged knowing glances with the other pilots while they changed into their flight suits. They were all experiencing the same thing, and they all knew better than to talk about it. Someone in higher would get scared and hold things up, and she didn't want any more delays.

She wanted to fly.

* * *

Lieutenant Colonel Grant Jessup was another former Air Force officer and pre-Contact Ancient, which made him the oldest person in the room with eighty years to spare. He looked pretty good for someone pushing two hundred; his complexion was a bit rugged, but that was about it. The years hadn't taken the edge off his skills or the casual arrogance with which he displayed them, either. The commander of Tenth Squadron had logged a little over a thousand hours on the War Eagle, which was three times as long as his pilots had. That amounted to over three hundred warp jumps inside the tiny craft.

The squadron leader looked over the briefing room, filled with the pilots and support personnel who had participated in the mission. Tenth Squadron had destroyed the *Bull Run*, performing six warp jumps per fighter in the process. Nobody had died or gone insane. The room's central holotank had shown all the details of the combat action in full living color.

"In conclusion, you all did great," he said after going over all the salient points of the sortie. "Perhaps a little too great."

Some of the pilots chuckled; the rest traded uneasy glances. They knew what he was talking about: even as they performed their attack runs, each fighter separated from the others by thousands of miles, all the pilots had shared a sense of awareness of what the others were doing. And Colonel Jessup had been at the center of it all, like a spider in its web. It was impossible, but the mission results confirmed it; they'd been able to coordinate the attack even though they hadn't communicated through conventional means. Nobody said so out loud, not with the ground crew officers in the room. They wouldn't understand.

"In any case, your performance has been on par with the other squadrons in the task force," he continued. "Confirmation of your new status is still pending, but unofficially, you are no longer trainees."

We made it, Lisbeth thought. They'd launched two successful sorties, engaged a target, and destroyed it. They now were part of the Marine Spacefighter branch, the tenth formation to be inducted into it. A part of her was as elated as she'd expected, but the rest was wondering about the price she and her fellow pilots were paying. They were being changed by the multiple warp jumps, the Spice drug cocktail, or both. Everyone joked how warp navigators were all weird, and pretty spooky to boot. She wondered what they would make of fighter pilots once their quirks started to become apparent.

Crazy or not, they are going to use us. We're going to be deployed, and soon. Ready or not, crazy or not, here we come.

And the funny part was, she didn't mind one bit.

Seven

Parthenon-Four, 164 AFC

"I think that makes it official."

Fromm nodded. "This sector is clear, and just in time for Christmas."

Not to mention the last stage of the evacuation, he thought. The Big Furries had been stubborn, but the destruction of their food stores at another handful of villages had driven home the lesson. Bravery could not stave off starvation. The end result had been mass migration away from the American facilities, the despoiled tribes falling upon those in the hinterlands. The natives were now too busy fighting amongst themselves to consider hindering American operations in the area. Whatever high-tech toys they still had were being used to drive off some other Big Furries from their lands. From satellite and drone surveillance, the ensuing wars of invasion were turning nasty, and would get worse still when the planet entered its winter phase, some ninety days from now. By then, all humans would be off-planet, leaving the natives free to live or die as they chose.

The evacuation had taken longer than expected, mostly because orbital transport had been at a premium and moving the heavy equipment deemed valuable enough to bring along had taken a great deal of time and effort. Even so, it was almost over. The last civilians were due to be evacuated by the end of the month, New Year's Eve in the Terran calendar. Fromm's company would get a well-deserved Christmas break, and a few days later they and the rest of the 101st MEU would be the last humans to leave Parthenon-Four.

All the Viper SF teams had been allegedly accounted for. There hadn't been many of them in the first place, a little under a hundred troops total, operating in small groups scattered around the planet. How they'd been inserted without anyone being the wiser remained something of a mystery, but a lot of trade passed through the system, including a great deal carried by alien-flagged ships. All from friendly polities, sure, but for the right price a tramp freighter's crew could be convinced to smuggle in a team of Nasstah infiltrators and their equipment. The Intelligence weenies were trying to figure out who and when. They'd probably find a culprit sometime after the battle to hold the system was over and the information didn't matter.

Fromm went over the take from the overheads one last time before leaving the command center. With the last group of insurgents in full retreat, he could afford to take some personal time off.

He read a new email from Heather he'd gotten that morning. From her account, Thanksgiving hadn't been much fun. Listening to a bunch of civilians grouse about how hard their lives were never was. Fromm wondered just how much worse it'd been before First Contact, when the vast majority of Americans never spent even a day in uniform. Of course, for the vast majority of US citizens, their Obligatory Service years were only slightly tougher than civilian life; it all depended on where and when you did your time. The current class would not be enjoying their term, that was for sure. They'd be sent out into harm's way as soon as their trainers were reasonably sure they weren't a greater danger to their own side than to the enemy. The newbies would be used as replacements and sent into battle, where they'd suffer disproportionately-higher casualties. That was the way things worked.

Conscription made sure there were always warm bodies to throw into the fire, but no laws or regulations could build the ships and guns they would need to actually fight. Heather's missive mentioned complaints of shortages in the civilian market, everything from car parts to grav-wave communication nodes. Ever since First Contact, the US had been desperately building up its industrial capacity, but most of it ended up supplying the military. Billions of man-hours and mountains of raw materials were spent to produce sophisticated devices that ended up shipped to remote parts of the galaxy and blown to pieces, with little to no benefit to the workers who'd made them – other than keeping alien ships from darkening Earth's skies for a second and final time.

Survival was great, but Earth's living standards were barely higher than they'd been before the ETs showed up; while his Marines relied on antri-gravity vehicles, most civvies made do with electric and internal combustion engines. And it was even worse in the exoplanetary territories and even some of the Star States; in many places ordinary people made do with imported horses or native beasts of burden. There just wasn't enough production capacity to go around, and the current war was squeezing the civilian side very badly. Fromm's sister had been complaining about that as well.

If the civvies had a clue of just how bad the situation was, though, they'd spend less time grousing and more praying. The news and even the Marines' tactical briefings were doing their level best to paint a positive picture, but anybody who bothered to do the math knew what the odds were. The Tripartite Galactic Alliance had such an edge in numbers and industry that they could afford massive losses and keep coming. The US had next to zero margin of error: the war could be lost in one or two battles. The coming fight for Parthenon System, for example. Lose here and the next few years would be nothing but the kicking and screaming of the condemned on his way to the gallows.

"Merry Goddamn Christmas," he muttered. He wrote Heather back, trying to be as cheerful as possible.

It wasn't easy. Part of him didn't think he'd make it to another Christmas.

* * *

"Your turn, Gonzo."

Gonzaga was looking at the colorfully-wrapped gift just the way he'd stare at a piece of unexploded ordnance. Russell didn't know what had possessed his buddy to bring the package to the Christmas party; a present from his latest ex-wife was something to be opened in private, if it was to be opened at all. Had Russell ever been married and gotten a package from an ex, he would have deep-sixed it without bothering to check what was inside.

Thing was, that had been Gonzo's only care package this Christmas, and he didn't want to be reduced to opening one of the generic gifts the battalion made available to grunts without presents, at least the ones who hadn't opted out of the holidays for religious or personal reasons. Russell had been happy with his random box, and he didn't care what anybody thought of him. Gonzo didn't, either, not really, but without a personal gift he couldn't make fun of the troopers who didn't get one.

The Christmas' Eve gathering was something of a tradition for the Marines. Anybody who wasn't on duty – most of the ones working that night were those who didn't celebrate the holidays – gathered together at the company's mess hall and everyone opened one of their presents after dinner. The ceremony was supposed to take the edge off being away from home. Sometimes it did.

"Here goes nothin'," Gonzo said, tearing into the wrapping. The box was big enough for an old-school book or some electronic device, but Russell didn't think it was anything Gonzo would enjoy. He'd met his buddy's ex, a bartender at New Parris who'd been cute enough to fuck, but way too much of a bitch to marry. She'd promptly gone on to screw a Jody or three when Gonzo was on deployment (he'd never found out, and Russell just didn't have the heart to tell him). Later on, her eating habits had overcome even the metabolic enhancers that kept most people trim, and she'd turned into a proper dependapotamus, without even the excuse of producing a litter of Devil Pups for the unseemly weight gain. Without children, divorcing her had been painless enough, and Gonzaga hadn't heard from her in years, until now.

As soon as the box opened, a life-sized hologram appeared over it. It was the ex, but sometime in the recent past she'd gotten back in shape: she looked at least as good as when Gonzo and every other grunt in the bar she worked at had tried to pick her up. Maybe even better; Russell couldn't be sure because he hadn't seen her naked until just now. The full-body hologram wasn't wearing a stitch of clothing.

"*Hola, mi amor*," the naked ex's hologram said. "Just wanted to let you see what you're missing." She wiggled her hips and smacked her own ass, and damned if she didn't look just fine.

Everybody burst out laughing. Even Gonzo.

All in all, it felt like Christmas. Russell's real present had come in early, almost a month ago. Waking up after being sure he was a goner had been a damn good gift. Waking up with a pretty nurse and an even prettier doctor hovering over him had been nice, too, although both ladies had been married and neither had been inclined to stray. That was okay. By the time he was discharged from the clinic, after they'd grown him a new set of limbs, he'd had plenty of hazard pay saved up, more than enough to have a good time at a discreet brothel that hadn't shut down for the evacuation. The establishment's owner had figured there was plenty of coin to be made servicing the Marines' needs. The ladies had finally left a few days ago, but it'd been fun until then.

He'd been lucky. Corporal Carson of Second Squad had bought it during the same fight. A good guy, and another veteran of Jasper-Five, which was still the toughest fight in Russell's career. Mostly because his platoon had been on its own, the only jarheads on the planet. This last fight had been about as easy as those things went. The fact that he'd almost gotten killed didn't change that. You could get killed during a complete cakewalk, or during a field-ex for that matter. The Viper operators had been tough, but they'd been outnumbered and outgunned, and their primmie puppets hadn't added much to the mix.

They were headed for Parthenon-Three, just after New Year's. That was going to be interesting. If the Vipers arrived in force, it was going to get a little too interesting.

Trade Nexus Eleven, 165 AFC

"Happy New Year," Guillermo Hamilton said with false merriment.

"I guess so," Heather said. She didn't give a damn about the new year, which promised to bring no happiness to anybody.

"Admit it, you're happy to be back in the field," her fellow spy said.

"If you say so." *I went from being a low-grade intelligence officer to the reincarnation of Jane Bourne simply because I didn't get killed during the Days of Infamy.* She kept that thought to herself, though. True, staying in New Washington and working as an analyst did not appeal to her; she liked field work and she thought she was pretty good at it. On the other hand, most of her achievements had been of the violent kind, the sort of stuff vids and games assumed spies did all the time and which real life intelligence officers avoided at all costs. When you operated in enemy territory, completely outnumbered and outgunned, the last thing you wanted was to pick a fight. She certainly hadn't enjoyed the times when circumstances had picked a fight with her.

Still, her survivor's luck had greatly advanced her career, although her superiors seemed to delight in putting her in dangerous positions, perhaps thinking that her winning streak would continue indefinitely. Remfie rat bastards. And Hamilton was one of said rat bastards, although he was at least sharing the risks with her on this mission.

Granted, the two Americans weren't in imminent danger, even though they were working undercover. Trade Nexus Eleven was neutral ground, under the control of the O-Vehel Commonwealth, which had assiduously stayed on the sidelines of the current galactic conflict and had enough muscle to make any of the belligerents think twice before antagonizing it. Heather had harbored some hopes the Vehelians would declare war on the Tripartite Galactic Alliance. After all, one of their embassies had been attacked and nearly destroyed during the Days of Infamy. Provocation or not, however, the Ovals weren't interested in joining what promised to be the losing side of a galactic war.

On the other hand, they hadn't joined the presumed winning side, either, and that was very helpful indeed. Among other things, it meant she and Hamilton could travel freely through Vehelian space. Humans were welcome to Trade Nexus Eleven, just like everyone else, as long as they behaved. All in all, her current posting was not a bad one. She and Hamilton were pretending to be private shipping sales reps, allegedly here to negotiate the services of a consortium of human-crewed merchant ships, a job that allowed them to interact with all kinds of potential sources of information. Even if they were caught, they would probably get off with a slap on the wrist, or at worst a few years in a minimum-security Vehelian prison, both of which were infinitely preferable to what awaited spies in Lamprey or Viper space. Or even the Imperium, which was nicer but not exactly forgiving towards enemy agents.

Heather was still glad for the hooded robes and face masks that concealed them from casual observation. Both the garments were necessities: although the titanic space station's life support systems were calibrated to accommodate Class Two biologies, their default oxygen level and temperature were both below comfortable levels for humans. The face masks helped them breathe without needing special nanite treatments, and the robes kept them warm in the fifty-degree ambient temps that Ovals considered ideal. The need to cover up made it harder to identify their species: bipeds their size could belong to any of a dozen different species. All to the good, since humans weren't exactly popular at the moment. It meant the two intelligence officers could wait for their contact in public without too many worries.

"She's late," Guillermo commented idly.

"She'll show up," Heather said with a shrug. To pass the time, she turned away from her fellow agent and checked the view from the station's promenade, which was rather spectacular. The miles-long space station was in a stable orbit around a black hole, a small one as those things went but still an impressive sight, not of the hole itself, of course, but of the effect around it. At the moment, the singularity was feasting upon a nebula unlucky enough to cross its path, creating an impressive light show beyond its event horizon. The colorful swirling lights coming from further out than Pluto's orbit around the sun were beautiful and almost hypnotic.

The black hole's effect on the fabric of spacetime had created fifteen ley lines connecting a good third of the known galaxy, which was the main reason the space station had been built there – and why the second largest Vehelian fleet in the Commonwealth made it its base of operations. A duo of dreadnoughts being refitted were floating not too far away; the five-mile-long cylinders, festooned with weapons and shields, were pretty impressive, easily three times the size of the equivalent American ships. Only the Imperium built bigger capital ships.

The view on the inside of the station was less awe-inspiring but just as colorful. The Ovals had gone for a bazaar-like atmosphere for the long promenade around its central hub. Open market squares, filled with vendors hawking their wares and haggling with would-be buyers had been a common feature of thousands of civilizations during their pre-Starfaring days, and the faux-primitive ambiance was a tourist attraction. Spacers, soldiers on leave and travelers taking some time off between warp jumps mingled with hawkers from all over the galaxy, all doing their best to part visitors from their money. On their way to the meeting place, Heather had spotted a dozen distinct species, despite the fact that many of them were partially hidden by heavy clothing and breather masks. Most of them came from Class Two biospheres, with a smattering of Class Ones and the odd Three or Four. Long-necked Wyrms growled at six-limbed Buggers; one stall over, a troupe of Puppy performers were in the middle of a complex sword-dance to the delight of a gaggle of Blue Men spectators. Food from hundreds of cultures was cooked over open braziers, making the stations' life support systems work overtime to clear out the smoke rising from them: the primitive spectacle was belied by the imp warnings that indicated which kinds of meat and vegetables were edible to her species, and which would be nothing but poison.

The chaotic environment would provide some cover for their meeting, although not from any serious security agency. Luckily, the Vehelians were taking their neutrality seriously and the enemy would be operating at an even greater handicap than the Americans. Supposedly. Heather had quickly learned that the opposition was perfectly capable of pulling assorted surprises out of its notional hat.

"I thought Scarabs were punctual to a fault," Guillermo said after a few more minutes passed.

"This one isn't exactly an exemplar of the species," Heather said, suppressing a sigh. Hamilton clearly needed to be entertained. Everyone dealt with nervousness differently. She handled it by quietly becoming hyper-aware of her surroundings; he apparently craved conversation.

"And here she is," she added, noticing the approaching figure before her chatty boss did. It belonged to the right species, but... "Or maybe not," she corrected herself as Guillermo turned around.

"I think this one's a drone."

The Kreck (a.k.a. the Scarabs) were a Class Two species descended from insect analogs that had evolved in a low-gravity planet, enabling exoskeletal lifeforms to grow to sizes that would lead to instant death in anything close to Earth-normal conditions. This particular specimen looked like a typical young neuter adult of the species: forty-six inches in length, with six long, spindly legs, a set of head-mounted fine manipulators that had evolved from antennae, and a pair of thicker arms terminating in pincers protruding from its upper thorax. Plates of plain brown-and-black chitin covered its body; the head resembled an ant's more than a beetle's, complete with large, multifaceted eyes and a beak-like mouth.

The ET was floating inside a bubble created by a gravity field projector that kept it from being crushed by the local 1.1 G environment. Most sophonts dealt with such inconvenience through a combination of medical implants and temporary cybernetics; a G-field generator that small was worth a cool half million Galactic Currency Units and about ten times as much in US dollars, where the facilities to produce that kind of tech were still few and far between. The casual display of wealth was not lost on either of the Americans. Neither was the fact that this Scarab was not the one they were looking for.

"A nova is a terrible thing to waste," the alien sent out through its implants: it was the code phrase they'd been expecting. The virtual ID showing up in Heather's personal display did not match that of their contact, however. This Scarab was at least fifty years too young, and its neuter-drone's carapace was not decorated, a clear sign of low-to-middling status among Kreck society. A personal assistant at best, despite its expensive personal carriage.

"Where's Honest Septima?" Guillermo asked. His brusque tone was probably wasted on the alien, but not the two steps he took forward, right next to the edge of the gravity generator's effect zone. Krecks liked their personal space; getting that close would make it nervous.

"I am Heavy Decimus, servant to Proxy-of-Ten-Thousand Honest Septima of Star System 2-9348," the Scarab replied. Kreck names consisted of an official nickname and the order in which they'd been hatched; the similarity to ancient Roman naming traditions had prompted translators to render the aliens' numerical praenomen into their Latin equivalent. "I am here to take you to her."

"That wasn't the plan," the intelligence officer protested.

"The Proxy conveys her deepest apologies, but she wishes to converse with you at some length. That cannot be done in a public venue."

A change in plans was almost always a bad thing. This meeting had been meant to be a simple burst transmission via their imps, serving both as a simple info dump and an introduction to Honest Septima's new handlers. It appeared that their agent had ideas of her own. Heather bit back on her own reply – a not-too polite 'Go to Hell' – and waited for Guillermo's response. He was team leader, and he already didn't care for having a newbie come along simply because she'd seen some combat action. Heather even agreed with his general assessment: she thought that killing people and breaking things were overvalued everywhere in the US.

The senior officer hesitated for a second. "Fine," he finally said. "Let's go."

Not what Heather had expected. Moving a meeting to an unknown and unexpected location wasn't a good idea. She went along nonetheless. The chance for actionable intelligence probably outweighed the risk, at least enough that she wasn't going to second-guess her superior.

And if worse came to worst, she had come prepared for trouble: a holdout beamer and a light force field were concealed under her hooded robes. She had recently learned she wouldn't hesitate to pull the trigger on anybody who threatened her. Maybe the remfies who'd sent her on this mission had known what they were doing after all.

They followed the floating Scarab through the crowded concourse, past clumps of ogling or chatting visitors. In their robes, they blended in just fine; their guide was the one that stood out, and not in a good way. The Kreck were one of the four Founding Races of the Galactic Imperium, and weren't popular outside its borders. Most people they passed by didn't react visibly; those who did exhibited various forms of hostile body language, from deliberately turning their backs on them to raised hackles from a group of Puppies and angry hoots from a passing Butterfly.

Heavy Decimus ignored the gestures. Nobody tried to do anything beyond that; a Scarab wealthy enough to afford its own anti-grav system would no doubt be well-equipped to defend itself, and the authorities would come down hard on anybody offering violence to a citizen of the Imperium. They made it to one of the station lifts without incident.

The double doors of the lift looked just like an oversized

elevator, although the car inside was capable of lateral movement as well, being suspended in a magnetic field as it moved through a complex system of shafts and tunnels. Heather gave her superior a look, but he simply shrugged and followed the Scarab inside. Half a minute later, the lift's doors reopened, revealing a nondescript corridor somewhere inside the station. Heather tried to ascertain their location and discovered she couldn't: the area was shut off from all communications. That was good if the meeting was friendly, but if it turned out to be otherwise, they didn't know where they were, couldn't call for help, and would have to hack into the lift's controls to go anywhere.

"We did not agree to be cut off!" Guillermo said when he discovered the same thing a few moments later. It was more than little too late to complain. The moment they'd gotten into the lift they had agreed to put their lives in the hands of their agent. *Idiot*, Heather thought. And she'd followed his lead; what did that make her?

"Security," was all the Scarab said as it walked to the single door at the other end of the corridor. "Be careful upon entering; the chamber is set up to accommodate Kreck's biological needs."

Heather appreciated the warning as they stepped into the opulent room; its local gravity was slightly less than half Earth's standard. Her Navy training had prepared her for this kind of environment, so she avoided making a fool of herself. Guillermo Hamilton didn't launch himself across the room or smack into the ceiling, either, so at least he wasn't that sort of idiot. Her face mask automatically tightened over her face when her imp sensed that the local oxygen concentration was both too high and at unhealthy pressure levels for humans.

The dwelling had been refurbished to fit the Scarabs' sense of aesthetics: there were no separate rooms, just one large circular chamber, with partitions made by fence-like walls that only reached halfway towards the ceiling, creating a ring of stall-like sections. The largest one was elaborately decorated with organic-looking furnishings made of plastic or chitin. Their host was waiting for them there.

Honest Septima lay on a reclining couch. A mature female past her breeding stage, she was half again as large as her servant; her carapace was painted a garish pattern of silver and gold and encrusted with jewels and decorative circuitry. She waved her pincer limbs in greeting.

"Human-Americans Hamilton and McClintock, welcome to this humble dwelling. I must beg your pardon for the change in plans, but I needed to discuss some things at length, which a brief meeting in public would not allow."

"You breached protocol," Guillermo said, pointedly not using the alien's titles and honorifics. Heather knew the Kreck liked to play verbal dominance games and had to be reminded who was the boss early and often. All the Imperium's founding races did: over three millennia of coexistence, the different species had come to adopt the same arrogant culture, a rarity in the galaxy, where there were usually a couple of distinct civilizations even within a given species. "This was supposed to be a brush-pass and a brief face-to-face meeting as a show of good faith. By leading us here, you have put us all at risk."

"My apologies once again. I believe you will find my reasons to provide sufficient excuses for my behavior." The alien's body language and 'tone' – as interpreted by Heather's imp – were contrite enough. "First things first, of course. Decimus, you may leave now."

"As you wish, My Proxy."

"Here is the information I was to convey to you, and quite a bit more," the Kreck female said after the servant had left. An imp-to-imp burst transmission sent Guillermo some fifteen petabytes of information, protected by heavy encryption. Heather watched the data dump through her imp; they'd been expecting a copy of the Imperium's latest economic figures, which Honest Septima's position in the Ministry of Wealth gave her access to. Whatever was in those files was a good thousand times bigger than the simple report they'd been expecting.

"In addition to the Ministry of Wealth report, I have given you the minutes of the last six conferences between the Giga-Proxy Council and the Imperial Troika," Honest Septima went on. "They include the meeting in which the decision to make war on humanity was made. At that conference, a detailed report of the Imperium's capabilities was presented by the Troika. That is also included in the report."

Heather fought to stay impassive; Guillermo went pale but also managed to maintain a poker face. Their minor contact – so minor that her original recruiter had handed her off to two relatively junior agents without a second thought – had just handed them the keys to the Galactic Imperium.

"That… that is very impressive," Hamilton said. "The data will have to be analyzed and verified, but if it proves to be accurate… How did you come upon this information, may I ask?"

"To answer your question, I must first ask one of my own,

distinguished human spy. Do you know how I came to be forced into your service?"

"Yes," Guillermo said, not bothering to hide the contempt in his voice. Both he and Heather had been briefed on exactly what kind of person their agent was.

Honest Septima was a pervert by the mores of both the Scarab species and the Imperium at large. Her secret vice was rather unpleasant: infant cannibalism, an atavistic behavior that had once been common among the Kreck thousands of years ago. Despite millennia of cultural and psychological conditioning against the practice, a small minority among the species still felt the urge to feast upon hatchlings, although they usually dealt with it through therapy or chemically-altered food substitutes. Honest Septima had used her power and influence to satisfy her hungers, paying a criminal gang to provide her with Kreck newborn. An American trader had somehow stumbled upon the secret – Heather didn't know the details, but they apparently involved gambling, murder and assorted mayhem – and he in turn had sold the information to the CIA.

Spies betrayed their countries and species for numerous reasons. Money was a common motivation, of course. There were also people acting out of spite, turning traitor because they'd been overlooked for promotions or otherwise slighted. Some even lashed out of twisted patriotism, after deciding their nation was headed in the wrong direction. And then there was blackmail. The Imperium's penalty for child cannibalism was death, preceded by a lengthy 'scourging' process involving the stimulation of the convict's pain receptors in assorted ways. The US had Septima over the proverbial barrel. Heather found the whole thing disgusting, but intelligence work forced you to deal with some of the worst people in the known universe, human or otherwise.

"I know that if humanity is destroyed, I will not survive it by very long," Honest Septima went on. "If you lose the war, I expect my… proclivities will come to light, either when the Imperium seizes all your data or when you decide to reveal any damaging information you have on its leadership, which regrettably includes me. Thus, I felt I had to provide you with some vital information, in the hopes that you may be able to forestall your downfall."

"I see," Hamilton said.

"To elaborate, even though I am but a minor Proxy, I discovered some time ago that one of the Giga-Proxies of the Imperium shares my regrettable vices. And much like your fellow spies snared me, I too came with an arrangement with said individual. He now provides me with information in return for my discretion."

Whatever works, I suppose, Heather thought. Their agent had in turn recruited an even bigger fish, apparently.

"I trust you will find the information useful."

"I'm sure we will. And you will be suitably compensated, of course."

Blackmail was the stick; discreetly-paid bribes provided a consolation carrot.

"Do the records explain why the Imperium chose to go to war with the US?" Heather asked. The data would be read and interpreted by a team of analysts back on Earth, but getting a little personal info couldn't hurt.

The Kreck made a crossed-pincer negative gesture. "The official explanation is that the Lhan Arkh and Nasstah surrendered several star systems to the Imperium to secure the alliance. This has prompted some Proxies to protest we are being used as 'mercenaries' by those polities. Those protests, as you will see in the reports, were ignored. The official explanation is rumored to be a pretext, however. The territorial concessions were actually the Imperium's demand to join the war. The real reason has not been divulged to the public."

"And do you know what it is?"

"This is only gossip, and you won't find it in the files I gave you. But it appears that a faction among the Dann, led by Princeps Boma, is responsible for the war. Their alleged reasons are... strange."

The Dann were a humanoid Class Two species, who, like the rest of the Imperium, had had very little direct contact with humanity.

"Boma's faction apparently believes you humans are some sort of demonic force. It's a... religious conviction," Septima said. Her antennae's movement revealed her emotions: a mixture of wonder and contempt. The Imperium had abandoned such 'superstitions' long ago, replacing it with a mixture of rational thought and a tradition of obedience – bordering in worship – to the nation-state itself. To refer to any motivation as 'religious' was very close to calling it insane.

"Boma is a scholar of sorts," she continued. "When humans revealed their incredible ability to withstand warp space, he spent decades delving into the records of the ancients. It was, as you must know, a monumental task."

Both intelligence officers nodded. Thousands of civilizations had existed in the outer arms of the Milky Way Galaxy for at least a billion years. The average lifespan of a Starfarer polity was five thousand years, give or take an order of magnitude During that time, it would spread from a few dozen to a few thousand worlds before their inevitable end: Transcendence for those that advanced to the next level of existence, abandoned their colonies and left for parts unknown, or Oblivion for those who died out through decadence, genocide or other catastrophes. There usually weren't more than thirty major Starfaring polities around at any given time: the current number was below twenty. The total number of known Starfarer nations was about ten thousand, spanning a billion years.

Nobody had complete records of the history of the galaxy. The amount of information any Starfarer nation would generate over its millennia of existence was enormous: multiply that by ten thousand, and throw in changes in information storage systems, losses due to war, Transcendence or accident, along with the unfortunate habit of victors to rewrite history to suit their needs, and what you got was a massive mess of contradictory accounts, legends, massive translation errors, and deliberate misinformation. Parsing through it was pretty much impossible, and most people never bothered to even try. Just trying to grasp the current affairs of the galaxy was enough of an ordeal.

"Humans are not exactly unique, you see," Septima said. "There have been at least a dozen similarly endowed species, according to Boma's research. The problem is, there aren't any detailed records about them, for one simple reason: their appearance coincided with major upheavals in the galaxy. Upheavals that led to the destruction of almost every civilization that existed during those times. It goes beyond mere political disruption, of however. There are always species that do not play well with the rest. The Horde, for example, and to some degree our worthy allies, the Lhan Arkh. But the beings in those stories, those warp-demons, they are worse than those miscreants. They bring forth supernatural entities, supposedly. Monsters and such. Apparently it became customary that any species that showed such traits be quickly exterminated before it could become a threat."

Heather and Guillermo exchanged a glance but remained silent.

"It is Boma's alleged conclusion that warp hyper-capable species are a plague that must be exterminated early in their development. The current alliance is meant to stamp humanity out."

"And what do you think, Proxy?" Heather asked.

"I think a few fragmentary records are meaningless: none of them are less than a hundred thousand years old, and all are woefully incomplete. The last such upheaval happened nearly a million years in the past. The Princeps and his followers are being foolish, that is what I think. Boma is over a thousand years old, one of the lucky few who has evaded death that long, and at that age certain mental peculiarities begin to show themselves."

"Would the rest of the Imperium go along with a madman's crusade?" Guillermo said. "Maybe spreading this information could change things."

Another negative gesture. "Whatever Boma's reasoning, he has convinced the Troika. The Proxy Assemblies cannot countermand the three Principes, and in any case they have been convinced, bribed or intimidated into acquiescing. Only a severe reversal in the course of the war would induce them to reconsider."

"Guess we'll have to kick the Imperium's ass, then," Guillermo said glibly.

Heather wished she could feel so confident. So far, there had only been a few skirmishes with Imperium ships; they were ponderously massing their forces, mostly on the Wyrms' borders. The US Third Fleet had been sent to buttress Earth's only ally in the war so far. The reports their agent had just handed them would reveal just how bad the odds facing them really were, but everybody already knew they were horrible. The Imperium by itself outweighed the Wyrashat and US combined. Throw in the other two members of the Tripartite Galactic Alliance into the mix and things went from bad to impossible.

At least we know more, Heather thought. She would make sure Guillermo added Septima's rumors to the rest of the data. Amazing how gossip learned from a perverted traitor might end up affecting the fate of nations.

Knowledge might not help much in this case, though. Knowing you were hopelessly outnumbered only meant you went into the fight with no expectation of victory.

Eight

Groom Base, Star System 3490, 165 AFC

"FNG-4, front and center!"

Call sign namings had been a long-held tradition among small craft pilots, and Tenth Squadron was going to carry it on. The main difference here was that everyone except the squadron commander – Lieutenant Colonel Jessup a.k.a. Jester – was a Fucking New Guy/Gal, and they were all getting a call sign tonight.

You didn't give yourself a handle; that was up to the rest of the pilots. The results would likely be hilarious; learning to live with them could be a bit of an ordeal.

FNG Number Four – Lieutenant Mark Giovanni – stepped back into the room. They'd appropriated one of the base's briefing rooms for the ceremony. Each pilot was forced to wait outside while the rest of the squadron deliberated. Alcohol was being consumed in copious quantities, adding to the solemnity of the occasion.

"Do you have any suggestions, FNG-4?" Captain Jaime Van Allen – now forever known as Belter – asked, slurring his words a little bit.

"I was hoping for Marksman," Giovanni said hopefully.

"I bet you were. What say you?" Belter asked the rest of the squadron. Boos and catcalls filled the room. "Sorry, Number Four. After careful deliberation, your call sign has been deemed to be… drum roll, please…" Everybody pounded on their tables. "Goober!"

"Goober?"

"Get used to it, Goober. FNG-Number Five, step out of the room, please."

That was Lisbeth's number. She dutiful walked out into the corridor. The door to the briefing room shut off the laughter and shouting on the other side, leaving her alone in the sudden quiet.

It was all official. Twenty-five squadrons were rated to fly missions. Two hundred and fifty plots, about a hundred a fifty from previous classes, the rest from Lisbeth's own band of volunteers. The two-hundred-plus candidates that had started out with her had been pruned down to less than half that number. Five of the washouts had been fatalities; six more were no longer fit for service, or much of anything else, at least until the shrinks figured out how to put their minds back together. And now the rest were heading out into harm's way, where they would find out what pesky little details the simulations and training had missed. Testing new weapons technology by using it in combat rarely went off as expected, and there were very few good surprises.

Lisbeth knew all those things, but they didn't seem to matter. It was time. She wanted to go into warp space knowing the enemy waited at the other end.

The door opened.

"FNG-Number Five, front and center!"

She went back inside.

"Do you have any suggestions, FNG-5?"

"Nope."

"Good answer. It is our considered opinion that from now on, you will be known as, drum roll, please…"

Lamia? I'm getting call-signed after mythological half-woman, half snake thingie?

"Lamia!"

The rest of the squadron thought her shocked expression was prompted by her call sign, rather than her knowing what it was before they said it.

Parthenon-Three, 165 AFC

"Who are those people in the big cars, Grampa?"

"Marines. Motorized platoon," Morris Jensen said, all but spitting the words in distaste. He scratched his close-cropped, mostly-white hair, feeling old. He looked it, too. Even well-to-do farmers had better uses for their money than spending it on the full rejuv package; his innards were mostly in good working order, but his face was wrinkled and weathered, and his joints ached whenever he pushed himself too hard. Keeping your internal organs from the ravages of time was expensive enough, unless you were rich or served multiple tours of duty in the armed forces. He'd never been wealthy, and his (unpaid) membership in the local militia was as close as he ever wanted to get to the military. He'd done his time in hell, and he was done with it.

"Marines. Like you used to be, right?" Jensen's granddaughter asked. Mariah Jensen was eleven, and was intently watching the advancing vehicles from the front porch of the farmhouse. There were few surprises around this neck of the woods, and the floating IFVs driving past his property were definitely a new sight.

"Yes, Mar. Like I used to be."

Like I never want to be again. Once a Marine, always a Marine, they said, but he was all too glad to be a former jarhead.

His time in the Corps hadn't been a happy time. Twenty-five years. Fourteen deployments. He'd seen too many of his buddies die. That had been the war against the Horde, and those fuckers played rough. His company had taken two hundred percent casualties in three years, hunting down guerrillas in Hawkins-Two. Sure, most of the dead had been boots who hadn't known what they were doing, but not all of them. When your number came up, even the most experienced grunts couldn't hold out on the reaper.

The sight of the sleek graviton-propelled fighting vehicles brought back memories. Back in his day, grav engines were too expensive to waste on ground-pounders, so his outfit had made do with ground-effect hover vehicles, but the basic lines were similar enough. Small turret on top, two side box launchers, bow and coax machineguns. The newer versions would be tougher and faster than the ones that'd carried him through fetid alien jungles, looking for insurgents to kill, but he bet the enemy would know just how to take them out. The enemy always did.

His gloves began to melt in the flames, the skin and flesh beneath blistering, but he didn't let go of Jim's limp form. He pulled him out of the burning wreck before he realized most of his friend's lower torso had been left behind. He'd burned his hands to the bone hauling out half a corpse.

Morris shook his head. Goddammit. He was in the Volunteer militia and spent a weekend a month in uniform, but those uniforms didn't trigger the bad memories. He hadn't thought about Jim's death in decades, even while playing war with his fellow Volunteers. But all it took was the Corps coming to town, and he was back in the jungle, the hideously appetizing smell of burning human flesh filling his nostrils. No sleep for him tonight. When he found himself back in the Suck, the only way he could bear to go to bed was after he'd downed a fifth of whiskey, maybe two. And he couldn't do that now, not with his granddaughter under his roof and him the only one left to take care of her. So no sleep for him; he'd just lie there in the dark staring at nothing. Goddammit to Hell.

He spat as the four-vehicle formation sped past his fields. Harvest was already in, but even if it weren't, those fancy anti-gravity personnel carriers wouldn't have disturbed the crops.

For the time being, that was. The Marines wouldn't be on Parthenon-Three if some damn big disturbances weren't on their way here.

"Those tanks are *big*," Mariah said. "Bigger then a combine!"

"Those ain't tanks, kiddo. Infantry fighting vehicles."

"Whassits?"

"They carry soldiers," Morris explained gruffly, resisting an urge to tell her to get back inside, to shout that the sight of those vehicles meant death was on its way. Scaring the girl would accomplish nothing, and she'd been through too much pain already.

He flashed back to a conversation from a little over a year ago. *"Honey, your Dad and Mom were in an accident, a really bad accident..."* Explaining to a child her parents weren't coming back had been as hard as anything he'd done in the Corps. He might as well let the sight of the gracefully gliding behemoths bring a smile of wonder to her face.

Morris softened his voice and went on. "The real tanks are even bigger. The box on the top, that's called a turret by the way, is twice that size on a tank, and the tube coming out, the main gun, is almost as long as the entire vehicle. The beams it shoots can hurt a starship in orbit, that's how big the gun is."

"Wow," Mariah said.

And when one of those big suckers blows up, there's nothing left of the crew but a smear on the wreckage. And they may be tough, but they ain't invulnerable. There's no can so big a can opener to handle it can't be found.

Death came for everyone. His son Otis and his wife Ruth had been driving home from a barn dance in Davistown when one of the local critters had made them swerve and drive off a cliff. That's all it took.

Sure, one could blame their deaths on the fact that most colonists in Parthenon-Three had to make do with cars only slightly better than what folk had used before First Contact. All the fancy graviton engines and force fields went mostly to the military or the uber-rich; the latter stuck around big cities like Henderson, New Burbank and Sunnyvale and wouldn't be caught dead driving on the plasticized-dirt roads of Forge Valley. He shrugged. Might as well blame the pseudo-lizard that had stepped in the path of his son's car. In the end, looking for someone to blame was useless. Sometimes shit just happened.

Some serious shit was about to happen right here.

While Mariah watched the five maneuvering IFVs before they got out of sight, Morris glanced over his property: fifteen thousand acres of prime farmland that he and his son and daughter-in-law had managed until the accident left him alone in charge of both farm and granddaughter. Robots did most of the hard work, along with temps hired from Davistown or nearby farms who could spare a son or daughter come harvest or planting season. Managing the property was a lot of work, but he didn't mind. He'd been happy here ever since he plowed his savings and his twelve-year pension into the dirt-cheap property nearly fifty years ago, back when Parthenon-Three had been an up-and-coming colony with less than a million inhabitants on the whole planet and terraformer engines were still ironing out all the kinks needed to turn the near-goldie world into a full one.

He'd been happy so long that he'd forgotten how all of it could be taken away at a moment's notice.

"A tank! A tank, grampa! That is a tank, isn't it?"

"That it is, sweetheart," he said after taking a glance at the massive follow-up vehicle. One of the new Stormin' Normans by the looks of it. During his idle time, he still perused military sites. His feelings for life in uniform didn't extend to the hardware. The Marines got the best toys, of course. His militia unit was mostly logistics and they drove wheeled trucks and a handful of halftracks; even ground-effect vehicles were beyond their budget. The fighting/security element of which he was part of was light infantry, a euphemism for relying on the Mark-One Shank's Mare or clambering on whatever truck had spare room for a squad of grunts. The Army and National Guard formations stationed around the big cities and the Planetary Defense Bases were better off, but not by much.

The Corps had the best tech, but lacked the sheer numbers they were going to need to hold Parthenon-Three against an attack. And his land was likely going to become a battlefield.

Beyond the fertile plateau of Forge Valley loomed a ring of mostly-impassable mountains. The aliens would likely land near the western mouth of the valley and push their way towards the nearest PDB nestled within another mountain range some ninety miles away, on the eastern end. And opposing them would be whatever the Marines could bring to the table – he'd heard a battalion plus attachments – plus the local Army, Guard and Volunteer units.

He shook his head. Most of the militiamen were kids fresh from their obligatory service who liked playing soldier a few times a year, along with a smattering of old-timers, most of whom had never seen combat. Morris spat again. You couldn't stiffen a bucket of spit with a handful of buckshot, and second-rate buckshot at that. The militia was unlikely to be asked to hold the line, that much was true, but he also knew how quickly the rear could become the front. Those summer soldiers could well be put to the test, along with Morris himself.

And they would likely fail. They said there was no 'fail' in the Corps, but he wasn't in the Corps anymore.

* * *

They had some big-ass cities here, but the way things were going Russell would never get a good look at them. The 101st had ended up deployed in the boondocks yet again, just outside the miles-wide force fields protecting Planetary Defense Base Twelve, and to get to anywhere fun, they would have to make a two-hour drive to New Burbank, the only big town nearby. And that was if they ever got leave and could beg, borrow or steal transport there. The only civvie settlements in the valley were tiny farming villages, the kind of place where everybody knew everybody and strangers weren't welcome. Russell had thought about trying his luck with some of the local farmers' daughters, but the communities around here were mostly Orthodox Catholics or Reformed Mennonites, which meant you could look but never touch, and on second thought you couldn't look, either.

Oh, well. The Skipper and the higher ups from the battalion were keeping everyone too busy to think about having fun. The Eets were coming. Any day now, or so they'd been saying for nearly a month since they deployed here. Another combat mission, but unlike the last couple ones, they weren't going to fight primmies with a few borrowed toys. They were up against the ET varsity now. Russell had never run into the Vipers, but from what he'd seen in the training simulations, they were no fun at all.

"Edison, move your team to the next ridge," Staff Sergeant Dragunov ordered. "And keep your heads down, fuck-socks! We ain't fighting barbs no more."

We ain't fighting nobody, Russell groused silently, but he understood the purpose of the exercise. Charlie Company had spent the better part of a year hunting Big Furries, and you started to develop bad habits after a while. They needed to be ready, just in case the shit hit the fan for real.

"You heard the man," he told his fire team. "Move it!"

They rushed forward, making sure to stay in defilade the whole way. They were practicing a movement to contact evolution against a notional enemy company. Their imps projected fake energy discharges straight into their eyeballs and blasted their ears with the appropriate sounds, adding realism to the maneuver. He saw and heard laser beams crisscrossing the air overhead as they reached their objective. They looked and sounded just like they did in real combat.

Russell dropped the portable force field he'd been lugging right on the reverse slope of the ridge; Gonzo and Nacle joined him, and they slowly crawled the last few feet to the top, pushing the shield ahead of them. A flight of drones made a pass overhead; most of them were (administratively) swatted down before revealing anything useful, but enough survived to provide them with some targets: a crew-served laser a klick and a half away.

Russell designated the target. "Let 'em have it!"

He opened up with the 20mm launcher while Nacle and Gonzo cut loose with grenades. The range was a bit long, but it was worth a try, plus the mortar section was busy with other targets and the exercise assumed all other heavy weapon assets were not available at the moment. The battalion's attached tank platoon was supposed to swing by, but it hadn't yet. They were out on the sharp end with near fuck-all in the way of support, in other words. Russell hated that kind of no-win scenario, Well, supposedly you could win them, if you did everything perfectly, but you mostly didn't.

The pretend volley hit a pretend force field without doing damage, and then it was the pretend Vipers' turn. The portable shield sizzled and crackled as it was overwhelmed by a direct laser hit. A second later, Russell's sensors went white and his armor's power cut off. The sudden weight of over a hundred and fifty now-inert pounds of battle-rattle and gear dragged him down as surely as if his brain had been vaporized by a real laser.

"You dead, Russet," Gonzo said. "Forgot to duck?"

"Go duck yourself," Russell growled. His commo was still working even though he was a notional casualty. Gonzo chuckled.

"What now?" Nacle asked.

"Now we hunker down and wait for support," Gonzo replied. "And here come the tanks!"

"Tanks for nothing," Russell said. He normally wasn't big on puns, but it was better than just lying there. The whole thing felt a little too much like the last time he'd gone down for the count.

He just hoped that the next time it happened for real it wouldn't be so bad.

"Give 'em hell, Shellies!" Gonzo cried out.

Russell couldn't see much from his prone position, but he sneaked a peek through his fire team's sensors and watched the MEU's tanks float into position. They didn't look like much, from two klicks away, at least until they opened up on the laser position. A 250mm graviton cannon blast looked like nothing else in creation, and even the simulated version was scary as hell. The inner core of the beam was the purest black; some egghead had explained to Russell that it was akin to looking into a black hole, not you could actually see a black hole. Black in the center, surrounded with an aura of twisted matter, space and supposedly even time. When four beams hit the laser's position, they turned it into a crater. Or would have, if it had been for real.

He'd briefly considered going into tanks. There was something to be said about being inside a hundred-ton metal beast with near-invulnerable force fields and armor and a main gun guaranteed to go through just about anything you could find on a planet. On the other hand, whenever a Shellie showed up, everybody on the other side did their level best to kill it. All in all, staying close to the ground and being able to duck for cover was better, he decided, even if sometimes you didn't duck fast enough.

They were sure handy to have around when the shit hit the fan, though.

* * *

"We bring you death!" Staff Sergeant Konrad Zimmer roared at the top of his lungs.

"We bring you DOOM!" chorused the rest of the tank crew as the *Fimbul Winter* unleashed twisted gravity devastation on the simulated targets downrange.

Zimmer had been a Kriegsmetall fan ever since he'd been a snot-nosed teenager and his older sister had grudgingly taken him to a Star Valhalla concert. He'd been lucky enough to find two kindred souls in his crew. Both Lance Corporal Mira Rodriguez and PFC Jessie Graves were war-heads. Well, Mira had been, and between the two of them they'd dragged Jessie into it. Now they marched to battle to the sounds of Star Valhalla, Molon Labe or We Own the Night, and they loved it.

Since this was a simulation and not the real thing, they could be a bit more casual about singing and fighting. Things got a lot quieter when it was for real.

"Target, three o'clock," Zimmer called out. A Viper field gennie, floating along on a weak graviton engine while providing protection to anything inside a two-hundred-yard radius around it.

"On the way! Hit!" Mira shouted. "DOOM!" The cannon blast punctured the force field and turned the generator into a fireball.

A volley of anti-armor rockets sped towards the tank, but Jessie had been alerted by the targeting warning sensors and made the tank lurch sideways fast and hard enough to slam Zimmer against his seat with bone-bruising force.

"Motherfucker!" Zimmer shouted. His armored vest absorbed most of the damage but that was still going to leave a mark.

"DOOM!" Jessie roared. Only one of the dozen or so missiles hit the tank, and it didn't even make an impression on its shields.

"We bring you Hell," Mira sang. She fired without calling out the target, but Zimmer had seen it too: a Viper rocketeer, standing up in full sight of God and radar. Were the real ETs that stupid? If they were, they would share the fate of the asshole who'd dared fire on the *Fimbul Winter*. The graviton blast drank away the lone figure, leaving no trace of the tango behind.

Most Vipers had scrambled for cover. Mira made sure they stayed down with a long burst from the coaxial 15mm automatic launch system. Plasma and frag grenades burst over the target area, showering the ETs with fiery death.

"Your Wyrd is here!" Zimmer sang on. His cupola ALS added some extra firepower to the mix. "Valhalla beckons!"

The rest of the platoon was spread over a mile-wide front, each of the four tanks creating a bubble of destruction where no living thing could exist without their permission. They had to be careful not to blue-on-blue the ground-pounders who'd been kind enough to fix the Vipers in place so the platoon could come sweeping down their left flank. Leg infantry had its uses, Zimmer supposed. If nothing else, they helped make sure any enemy grunts couldn't get close enough to the tanks to become a nuisance.

First Lieutenant Morrell called out the all-clear. The platoon had run out of aliens to kill.

"And Death claimed them all!" the three crewmembers went on singing, mercifully only in their vehicle channel. The rest of the platoon didn't share their passion for metal.

This was the life. Zimmer couldn't wait for the real aliens to show up.

Sixth Fleet, Parthenon System Warp-Lane, 165 AFC

The courier ship didn't bring any good news.

"That's it?" Admiral Sondra Givens said in a soft voice. No sense scaring everyone inside the Tactical Flag Command Center, deep in the bowels of the *Admiral*-class dreadnought *USS William Halsey Jr.* Shouting would be bad for morale. Despite her best efforts, her voice rose slightly as she went on. "We know the Vipers are going to hit us here, and at any moment, and that's all the reinforcements they send us? A squadron of *Presidents* almost as old as I am, and a smattering of frigates and destroyers?"

"Seventh Fleet is still coming together on Wolf 1061," Rear Admiral Farragut said diffidently. The skipper of Sixth Fleet's flagship didn't sound any happier than Givens felt, despite the vain attempt to reassure the fleet commander.

Givens repressed a string of curses. *Maintain an even strain*; that saying was as true now that humankind had spread to the stars as it had been during the early days of the space program. This war was putting her normally-unflappable demeanor to the test. The fact that her own grandson had been killed during the opening salvos of the conflict – before the US even knew it was at war – didn't help. She'd buried her dead, and she was more than ready and eager to bury the enemy next. But she needed the right tools for the job and she was getting a lot less than she'd expected.

Onscreen, Sixth Fleet was an impressive formation. Two dreadnoughts, six battleships, twelve battlecruisers, twenty-four light and medium cruisers that unfortunately included the six *Presidential*-class antiques that had just arrived and four converted Puppy light cruisers the GACS had sent along, thirty-six destroyers, six assault ships (currently mostly empty of Marines and serving mainly as missile-defense platforms) and sixty frigates.

Impressive, that is, until you considered that Fifth Fleet had been stronger in capital ships (four dreadnoughts and seven battleships) and had fielded about twenty percent more tonnage in all other vessel classes, and yet it'd been defeated and forced to run with its tail between it legs. It'd lost one irreplaceable dreadnought and three battleships, suffered even worse casualties down the rest of the battle line, and was now trying to pull itself together at Wolf 1061 after Givens had relieved it at Parthenon. The damage wasn't just physical; a brief talk with Admiral Kerensky had made it clear to Givens that the fleet and its commander were beaten, thoroughly demoralized after being forced to abandon a major inhabited system to the Vipers. If Fifth Fleet had to fight again anytime soon, it wouldn't fare well.

And Sondra Givens wasn't sure her own ships would do any better.

Kerensky was a gifted commander, forged in the same cauldron where Givens' own career had begun, fighting the Snakes into extinction. Both admirals were fighters who had eschewed advancement beyond fleet command because they belonged out in the dark of space, trading broadsides with any alien foolish enough to threaten America. Neither of them had met with defeat in nearly a century of service, broken only by the occasional forced retirement periods meant to give others their chance to learn the tricks of the trade. And yet, despite his skill and resolve, Kerensky had failed; he was a shadow of his former self, at least for the time being.

"Seventh Fleet is expected to arrive no later than three months from now," Farragut went on, breaking the string of dark thoughts running through her mind. "When it does, our strength will more than double."

"Except many of those ships are still being *built*," Givens said. "Their flagship, the *Zeus*, was still having its main warp drive assembled when we left Wolf 1061. Sure, they were almost finished when the war began and the Sol and Wolf shipyards are doing their best to get them ready, but it takes more than a launch ceremony to make a ship, and you know it."

Farragut didn't even try to argue the point. The fact was that putting crews together for those ships and getting them ready for action was going to take a lot more than three months, even if the paperwork was expedited. Normally a starship wasn't deemed fit for service until a lengthy shakedown cruise to work out any kinks the engineers had missed, not to mention making sure the crew learned how to work together in an unfamiliar environment. Even if it arrived in time, Seventh Fleet's effectiveness would be far lower than a landlubber would assume.

But they weren't going to arrive in time. Three months was a wildly optimistic estimate, and she didn't think the Vipers were going to give them three months to prepare. She'd sent a steady stream of scout ships into Heinlein System; the little stealth destroyers had taken losses from enemy pickets but their efforts had formed a picture of the aliens' activities. Heinlein-Five was gone, all defensive bases and every city burned to the ground. There were probably scattered survivors in remote areas, but for all intents and purposes the planet had been lost.

The enemy fleet was replacing the losses it'd incurred taking that system. Her scouts' reports indicated the Vipers would be at full strength in fifteen to twenty days. For most intents and purposes, they were ready now.

They didn't have three months. She didn't think they had three weeks.

Nine

Trade Nexus Eleven, 165 AFC

"Isn't this interesting?" Heather said.

"What's interesting?" Guillermo Hamilton asked. He'd been busy poring over the latest Imperium production figures he'd gotten from a friendly Oval trader who was amenable to taking bribes and sharing information.

"The *GACSS 1138* docked onto TN-11 earlier today."

"And this is important because...?" the station chief muttered instead of bothering to do a search of the name. Heather sighed and sent him the info directly, imp-to-imp. Remfie.

"Oh," he said after reading the data dump.

"Yeah. That ship played a role in the Days of Infamy. More specifically, in the attack on Jasper-Five. We even got some eyewitness accounts from the natives after we made a deal with the new government; they testified that the ship unloaded the components used to destroy two American corvettes. Which in turn almost cost the lives of every human on the planet."

Including my own, but let's not make this personal, not quite yet.

"I see. And why haven't our good friends the Pan-Asians turned them over to us?"

"They tried. I know they usually don't like cooperating with us, but the situation has changed." The realities of the situation couldn't be ignored. Like every other human nation in the galaxy, the Greater Asian Co-Prosperity Sphere was at war with the Tripartite Galactic Alliance, and only the US could protect their space colonies. "They issued arrests warrants for the ship's captain and her crew. Someone warned them, however, and they've gone rogue. For the past year, they've avoided human space, and anywhere else that will extradite them. Which unfortunately doesn't include the O-Vehel Commonwealth. The Ovals don't like bothering traders. Too much of their economy depends on the 'free passage of goods and information.' Free except for their tariffs and fees, that is."

"Despite the fact that the ship's actions got a number of Ovals killed on Jasper-Five?"

"A lot of human pilots are working for the Vehelians," Heather explained. The ability to handle warp space better than any other extant species in the galaxy made human-crewed vessels rather valuable. Enterprising Earthlings could write their own ticket crewing alien ships. And many of them didn't bother paying US taxes on their income, which made them outlaws in human space. Thousands of those rogue pilots were happy with their status as exiles, though. "The Ovals don't want to antagonize them by turning on one of their own. On the other hand, they aren't likely to join the Tripartite Alliance for pretty much the same reasons. They consider humans a valuable asset."

"All of which means there isn't much we can do," the chief spook said. "They don't let bounty hunters operate in their territory, either. If they won't turn them over to us, that's the end of the matter. I guess we can report their passage, maybe try to find out what their next port of call will be. We don't have any other options," he concluded, clearly intent on forgetting about the Pan-Asian rogue ship and getting back to work.

"Our *legal* options," Heather said.

"Uh, oh. I smell cowboy crap. We're not set up to do wet work, McClintock."

"We are authorized to sanction enemy assets, as long as such operation can be safely disavowed," she reminded her boss. 'Sanction' was spook jargon for killing. While the CIA was primarily in the info gathering business, it also helped deal with enemies foreign and, under certain circumstances, domestic.

"What do you propose?"

"Well, I have been gathering contacts with the local underworld."

"Criminals," Hamilton said with disdain. "Unreliable, dangerous. I thought you had more sense than that."

"They have their uses. My report on those Viper fleet movements came from smugglers, in case you forgot."

"You got lucky. Next time, they'll probably try to sell you garbage. I don't know, McClintock. I don't like improvising an op on the fly. Could this be a trap?" Guillermo was trying to be the voice of reason, and was coming off like the voice of a chickenshit.

"I checked their travel records. They've made stops at TN-11 seven times over the last six years. They are currently delivering Lamprey foodstuffs to a couple high-rent restaurants that serve Class One delicacies at ruinous prices. Doesn't smell fishy to me. Except maybe the food."

"How long do we have before they're gone?"

“They’ve paid docking fees for the next seventy-two hours, with an option to extend. Probably trying to negotiate for new cargo. So figure we’ve got two, maybe three days minimum.”

“Not exactly a surfeit of time. What do you propose to do? We can’t bring the Marine security detachment into this. We’re not going to instigate an act of war against a neutral just to get some pirates.”

“I know,” she said, trying not to let her impatience show. Yes, this was personal, but it also fulfilled their professional duties. Traitors to humanity couldn’t be allowed to live. “Like I said, I’ve made some useful local contacts.”

“Again with the thugs,” Guillermo said. He preferred to work with high-class criminals, like corrupt government officials who could be bribed and blackmailed. He didn’t quite get that regular criminals could provide a great deal of support. Too many CIA operatives came from the wealthier and more ‘civilized’ sections of the US, on Earth or off, places where getting your hands dirty or bloody just wasn’t done. Heather might have been raised in that community, but contact with the real world had changed her. Maybe Guillermo would get it too, eventually.

“I can handle it, Gill. I’ll take care of it, and if anything goes wrong, you can disavow me. If everything works out, you get the credit. I don’t care about credit. I just want to get those bastards.”

Hamilton thought about. In the end, she guessed the chance of getting rid of her was as much an incentive for him as pulling off a major covert operation. The two intelligence officers hadn’t warmed up to each other. “All right. Let’s keep it off the books. Completely off. Can’t leave any sort of trail on this one.”

By which he meant that he didn’t want CIA funds to show up anywhere near the operation. They wouldn’t. Heather had been accumulating a decent stash of ‘unofficial’ funds during the past six months. She’d used her own money to start with, and made it grow via a variety of investments, some legal, some somewhat questionable. She’d learned from her time in Kirosha that relying on her official budget could leave you high and dry in the field. Sometimes you needed to be able to pony up some cash up front and there wasn’t time for some bean counter up the chain of command to approve the expense. And she’d discovered she had a not inconsiderable talent in business. When or if she retired from public service, she’d probably be able to supplement her pension rather handsomely.

Her family would be proud, the day she got a ‘real’ job. Assuming she lived that long.

"I've got it covered," she said. If the op went well, he'd make everything 'official' and reimburse her for the expenses, along with getting all the credit. That was fine by her.

She had a score to settle.

* * *

"How about a discount, *jingjing* girl?" the Korean spacer said for the third time as he allowed the hooker to drag him into an alleyway between two dive bars in the low-rent section of the station, so low-rent you needed to bring your own oxygen along unless you came from a *very* light-atmosphere planet. He and his buddy – you didn't wander the more disreputable parts of TN-11 on your own – were drunk, stoned, and ready to play. Their facemasks and inebriation slurred their words as they shared a joke and laughed.

The 'girl' – a member of the Blue Man species who might pass for human in poor lightning and resembled a human female only if the beholder was legally blind – rocked her head in a circular motion that was her culture's equivalent of a shrug.

"'Oo pay, I pop." She extended one of her four thick fingers towards the leader of the pair. "Wee nego-tee-ate," she finished in atrociously-accented English. Neither party had sophisticated imp translator apps, so they were relying in the one language they had in common, more or less. Fortunately, both of their limited vocabularies specialized in this sort of transaction.

"Yah, yah, negotiate," the designated haggler said. "Good girl. You pop me good, okay? Then mah friend. Ten Gee-Cees."

"Pop 'oo good, 'kay. Freen pop, thees many extra." She stuck out three fingers. Blue Men – or Women – weren't exactly sexually compatible with humans, but certain body parts would do well enough as field expedients. Thirteen Galactic Credit Units was a fairly reasonable price for a twosome, even though it probably represented several months of banked pay for the Pan-Asian spacers.

"Good. Thirteen Gee-Cees. Less whining, more suckey-fuckey, okay?"

And they say romance is dead, Heather thought as she watched the unfolding scene from her hiding spot at the end of the alley. Luring the unfortunate Gack crewmembers into the ambush had been child's play. As soon as the hooker led them out of sight of the main passageway, she and the rest of her ad hoc team pulled aside the stealth blankets they'd used to conceal their presence.

Her imp jammed the Pan-Asians' commo systems, ensuring they couldn't call for help. The two spacers were surrounded by hostile aliens before they realized their planned sex party had turned into something completely different.

The Boothan Clan was that rarity in galactic criminal circles, a multi-species organization. Most underworld gang stuck to a single species, or even an extended family within that species, on the grounds that outsiders were intrinsically untrustworthy. Major trade junctions like TN-11 were the most likely places to find exception to the rule. The clan members' loyalty was insured through fear; betraying the Boothan was punishable by death, but only after several weeks of methodical torture and mutilation.

Four figures rose from hiding and blocked both ends of the alley. Two were Blue Men like the prostitute they'd hired as bait, vaguely humanoid, their hairless, narrow bodies covered with slick-looking skin that ranged from sky blue to deep indigo in color. Their yellow eyes seemed to glow in the poor lightning of the alley. One was a Crab, more like a scorpion analogue really: eight legs, two arms with skeletal hands at their end, and two fighting pincers. The last one was a Class Three alien of an unknown species, his physical features completely covered up by a metallic environmental suit reminiscent of medieval plate armor, if a suit of armor had been designed to fit something shaped like a fireplug with three stubby legs and three long arms.

The alien gangsters were armed with a variety of death-dealing equipment, from laser pistols and beamers to the Class Three ET's sidearm, which looked like a hose at the end of a backpack container and which Heather had been told could spit out a combination of liquid nitrogen balloons and self-propelled solid darts. The Vehelian authorities allowed weapons to be carried on their trading posts – force fields minimized danger to the facility as a whole – but their unlawful use was harshly punished. This gang of thugs didn't seem to care. Of course, this area had next to no police presence and minimal and easily-bypassed surveillance systems.

"Wha…? Wha…?" the chatty Korean spacer said.

"Be quiet or die," Heather said in Mandarin, the common language of the GACS. Even the Russian members of the loose confederation had been forced to learn to speak it in the aftermath of First Contact.

"Who are you?" the less talkative one blurted out in the same language.

Heather made a curt head gesture. The armored three-legged

fireplug cut loose with his weapon. The center of the Korean spacer's chest was frozen solid by a splash of liquid nitrogen; a fraction of a second later, a kinetic projectile shattered the frozen flesh, leaving behind a hole large enough to accommodate a human head. The dead Pan-Asian fell to ground without making another sound.

"Be quiet or die, I said," Heather repeated. The surviving spacer kept his mouth shut. His wide eyes regarded the motley group with growing horror. He glanced at the prostitute, who impassively met his stare, and then desperately looked about for a way out. He needn't have bothered. There was no hope or mercy to be found anywhere on that alley.

It took a few seconds to break into the living crewman's third-rate implant system and access his personal records, which included a moment-by-moment video feed of his entire life, beginning with his implantation at age fifteen in Ryanggang Province and ending forty years later here, in a back alley on a far-off space station. The records had all the information Heather needed. Imps locked up when their wearer died, which made hacking into them more difficult and time-consuming. That little fact had earned the surviving Korean a few extra seconds to live. As soon as she got what she needed, his time was up.

She found that having people killed in cold blood was even more unpleasant than committing murder in the heat of the moment.

Another head gesture. Another blast of nitrogen and a kinetic coup-de-grace.

Unpleasant, but part of the job.

* * *

Harry Routh spent his last moments bitching about his life.

Life aboard the *GACSS-1138* had never been pleasant, and it had only gotten worse. The freighter's owners and operators were a Korean family who had sunk their life savings on the small and run-down vessel and aimed to get their money's worth by any means necessary. To that end, they would do business with anybody, and skimp on such luxuries as proper life support and spare parts.

The Greater Asian Co-Prosperity Sphere was a funny country. Harry still barely understood it, even after working in a GACS-flagged ship for what felt like a lifetime. The loose coalition of Russians, Chinese and assorted Eastern nations had come together after First Contact had largely depopulated their entire hemisphere. The resulting coalition of semi-independent governments generally cooperated with each other, especially when dealing with outsiders. China and Russia dominated the Sphere and were in fairly good shape. Harry was in a Korean vessel, unfortunately. Korea had been holding the short end of the stick ever since aliens had wiped out most of the South and left the survivors at the mercy of a gaggle of low-level northern officers who'd been lucky enough not to be in Pyongyang when it went up in flames. The *1138* was one of maybe a dozen Korean-flagged merchantmen, and Harry had been terrified to learn it was considered one of the better vessels of the bunch.

Captain Minh, the head of the family as well as of the ship, enforced discipline on his first- and second-cousins with gleeful brutality, and only the fact that his crew had literally nowhere else to go kept the desertion rate to a minimum. Harry had ended up as first mate of that floating disaster through a series of extremely unfortunate events. Like everyone else in the freighter, he was out of choices and out of luck. Except that, as an outsider, kept alive only because he knew how to keep the ship's systems running, he had to take crap from everyone all the time.

The previous year, he'd put another nail on his coffin by participating in a Lamprey covert operation against the US. He'd never planned to return to American space, but now even the Gacks wouldn't have him anymore. If the Pan-Asian authorities caught him, or anybody on the crew for that matter, they'd send him to the US for a short trial and a quick execution. As the only American in the crew, he'd earned the dubious honor of having the highest price on his head. Only the fact that the rest of the *GACSS-1138* spacers were in the same boat, pun intended had kept them from selling him out. The ship was doomed to spend its days wandering from one alien port to the next.

Their stay on TN-11 had been typical of his life on the Korean ship. Harry never got any shore leave and was stuck on deck the entire time. Then again, maybe he'd been lucky; two crew members hadn't come back. Desertion was a possibility, but Harry's guess was that they'd fallen afoul of one of the local criminal gangs that infested the shittier portions of the space station. The captain hadn't even bothered reporting the disappearances to the authorities. You never wanted to attract the local cops' attention, not when you sometimes engaged in activities they might not approve of.

Captain Minh had made a half-hearted attempt to find

replacements before leaving, but no human in TN-11 would even consider joining the outlaw ship, and aliens were out of the question. It wasn't because of the life support issues involved in having another species aboard, although that didn't help. Minh and his crew just couldn't abide the thought of having nonhumans working and living with them. They were disgusted enough by the presence of an American, although to be fair they would have been just as revolted by a Russian or Thai. Koreans didn't play well with others, probably because they'd been bombed back to the Stone Age during First Contact and many of the survivors had spent years on an enforced diet of tree bark and long pig. The resulting culture was extremely hostile towards outsiders. Minh's allowing Harry to stay alive on his ship made him a paragon of tolerance.

With no replacements available, they'd be leaving with a short crew. Which meant someone had to pick up the slack, and as usual Harry got the short end of the stick. On top of getting no leave time, Captain Minh had him supervising the loading of their next shipment. Their last delivery had consisted of a thousand tons of Class One foodstuffs, and that had been a mess. The *1138*'s new cargo was not biological, thankfully: electronic components, fairly valuable stuff, and the shipping fees for delivering it to a Crab colony would keep the little merchantman running for a good while. On the down side, the trip would take about ninety warp-hours spread over five weeks, and Harry would be busting his ass for most of it.

"Watch it, Sagong!" he yelled at one of the crewmembers, who was about to drive a mag-lev forklift into a bulkhead. Sagong glared at him but slowed down and maneuvered the container through the door without breaking anything. The last thing they needed was damaged cargo. The Captain would take any penalties out of the shares of all crewmembers involved.

I can't live like this, he thought, not for the first or the thousandth time. He had a plan of sorts: save enough to buy his way out of his contract, and then find some ETs willing to pay what he was worth. Failing that, he intended to jump ship with the clothes on his back and take his chances. So far, neither opportunity had presented itself. But some day, hopefully soon…

A sudden flash of light interrupted his thoughts. Next thing he knew, Harry was crumpled against a bulkhead, trying to blink away the afterimages dancing in front of his eyes. He couldn't hear a damn thing.

Explosion.

The concept felt dull and distant, much like the sound that eventually got through the temporary deafness. The whine of charging capacitors and sizzle of energy blasts. Shooting. Someone was shooting inside the ship.

Someone screamed loud enough to be heard over the beamer discharges. Harry thought he recognized Sagong's voice, but the scream had been too distorted with pain to be sure, and it was quickly cut off.

We're under attack.

The thought brought back memories of life in the Navy, drills and battle stations. Captain Minh should be on his imp, screaming at the Port Authority. Who would be crazy enough to attack a ship here?

A figure loomed over him. Its head was hidden behind a helmet, but the eyes looking down at him from a transparent visor were human.

"Wait..." Harry croaked.

Human, yes, but there was no mercy in those eyes as the attacker leveled a beamer at him.

A shitty end to a shitty life.

* * *

"And you're sure this isn't going to come back and bite us in the ass," Guillermo Hamilton said. It wasn't a question, more of a combination of a statement and a veiled threat.

"The *GACSS-1138* left on schedule and will complete its delivery," Heather said. "Nobody at their next stop will care what species the ship's crew is, even assuming they can tell humans from Blue Men. After that, the ship will quietly disappear. The Boothan Clan Lord assured me neither the vessel nor the bodies of its crew will ever be found again."

"Kind of unsettling, how easy it is to steal a freighter, even a small one, in the middle of one of the busiest warp lanes in the galaxy."

"It wasn't that easy. Without my implants making sure the local security sensors didn't notice the commotion, it would have been impossible. And we wouldn't have pulled it off at the common docking stations. Security is a bit lax in the low-rent docks. You truly get what you pay for around these parts."

"I guess we're clear, then," Guillermo said. He didn't look happy about it.

"Yes. I figure someone in the State Department will eventually let the Pan-Asians know they shouldn't bother looking for the ship. That it's been taken care of. They won't like it, but having it vanish into hard vacuum makes things easier for everyone. Word will get around that working with the enemies of humankind isn't conducive to a long or healthy life, and there's plenty of plausible deniability to go around."

"You've thought of everything, haven't you?"

"I made sure the entire thing was done off the books, as per your instructions. As far as everyone is concerned, the Company had nothing to do with the mysterious disappearance of a Gack freighter. The Vehelians have no indication a crime was committed in their territory, and their records show that the ship departed TN-11 without incident."

"Not bad, I suppose," Guillermo conceded. "I'll send off a report with the next courier, eyes-only. We'll both get an unofficial attaboy and the usual reward for a job well done."

"Good."

Revenge hadn't been as satisfactory as she'd expected, but she at least felt a sense of closure. Of course, that still left the Lampreys. Hopefully she'd get a chance to settle that score, too.

Ten

Parthenon-Three, 165 AFC

"I can't believe we're off to see a witch," Gonzo muttered. "Sometimes I don't believe the shit we do for pussy."

"No hookers anywhere around here, so the witch will have to do," Russell said as he drove the civilian vehicle he'd rented for the night. The car's handling was terrible, the IC engine made a continuous roaring noise that annoyed the shit out of him, and he felt every bump on the poorly-maintained road all the way up his spine. He'd shelled out twenty bucks for the privilege of driving this POS for the night once it became clear they weren't going to let him borrow the platoon's LAV for this recon mission. He didn't mind the expense; he had some money to burn, courtesy of Dragunov's pathetic attempt at bluffing, and nowhere else to spend it. It'd been three months after they'd arrived to P-3, three months of hard work and no play. Hard to believe he'd gotten laid more often in P-4, which had held less people in total than any of the top five cities here. Being deployed in this hick-ridden valley sucked ass.

He'd been on a quest to find loving companionship at reasonable rates since day one, spending time and money among the local yokels to see if anybody could point out a discreet cathouse in the area. All he'd gotten from his efforts had been lots of blank stares, some cussing and a couple bar fights. Until now.

"There's this woman. Might be she can help you," the local bartender had said reluctantly after Russell plopped down an obscenely-large tip in front of him, all in anonymous cred tubes that the IRS didn't need to know about. Even so, getting the story out of him had been like pulling teeth, but Russell had been relentless. VR porn could only get you so far in life.

"Are you sure she's down to fuck?" Gonzo asked as they turned into a tiny country road leading up into one of the gazillion hills that dotted Forge Valley.

"Dude said she'll do a reading first, some witch stuff with cards or whatever, and if she decides you are worthy, she'll do whatever she thinks you need," Russell explained. "He made it sound like she was willing to go full service."

Or maybe the dude had steered him wrong and the woman at the other end of the road would be an old spinster with a large collection of pets or someone who'd get Russell in trouble otherwise. Russell had been a little too persistent, so maybe this was a way to try and get rid of him. In which case that bartender would get what was coming to him. He didn't say any of that out loud, though. Best to have a positive attitude.

"And if you ain't worthy?"

"Not gonna happen," Russell said confidently. "I know how these scams work. She'll do a 'reading' of my credit stick and will know I'm worthy. Here in the boondocks, she can hardly hang out a shingle announcing she's a whore, can she? The local Bible-thumpers would run her out of town. But doing it this way, all them horny farmers can say they're just getting their fortunes read. Everybody wins."

"Whole thing doesn't sound right," Gonzo said. He'd only agreed to come along because he'd been just as bored as Russell. "How much business can she do anyway? She's in the middle of nowhere, even for this one-cow town."

Gonzo had a point. The 'fortune teller' lived well off the beaten path. Their drive was taking them to the very edge of farmland and imported Earth plant life in the valley; the trees around here were a mixture of native and terrestrial species. The local varieties were tall and spindly, their long pointed leaves arranged in a circle on top, a little bit like palm trees, except the trunks were studded with sharp hollow spines filled with poisonous sap. You didn't want to frolic around them woods without some high-grade nano-meds on you. The witch liked her privacy. Maybe the remote location made it easier on the locals, too. Out of sight, out of mind.

They almost drove past the path leading to the witch's hut. The winding private road was barely wide enough to fit their civvie car and it had been barely graded; it made the pothole-ridden country highway they'd taken on the way there look great by comparison. You'd think that someone providing a vital service would make it easier for prospective customers to find her.

"Doesn't look like she gets much traffic," Gonzo said, echoing his thoughts.

"They just don't want to make it too easy to step out on their wives is all."

"We could just turn around, Russet. There's always the waitresses at the Boar's Head and Smiley's. Or the new enlisted joint they just opened."

"Yeah, sure. Half those girls just won't put out, and the other half have a dozen Marines apiece chasing them. Good luck getting anywhere."

Gonzo glanced at the woods. "Not liking this, Russet."

It wasn't like Gonzaga to get nervous, but they were way off the grid out here, and if that bartender had been doing more than bullshitting Russell, this was just the kind of spot where a couple of idiot grunts could get bushwhacked. The alien trees grew thickly alongside the road, their canopy obscuring the stars above and darkening the area to the point they might as well be driving down a tunnel. The car's headlights cast a small patch of illumination ahead of them, and Russell had his imp run a low-light app, which helped a little. It still felt like they were going into hostile territory.

"Almost there, brah."

A house loomed at the top of the hill, its slopes too steep for the trees to continue crowding the road; only few brushes and wind-bent saplings grew on the final stretch. Russell noticed that someone inside the house would have a clear shot of the approaching vehicle most of the way up. The impression that the place had been set up with an eye for defense got stronger as they reached the house proper, a three-story old-school wooden structure with peaked tiled roofs and narrow windows, its dark colors fading into black in the faint starlight. There was a footpath leading up to the porch, too narrow and steep for a wheeled vehicle, and not coincidentally in full view of several of those narrow windows. Russell wouldn't want to storm that place with less than a squad in full battle-rattle, even if there was only one person inside. A less-well equipped force – a mob of angry townies, say – could expect to take some losses before even getting to the front door.

They parked in a cleared area some twenty feet below the summit, and walked the rest of the way. Out in the open, the forest below seemed too quiet for comfort. Russell didn't like this one bit. That bartender had screwed him. It'd be just the thing to do to some outsider trying to get laid: send him somewhere where asking for sex might get him shot or arrested for attempted rape.

"Let's play it smart, Gonzo," he said as they paused in front of the door. "Be very polite-like. Maybe we got played, so don't be asking for her rates just yet, okay?"

"I feel you," Gonzo replied. "If this is a whorehouse, it's the worst one I've seen. Makes you feel as welcome as a Snake at a Puppy festival. Tell you what, even if she is hot to trot, she's all yours, man. I'll just catch up on my reading or whatever."

"Roger that."

Russell was looking for a doorbell or intercom while his imp searched for the contact info associated with the property. He drew a blank on both fronts, but the door swung open on its own anyway.

"Spooky."

"Just an automated door," Russel growled. "Like they got everywhere."

"Here, it's just fucking spooky."

They went in.

The door opened to a narrow hallway leading in, with a small table built into a wall and an antique-looking mirror above it. Russell noticed yellow wallpaper in a twisting pattern that caught his eye and wooden slat flooring with a homey welcome mat by the entrance. He carefully used it to scrape any dirt from the soles of his boots. Like he'd told Gonzo, he planned to be very polite. Worst case, he'd get the cheapest fortune reading available, and then head home and figure out some payback for the dickhead who'd steered him here.

"Good evening," someone spoke from deeper inside the house. A female voice.

She was waiting for them in an old-fashioned parlor. All the furniture appeared to be hand-made and locally-produced. He'd noticed the same styles around Davistown; hardly any fabber stuff around. The woman appeared to be in her thirties, not that looks meant anything nowadays. He noticed her jet-black hair, long but tightly wound in a bun over her head, its lustrous sheen making Russell wonder what it would look like loose and whipping around while she swayed back and forth in time with his rhythmic pounding…

Shit, he thought, noticing his mouth was hanging open, making him look like some yokel on his first trip to the big city.

"Good evening," the woman repeated. Her face was a pleasant oval shape, her skin pale, in sharp contrast with the dark hair. The lips were a bit thinner than Russell liked, and the grin had an edge to it that made him wary; something about her told him she could take care of herself.

"Evening, ma'am," he said while he tried to access her public profile with his imp. PRIVATE PROFILE was all he got. Weird. It was hard to avoid providing at least a name and birth date, and people who went to the trouble of hiding those were automatically met with suspicion.

"I assume you are here for a reading, Lance Corporal Edison, Private First Class Gonzaga."

Nothing supernatural about that. Their public profiles were

pretty much open to inspection by anybody with an imp. Russell's Facettergram page was short on personal details and long on adult content clips and pics.

"Yes, ma'am. We were told you did that sort of thing."

"Is that all they told you?"

Ordinarily, Russell would have used that question to start testing the waters about any 'special services,' but he simply shrugged. "Pretty much, ma'am. Psychic reading, fortune telling."

"I see." Her smile shifted a bit as she spoke, her dark-blue eyes glimmering with a mixture of humor and something else. Russell had never been the kind to look away from someone's gaze, and he didn't do that here, but it took some work. She was unsettling. A witch. He could tell without looking away from her eyes that Gonzo was getting tense, and when Gonzo got tense things could get ugly fast.

At ease, he sent through his imp, and his buddy relaxed minutely.

"Very well. Let us get started," she said, getting up. She was wearing a plush bathrobe, and the movement revealed something satin and sleek underneath, bright blue against pale skin, and the little flash stirred Russell up more than a full frontal squat at a strip joint.

"Ah, well, about your rates. Uh, for a reading," he stammered, feeling about as sure of himself as he'd been his first time at a cathouse, back when he'd still been an Obie.

"You will pay me what you think the experience was worth. Does that sound fair?"

He glanced at Gonzaga.

"All yours, bro," Gonzo said with a shrug.

"Follow me," she said.

He did.

Most of the interior of the house was unlit. A lone lamp illuminated the parlor. The hallways leading deeper into the house had no overhead lighting, and the only break in the darkness was an open door at its end, where another lamp cast a small square of light. They went through that door, into a smaller room filled with a table and four chairs.

"At ease, Marine," she said. "Have a seat."

Russell did so automatically, following the orders as if they'd come from an officer. Which clearly was who he was dealing with. Miss Private Profile had commanded troops at some point. He suspected bubblehead rather than Marine, but an officer was an officer.

He'd always wanted to fuck an officer. But in this case he wasn't sure if it was a good idea.

"So what did they tell you about me?" she asked as she sat down on the other side of the table. "Did they call me a fortune teller? A witch?" She tilted her head, and her smile vanished. "A whore?"

"All of those," he said. Lying came as naturally to him as breathing, especially lying to an officer, but it didn't even occur to him to say anything but the truth to her.

"They would say that. Witch. That's almost flattering, if by that word they meant a follower of one of the Old Religions. As far as belief systems go, most of theirs aren't bad at all. But no, I'm not a Wiccan. I was raised Catholic. I even attend Sunday services."

How about the whore part? The thought came up as automatically as a fish darting for a lure.

"No, I do not sell my body for money, either," she answered the unspoken question, and laughed at the way his expression changed. "And no, I didn't read your mind. You have a decent poker face, Lance Corporal, but not good enough, that's all."

"Understood, ma'am." Well, this had been a waste of time and money. But he wasn't sorry he'd come here. The woman was…

"Hold out your hands," she said in the same voice of command.

Orders were orders. She reached out towards him. Her skin felt cool to the touch, almost cold. *Cold hands, warm heart.* His mother had used to say that, in between the periods of incoherent, blissful stupor when she got her hands on a dose of her medicine, and the bouts of brutal, also incoherent cursing when she was going through withdrawal.

She closed her eyes, still holding his hands in hers.

"Sometimes it works, sometimes it doesn't," she said. "It's easier if you're warp-rated, of course."

"Wha...?"

At first, he dismissed the slight tingling feeling as just nerves, at least until he started seeing things.

It was like being in warp space. Scratch that. It was exactly like being in warp space, except he wasn't going anywhere. But he was watching bits and pieces of his life. His first kill. Getting blown to hell on Parthenon-Four. Sex. Death. The highlights of existence. It seemed to last forever, but took no time at all.

She let of go of his hands and he slumped on the chair, blinking back tears, feeling worse than that time he'd tried some alien drugs that he'd been told were 'better than peyote' and had almost killed him.

"Interesting," she said.

"What the fuck are you?" he said, but in a tone of voice far softer than the words themselves. His normal reaction to something like that would have been to bury the emotions and memories she'd woken up under a tsunami of violence. Not now, though. Now he wanted to know what she thought of him, after seeing what kind of man he was. For some reason, he wanted to know that very badly.

"My old naval designator was 6611," she said. "Warp Navigator."

"Holy fuck." That explained a lot. Warp-Navs were all a bit nuts. It came with the job of having to hold things together while they made sure their ship came out of the other end of warp transit. They usually worked in teams of no less than three in military vessels, two in civilian ones, because they tended to burn out, sometimes without warning. In theory anybody with a brain could help the nav systems lead a ship through FTL, but it took someone special to make it work a hundred percent of the time. Warp-Navs were special, but a lot of them ended up with…

"… a medical discharge," she completed the thought. "You see, what our normal senses perceive as reality is just the tip of the iceberg. Accessing warp lets you see deeper into the reality spectrum, as it were."

"And now you can do magic," he said. He should be worried, the way you'd feel when you realized the person you'd been chatting with was totally insane, but he wasn't bothered by this conversation.

"I can see things a little differently, that's all. There's quite a few people like me. The dumb ones end up in glorified insane asylums. The rest of us, we learn to smile and say the right things, and they let us go in peace. Out here in the colonies, you can be weird and most people leave you alone. At first, I hid from everyone, but I helped someone out, and that led to someone else asking for my advice, and so on. Most of my neighbors have come to appreciate my services, although they prefer not dealing with me except when they need something." She shrugged. "That's fine with me. I prefer to be alone."

"Yeah," he said. He would have agreed with her if she told him the local star was made of nacho cheese.

"But I do get lonely sometimes," she added. The smile was back, along with the glimmer in her eyes. "And you are a not a good man, but you aren't rotten in the middle. A hard man. Good to those you think deserve it. Those happy few. The rest of the world doesn't really count. Not a great way to live, but it's what you are. It doesn't bother me. And I do get lonely sometimes."

No, he wasn't bothered at all.

"You only have two hours or so, so better make them count, Marine."

He didn't know what she meant about the two hours, since his liberty didn't expire for another forty-eight, but right now he didn't care.

They lunged at each other, knocking the table to one side.

* * *

Afterwards, he didn't fall asleep or grab his shit and head out, the way he always did, especially the latter, because falling asleep next to some stranger was a great way to end up broke or dead. He lay next to her instead. There was something he wanted to say, and he wasn't sure how to say it.

The actual words were easy enough. He'd whispered them to plenty of chicks along the way, whenever paying for it was beyond his means or too much trouble. Not that the 'good girls' didn't get paid. The coin was different: dinner and presents, yeah, but above all, lies. *Let's do this again. I really felt a connection, baby. Didn't you? I think this could really be something. You're different from anyone else I've been with.* He'd said all of those, and more. It was the coin of the realm when you dealt with amateurs.

And now he couldn't make himself say them.

"You're sweet," she said. "But you're going to be too busy to worry about that. Your two hours are just about up." She grinned and threw his jumpsuit at him. "They were two very nice hours, granted. But you better get dressed."

Before he could open his mouth to ask what the fuck she was talking about, a FLASH message came through his imp.

ENEMY WARP EMERGENCE DETECTED. THIS IS NOT A DRILL. ENEMY WARP EMERGENCE DETECTED. ELEMENTS OF NASSTAH FLEET HAVE ENTERED PARTHENON SYSTEM. ALL LEAVES ARE CANCELLED. ALL PERSONNEL REPORT TO DUTY SOONEST.

His personal orders came through. He and Gonzo were going to have to drive their rented piece of junk as fast as it could and get back to the FOB.

"You *are* a fucking witch," he said as he scrambled back into his field grays.

"Depends on your definition, I suppose."

"Will I see you again?"

"Maybe. If you want to. If we both make it through what's coming."

Russell almost asked her if she knew what was coming. If they'd both make it. He rushed out instead. Gonzo had already left and had the car running.

He wasn't sure he wanted those questions answered.

They'd been driving for almost an hour before he realized he'd never gotten her name.

Sixth Fleet, Parthenon System, 165 AFC

"Eight dreadnoughts, all with multi-missile boxes. Fifteen battleships, five of them also missile platforms. Eighteen battlecruisers and forty cruisers; twelve of the latter are volley ships, the rest are fast-attack models, light on armament and shields but capable of exceeding .001 *c* by some five to ten percent. Seventy-five fast-attack frigates, outfitted likewise; fifty standard frigates, and fifty destroyers. Plus thirty planetary assault ships and the usual support elements."

"Hey, we outnumber them in destroyers," Admiral Givens said, eliciting a chuckle from everyone in the Tactical Flag Command Center. "They're serious this time," she went on, her calm tone belying her true feelings.

The disparity in tonnage was even more hideous than the ship numbers indicated. Their destroyers alone were thirty to fifty percent more massive than the American equivalents. The US Navy had faced worse odds and come out victorious, but the Vipers were using weapons and tactics designed to counter their normal advantages. They'd all but crushed Fifth Fleet, and now it was her turn to find out just how effective the ETs' new toys were.

"Execute Attack Plan Epsilon." There were grimaces among the crew at the orders, but everyone did as they were told.

The two forces played the elaborate dance the preceded a space battle, selecting a place to fight and meeting each other there. The Vipers armada's final emergence point was one light-minute away from Parthenon-Three. Sixth Fleet met them there.

Standard operating procedure was to appear in normal space at half a light second away from the op force, taking it under fire before the ETs had fully recovered from transit. Most alien species needed a minimum of thirty to sixty seconds to fully overcome even a short jump. That was a long time to rely only on automated systems that couldn't be very sophisticated or they, too, would be affected by FTL travel's unavoidable side effects. The ability to strike after emergence with near-impunity had been the key to multiple American victories.

The enemy had emerged from warp in a vertical formation forming a wall of ships that launched thousands of missiles as soon as Sixth Fleet came out of W-space. The volley, travelling at around 1/100 of c, would have taken less than a minute to reach its targets, had the Americans appeared at the usual range. They hadn't.

Sixth Fleet emerged two light seconds from the enemy formation, sacrificing its normal advantage to quadruple the time the missile storm would take to reach her formation. Givens knew they were going to need every bit of those extra two or three minutes to avoid sharing the fate of Admiral Kerensky's ships. There were a lot of missiles. Even after being whittled away for their entire two light-second trip, some were bound to get through. At least the Viper fleet would be too far away to pile on with beam weapons after they recovered from transit.

Admiral Givens realized she was grinding her teeth together hard enough to hurt. She forced herself to unclench her jaw.

The next few minutes would tell if she'd been right challenging the enemy in deep space, or whether her fleet would be too badly mauled to help defend Parthenon-Three.

Whatever happened next, it was going to be a long day.

Parthenon-Three, 165 AFC

"Sixth Fleet is engaging the enemy, trying to cut down their numbers as it falls back towards Parthenon-Three," Colonel Brighton said. "They aren't going to stop them unless we're luckier than we deserve. The Vipers will get here sooner rather than later. Best estimate is sixteen to eighteen hours from now, but they could make another warp jump and drop in on us within minutes."

The 101st MEU was having a final officers' meeting before the inevitable arrival of the ETs. It was a virtual meeting, relying on imp-generated holograms; everybody was already at their assigned posts, and nobody wanted to be shuttling back and forth when the Vipers could make landfall at any time.

"Based on the correlation of forces involved, Sixth Fleet will attrite but not destroy the enemy formation. Parthenon-Three's defenses will add their firepower to the mix once the Nasstah reach orbital engagement range. That may be enough to destroy or successfully repel the Vipers, but our estimates are they will not. Once they reach Parthenon-Three, the enemy will deorbit land forces with the purpose of reducing the twenty-four Planetary Defense Bases protecting the planet. Their secondary objective will be to destroy all major cities' force field systems, in order to allow the deployment of starship-launched genocide weapons."

Images of burning Detroit danced in Fromm's mind.

"The Hundred-and-First's primary mission is to defend PDB-18 and the cities of New Burbank and Henderson, working in conjunction with Army, Guard and militia units in-theater. In addition to Marine assets, we will be assisted by two divisional-sized forces, including a field artillery brigade. Additional units are being mobilized and assembled in New Burbank, but they will take as long as two weeks to be ready for action.

"Our primary theater of operations will be Forge Valley," Brighton went on, reviewing the battle plans they'd all been working on in the past couple of months. The holographic display provided a detailed 3D rendition of the central plateau, a roughly football shape surrounded by mountains and running on an east-west axis, wider around the middle and with two main gaps at each end. At the end of the eastern opening – Miller's Crossing – lay PDB-18. Two villages – Davistown and Paradise Creek – and several hundred square miles of farmland filled most of the valley proper, broken up by expanses of hilly terrain and a mix of native and imported forests. A chain of hills nearly tall enough to be called mountains divided a third of the eastern side of the valley into two distinct regions; the villages were on opposite sides of the range. The other major terrain features in the plateau were two rivers – White River and Miller's Stream – running west-to-east until they came together at the end of the dividing hills, near Miller's Crossing, and then flowed towards the south. Five bridges spanned them at different points, and Fromm figured most of them would end up going down; orders were to blow them as soon as enemy forces came within a mile of them. Hills and rivers presented little obstacle to anti-grav vehicles, but Viper assault forces consisted mostly of light infantry; they would be severely inconvenienced by both.

On the other hand, there was a lot of terrain to cover, and not that many troops to do the job. Given the width and length of the valley, and assuming the enemy landed on the next plateau over, on the western side, a Marine battalion and attachments, plus two ad-hoc divisions and other dribs and drabs weren't enough to plug either gap, let alone the plateau between them. The western pass was the worst one; it was wider and too far away from the planetary defense base to expect any support from it. The conservative play would be to evacuate the entire valley and make a stand on Miller's Crossing, the eastern pass, which was narrower and far more defensible. But surrendering the plateau to the enemy would give them the chance to concentrate and hit the human defenders with everything they had, at a time of their choosing. You didn't want to surrender the initiative to the opposing force; waiting passively for an attack was a last resort and an admission of weakness or sheer incompetence.

"The 101st and attached units will engage and destroy any enemy forces entering Forge Valley. If the landings' strength makes that unfeasible, we will conduct a retrograde operation, using maneuver and movement to disrupt and slow down the enemy's advance while we gradually fall back in an easterly direction. In that case, our primary goal will be to attrite the enemy through ambushes and counterattacks. We will maintain contact with the alien forces while avoiding a decisive engagement unless local conditions favor us.

"Once we reach the strongpoints at Miller's Crossing, we will revert to a fixed defense, with mobile elements remaining in play to threaten the enemy's flanks. At that point, our orders are to hold until relieved. Local commanders have latitude in ordering tactical retrograde maneuvers, but their units must not move beyond the outermost force field perimeter of PDB-18 unless such movement is approved by higher."

Colonel Brighton leaned forward; the holographic projection showed the lines of tension marring his face. "I am not in the habit of giving suicide orders. If the situation becomes well and truly untenable, I will order a retreat and evacuation towards New Burbank, the closest city in the area. I will be the sole judge of what I consider to be an untenable situation. To make things abundantly clear, any unit that falls back beyond their assigned final protective line without my personal approval will be denied force field coverage and artillery support, and, if deemed necessary, will be engaged by our own artillery in order to close the gap in our defenses created by their unauthorized retreat. Make that clear to everyone under your command. To run means death. Is that understood?"

There was a chorus of imp acknowledgments. Fromm didn't like the directive, but he realized it was aimed mostly at the Army, Guard and militia units that would be providing the bulk of the manpower for the final defensive battle. After months of joint training exercises, it'd become clear that many of those formations could best be classified as 'shaky.' Parthenon-Three had been a peaceful, prosperous world for far too long; the state government had grudgingly supplemented the federal funds needed to maintain the defensive installations on and in orbit around the planet, but had done the bare minimum to support the ground forces that were supposed to defend them. The Guard was poorly equipped and supplied; even worse, their training left a lot to be desired. The volunteer militia was a hodgepodge of units ranking from useless to somewhat better than the average Guard ones. The federally-funded Army was only in slightly better shape. The previous few months had not been enough to make up for those deficiencies, and there were serious doubts as to how well they would fare when exposed to combat, in most cases for the first time.

"A relief fleet is being assembled at Wolf 1061, comprising elements from Fifth Fleet deemed fit to return to action, alongside reinforcements from other sectors and newly-commissioned vessels. It will come to the system's defense when it is ready, but the most optimistic estimate calls for no less than twelve weeks.

"We cannot afford to lose Sixth Fleet, so if it is facing annihilation, it will retreat from P-3's orbit and assume a blocking position next to the warp valleys leading out of the system. At that point, it will be up to the forces on the ground – to us – to make sure that there is something worth saving when the fleet is reinforced and comes back."

Before First Contact, human strategists and science-fiction writers had assumed an enemy who gained control of a planet's orbitals would enjoy total supremacy. Ground defenses could do little to prevent orbital strikes that would utterly wreck a world's biosphere; dropping large rocks on its surface would do the trick. The realities of Starfarer combat were different, however. Because of the simple but strictly-enforced rules imposed by the Elder Races, space-borne attackers had a limited choice of weapons they cold deploy against a planetary target. 'Dinosaur-killer' asteroids, nuclear or kinetic devices above one kiloton in yield, and energy weapons beyond certain numbers and intensities were all outlawed. Those rules put starships at a disadvantage when exchanging volleys with ground installations, which had many fewer restrictions. The best way to handle those installations was to send troops down to take them out.

Without Sixth Fleet providing cover, and even after its orbital fortresses were destroyed, Parthenon-Three and its twenty-four Planetary Defense Bases could hold off the Viper fleet. For a while, at least, assuming the ground forces protecting them did their duty.

"That is all."

Someone shouted "Oorah!" Others echoed the battle cry, but Fromm remained silent; his mind was too busy mulling over things. Terrain, fields of fire, logistics, the men and women he would send out to do or die. The basic tools of war.

Concentrating on the details made it easier to ignore the big picture, especially when the big picture was almost too terrible to contemplate.

Eleven

Sixth Fleet, Parthenon System, 165 AFC

From a merely human perspective, space combat is silent and lonely. Even in 'tight' formations, ships are too far apart to be seen with the naked eye. Missile launches are all but invisible even in the infrared spectrum, and beam weapons for the most part produce brief bursts of illumination, when they produce anything at all. An outside observer would be unable to tell a battle was happening – until the enemy volleys started impacting on his position, producing a far more impressive – although still deathly quiet – show.

The Vipers started the dance with an expected and dreaded massive missile launch. Over a hundred and sixty thousand vampires erupted from the alien armada and sped towards Sondra Givens' ships. A similar deluge had wrecked Fifth Fleet at Heinlein and turned Admiral Kerensky into a shadow of his former self. Admiral Givens had studied every last bit of data about that battle and the smaller but still significant Lamprey attack on Melendez, and she'd come up with new tactics to deal with what some wags were beginning to call 'the Sun-Blotter' after the Persian boast at the battle of Thermopylae.

The first thing she'd done was have every anti-missile in Sixth Fleet reprogrammed for point defense. The slower-than-light weapons weren't designed for defensive purposes, since beam weapons did a far better job, but they could be effective with some adjustments. The ten-thousand-strong volley her ships could fire was saved for the last ten seconds of the attack, when the enemy ship-killers would be entering relatively-fixed trajectories and Sixth Fleet's energy weapons had whittled down the swarm.

Every weapon platform capable of engaging an anti-ship munition had also been modified to excel at that job. Active sensors working at maximum power swept the space between the two fleets, detecting the incoming swarm at twice their normal range and allowing every ship's main guns to engage it from well over a light-second away. An entire set of hastily-drafted defensive procedures were tried for the first time in the interplanetary depths of Parthenon System, a trial run where failure meant the savaging of dozens of vessels and thousands of deaths.

At Heinlein, Fifth Fleet had only managed to destroy about a hundred and twenty thousand vampires out of one-fifty; the remaining thirty thousand had destroyed seven ships outright and damaged every one of the survivors, many of them critically. Givens' crews accounted for a hundred and thirty-six thousand before they made their final sprint – and were met head-on by her own missile swarm and every weapon in the fleet, resulting in an orgy of destruction that claimed over nine tenths of the remaining missile storm.

The survivors – still over a thousand strong – darted past the American vessels' warp shields, aiming at the exposed sections between them. In most cases, they failed to get through their target's force fields and armor plating. But some did.

Admiral Givens grimaced as the first fleet damage reports trickled in. The *USS Baldwin* took six direct hits; the unlucky destroyer broke apart with the loss of all eight hundred souls aboard. A frigate fell out of formation while its crew desperately tried to restore power to its graviton drive. Several other ships suffered non-critical damage. And that was all. They had weathered the largest missile launch in recent galactic history, and survived. She found herself breathing freely again, and smiled when the TFCC personnel cheered briefly before getting back to work.

Her crews had done an incredible job, but this had been the opening salvo, fired without the assistance of sapient control. The Vipers had recovered from emergence and were rushing into beam weapons range. The primary purpose of the missile swarm, to allow the aliens to emerge from warp unmolested, had been achieved, although without inflicting the heavy casualties their previous attacks had. The aliens' external box launchers could not be reloaded during combat, so any follow-up barrages would be a fraction of the size of first one, but they would be more accurate, as well as impossible to engage with missiles of her own.

The only easy day was yesterday, she thought as the two fleets moved into direct fire range. She was starting the battle in much better shape than Kerensky. While victory was still unlikely, decimating the alien formation in a running battle towards Parthenon-Three would count as a solid win in her book.

Some ten minutes after the last Viper missile was dealt with, the ships entered ideal fighting range and began firing their main guns. Sixth Fleet stopped moving forward and reversed course, maintaining the range at which its warp shields rendered them nearly invulnerable to frontal fire. This was the kind of battle

American space forces excelled at, an energy-weapon slugfest where they could face and destroy several times their tonnage in enemy vessels while taking minimal losses.

The Vipers had an answer to that as well.

Besides the new missile platforms, the fast-attack cruisers and frigates moving around the edges of the Vipers' formation worried Admiral Givens. Those ships had no missiles and relatively light weapon mounts and shields; most of their tonnage was dedicated to gravity thrust systems. Once they reached one thousandth the speed of light, reactionless graviton thrusters hit steep diminishing returns, but you could make enough marginal gains to make a difference. By tripling their propulsion energy budgets, the Viper fast-attack ships could increase their flank speed by about five percent to ten percent, which meant they would eventually overtake Sixth Fleet's, envelop its position, and engage it from multiple angles, allowing them to bypass the American ships' warp shields. Even with their lighter armament, those fragile but swift vessels would make Givens' position untenable unless she did something about them.

Admiral Givens ordered all ships to concentrate their fire on the fast-attack classes. The losses among them started to mount, but that meant ignoring the enemy's capital vessels, the dreadnoughts and battleships that kept pounding on the American formation with their main guns. Direct hits were nearly impossible, but carefully-aimed glancing shots would impart some of their energy into their targets even in the poorly-conductive vacuum of space. The damage inflicted in that was minimal, but it would build up over time, damaging shields and stressing other systems.

And a second volley of missiles erupted from the Vipers fleet of the line. A mere thirty thousand this time, but those ship-killers had a lot less distance to cover, and dealing with them meant diverting Sixth Fleet's firepower away from the fast-attacks that were closing the distance at a steady fifteen miles per second. It would take some eighteen hours before they could overtake Sixth Fleet, but they would start scoring telling hits long before then.

The *Halsey*'s command center trembled under her feet. Something had applied enough momentum to overwhelm the dreadnought's stabilizers, however slightly. A missile strike had made it through. A quick check revealed no damage to the ship. She didn't bother to look any further into it. Fighting the flagship was up to the *Halsey*'s skipper, and she had a murthering great battle to conduct.

For eight hours, it went on. Sixth Fleet moved backwards steadily and traded salvos with the inexorably approaching enemy. Protected by warp shields, the American vessels were able to survive multiple hits from the fifty- and sixty-centimeter graviton cannon mounted on the alien heavies; most of those shots were absorbed by the impenetrable barriers protecting close to seventy percent of their surface area. The *Halsey*'s 20-inchers, on the other hand, only had to contend with conventional defenses, and they scored devastating hits on her targets. Which unfortunately consisted mainly of fast-attacks rather than capital ships.

One by one, the nimble alien tin cans fell out of line with heavy damage or blew up outright. Eight frigates and five cruisers were down or out already, versus one American destroyer and one frigate. That was the sort of exchange the US Navy was used to. Except this time it wasn't going to continue much longer.

The lighter Viper ships were paying dearly as they closed the distance, but they kept advancing. By the time they'd closed to within a quarter of a light second, they had targeting solutions that even their relatively weak armament could exploit. Direct hits from their 100mm popguns began to impact on ordinary force fields and armor, hardly a threat for her heavies, but enough to start damaging cruisers and lighter vessels. And as soon as the first fast-attacks reached those improved firing ranges, the rest of the alien line unleashed an even heavier missile volley. Forty thousand vampires: they'd been saving them for this moment. A thousand made it through, and an American destroyer and two frigates broke apart. The death of *USS Dickson* marked the point where the tide turned. Sixth Fleet claimed another cruiser and four more frigates minutes later, but an American light cruiser drifted to a stop almost at the same time, its status light flashing yellow. That was a death sentence for its two thousand crewmembers; rescue operations were impossible at flank speeds.

We are done here, Givens realized, seconds before a new Sun-Blotter launch was detected. 'Only' twenty-five thousand vampires this time.

The cold equations of the fight were obvious. She couldn't afford the losses the enemy was inflicting, and the exchange ratio would only get worse.

No choice. "Prepare for warp transit. Sixth Fleet will fall back to Parthenon-Three."

She had expected her ships to launch multiple hit-and-run attacks on the enemy, hammer the Vipers every step of the way and bleed them dry before the two forces arrived at Parthenon-

Three. Instead, her ships would have to disengage after inflicting minimal losses, allowing the enemy to effect repairs, reload their magazines and rejoin the battle at a time of their choosing.

Kerensky had warned her about this. She'd thought that dealing with the initial missile barrage would allow her to fight longer and do better than her fellow commander. And she had, but not enough. Not nearly enough.

Retreating this early in the game stuck in her craw, but keeping her command intact was paramount. Last stands made for great drama, but only if there were any survivors to appreciate the stories. As long as Sixth Fleet remained to block the warp-lanes leading deeper into American space, the enemy could be held in the system. In retrospect, she probably should have declined a deep space engagement and kept her ships close to P-3. Effecting a warp retreat while under fire was neither easy nor painless.

Her orders were transmitted and Sixth Fleet prepared for transition before the missile storm could reach it. Their warp shields flickered for a fraction of a second before they could leave ordinary space-time, and that was enough for the Vipers to score several hits. Two destroyers and another cruiser – one of the last *Presidential*-class vessels still in service – became rapidly-expanding gas and debris before the chaos of warp space swallowed the retreating formation.

Givens' warp nightmares were always informed by her deepest fear: failure. During the few seconds before she and her ships emerged in orbit around Parthenon-Three, she was regaled with images of the planet burning while the lifeless hulks of Sixth Fleet drifted idly above its skies. Her grandson Omar appeared before her, wordlessly expressing disapproval as he beckoned her to follow him into the dark. She shook her head and willed the waking nightmare to go away.

Had that been just a hallucination, or a vision of things to come? She'd find out soon enough.

Parthenon-Three, 165 AFC

"Come with us, Grampa!" Mar cried out from a passenger window of the ground-effect bus carrying the last load of refugees out of Davistown. Tears were running down her face.

"I can't," Morris said. His eyes were burning and his voice came out harsher than he intended. "I'll see you when it's over."

"You won't. You'll go to Heaven like Mom and Dad, and I'll never see you again!"

"Child…" he began to say, but the bus lifted from the ground and the whine of its fans made speech impossible. He waved to his granddaughter as the bus lurched forward, heading to the relative safety of New Burbank.

Very relative safety. If the regional force fields and planetary defense bases went down, Mariah and everyone in New Burbank would burn to death in the glare of Viper city-melters. That would only happen over Morris' dead body. Which didn't mean it wouldn't happen.

Morris watched the line of fleeing vehicles for a few moments before rubbing his eyes and looking around. He was far from the only militiaman saying goodbye; two dozen others were there, about half of his platoon. They were all in uniform; there weren't enough field long-johns to go around, so his unit made do with locally-fabbed fatigues made of tough fabric but lacking all the sophisticated systems of real uniforms. At least the militia's combat element had been issued clamshell breast plates and sealed helmets, the kind of stuff the Marines had worn about a hundred years ago, without any exoskeletal reinforcements and only light force fields that would stop shrapnel and a glancing beam but not a direct hit unless you got lucky. Better than nothing, but if it came to a serious firefight they were going to take big losses.

Good thing that the Marines were expected to do most of the fighting.

Morris' platoon and the entire Forge Valley Volunteer Regiment would be providing support to the 101st MEU, along with the US Army's 323rd and 331st Brigades and three National Guard regiments. For most of those troops, that meant being in the rear with the gear, doing the work the trigger-pullers needed done so they didn't run out of power packs or snacks at the worst possible time. If the Volunteers had to fight, it meant the shit had well and truly hit the fan. Morris was still glad he and the rest of his platoon were being issued IW-3s when they reported in, because he expected the shit to hit the fan at some point. Probably sooner than anybody expected.

The troops of Bravo Company were scheduled to assemble at the town's Green at 1200 hours. It was still early, but Morris headed there. The walk from the bus station to the Green was short; it was a short walk to anywhere in Davistown, given that downtown comprised of a whole four city blocks. Most of the stores and buildings were closed and shuttered; the only men and women he saw out and about were in uniform. The three churches around the Green were also closed. The only establishment still open for business was the Irish pub across from City Hall, and that would only last until the troops headed out and Davistown became a ghost town. The rats at City Hall had left hours ago, of course, except for the mayor and the sheriff, who were both officers in the Volunteers and pretty good people, for rats.

A largish group of militiamen were clustered around the Green, smoking or drinking coffee – or rather, Parthenon chicory, which was close enough for the name as long as you'd never had the real thing. Something in the planet made the real stuff impossible to grow, despite the fact the climate on the plateau should have been ideal for it. Morris had enjoyed Earth coffee during his time in the Corps, but since he couldn't afford it anymore, he'd grown used to the local version.

"Heya, Gator," one of the men in combat gear said.

Gator. It'd been a while since he'd heard his old handle. Not since Otis and Ruth had gone and gotten themselves killed; after that, he hadn't been able to make it to town to drink with his old buddies.

"How goes, Lemon?" he said.

Boris 'Lemon' Nikolic smiled at him from under the raised visor of his helmet. The big guy was another retired leatherneck. He and Morris hadn't served together but they had exchanged life histories over some fine booze during an American Legion-sponsored shindig, shortly after arriving to Parthenon-Three. They'd both been out on the sharp end: different planets, different wars, but in the end it all came down to killing the sorry bastards trying to kill you. Along with all the other combat vets in town who'd volunteered for militia duty, they'd been assigned to the recon-escort platoon in Bravo Company.

"Fair to middling," Lemon said. "Sent the kid away?"

Morris nodded. "Should be safe enough at New Burbank."

"Yeah." Lemon didn't sound convinced, but Morris didn't mind; he was whistling in the dark, and they both knew it.

"Any scuttlebutt?"

"Sixth Fleet is in orbit now; gave the Eets a bloody nose but had to retreat. An old Chief I know – retired, but still plugged into the Chief's network – tells me our fleet got a pretty bloody nose, too. He heard the Vipers met up with a supply squadron three days after they kicked Sixth Fleet's ass, and have been fixing their cans, getting ready for round two."

"They didn't really kick our ass," Morris protested. "They lost more ships than we did."

Nikolic shrugged. "It's all bubblehead BS to me, Gator, but that's how Chief Hoover called it. Sixth Fleet should have kept up the pressure on the Vipers rather than running back here. They didn't because they couldn't."

"Yeah. Guess the Chief's right." Being outnumbered had rarely been a problem for the Fleet before, except when the odds were completely insane. But now they were outgunned, and that wasn't good. The orbital and planetary defenses on Parthenon-Three were first-rate, but would they be enough to help Sixth Fleet keep the Vipers out? He didn't think so.

Urgent FLASH traffic from his imp interrupted his musings. WARP EMERGENCE IMMINENT. ALL MILITARY PERSONNEL REPORT TO THEIR ASSIGNED STATIONS. THIS IS NOT A DRILL.

Morris glanced up at the green-gray skies. It was close to noon, but he thought he saw a few lights blinking up there. Real or imagined, it didn't matter. For the defenders out in the black, the light show would start soon enough.

"Guess it paid off to be early for the muster," Lemon said, gesturing at the other militiamen running towards the Green.

Morris shrugged. "We should have a day or two before the Vipers can deploy any ground troops. We won't be needed before then."

He wasn't sure he had another fight left in him, but the aliens weren't giving him any choice.

* * *

"Drones gonna be doing a spot check in three, people," Staff Sergeant Dragunov said. "Them camo blankies better be good and tight over everything or I'll make you sorry your mama didn't smother you in your crib."

"I'm already sorry," Russell muttered to himself. He wasn't worried, though. His squad knew what they were doing; they'd broken in all the boots even before they left New Parris, so by the time they got into their first firefight on Parthenon-Four everybody knew what was what. Of course, that shindig had been against barbarians with a few Starfarer special ops types. Things were going to be different now.

"Should I go outside to make sure?" Nacle asked.

"Nah, we're good. Nobody can spot us from overhead."

They'd spent a good bit of time and effort camouflaging their position. There was an FOB back some ten klicks that was slightly less-well camouflaged on purpose, so when the Vipers came down they'd figure that was where the defensive line was. The idea was to give the Eets a nice surprise when they tried to enter Forge Valley, which as far as the aliens were concerned would soon become the valley of the shadow of death.

The camo nets covering all their prepared positions blocked all kinds of signals, everything from IR and radio to graviton waves. Nothing could get in or out, which meant the fighting holes could get mighty hot even with the air conditioners and heat sinks working overtime. But the enemy would end up in a much hotter spot once they made contact.

To keep the camouflaged positions in touch with the rest of the battalion, the combat engineer platoon with the MEU had set a network of laser transmitters which sent out the take of observation points, drones and satellites. Being line-of-sight only, they couldn't be easily tracked by the enemy. Russell used them to check on the drones checking on them. The little machines were flying over Charlie Company's position, but all they were detecting was the local flora, a mix of local palm trees and gene-modified spruce oaks, with patches of competing grass species in between. There was no sign of Russell's squad, or the rest of the company, spread out in a shallow C-formation, covering one third of the mile-wide prairie leading towards Davis' Gap.

The drones went by without spotting anything. Russell tried to check the situation up in orbit, but higher was keeping a tight lid on news about the space battle raging overhead. At night you got so see all kinds of flashes, which could mean many things, few of them good. When the battle was close enough to be visible from the ground, it meant the enemy was too close. The Vipers had arrived to Parthenon-Three two days ago, and they'd been slugging it out with Sixth Fleet and the local defenses ever since. The fact the ETs were still up there meant the good guys hadn't won yet. Or were losing, which was another way to put it.

He couldn't blame the bosses for keeping things quiet. There'd been too many civvies on P-3 to evacuate – barely five million, mostly children, had managed to escape before the Vipers showed up – and if they heard too many bad news they might panic and make things worse. The local authorities had put as many people as they could in uniform, and organized the rest to assist in the defense of the planet, but too many pogues treated their four years of obligatory service as an extra-long round of summer camp, and any lessons they'd learned hadn't sunk in. The local remfies had even elected a Federalist to the Senate, the kind of shit only the most coddled star systems and shithole states like Vermont ever did. Anybody who didn't vote the straight Eagle Party ticket believed in a universe that wasn't full of murderous ETs. Well, they'd learn soon enough.

The visual feed from the drones disappeared, replaced by a FLASH message: LANDINGS IMMINENT. He switched to the observation posts' visuals and watched a swarm of landing pods coming down from the sky.

Since no living ET species other than humans could launch warp assaults, Starfarers had come up with their own techniques. The Vipers' way was to send down thousands of pods, aimed at uninhabited areas protected by terrain features. Thousands of missiles were coming down as well, aimed at the closest Planetary Defense Bases and any city near them. The PDBs and other anti-air assets blasted the incoming with lasers, hypervelocity munitions and plasma bursts. A lot of pods were blown away, but the defensive fire had to concentrate on the missiles, because if enough of those hit, some might get through the defense shields and blow up some innocent civvies. ETs didn't use nukes, but a few dozen plasma warhead impacts would be almost as lethal.

The sky was full of descending contrails, along with scattered bursts of light and smoke as an ADA round hit a target. Somewhere to the rear, the 101st's own air defense artillery guns got into the game: 12mm lasers swept their assigned sectors with thousands of high-intensity pulses. The targets had force fields, but a few bursts would chew through them. The poor bastards inside a pod hit by one of those would either die quickly if in the direct path of the beam or would get the chance to scream all the way down as the pod's braking and steering engines died and they plummeted to the surface. Either way, they wouldn't be a problem.

A lot of pods ended up that way, but not enough. Vipers organized their drops expecting to lose as many as sixty or seventy percent of their troops on their way down. Their assault troopers were a gene-engineered sub-breed of their species, designed to be about as smart as a dog. An assault ship carried millions of embryos aboard, threw away the ones that died in warp transit, and force-grew the others in about eight hours. The vat-grown instant soldiers were 'educated' via direct neural cortex downloads and programmed to fight and follow the orders of a portable computer that was about as smart as the systems controlling your typical video game. Russell had played enough games to know that even a dumb system could beat you if it had enough firepower on its side.

The contrails – hundreds of them – descended behind Kacey's Ridge, a line of tall hills some twenty klicks away from Davis' Gap. Russell's imp did the math for him: thirty minutes for the

Vipers to come out of their pods, assemble their vehicles – modular designs that used portions of the landing pods for many of their parts – and head out towards the valley, mostly on foot. Figure two hours to make it through the rough terrain. In a hundred and fifty minutes or so, things were going to get downright interesting.

Things were going to get interesting for the ETs a lot sooner, of course.

* * *

Fromm watched the battle's progress from his command vehicle, forcing himself not to squirm in his seat. The urge to be doing something was still there, but he was learning to control it.

The first salvos from the 101st's artillery hit the Vipers' landing zone before most of the surviving pods had landed. Cameras built into the rounds showed several hits before the enemy deployed area force fields and blocked the rest of the incoming. The next barrage consisted of a combination of shield-busters and anti-personnel. That would whittle down the enemy force, but wouldn't destroy it. The MEU had a full battery of multiple-launch rocket systems, plus an Army artillery brigade with four batteries of slightly antiquated but still fairly good 200mm howitzers. Twenty-eight guns could cover only so much ground, however, and their mortars and other long-range assets were being held back for the time being.

"They're estimating a reinforced brigade-size force is assembling behind those hills," Lieutenant Hansen said as swarms of drones crested the obstacles and died in droves for a few seconds' worth of visual footage. "About five thousand effectives, not counting casualties."

"Sounds about right."

The Vipers had tried to land close to a division's worth of troops on this sector and they'd lost over half of them in the process. That translated to about three, maybe four thousand combat troops still able to fight out of the estimated five thousand; the Viper ground-assault formations were almost all teeth, with very little in the way of logistical 'tail.' And facing them was the Marine Expeditionary Unit, about a thousand combat troops, plus the Army's arty brigade, and a local militia regiment, two thousand strong but providing only a couple of hundred fighting men, lightly armed and equipped. The artillery would help a lot of course, and the rest of the troops would take care of most of the

Marines' non-combat needs, but the fact remained that they'd be outnumbered three to one. The enemy would be short of artillery and combat vehicles, but Viper assault troopers were bred for strength, speed and endurance. They could advance on foot at a steady twenty miles an hour on anything like level terrain, close to thirty on roads. Artillery would slow them down, but their mobile field generators were better than American models, and that would minimize their casualties.

Fromm shrugged. The greater tactical situation, let alone the strategic one, were not his problem. His problem was to ensure that the ambush he'd prepared was carried out as effectively as possible, followed by a retreat under fire towards their next defensive position, where Bravo Company would launch its own ambush. The plan was to lead the Vipers on a merry chase through the valley before throwing them out through a series of counterattacks, or, failing that, stopping them cold at the other end, the point beyond which the enemy could not pass, because that was where PDB-18 guarded the cities of New Burbank and Henderson, with a combined population of three-million-plus civilians.

He went over his assets automatically. His infantry and weapons platoons were all concealed and dug-in, including their combat vehicles. His own command vehicle was also under cover, a thousand meters back from the firing line, along with his Hellcats, which he was keeping as a mobile reserve. So far the battalion's FDO was letting him keep control over his mortars, for what that was worth: most 100mm munitions wouldn't punch through the Viper's force fields, and the ones that could were in short supply. If he sent them in slowly enough to bypass the shields, they'd be easy meat for the swarm of fireflies the enemy would have floating over their heads, not to mention their swatters, which were already doing a number on the battalion's fleet of recon drones. He'd hold off on using the mortars until the ETs were well and truly stuck in.

As always, the hardest part was the waiting. He'd done everything he could do. Once again, he was playing defense, a role that went against his instincts. Fromm didn't like having to wait on the other guy to make the first move.

Although, come to think of it, his troops would be making the first move this once.

* * *

Vipers had eight multi-jointed limbs, arranged symmetrically around a long-tailed body similar to an alligator's. The scaly bastards had originally been tree-climbers, so they had hands at the end of every set of arms/legs, although the lower two pairs weren't good for playing the piano or similar fine control stuff. The ugly bastards moving towards Russell's position were using their lower four limbs to trot at a good clip, occasionally using a couple of their other four arms to add a little extra speed or support while their long torsos twisted in an up-and-down fashion that was like nothing that'd ever evolved on Earth. Watching them move made Russell feel a little queasy. There was something wrong about the way the four to six leg-things worked.

Well, pretty soon he'd be doing his damnedest to make sure they stopped moving. And his damnedest was usually pretty good.

The ET assault troopers weren't wearing body armor, although their scaly skins were tough enough to turn light shrapnel. They had force field harnesses that Woogle claimed were about fifteen percent better than what he was wearing, and their heads were completely encased in helmets that allowed them to breathe the local air without dropping dead. The power packs providing juice for their weapons, shields and breathing system were on their backs, and they were good for a week of combat ops. Fucking ETs always got the best toys.

Toys like their 2mm laser rifles, which were better than Lamprey models, about as good as what the Ovals used. Russell had seen Oval lasers in operation back on Jasper-Five, and he'd gained a great deal of respect for them. He didn't want to be on the receiving end of those. And the Vipers' primary support weapons were even nastier: four-tube 30mm launch systems, each tube holding ten stacked rounds that could be shot individually or ripple-fired; the latter option meant forty guided explosives would sally forth in quick succession, each one perfectly capable of ruining a jarhead's day or putting a big ding on a LAV. Taking down the alien rocketeers was their top priority.

Russell watched the advancing ETs without having to poke his head up, courtesy of the dwindling swarm of drones overhead and the tiny eyeball-wires they'd placed ahead of their line. The little sensors sent their feeds via fiber-optic cables and were nearly undetectable. The alien horde was still over two klicks away, but he could see them coming as if they were at arm's length.

They weren't coming in dumb like so many primmie barbs, either. They were doing a classic bounding overwatch advance, rushing from cover to cover and watching over the next batch coming forward. Their point men were well ahead of the main groups, and they were moving in an open order formation to minimize casualties when the fireworks started. Interspaced among them were little floating cars, open-topped and barely big enough for one or two ETs apiece. Some were gun platforms, heavy lasers or grav guns meant to take out tanks and IFVs with a couple of shots, but also good to dig out entrenched grunts. The other floaters were support units, projecting area force fields and sending out pressure waves that exerted as much pressure as an infantryman or vehicle would, designed to detonate any mines the Americans might have placed in their way. Gadgets like that were the main reason the battalion's engineers hadn't placed any mines in front of them. They had some behind the ambush, though, the kind that didn't go boom when you stepped on them but went off when activated via a laser signal. The Vipers would be making their acquaintance soon enough.

"Fucking arty's hardly scratching 'em," Gonzo groused. Most explosions were going off overhead and bouncing off the big force shields acting like giant umbrellas for the ET horde coming their way. Here or there one shell made it through and knocked down a couple of bastards. The bad thing was, they often got back again and kept walking. Those personal shields were good.

"Don't worry about it," Russell said. "We'll scratch them plenty once we're inside their field perimeter."

Which would happen when the ET lead troops, which marched outside the area field's edge, had gone past the ambushers' position, which would lead to all kinds of fun stuff. There were only two ways to deal with area force fields: you could overwhelm them with enough ordnance, or try to get inside them by walking past them or hiding until it moved past your position. The second way meant a short-range firefight, just as exciting as a knife fight inside an elevator.

They'd set up the ambush accordingly, digging in on top of a natural ridge with a ravine on the left side and a steep trail on the right. The enemy point would have to take those paths unless they wanted to scale the nearly sheer wall from which Russell and the rest of First Squad waited to begin the dance. The rest of Charlie Company was similarly positioned and camouflaged, getting ready to hit the leading enemy formations from inside their force fields.

The Vipers got closer, taking a few casualties, but not many, thanks to their damned force fields. Russell's imp estimated it would take a good five or six hits with his Iwo's 4mm plasma rounds to take out a tango. Even a 15mm grenade had a fifty-fifty kill chance. Only the twenty mike-mike in his IW-3a was a guaranteed one and done. Fuck. They'd gotten spoiled fighting primmies. This was going to be rough.

"Dibs on the field gennie up front," Gonzo said.

Russell checked. "The assaultmen have tagged it already. Go for the missile guys."

"Copy that."

Off to Russell's left, Nacle was softly humming some tune he didn't recognize at first. After a few bars, it came to him: it was a Toby Keith song, an oldie from pre-Contact days, not that the old bastard's style had changed much; he was pushing two-fifty and still playing large venues all over American space. And "Courtesy of the Red, White and Blue" was as applicable as it'd been back in olden times, even now when there were seventy-nine stars on the flag.

Russell wasn't a big flag-waver – he'd seen too much shit, done too much shit, to care much about that sort of thing – but the idea of those motherfuckers with their too-many legs and nauseating way of walking depopulating this planet just made the carnage he was about to unleash feel more than just enjoyable. It felt right. Righteous, even.

He wondered what the witch-woman would have made of the thought. And he hoped she'd gotten to somewhere safe. Things had been too busy to try and get in touch with her, and he couldn't find any way to reach her with his imp. This would be the first time he'd go into combat thinking about a woman. He hoped it wouldn't get him killed.

The tangos were less than a klick away. That put them in range of most of their weapon systems, but still on the wrong side of their force fields. Russell kept watching them as they came closer and closer. This was the kind of situation where you needed hardened combat veterans. All it would take to turn the ambush into a disaster would be one asshole opening fire too soon. Everybody on his fire team was steady. Staff Sergeant Dragunov had told a couple of the boots in the squad to remove their guns' magazines, just in case, and the same had probably been done to a handful other guys in the company, but only a handful. The rest would keep their cool and fire when ordered to, because they knew that trusting their buddies and their officers was the only way they had a chance to make it out alive. It took a lot of work to create that sort of trust, and it didn't take much to undo all of it, either.

The lead Vipers got to within a hundred yards. Fifty. Twenty-five. He ignored the up-close tangos as they started going around their position, taking the path of least resistance, just as expected. There were other Marines further back, tasked with dealing with them.

"Shit," Gonzo muttered. "One of them is climbing the ridge."

"'S okay," Russell said through gritted teeth. "I got 'im."

He sent out his suggested solution to higher. Captain Fromm approved it and sent out an instant fragmentary order with the changes; the whole thing took ten seconds, long enough for the Viper to get halfway up the ridge. Russell would open up the festivities. That was an honor he would have happily declined.

"Back away," he told his buddies. "This is gonna be fucking danger close."

The edge of the area force field slid over their position just as the Viper scout made it to the top of the rock wall, which had turned out not to be sheer enough. The ugly motherfucker touched the camo netting and realized it didn't feel anything like the stone surface it looked like.

Russell shot him in the face with a 20mm plasma round.

He'd had to do some fast reprogramming via his imp to get the warhead to go off at that range; the mini-missile usually wasn't armed until it'd traveled a good five yards away from the muzzle; five inches was a tad close.

The Plasma Armor Piercing round hit the alien's personal force field and went off, spewing a jet of superheated matter that tore through the energy barrier and the high-density alloy of the helmet beneath it. The alien's head disappeared.

A backscatter of plasma, sublimated metal and vaporized Viper brains and bone hit Russell hard, just as he'd expected. His own force field handed the diffuse impact well enough. It still wasn't pleasant; about as much fun as being lightly steamed, not to mention getting hit by a hefty pillow wielded by someone with muscle enhancements. He was nearly bowled over, but he held on and was up and firing a moment later.

"Shit, I felt that," Gonzo said as the headless corpse fell off the ridge. He was shooting as he spoke, along with the rest of Charlie Company.

The world narrowed down to Russell's field of fire. As soon as he recovered from the explosion, he found a target and fired. One of the rocketeers took a burst of 4mm and one AP grenade at fifteen yards, fucking knife-fighting range. The tango went down, but his ammo load didn't blow up like Russell had hoped. Fuck it. Next target. A burst and two rapid-fire 15mm grenades. Miss. He tried to lead a scurrying alien but wasted another grenade without scoring a hit, the last one in the tube magazine. Shit. Something big blew up somewhere, the flash of light intense enough to get his attention. He glanced around while he reloaded the 20mm launcher and saw the Viper force field gennie going up in smoke. Its power plant had gone off, doing more damage than a ground-bursting 200mm artillery shell. A bunch of Vipers nearby were down, and several of those weren't going to get up again.

The enemy froze for a second or two, plenty of time for the Marines to put a good hurting on them, but they reacted soon enough, going to ground, returning fire, and maneuvering around the unexpected obstacles. Their little floating fireflies spat out laser beams, detonating grenades in mid-flight and targeting the grunts firing them. The puny lasers didn't do any damage to their human targets; they were all behind their own portable shields, the kind of gizmo you could set up in place but couldn't walk around with. Just one of the many bennies of playing defense.

Russell spotted another fucker with a rocket launcher, leaning out behind a falling tree and taking aim. He hit him with a 20mm round, and this time he got a nice sympathetic detonation as at least some of the ET's forty-missile load blew up.

One of the platoon's LAVs fired down the path to the left of Russell's position, its 30mm graviton cannon turning a squad of Vipers into a twisted mass of metal, plastic and meat. Artillery and mortars hit other enemy concentrations; the tangos had been left high and dry by the destruction of their field generator. Other gennies were floating forward to fill the gap in the defenses, but one of them was taken under fire by a beautifully-coordinated LAV and mortar volley that knocked a hole through its shields and destroyed it.

The Vipers were slower on the uptake than Marines, but they had numbers and enough training to fight back. Rockets and lasers began to hammer Charlie Company's position, and their mobile guns were moving up. The fallback order went out.

First Squad backed up from the ridge, crawling and dragging their portable field gennie along while 100mm mortars blasted the unprotected aliens on the other side, forcing them back and allowing the Marines to break contact. A minute or so later, they were inside their squad LAV and headed back to their secondary position, one comfortably behind their own area energy bubble.

"Like the man said, I love it when a plan comes together," Russell said.

"What man?" Nacle asked.

"Some pre-Contact grunt." He'd Woogled the phrase a ways

back, but he didn't feel like checking it again. "John or Joseph Smith, I think. Or maybe it was the elephant guy, Hannibal."

"Joseph Smith?" Nacle said, awe in his voice.

"Fucker sure got around," Gonzo said.

* * *

Only two carats in the company roster were yellow, indicating Wounded in Action, which meant people hurt too badly to continue fighting; any lesser injury would be handled by the Marines' nano-med packs. No KIAs, not yet. Enemy casualties were just over a hundred dead from the ambush and artillery fire combined, and maybe as many wounded, although those casualties were harder to identify. It was as good as it got, and the only problem was, it probably wasn't going to be good enough.

Fromm watched the orderly retreat to the next line of prepared positions. The Vipers pushed through the mortar bombardment, taking another dozen casualties, and tried to mount a pursuit, only to get hit on their right flank by a surprise attack from Fourth Platoon's Hellcats. That had knocked the wind out of the advance, allowing the ambush forces to break contact cleanly and make it to safety without taking hardly any fire.

His main concern at the moment was keeping contact with the enemy forces to make sure they didn't pull out any surprises of their own, and to lure the aliens towards the forest to the north, where Bravo was waiting for them. The fixed sensors the Marines had left behind had been systematically destroyed as soon as the Vipers consolidated their position. The battalion's other recon assets were being destroyed at unsustainable rates; the ETs anti-drone tech was better than they'd estimated. And all the overhead satellites were gone, destroyed during the ongoing space battle still raging overhead. Fromm supposed the Colonel could ask some of the starships or orbital fortresses to take some time off from fighting for their lives and conduct a sensor sweep of the ground below, but he didn't think he'd get much of a response. The fog of war was alive and well on P-3. For now, he would use the Hellcats much like old-fashioned cavalry, screening the enemy advance and keeping them under observation. It was going to be hard on the mechanized kitties, though.

After a brief lull, punctuated only by a continuous artillery barrage over the aliens' rally point, the Vipers began moving forward again. A few hundred infantrymen, along with a handful of field projectors and mobile energy cannon, dutifully pursued

Charlie right into the next ambush. Fromm's implants manipulated what he saw, making lasers visible and reducing the glare of plasma explosions to tolerable levels, but they did little to obscure the horrors of battle. Vipers collapsed under multiple hits, or were torn apart under the impact Bravo's heavy weapons. The occasional artillery shell or missile broke through and delivered a brief moment of carnage. The enemy's relatively few vehicles were targeted by multiple heavy weapons. Their defensive shields didn't last long, and they had little or no armor underneath. One by one, they fell; area force fields were knocked down, leaving two Viper companies to the mercy of artillery and direct fire. A final charge from both companies' Hellcats wiped out the last few survivors before enemy reinforcements could arrive.

The exchange wasn't one-sided. More roster carats turned yellow. Three of them turned red, and two of those went black when a multiple rocket volley tore through a portable force field and obliterated Private First Class Greg O'Malley and Sergeant Fernando Uzcategui from Bravo Company. The casualty ratios were terribly lopsided in the Americans' favor, though. At those rates, the ETs would run out of warm bodies long before they could even decimate the battalion facing them. Sooner or later, that reality would sink in.

It didn't take long. Even the low-intelligence assault troopers weren't suicidal. When a follow-up attack was hit from both flanks, the aliens retreated in good order and took positions near the mouth of the valley while they waited for additional forces to arrive. Fromm wondered if Colonel Brighton would try to retake that position. Even after their losses – running close to three hundred now – the enemy still heavily outnumbered the Americans. The battalion's single armored platoon hadn't joined the fight yet, however, and the MBT-5 'Schwarzkopf' grav-tanks were absolutely deadly. Those four behemoths would blast the hell out of the enemy's light infantry. It looked like the enemy had underestimated the levels of resistance they would face. Maybe...

An alert signal chimed in. Fromm accepted the linked video feed and watched another artificial meteor shower coming down. A new wave of assault pods had been launched, including dozens of larger drop ships. Once again, half of them or more were destroyed in transit. But their landing zone was now heavily protected by force fields, so artillery did little damage to the enemy once it'd arrived. The initial incursion had prepared a relatively safe beachhead for the main push.

They'd been facing a brigade. The second wave was estimated

to comprise an entire corps.

Twelve

Parthenon-Three, 165 AFC

Morris Jensen suppressed a yawn as he stood watch.

The Forward Operations Base consisted of a thinly-manned defense perimeter, a vehicle laager, some hastily-erected tents, and a mass of weekend warriors and civilian volunteers unloading and organizing supplies. Everything from power packs to toilet paper was being stored there to support the Marines trying to keep the aliens from pushing deeper into Forge Valley.

Trying, and failing. Morris had been listening in on their comm chatter, courtesy of his prior service; when they'd activated the Volunteer Regiment, somebody had screwed up and granted him the same network access he'd had as an E-8, First Sergeant, rather than his current rank, two grades lower, not to mention in an auxiliary branch of the military. Under normal circumstances, he would have been booted out of the network, but nothing was normal. Which had given him a front-row seat to the battle being fought a hundred miles east of his position.

A Marine Expeditionary Unit packed a lot of firepower, but it was still nothing more than a reinforced battalion, and that just wasn't enough to hold off two division equivalents, even if they were mostly light infantry. They'd had to pull back to their third prepped position over the last twenty-four hours, which hadn't been supposed to happen for two or three days. They'd had no choice: the Vipers were tough, and they were getting through natural obstacles that would have slowed down or even halted human infantry. The 101st kept being threatened with encirclement and forced to fall back. Not retreat, mind you. Marines never retreated. They were just relocating backwards at a rapid pace.

The Volunteers might end up having to load the supplies back into the trucks and drive back to the east end of the valley. Militia didn't have any problems with retreating. As long as their families were safe, they'd be happy to run away. Came with having a brain and something to lose.

"Second Squad, we just got a report of enemy activity somewhere near Lover's Leap," Lieutenant Cassidy sent out through the platoon's net. "Go check it out."

"Roger that," Morris said.

"Sending you the report."

Morris reviewed the imp footage while he led the ten men in the squad towards the cliff commonly known as Lover's Leap, named after an urban legend involving a couple of teenagers who'd allegedly committed suicide by gravity shortly after the town's founding, the kind of place the current crop of teenagers liked to frequent to fool around. Morris was grateful Mariah hadn't yet reached the age where that kind of thing would be an issue.

The imp recording came from, unsurprisingly enough, two teenaged civvies, a boy and girl, who'd taken a break from helping out at the FOB to spend some quality time together. The footage showed something big moving through some brushes: the kids had panicked and run back screaming, and luckily the girl had retained enough presence of mind to send out an alert. The shaky video wasn't clear enough for an ID, though: there were a few large critters out in the wild, and whatever had been crashing through the foliage could be any of them. Better safe than sorry, though.

"Any chance of drone coverage?" he asked the El-Tee.

"That's a negatory, Jensen," the company commander replied. "Drone losses have been heavy and the gyrenes don't have any to spare."

The goddamn officer hadn't even bothered to ask the Marines about the drones. Lieutenant Cassidy was pushing fifty, but had zero combat experience and was an officer only because his pappy was a wealthy donor who'd paid for a lot of the Volunteers' equipment. Morris thought about pressing the issue, then sighed and carried on. They'd find out if there was anything to worry about soon enough.

They ran into the young couple about halfway there. The two fifteen-year olds were out of breath and clearly scared shitless.

"Oh, thank God!" the girl cried out and she and her boyfriend all but collapsed at their feet.

Her Facettergram profile popped up in Morris' field of vision, providing him with her name.

"Hey, Becky. Becky Cunningham – I know your dad, he runs the general store, doesn't he?"

She nodded, panting from fear and exhaustion.

"Just tell me what you saw."

"We heard something, I, uh, tried to take a look, but Tommy pushed me down and we crawled away. I'm sure it was an ET! He woulda shot us if we hadn't run!"

Tommy confirmed the story, with a lot of extra profanity thrown in.

"All right, head back to the FOB, and next time don't wander out into the woods, all right? We're having us a war here, in case you didn't notice."

Becky and Tommy nodded emphatically and took off.

"Think there's anything to it?" Lemon asked.

Morris shrugged. He couldn't believe the Vipers could have made it this deep into the valley, but you never knew.

"Only one way to find out. All right, people! Spread out, skirmish line. Let's act like it's for real."

All the men in the squad had been in combat and knew the drill. They moved forward in a staggered double line, half the squad hanging back and providing cover while the other half advanced. Everyone knew the area; they headed for a slight rise that overlooked Lovers' Leap, staying low and quiet.

Lemon was the first to spot the ETs.

Vipers, he sent out via imp.

And there they were, half a dozen aliens in a half circle next to the cliff. As they watched, a couple more scrambled up. Becky and Tommy must have spotted the first one up.

The six-hundred-foot cliff was nearly sheer, but it could be climbed. A couple of mountaineering enthusiasts did so every once in a while. And Vipers were like spiders when it came to climbing stuff.

Another alien made it to the top. Now there were nine. Less than a klick away from the FOB. No time to wait for orders.

"Light them up!" Morris said, drawing a bead on a Viper with a rocket launcher and double-tapping him with two armor-piercing grenades. The bastard went down.

Their first fusillade took out four Eets. The others managed to duck for cover and return fire. An eighth Viper poked his head over the edge of the cliff and Morris put a couple of bursts of 4mm explosive into him. The alien's force field failed and he went back the way he came. It was a long drop to the bottom. Problem was, Morris didn't need drones to tell him there were plenty more where he came from; the cliff face could well be crawling with hundreds of Echo Tangos.

It took a bit of yelling to get through to the El-Tee, but word went out. A flight of drones got sent out, along with a promise that help was on the way. Morris and the squad kept the aliens pinned down, but more were coming up, and they couldn't take them out fast enough. At least the enemy didn't seem to have any fireflies with them.

Drones arrived, and Morris got their take as they flew over

Lovers' Leap. It wasn't as bad as he'd imagined. It was a lot worse.

A reinforced company's worth of Vipers were on the cliff's face, scrambling up like so many spider-monkeys. Two hundred, maybe more. And that wasn't the real bad news.

An entire infantry regiment was at the foot of the mountain range, headed for a narrow pass some ten klicks to the southeast. How the aliens had managed to make their way through the largely impassable mountains, Morris had no idea. Maybe they'd had some grav vehicles along to help them through the rough spots. None of that mattered, though. If someone didn't stop them, they would flank the entire blocking force.

Morris ducked when a laser shattered a piece of rock and peppered him with stone shards. His shields caught them, but the whole thing reminded him why he'd left the Corps.

* * *

Fromm and Charlie Company raced to beat the devil.

Colonel's Brighton's orders had been terse and to the point. Head back towards FOB Sentinel and use his command to stop the flanking force that had managed to bypass most of Forge Valley. Success was going to depend on who reached their objective first. Fromm's troop carriers had more ground to cover but their LAVs could move at two hundred miles an hour if they rose above any obstacles and they left the slower Hellcats behind. They did both. There was a chance the extra elevation would allow some of the ETs on the west end of the valley to take a few shots at the vehicles, but he had to risk it.

The twenty Light Assault Vehicles ferrying Charlie and elements of the battalion's weapons company rose some twenty feet off the ground and got moving. Someone sent a full flight of forty mini-missiles after them, but they were intercepted mid-flight by the battalion's air-defense battery. Charlie Company kept going, only slowing down when it approached the area force fields protecting the FOB; going over sixty mph would lead to a crash against the energy shields.

The base was in chaos. Some militiamen and civvies were still doing their jobs, but some fobbit was trying to organize a perimeter defense by handing out rifles to a bunch of militiamen who hadn't fired a gun in anger since Basic. Fromm could only hope they wouldn't end up with a bunch of friendly fire incidents. Not his problem. If the Vipers got to the militia's defensive perimeter, they were toast. Of course, his command would be long gone if that was the case.

For once, things went as planned, and Charlie Company got to the pass before the Vipers, thank God for small favors. To call the narrow footpath between a series of rough natural ladders on a mountainside a pass was something of an exaggeration, but apparently the aliens had thought they could move a regiment through it. Fromm intended to disabuse them of such notions.

The troops came out of their vehicles and got to work setting up a hasty defense. The LAVs retreated back a ways and positioned themselves hull-down, only the tops of their turrets protruding from view. Fromm thought about using camo netting to hide the company, but dismissed the idea. He wanted the area force fields deployed and working, and they would be detected right away by the Vipers. The first ambush had been risky enough, keeping their energy shields down until the enemy was nearly on top of their positions, and that kind of trick was unlikely to work twice. The alien assault troopers might be dumb, but the expert systems leading them were smart enough to learn from their previous mistakes.

His troops had just enough time to dig in and prepare to receive the enemy. Strips of explosive 'diggers' did most of the work, blasting holes into the rocky soil that the soldiers improved with their classic entrenching tools. A mile behind them, a company from the Volunteers were working on a secondary line of defense. Fromm hoped they wouldn't need it. Their current position was the narrowest point in the pass, barely wide enough to deploy a squad in a line, the place where his company could concentrate the most fire, where the enemy would have to concentrate and take fire from up high for pretty much the entire length of their formation.

It was still a matchup between a regiment and a company. Fromm concentrated on the positive. It was a lightly-armed regiment. This particular group only had three field generators in support, and no heavy weapons other than their rocket launchers. Their lasers outranged his Marines' small arms, but that wouldn't matter here; the twisting pass wouldn't allow direct fire from more than three, four hundred yards. And he had two artillery batteries backing him up.

The Vipers' fireflies began to shoot down drones as the enemy force approached. Somewhere ahead of him, the main gun of one of the LAVs opened up, the stream of gravitons making a thunderous sound as it warped space-time on its way to the target.

The battle was joined.

* * *

The ETs' lasers were like a rainbow.

At least that was how they looked to Russell; his imp turned the normally invisible energy streams into lines of red, yellow and green, color-coded to indicate how close they were to his position. Red was the worst, of course. And there was a lot of red.

When the red lines became dots, it meant they were aimed straight at you, and you ducked, even if you had three force fields between you and them, because you never knew if one of those beams was going to punch through them and punch your ticket. The alien bastards were going continuous beam at the moment, pouring it on in other words, massive amounts of energy concentrated on a point a couple millimeters wide, and the area force fields started to flicker and sparkle when multiple beams converged on them. Somewhere down the line, the status carat of a trooper from First Platoon went yellow. Morales, one of the boots. The poor bastard hadn't remembered to duck and gotten tagged. He wasn't dead, but your carat didn't go yellow from a first-degree burn or a scratch. Somebody had put a hurt on him.

The detached part of Russell that dealt with such things processed the information and set it aside. The rest of him was busy servicing targets in between ducking lasers, shooting at designated aiming points just like the Vipers were. Aim at the virtual dot and fire when ordered: his 20mm shield buster hit the Viper's area field at the same time as a grenade from Nacle, opening a temporary breach that Gonzo filled with a long burst from his ALS-43. Most rounds were wasted on the shield, but a handful made it through and potted an ET who'd stepped out of cover, and that was enough to send him to hell, personal force field or not.

Fucking ETs. Behind their area field, it took an entire fire team to get one of them, more like two when you were talking about regular Marine infantry. Russell and his team were more heavily armed than the average leatherneck, but chewing through the enemy defenses still took some doing.

First Squad's LAV opened up over their heads, firing behind a massive boulder that added its bulk to the vehicle's own force field and composite armor. Its 30mm grav cannon was part of a volley aimed at a Viper field genny. Knocking those out would make killing the ETs a lot easier. There was no big boom among the scurrying scaly critters filling up the pass, though; no joy this time.

Russell got another target, and he and his buddies dutifully tagged it. The Viper staggered but made it behind cover, and his alien pals' lasers got through the platoon's big shield before being stopped by the squad's portable one; everyone in the fire team ducked before that. The aliens were getting closer, down to three hundred yards. Some artillery would be nice just about now, but Russell hadn't seen any explosions overhead for a while. Things must be getting livelier on the other side of the valley, there a couple alien divisions were chasing the rest of the 101st all over the place. He'd chanced a peek during a lull in the action, and he'd watched some short-lived drone footage. The second wave of Vipers had included a company of Turtles. Light tanks, small and not even as tough as a LAV, let alone a Stormin' Norman, but a lot more dangerous than the leg infantry they'd mostly been fighting so far. That wasn't going to be any fun.

He ducked as multiple red dots joined together towards him. The portable force field dissolved in a shower of colorful sparks and a chunk of rock over his head exploded as a laser superheated it and turned it into a good imitation of a hand grenade. Fragments peppered everyone, but their personal shields kept them in one piece.

The squad's portable shield didn't come back.

"Drained battery," Gonzo said while he fired a short burst before ducking for cover.

"I got it," Nacle called out; the Mormon started crawling towards the genny, a boxy contraption they'd set on the ground some five yards behind their position. It would take him about a minute to grab a power pack from the supply box and replace the spent one, and Russell and Gonzo couldn't hunker down and wait that long. The squad's fire computer was calling out more targets; they were going to have to do without a shield and start shooting. All in a day's work.

"Ready?"

"Ready," Gonzo said, sounding as happy as Russell felt.

Tango at two-fifty meters. Another rocket-launching mother lover. Russell and Gonzaga leaned out and let him have it, full bursts and a 20mm plasma round that reached out and tore the fucker apart – just as he ripple-fired a full load of missiles their way. Russell had just enough time to see a wall of flame blossoms smash against the platoon's area force field before a leaker got to his unprotected fighting hole.

The world turned white, then black.

He was on his hands and knees, blood filling his mouth, clogging his nose. Everything hurt. He hawked, snorted and spat until he could breathe again, ignoring the bloody phlegm dripping on the inside of the helmet and running down his chin. It took him a moment to remember who he was and what was going on, and another moment to query his imp and get a status check. Green. Well, greenish. He had a mild concussion, but the nanomeds were on the job. Nothing else was broken, other than his Iwo: the infantry weapon had taken the brunt of the explosion, and it was no longer usable.

Russell checked on the rest of his fire team next. Gonzo's carat was yellow. A piece of his own body armor had spalled under the explosion. The fragment of high-refractory carbon-ceramic alloy had stabbed him in the chest and perforated a lung. The wound was being serviced by the nanomeds but it was going to take a full regen tank to fix. Nacle had been knocked silly by the overpressure but was back on the job. By the time Russell regained his bearings, the squad's force field was active again.

Two bubblehead corpsmen put Gonzo on a static lift stretcher and crawled away, the stretcher floating an inch off the ground. He'd be all right, assuming their position didn't get overrun.

"Nacle, check on Gonzo's Alsie," Russell ordered. According to his imp, the ALS-43 was in working order, but it was best to be sure.

"On it." Nacle crawled to the spot where the Automatic Launch System had been flung aside when the Viper missile volley had blasted their position. The fighting hole had been chewed up to hell; Russell and Gonzo were lucky to be alive.

"It looks good, Russet," the kid said after a quick manual check. They'd all cross-trained on the squad's weapons, just for occasions like this.

"All right. Hand me your Iwo. The All-Good's yours for now. You know what to do."

"Kill bodies, oorah."

"Yep."

At some point, the Vipers' leading field genny had been taken out, and the Vipers had been showered with 100mm mortar munitions. There was at least a company's worth of dead ETs in front of Russell's sector, and the live ones were all hunkering down while the last alien field projector reached them. He picked out a tango who wasn't as well-covered as he thought, and he and Nacle sent him to hell, followed by another, and another. They scored five stepped-on kills and half a dozen probables before the rest were saved by their replacement shield, and they weren't the only ones reaping aliens. The Vipers were having a pretty bad day.

There were five yellow, two red and two black carats on the company's roster, though, and those guys were having the worst day you could have.

"Getting hot in here," Russell muttered as he opened up on the next target.

Sixth Fleet, Parthenon System, 165 AFC

"Instruct Sixth Fleet to commence warp transit," Admiral Givens said, nearly choking on the words.

For two days, her ships and Parthenon-Three's defenses had traded salvos with the Viper armada. Losses had been high on both sides, but they were becoming unsustainable for the Americans. All the STL monitors had fallen; the orbital defense ships were tough, but they lacked warp shields and they'd been taken down one by one. One orbital fortress had broken apart under the Vipers' relentless hammering and the remaining five were all heavily damaged.

Sixth Fleet hadn't fared much better. Three battlecruisers were gone, along with one third of her frigates and destroyers. The fact that the enemy had lost three times as many ships did little to change the realities of the situation. To stay any longer meant to die in place, and her orders were to preserve Sixth Fleet as a fighting force. She'd pushed things to the limit, and perhaps a bit beyond it.

The Fleet Operations crew grimly followed her orders. They knew they were leaving Parthenon-Three to the aliens' tender mercies. Each Planetary Defense Base packed as much firepower as a dreadnought, and they would keep the enemy fleet at bay, but only until the alien ground forces took them out.

Sixth Fleet entered warp while under fire for the second time in a few days. Two destroyers were lost in the process. More deaths on Givens' conscience. Warp ghosts howled at her for a brief eternity before she and the rest of the formation emerged one light minute away, far enough to be safe from enemy pursuit, and close enough to remain a threat and block any attempts to reach the warp valleys that would let the enemy attack other systems.

The enemy spent two hours blasting another fortress into burning ruin before they executed their own warp jump, heading back to a rendezvous point where they would meet their supply fleet. Another milk run, Givens realized. They would make repairs, reload their massive missile boxes, and come back. Their new weapons and tactics were more logistics-dependent than normal. Something could come of that, although she couldn't risk trying anything fancy at the moment. Sixth Fleet would have to do nothing other than lick its wounds while it waited for reinforcements.

And if those reinforcements didn't come in time, Parthenon-Three would fall. Givens didn't think she could abandon thirty million people to their fate. The temptation to launch a warp-kamikaze attack was strong, but she knew it would be worse than futile. Unlike the Lampreys at Melendez, the enemy here would not be caught off-guard. And the useless sacrifice would doom every world down the warp-chains leading out of Parthenon System.

Admiral Givens left the TFCC and headed towards her cabin.

She needed to scream and break something, and she couldn't do it where the crew might see.

Parthenon-Three, 165 AFC

The Vipers finally got tired of dying and broke away.

Retreating while stuck in a decisive engagement was tough, but the aliens performed the maneuver as well as anybody Fromm had ever fought, using their dwindling supplies of fireflies to keep the Marine drones at bay and pulling back to where artillery could no longer be efficiently targeted on them. In so doing, they abandoned the pass without achieving anything other than filling it with their corpses.

Charlie Company hadn't budged from its starting position. His own butcher's bill hadn't been very high under the circumstances: ten casualties, including two dead; five of the wounded would be back on active duty within twenty-four hours. The aliens had lost well over four hundred KIA. Most combat units would lose cohesion after that sort of rough handling, but the Viper assault troopers were stubborn.

Fromm shook his head. He was getting tired of fighting suicide troops. The Lampreys would have never kept coming into the pass once they realized surprise had been lost. From what he'd heard about the Imperium, it also wasn't in the habit of shoving troops into meat grinders. That sort of warrior culture was usually found among barbarians, usually pre-Starfaring ones.

Or humans, he conceded. CRURON 56 had proven that at Melendez System. By the same token, if holding the pass had required him to endure those losses, he would do it, and his

Marines would stand by him. It helped when the only alternative to fighting was death, of course. The Vipers didn't take prisoners.

He was still watching the last enemy forces as they disengaged, taking more casualties along the way, when a FLASH message arrived. The news helped explain the sudden decision by the Vipers to pull back. Sixth Fleet had been pushed away. The enemy would be able to operate closer to the planet, and to drop more troops. No sense in taking losses when they would soon be able to storm the Marines' positions with overwhelming force.

A virtual meeting with all company and attachment officers was scheduled for the morning. Fromm hoped they would be able to hammer out a plan that wasn't doomed to failure.

Death he could handle. Failure was unacceptable.

New Washington, District of Nebraska, Earth, 165 AFC

The JCS were getting a little riled up.

Tyson Keller watched the assembly in stony silence. Nobody shied away from his gaze, a big difference from the cabinet meetings he usually attended; the Joint Chiefs of Staff were made of sterner stuff, and they might respect Tyson but weren't scared of him. They were all fighting commanders who'd gotten their stars the old-fashioned way, even the Army Chief, who was the low man on the totem pole, given that the universe belonged to the Navy and the gyrenes. Hell of a thing, in Tyson's opinion, but what could you do? In any case, even the Army Chief of Service wasn't really afraid of him; you didn't make this far without a full set of balls, even if two of the JCs were female.

"This diversion of resources could be disastrous, Mister President," the Vice Chairman said. Admiral DuPont had started out in the wet navy before First Contact, and, ironically enough, had been one of the few carrier guys who'd adapted to the Space Navy's battleship tactics. Ironically, because he was now arguing against the introduction of carrier operations to space combat. Tyson figured that a hundred and fifty years of active service later, he was too hidebound to even consider carriers something other than an antiquated, useless concept, about as applicable to modern warfare as galleys had been in the 20th century.

"You are talking about re-tasking the better part of three support squadrons at the last minute, and hoping an untried combat platform will perform as advertised," DuPont continued. "Which is highly doubtful. Sir."

"I strongly disagree," the Marine Corps Commandant said. He

was another Pre-Contact Ancient who'd distinguished himself at Fallujah back in the day. "The fleet exercises have all been successful and exceeded even our most optimistic estimates. I think the Lexington Project is a go, if we give it enough support. All the elements are in place, except for logistics, and, frankly, two more battlecruiser squadrons, which is what we'd be replacing with the Carrier Strike Group, are not going to make a crucial difference."

The rest of the JCs looked askance at the lone Marine; they usually tried to present a united front when meeting with the Commander in Chief. But the Lexington Project had been the Marines' show, mostly because the Navy had given up on it early on. Things would change as soon as the new tech proved its worth, of course, but Tyson and the President would help keep the ensuing turf wars down to a dull roar. This wasn't the time for that kind of bullshit, not when the human race was two, maybe three defeats away from being exterminated like so much vermin.

The Chairman spoke up. "Mister President. I agree with General Forsythe that Project Lexington looks promising. On paper. It even appears as if we might be able to deploy the… Starfighters, I guess, deploy them in enough numbers to make a difference. But I don't know if Parthenon-Three is the right place to deploy them." Admiral Carruthers' opinion was always worthy of respect, of course. The man had fought and won the first two conflicts against Starfarers. "The Navy has a tradition and a future," he quoted. "If Lexington is indeed successful, we should try to use it to our maximum advantage, to extract as much benefit from it as possible. After we use the carriers in combat, strategic surprise will be lost."

President Hewer stared steadily at the top brass as he spoke. "We have next to nothing to put up against the Vipers' thrust at Parthenon. Four warp transits from our doorstep, Admiral. Do we have enough conventional forces to stop them? What good is preserving strategic surprise if we lose the whole damn war?"

Carruthers looked down. Everyone knew the score. They were throwing every hull they could scare up into the relief force, the so-called Seventh Fleet. They were even going to commission the first *Pantheon*-class superdreadnought, the *Zeus*, which was less than eighty-percent operational. At this point, if it could maneuver and it could fire at least some of its guns, it was considered good to go. But you couldn't assemble a fleet from scratch. The new ships' crews were mostly reactivated veterans riding herd over the current conscript class. And Fifth Fleet, which was supposed to serve as the core of the new formation, was still in terrible shape. Most of those warships were too heavily damaged to return to combat in time to make a difference.

On paper, Seventh Fleet looked pretty good, with enough firepower to save the day. On paper. When the chips were down, Tyson knew the green, untrained formations would be lucky to perform half as well as they should.

"Well?" Hewer said when Carruthers took too long to answer.

"Even if we lose Parthenon, the war is far from lost, Mister President. We could still fall back into a defensive posture. Trade space for time." From the look on his face, Carruthers found that proposition barely more palatable than suing for unconditionally surrender.

Going defensive was the smart play: abandon Parthenon System and have Sixth and Seventh Fleets make their stand at Wolf 1061. Doing so meant giving up over a dozen other systems down the other ley lines emanating from Parthenon. Most of those were smaller colonies which wouldn't be able to defend themselves from even a single enemy cruiser. None of the larger colonies were as heavily fortified as P-3; the aliens would have them for breakfast. There would be no way to evacuate those planets. A hundred million Americans would be left out in the cold. The smart play involved trading those lives for time.

"Abandoning Parthenon is not acceptable," Hewer said. "The American people won't stand for it. *I* won't stand for it. What are our chances if we send everything that is ready this minute to support Sixth Fleet?"

"Lower than fifty percent, Mister President. And our losses even if we win are likely to be severe. Perhaps even catastrophic. We would likely lose all the worlds we'd be trying to protect, and weaken Seventh Fleet enough that we couldn't guarantee the safety of Wolf 1061 against further attack. Even Sol System wouldn't be safe in the aftermath."

"As I see it, and please correct me if I'm wrong, we have three choices," the President went on. "First, order Sixth Fleet to fall back to Libertas System and protect the warp chain leading to Wolf 1061, abandoning the other chains to the Vipers, while we finish readying Seventh Fleet. Which will take… how long?"

DuPont began to speak, but Carruthers interrupted him. "Two more months, Mister President."

The latest estimate claimed five weeks, but Carruthers knew better than blow smoke up the Prez's ass.

"Yeah, that's what I thought. Two months, plenty of time for the Vipers to depopulate all the systems along the other four warp chains leading out of Parthenon."

Nobody had anything to say to that.

"Second option, throw every ship that's combat-ready into the fray, and hope the reinforcements are enough to make a difference. That, as you said, has a fifty-fifty chance to succeed, maybe less, because the Vipers are likely being reinforced even as we speak."

Carruthers nodded.

"And finally, divert enough support to the carrier task force to make it operational, and send it forward to reinforce Sixth Fleet along with anything else we can send. Which will increase the timetable to ready Seventh Fleet by how long?"

"At least another two weeks. Maybe three," Admiral DuPont said. "And it would reduce the number of conventional reinforcements we can send immediately by two battlecruiser squadrons, nearly half the ready force. If the carriers don't work as advertised, the odds of success go from fifty-fifty to about one in ten."

"We'd be betting everything on those carriers making the difference," Carruthers concluded.

"It's better than abandoning a hundred million Americans," Tyson said. Nobody was happy to have the President's Chief of Staff at the meeting, let alone having him pipe in with his opinion. He didn't care. The ghosts of the dead wouldn't let him stay quiet. Too many had died by his hand, simply because they had been obstructing the steps they'd had to take to keep humanity alive, in many cases with the best of intentions. He'd be damned if he allowed millions of innocents to die because it was too risky to save them.

"Even if Sixth Fleet is defeated and wiped out, it will buy us time," he went on. "The Vipers' losses will be severe as well. Send the goddamn carriers, send whatever else you've got. Admiral Givens knows the score. She'll make the Vipers bleed at Parthenon."

Maybe. Shoulda coulda woulda. Wars were uncertain affairs; that was why it was best to avoid them if possible. But there was no need to say that. They all knew it.

"It is a risk," General Forsythe said. "But it provides some hope for Parthenon and doesn't abandon the rest of the warp chains."

There was some more arguing about the particulars before the President said he would announce his decision the next day and called the meeting to an end.

"They really don't think the fighters are going to make a difference," Al Hewer said when they were alone.

"'Not Invented Here Syndrome,'" Tyler said. "The Navy rejected the whole idea and the Marines ran with the ball, and even on a shoestring budget they've done some amazing stuff. I've made sure nobody's padding the performance reports, Al. Unless I'm missing something, those little flying cannon are going to be as decisive as warp catapults were."

"Yeah, I read the reports too. The actual reports, not the summaries. Cost me a good deal of sleep, but sleep hasn't come easy for a long time. What worries me are the psych evals, the reports of ESP, telepathy, the sort of bizarre crap we've been assured by our Starfarer friends is the stuff of fantasy. Half of it sounds like mystic mumbo-jumbo, and the other half is like something from a horror movie. Did you read the brief explaining why the Imperium decided to pick a fight with us? They think we are warp demons, or demon-summoning sorcerers."

Tyson nodded. "It's an economy-size witch hunt. Or a crusade. And we're the Great Satan. Not exactly the first time we've been called that."

"What if in this case it turns out to be the literal truth? Those reports jive a little too closely to some of the weirder Starfarer legends out there. Warp demons. Save our bodies, lose our souls."

"Kinda late to worry about your soul, Al, or mine for that matter," Tyson said. "We've been baptized in the blood of innocents, you and I. All to save humanity, and America. If it turns out we're calling forth the Dark Side of the Force, we'll have to hope our descendants fix that. As long as there are descendants, there's hope."

"Heh. I hated *Star Wars* just as much as *Star Trek*. Lucas was a moral imbecile."

"Maybe. The thing is, the dead don't have moral agency. Survival trumps just about everything else. And I may not have much of a soul left, but I can't have a hundred million deaths on my conscience."

"Neither can I. There are lines that can't be crossed. And I suppose the Lexington Project isn't one of them. The final reports indicate they have a handle on the pseudo-telepathy and the pseudo-demonic possession, and the last set of fleet exercises went off without a hitch. I suppose that'll have to be enough."

"Made up your mind, then?"

Al nodded. "I did when I said I wouldn't allow Parthenon to be abandoned without a fight. We'll go with the carriers, and if they bring pandemonium to the galaxy, too damn bad. We'll send them and everything else we've got to give Sixth Fleet a chance at victory, or at worst to give the Vipers a Pyrrhic victory. Should take a week if we drop everything and rush those ships out, maybe five days if everything works perfectly. Hopefully Parthenon-Three can hold on that long. It's all moot otherwise."

"They will."

Thirteen

Groom Base, 165 AFC

"We probably should bring back the Air Force," Fernando Verdi said. "Although we'd have to change the name. Space Force, maybe? Star Force?"

Lisbeth Zhang was feeling pretty agreeable; Fernando had taken her to what he referred to as 'the heights of ecstasy' and was now following up their lovemaking with a very thorough back massage. But there were some things she just couldn't agree with.

"Nope. Just nope."

"I'm just not sure keeping the fighters in the Corps is a good idea, though. Much as I love the gun club, they might need their own branch of service."

"Anything's better than bringing back the Air Farce," Lisbeth said. "Now, turning the fighters over to the Navy makes some sense, and that's probably what will end up happening. They are going to deploy from Navy ships, after all. But so do the Marines, either from shuttles or warp catapults, shudder, groan," she finished mock-grimly.

Fernando' laugh at her last comment was a bit shaky. They'd all experienced more warp jumps in training than most Marines did in their entire careers, and the experience hadn't improved one iota with practice, even with the newest batch of Mélange keeping them sane and alive through the process.

"So anyways," she went on. "Given that Marines are meant to conduct offensive operations off naval vessels, I would argue that there should have never been a Naval Air Force in the first place; it should have been the Marines' show from the get-go. Well, except maybe for Search and Rescue or flying big wigs around or whatever. But the fighters and bombers should have always been under Marine control. Screw the bubbleheads."

"That's funny, coming from a former bubblehead."

"Bah, I say. The Navy didn't want me, and being a Marine suits me fine. Well, being a Marine pilot, that is. I did my share of ground-pounding shit, and the 03s can keep that job. But I like being the skipper of my own little warship. If I screw up, the only one who pays the price will be little old me, instead of…"

They appeared around her from one heartbeat to the next, the dead crewmembers and passengers of the *Wildcat* and the *Bengal Tiger*, and she was able to see each of their faces as they started mutely at her.

"Oh, shit. I see them," Fernando said.

That had been happening with growing frequency. Shared flashbacks. Most of the pilots weren't reporting the increasing number of incidents, and the stories from those who did had been dismissed as the product of 'highly suggestive states.' They weren't affecting anyone's performance, and at the moment that was all that mattered.

"Yeah. Not a pretty sight, are they?" Lisbeth said. The dead didn't scare her anymore. She mostly felt sad. And guilty. She was past being afraid of ghosts.

"It wasn't your fault," Fernando told her. He turned to the staring dead. "It wasn't her fault."

One by one, the ghosts nodded and vanished.

"Did you see that?" Lisbeth gasped. That was new, getting a reaction from the spirits.

"They heard me. You saw that, didn't you? They heard me."

"And they agreed with you. I think. Pretty fucking responsive, for a shared hallucination."

"*Ave Maria,*" Fernando said. He crossed himself. "Makes me wish I'd paid more attention during Sunday school."

"You're Catholic, aren't you?"

"Yep. You?"

"Nothing. Not really an atheist. Just don't give a crap either way. You live and you die, and whether or not there's some big old beardo watching you from on high doesn't matter until after you're dead. In my humble opinion. At least, that's what I used to believe."

"Yeah. Well, maybe you should start praying."

"Yeah."

The next morning, they heard the news. They were going to war. Just a few weeks after qualifying, without even a shakedown cruise under their belt, and they were going to war. Things were so bad they were throwing them into the fray, fresh out of R&D. She thought she was ready for the real thing, but it would have been nice to get a little more practice before rolling hot.

Maybe she *should* start praying.

* * *

Rear Admiral Leroy Burke watched the ships of Carrier Strike Group One and was nearly overwhelmed by a disturbing mixture of pride and terror.

Born in the rough streets of Chicago, Leroy had managed to claw his way out, helped along by his implacable mother, who had made all kinds of sacrifices to provide him with an education at a charter school. He'd made it to college and become a naval officer and eventually a Navy pilot. He'd flown missions all over the world, survived through several close calls, and risen through the ranks. It'd been a long road, from Tailhook to US Central Command, with even a stint with the Blue Angels along the way. He'd killed and watched good men die, had learned many harsh lessons, and taught many more.

The day the aliens had come he'd been the captain of the *USS Nimitz*, cruising alongside the rest of CSG-11 in the Indian Ocean when the impossible news began to pour in. His fleet had gone to DEFCON-TWO just before cities all over the world began to burn. The supercarrier and the rest of the group had scrambled their fighters, but there was no enemy to engage, nothing anybody could do as half the world was massacred by an enemy only glimpsed through telescopes and the doomed International Space Station in the brief moments before it was contemptuously swatted from orbit by the unknown attackers.

The shock of discovering that the most formidable surface force on the planet was utterly helpless had been bad enough. The disjointed reports of death and destruction that filtered in as the fleet wandered around aimlessly and waited for orders had been much worse. Leroy's wife and children had survived – Kitsap Base was spared from the horror of the fire domes – but his mother and everyone in Chicago had not. Those losses, combined with witnessing the darkest period in the planet's history, had scarred him for life.

America had survived, for some values of America. Leroy, like most men and women in uniform, had followed the new President's lead. CSG-11 had headed back to North America, to help the survivors of the attack. Less than half of the US pre-Contact population had survived, and millions more perished in the aftermath, particularly the elderly and infirm. Disease and civil unrest had been almost as deadly, and Leroy had the dubious honor of being the first US carrier commander in history to order air strikes over American soil, targeted at fellow Americans.

Eventually, the nation pulled itself together, although it was a different country in many ways. Leroy and most of the military were too busy to dwell on the political changes, however. The enemy that had nearly exterminated humanity was still out there, and the US Armed Forces had to undergo a systematic transformation to deal with it. The Navy ceased to exist as a seaborne service, and became the Space Navy. The change affected everyone, from the lowest Seamen – soon to be renamed Spacers – to the topmost admirals.

Most people believed the slang term for Navy personnel – bubblehead – came from the NASA-designed helmets that became part of their uniform during the early phases of the post-Contact space program, and to some degree that belief was true. But the term had existed before then, and was used among military circles long before the general public saw the first generation of Navy spacers. Submarine crews were called bubbleheads, and sub commanders quickly dominated the early Space Navy. It made perfect sense: submariners were used to dealing with self-contained vessels surrounded on all sides by a hostile environment. When the first American starships were built, the highly-coveted command assignments went to bubbleheads.

The Old Navy balked, but President Hewer had no patience for what he considered petty concerns. Seniority be dammed; the admirals who didn't get with the program were encouraged to retire, their only other option being to be fired outright. Most realized the wisdom in letting the bubbleheads lead the way, and changed with the times.

Leroy managed. He spent years without a ship of his own, after the heartbreaking task of overseeing the breaking up of the *Nimitz*, her power plant and other parts used for crude spaceships that went to other captains. His first space command, well over a decade later, was the *USS Whipple*, a cheap, light frigate that later would be reclassified as a corvette, tiny compared to the *Nimitz*, let alone the ships of the line the Space Navy was beginning to sail. Those were tough times: the Puppies' technical advice notwithstanding, they'd all had to learn by doing, and the inevitable mistakes that ensued cost lives.

His tenure on the *Whipple* taught him a great deal as he was faced with hazards and complications he'd never encountered at sea. And by the time he learned how to handle them, new technologies came into play: warp shields, something other Starfarers had never used in recorded history. Like all new things, they came with their share of unintended consequences.

Over half of Leroy's pre-Contact fellow captains were even less fortunate and died in combat, fell prey to accidents, or vanished in warp transit, never to be heard of again. The Navy's old guard was essentially wiped out during Earth's first interstellar conflict. The bubbleheads, to the surprise of no one, had the highest survival rates. After the Risshah were dealt with, he retired, spent thirty-five rather boring years in the private sector, and rejoined the service for another war, this time against the so-called Gremlins.

He'd always regretted the realities that spelled the end of small craft in combat. Against weapons that could span tens of thousands of miles in a fraction of a second, only mass and armor provided security. Fighters had gone the way of the horse-borne warrior, relics with no place in the present. Until now.

Twenty-six ships prepared for departure. Five light carriers that were little more than refitted Marine Assault Ships, each fielding two squadrons of twelve War Eagles each. Their pilots averaged a hundred hours and forty warp jumps. The guidelines he'd helped craft required at least two hundred and fifty hours and a hundred jumps before being considered fit for combat operations, but circumstances had forced everyone to cut corners. Besides the carriers, the group consisted of eight *Aegis*-class destroyers, most of their armament dedicated to point defense, and twelve logistics ships. The support vessels had just arrived, diverted from Seventh Fleet to allow the strike group to sail into combat.

Leroy was on the bridge of the flotilla's flagship, a converted battlecruiser that had been stripped of her main guns but retained her armor and heavy force fields; she held five War Eagle squadrons. They'd planned to name her the *Enterprise*, but the group commander had fought hard to get his way, spending every favor he had left for the privilege of naming his ship.

The *USS Nimitz* sailed towards her baptism of fire. Admiral Leroy Burke set aside his fears and doubts and savored this moment.

"We are cleared for departure, sir."

"To all Strike Group Elements: Engage."

Parthenon-Three, 165 AFC

Charlie Company left the narrow pass for resupply and a new mission. Which from the looks of it would be a redeployment from the frying pan into the fire.

The job of blocking the pass was now in the hands of the Volunteers' Regiment, along with an ad hoc company of private contractors cobbled together from the ranks of several New Burbank corporations' security teams. As usual, the mercs had a large number of combat vets among their ranks, and they'd been issued enough heavy weapons to put that experience to good use. Alongside militiamen who were literally defending their homes and families, they should be able to hold off any further enemy incursion. Fighting from fixed positions along a narrow front that couldn't be flanked was as easy as it got, combat-wise. Charlie Company couldn't be spared for the easy jobs.

They'd had two quiet days. The Vipers had pulled away from P-3's orbit and were refitting and resupplying in deep space. Sixth Fleet was playing games with them, feinting via warp jumps that forced the enemy to deploy for combat. Hopefully that would buy them a couple more days, but sooner or later they'd be back.

On the ground, two enemy assault troop divisions and tanks had chased the 101st's other two companies and their Army attachments halfway through the valley, taking heavy losses, before pulling back to Davis' Gap and assuming a defensive posture. Alpha and Bravo had been glad to see them go and were regrouping in the neighborhood of Davistown. The push into the valley and the doomed attempt at outflanking their defenses appeared to have been part of a reconnaissance in force rather than the main thrust they'd feared. The western half Forge Valley had become a no-man's land of sorts. The aliens were waiting for further reinforcements while securing their staging area.

Fromm's company was going to head west and poke that hornet's nest.

"Do you understand your orders, Captain?" Colonel Brighton asked him.

"Yes, sir. Take command of a task force comprising Charlie Company, the BLT's armor platoon and Bravo's Mobile Infantry platoon. Advance towards Davis' Gap. Ascertain enemy dispositions there and provide forward observer support for artillery attacks. Attempt to provoke an enemy sortie and lead it into a series of ambushes, with the goal of weakening the landing zone holding force."

The ideal goal would be the destruction of the landing zone, but they didn't have forces to fight a set-piece battle against the better part of a corps. This sortie would be risky, but weakening the enemy was worth it, as long as the cost wasn't too high. And making the other bastard react to your actions was central to the Corps' doctrine.

"We can't afford any serious losses, Captain, which is the reason I'm sending you. I know you will make sure you preserve your command." The other two company commanders, Jimenez and Bradford, were a little too enthusiastic; Fromm had seen that during the previous week's engagements. This mission required a good sense for when it was time to run away; stay in place too long and the Vipers would overrun and destroy his unit.

"Don't get caught in a pitched battle. Sting 'em and break contact, rinse and repeat. If they chase you all the way into the valley's central ridge, where we can give them a good pounding, all well and good. If not, we'll at least give them a bloody nose. All the fabbers in New Burbank are working three shifts, so we've got plenty of ammo. Burn as much of it as you want, but spare the men."

"Understood, sir."

More troops were mobilizing at New Burbank. A city of two million, where all of its adults had undergone at least four years of military service, could easily put together several divisions' worth of troops, but easily did not mean rapidly. Not to mention those improvised divisions would be lightly equipped and shaky as hell, far worse than the regulars or even the militia. When those units faced Viper assault troops, it wouldn't be pretty.

They needed to buy time, and disorganizing and damaging the enemy forces on the ground would make things harder for the ETs when their reinforcements arrived. It was a gamble, and a reinforced company was just strong enough to do some damage, and small enough that its loss wouldn't cripple the defense effort.

All he had to do was accomplish the mission with acceptable losses. Acceptable, that is, to everyone except the human beings that would be left bleeding and broken on the field.

Trade Nexus Eleven, 165 AFC

"Got dispatches about the war," Guillermo Hamilton said as he walked into the station house.

The local nest of spies – spies preferred the term 'intelligence officers' but Heather preferred the plain unvarnished truth, at least inside her head – looked like any mundane office would, both befitting their cover as traders and because most of what they did was in effect office work: their time was spent reading, analyzing and collating information. She gratefully accepted the imp-to-imp download and settled down to catch up on the big picture. Guillermo didn't look happy, so the news was probably all bad. He'd finally begun to act like his old confident self, after weeks of being a nervous wreck following the sanctioning of the *GACS-1138* and its crew. Expecting the other shoe to drop, she supposed.

She herself hadn't lost any sleep over it. She'd helped prosecute and kill an enemy Sierra, just as a tactical officer on a warship would have. Those crewmen had been enemies and they'd been disposed of accordingly. The methods had been more underhanded than in a naval battle, but dead was dead.

And if things continued the way they were, dead was what she, Guillermo, everyone in the US and very likely every human in the galaxy would soon be.

The news was indeed bad. Terribad, even; her mother had been fond of using that made-up word and it fit the situation to a t. Fighting a three-front war was never easy, and developments on all three theaters made it clear just how desperate things were becoming.

On the Galactic Imperium front, things were still relatively quiet. The Imperials didn't have direct access to human space, and were currently negotiating passage with the polities in between, using a combination of bribes and threats. Their methods were working. According to the dispatch, the Crabs had geeked and granted full access to their former enemies. The Imperials would be in a position to threaten half a dozen American systems sometime in the next two or three months. Fourth Fleet, the force tasked to defend that region of the galaxy, was fairly strong, but it probably wouldn't be strong enough. The war might be lost right then and there.

The Lampreys had gotten beaten like a drum twice in a row, first at Paulus and then Melendez, but the US allies who were in the best position to exploit those defeats were dragging their feet. The Wyrms had delayed their expected – and promised – offensive and there were hints that they might be considering making a separate peace. Which would be awkward for everyone concerned, most particularly the Allied Task Force, a collection of US, GACS and Puppy volunteer ships currently operating in Wyrm space. If the Wyrms stabbed the US in the back, the war was as good as lost.

And finally, the Vipers' push into human space had netted them Heinlein System and they were well on their way to overruning Parthenon. After which the war would be… well, one got the picture. Three point-failure sources, all with damn good chances of failure. No self-respecting gambler would play those odds.

The battle for Parthenon had a personal element for her as well. Peter Fromm was stationed there. He could be dead already.

And there is nothing to do about that, she chided herself. *So concentrate on the things you can affect.*

She had plenty of things to do. Honest Septima kept sending a steady stream of information from the Imperium, some of which had a great deal of potential, provided the Powers-that-Be chose to do something about it. The combined power of the Tripartite Galactic Alliance was very alarming to other Starfarer polities, who rightfully worried about becoming the next target in line once humans were dealt with. Many of them, including the Vehelians, were having second thoughts about their neutrality.

A victory at Parthenon might just show the rest of the galaxy that the US wasn't doomed, and that might be enough to gain humanity some new allies. Or even some old ones; the Puppies were getting close to going all-in instead of merely providing funds and materiel, along with a trickle of 'volunteers.' But it was going to take something decisive, in a fight where survival would be close enough to a miracle to call it one.

Hope. Willful self-deception.

It was at moments like this when she wished she could believe in something that might listen to her prayers.

Parthenon-Three, 165 AFC

"They've been busy," Russell commented as he took in the sights.

About a mile from his prone position on top of a ridge, the Viper landing zone sprawled between three large hills, tall enough to make the position a tough artillery target. Multiple area force fields, set up in successive layers, made it even tougher. The Viper remfies that had been left behind on the LZ while the alien grunts got their heads handed to them hadn't been sitting on their alligator-like asses; they'd set up a damn good defensive perimeter, not only shields but also fast-firing lasers capable of destroying hundreds of supersonic artillery shells.

Part of Charlie's company's mission had been to find some good arty targets. From the looks of it, the cannon-cockers might as well save themselves the trouble and the ammunition. At least until Charlie lured some ETs out of their safe zone. That was part of their mission, too.

Russell crawled back down the slope. He'd used his helmet passive sensors and a laser-transmitter to send his observations over to the rest of the squad, which in turn would send it to the company CO. They were being cagey; the Vipers could detect normal gravity-wave communications like nobody's business, and they'd gotten some artillery of their own, mostly tubby 89mm mortars firing from a 20-shot rotary launcher that would plaster any comm emissions within seconds of spotting them. Their bombs packed about as much punch as the Marines' hundred-mike-mikes, or maybe a little more, not that anybody in the task force wanted to find out exactly how big a boom they made.

"All right, the dance is about to start," Staff Sergeant Dragunov announced on the squad's channel. "Keep your heads down until I give the word. You know the drill."

That they did. Hit 'em hard and fast, and then skedaddle back into their waiting LAV for a quick drive to their next rally point. They couldn't afford to get into a serious fight with the ETs, who could steamroll the company in a matter of minutes if they cornered it somewhere. There was a fine line between conducting an effective ambush and making a glorious last stand, and Charlie Company was going to be tap-dancing all over it.

They had no drones doing recon for them – too easy for the Vipers to spot, which would spoil the surprise – so Russell didn't get to see the tank platoon they'd brought along poke their turrets over a couple of hills about three klicks away and give the alien LZ three rounds of rapid fire with their main guns. The sound of twelve blasts from the Normies' 250mm graviton guns echoed through the entire canyon like the drums of an angry god. He didn't need visuals to imagine what it would be like on the other end of those shots. Even multiple energy shields couldn't stop a dozen aimed blasts; at least two or three would get through and hit something or someone. The duller roar of a power plant explosion followed up the volley, and smoke billowed out towards the sky, visible even from the reverse slope where First Squad of Third Platoon waited for its turn to join in the fun.

"That's gotta hurt," he said.

"I bet," Nacle agreed. Gonzo wasn't around to come up with something funny in response; the little guy was still in the rear getting patched up, the lucky S.O.B. Nacle had turned out to have a good handle on the ALS-43, but Russell still missed his buddy. Hopefully his fire team would be made whole after they came back from this field trip.

"Here they come," Dragunov said. "Get ready."

The Vipers were reacting to the attack, although not as quickly as Marines would. The crackle of heavy lasers and their own grav cannon broke out in the aftermath of the big explosion. The return fire might have even been fast enough to hit some of the tanks, but Russell doubted it, not that he would find out one way or another until they played the tapes during the after-action report. The aliens' infantry couldn't hope to catch the Stormin' Normies, so they'd have to send their vehicles after them while their mortars pounded the tanks' former positions, where they'd hit nothing but rocks. The tank platoon had taken off at flank speed as soon as they'd delivered their graviton greeting to the ETs, and were racing towards their next firing position.

And before the Vipers could catch up with the Normies, they'd be getting a new surprise.

"They're in the kill box," the squad commander said. "Move it!"

First and Third Platoons scrambled up the slope towards their firing positions on top of a ridge overlooking the path the enemy Turtles were taking in pursuit of the MBT-5s that had blasted their encampment. Russell got his first good look at the Viper combat vehicles through the aiming point of his helmet sensors: they sort of looked like an egg lying on its side with a straw poking out of its front, narrower end. Not much to look at, other than the fact that their shields were about as good as their own LAVs, and their 120mm railgun fired a steady stream of hypervelocity sabot-discarding darts that could peck through a mountain if given enough time, and would do the job just fine on any tank or infantry fighting vehicle that stuck out in the open for too long.

The enemy was sending a dozen of the floating eggs forward. They stuck close to the ground because to rise too high risked being acquired by the heavy guns of the closest planetary defense base and earning a shot from an anti-starship weapon as a door prize. They were moving as fast as Normies or LAVs, maybe a little faster, something to keep in mind when it was their turn to run from the damn things.

At the moment, they weren't looking to run from them, though.

Russell's targeting carat came to rest on the lead vehicle; he waited patiently while the rest of the designated hitters had zeroed in on the same target. As soon as the aiming symbol turned green, he opened up, sending a 20mm micro-missile towards the alien death-machine. His shot hit home, along with three LML-10 armor-piercing rockets and a long burst from Nacle's ALS-43. The multiple, near-simultaneous impacts breached the Turtle's shield, and one of the missiles pierced the tough but thin shell of the flying egg, cracking it and scrambling the living crap out of anybody inside. The tankette's crew consisted of a driver and a gunner, and both of them were probably evenly spread around the interior of their vehicle as its fast hover turned into an ungainly roll on the ground, bouncing off it several times before hitting a boulder and coming to a full stop. Greasy smoke poured out of a hole on its side. No big ka-boom ensued; the aliens built 'em tough.

"Not tough enough, though," Russell muttered as he ducked for cover; he knew what would happen enxt.

The two platoons' combined fire had accounted for three enemy vehicles; a fourth one looked a little bit wobbly. Before the aliens could react, Charlie Company's three 100mm mortars dropped thirty thermobaric bomblets over the enemy formation. Each shell sprayed a cloud of atomized fuel two hundred yards wide and ignited it.

Light and overpressure washed over Russell despite being behind cover and nearly a klick away. He ignored the sensations; he didn't need Dragunov's yelling "Move, move, move!" to know it was time to go. The fuel-air explosions were unlikely to kill the enemy vehicles; force fields and sealed armor were the most effective counters against thermobaric detonations. But they made for a hell of a distraction.

Even so, the enemy vehicles lashed the ridge with their railguns and coaxial lasers. Rock and dirt came apart as multiple shots shaved a good foot off the top of the hill. Even with portable force fields, the Marines wouldn't have made it through that storm of fire unscathed. Which was why they weren't there anymore.

Russell slid down the hill, letting gravity do most of the work as he and First Squad moved towards their getaway vehicle. Even though his ears were ringing a little from the massive explosions, he could hear the lesser blasts of grav guns and missiles from Second Platoon's LAVs as they took the Vipers tank company under fire from yet another ambush position, five hundred meters further back. Just as the hatch of the infantry carrier swung shut with all of First Squad inside, without any casualties for a change, Russell heard yet another boom. At least one more Viper mini-tank had bought it.

And this was just the beginning of the party they'd planned for the aliens.

* * *

"Target!" Staff Sergeant Konrad Zimmer shouted as he highlighted a Viper tank emerging from behind a hill.

"On the way!" PFC Mira Rodriguez yelled back. A graviton bolt speared the ET vehicle sometime between the second and third word of the standard response. Nothing with less than starship-grade shields and armor could take a direct hit from the Norman's main gun. The Viper's light tank fluoresced brightly for a brief instant before shattering like a dropped glass vase.

"Hit!" she said, and started humming the chorus from 'Valhalla Is Burning' by Gotterdammerung.

A couple seconds later: "Hit!" A force field generator this time. It was frantically darting for cover, but Mira caught it with time to spare, the shot going through two layers of shielding before blowing a hole through its thin outer armor. The bulbous vehicle's floating motion ended abruptly as it dropped like a rock, although it didn't blow up.

"Give him another," Zimmer ordered. The gennie might still be salvageable; no sense giving the tangos a chance to fix it later.

"On the way." No force fields attenuated the second shot, and the generator's power plant let go, the strange matter inside it reacting with the environment to produce a detonation that shook their two-hundred-ton tank from a mile away.

"I felt that," PFC Jessie Graves commented from the driver's compartment.

"We'll reap your souls!" Mira sang. "We'll drink your BLOOD!"

"Back up!" Zimmer told Jessie as the tank's threat designator sent an alarm. "Hull-down!"

"Hull-down, aye."

The tank darted behind a ridge, exposing only its turret. Jessie finished the move as quickly as he could, but a Viper self-propelled gun tagged them a couple of times, its 25mm laser beam making their frontal force field spark in a furious multitude of colors.

"Target!" Zimmer called out, marking the energy cannon.

"Hit!" Scratch one self-prop gun.

The platoon broke contact behind a hill while Charlie Company plastered the Vipers' vanguard with more mortar-delivered thermobaric goodness, just like Mama used to make. That was good, because *Fimbul Winter*'s gunnery pack was just about empty and the brief lull in combat would allow its internal stores to cycle a new 50-shot pack into the base of the gun. Their second and last 50-shot pack, as a matter of fact. After you fired all hundred 250mm death-rays in your twin power packs, you needed to head back home and replace them, or wait three hours for the tank's gluon power plant to recharge one of them. Either way, you'd been busy enough to deserve a break.

Damn, this is beginning to feel like work.

They'd been playing tag with the Vipers for a good four hours, poking them, making them chase the tanks into ambushes set up by the Marine crunchies, and when the aliens were taken care of, going out and doing it all over again. The canyon separating the alien landing zone from Forge Valley was filled with corpses and busted vehicles. Mostly alien, although a fire team from Charlie Company had zigged when they were supposed to zag and eaten a laser volley that hadn't left enough of the four poor bastards to bury. Other than that, though, the Marines had things go mostly their way, and a Turtle company and half a battalion of infantry had gone to whatever second-rate Valhalla they deserved. *Fimbul Winter* and her crew had accounted for a good many of the dead.

But the Echo Tangos were getting smarter. A second mini-tank company with a regiment of infantry and self-propelled guns in support was on the job now, and their mobile artillery was making ambushes a lot riskier. Those guns were meant to engage fortifications, but they made fairly effective tank destroyers. *Butcher and Bolt*, the platoon's lead tank, had taken a direct hit when a heavy laser got through her shields, and there was a still-glowing crater the size of a dinner plate on its front armor. Its normal 500mm thickness was down to maybe three or four inches on that spot. The next Viper gunner who took a shot at the Normie would make that crater its aiming point. The *B & B* needed to RTB and get that hole patched, pronto, or her crew would end up on the express train to Valhalla.

With more enemy troops pouring into the hills, the chances that one of their units would end up getting cut off and surrounded were going up fast. Assuming the task force's commander's head wasn't up his ass, he should see that soon.

"We're breaking contact and returning to base," Lieutenant Eddie Morrell said through their imps. "The Viper fleet is coming back. A second wave of landings is likely."

"Roger that."

"Reap their souls," Mira sang softly, but her heart clearly wasn't in it anymore.

They'd all known more ETs were due to arrive; the force they'd been harassing was clearly set up to receive reinforcements. Chances were they would drop enough troops to stop screwing around and finish the job. The casualties the Marines had inflicted had done very little to change the odds.

"We'll just have to kill more," Zimmer said, trying to sound confident and just barely pulling it off.

Fourteen

Parthenon-Three, 165 AFC

"The replacements are here, sir," First Sergeant Goldberg said. "We got four guys from Logistics and one from the engineers, all of them former '03s who switched MOS their second time around. "I've worked out where to put 'em, pending your approval."

Fromm went over the files. The new troops had been moved from non-combat positions in the 101st support units to take the place of the company's dead and maimed. A moment's bad luck had cost him five men, an entire fire team, and he wouldn't have the time to write emails to their families until after the battle for Parthenon-Three was over, not that any mail was moving off-planet at the moment. Between these losses and the casualties suffered during the fight for the southern pass, he was down a squad's worth of troops and getting enough replacements to fill less than half those empty slots.

"It all looks good to me," he said, knowing it wasn't good. Newcomers wouldn't be welcomed with open arms by soldiers who had lost their buddies. Goldberg had shuffled people around to reform the destroyed fire team and used the replacements to fill in the vacancies he'd created in the process. Each newbie would be paired up with two to four regulars, which would hopefully minimize the inevitable disruption and loss of effectiveness. They'd be seeing combat soon, and combat had a way of increasing unit cohesion – assuming all its members survived, of course.

Under ordinary circumstances, he would have preferred to wait on replacing his losses until current operations were over, but given how desperate the situation was, those extra warm bodies might make the difference between losing more men, or preserving his command. They were spread very thin as it was, and the main event had yet to begin.

The Viper fleet had received reinforcements, including ten more planetary assault ships, and was advancing on Parthenon-Three at a leisurely sub-light pace, daring the Navy to come back and try to stop them. Sixth Fleet wasn't taking the bait; it hadn't been reinforced yet, and the outcome of a second round of fighting would risk its total destruction. Which meant the enemy would soon launch a massive ground attack, possibly with orbital support. ETA for the invaders was less than two hours. Fromm had been lucky the news had arrived in time for his company to break off from the running fight and head back to their FOB. Being caught on his own when the second wave landed would have been unfortunate.

"Anything else, Sergeant?"

"Lieutenant O'Malley, sir."

"I know." Third Platoon's commander continued to be the weakest link in the company. He'd gone from leaning on his platoon sergeant to basically dumping the running of the unit on Gunny Wendell's shoulders. Since most of the weapons platoon had been spread out to support the infantry elements of Charlie Company, O'Malley's lack of initiative hadn't been obvious at first, but his handling of the mortars section had made it clear that his promises to mend his ways had been a big load of Bravo Sierra. The supporting fire had been sluggish; Gunny Wendell had been out with the rest of the units, leaving O'Malley in charge, and the lieutenant seemed to be unable to stop dithering at the worst possible times.

Goldberg waited quietly, letting him make up his mind.

"All right," Fromm finally said. "I'm having O'Malley reassigned to act as our liaison with the militia. Lieutenant Hansen will take over Third Platoon." Which would leave him without an XO, but he would do better without a second in command than Third Platoon under an officer that couldn't act in a decisive manner. After this was over, he would make sure O'Malley's days in the Corps were numbered. But for now, he probably wouldn't do a lot of harm lording over the militia regiment providing support for his Marines.

Probably.

* * *

"It would have been a whole three minutes out of our way," Russell groused.

"It's a hard life, Edison," Staff Sergeant Dragunov said. "It must suck to find out the squad's LAV isn't your personal vehicle. My heart bleeds for you. Did you actually think we were going to take a detour so you could check on your girlfriend? I oughta give you an NJP just for asking!"

"You are right, Staff Sergeant. No excuse, Staff Sergeant."

"Damn right. I never expected this kind of bullshit from you, Edison. Now get busy or I'll make you busy. Get out of my sight."

Russell had known it'd been an idiotic thing to ask pretty much from the moment the words had come out of his mouth. They'd been moving to their new positions when it'd occurred to him they would be passing mighty close to the witch's house. So he'd asked to make a pit stop there, with utterly foreseeable results. The rest of the squad would never let him live it down. Russell Edison, the guy who never shouted a girl's name while fucking, because chances were he'd utter the wrong name, had gone and fallen for some woman. About the only thing that was normal about the whole situation was that he didn't know the woman's name.

She put some voodoo hex on me, he thought sourly while he headed to his tent. Warp navigators were crazy, everyone knew that. But this chick was in a class of her own. Unless the other warp-navs simply were better at hiding their true natures; she'd claimed that was the case. He wasn't sure either way, but he knew he'd never invite one of those spooky bastards to a card game.

The woman still haunted his dreams, three nights later. He'd looked for her, tried a bunch of different ways to get her name, and nothing had worked. The bartender who steered Russell her way was gone, evacuated to New Burbank, and he wasn't taking any calls. There'd been no liberty since the landings began, so he couldn't go visit her. Besides, she'd probably had been evacuated with the non-combatants. The disturbing little house where he'd met her would be empty now.

All he had to do now was stop thinking about her.

"I'm sure she's all right," Nacle said. The kid was trying to reassure him, confirming Russell's fear that he had finally hit rock bottom.

"Yeah, sure she will," Private First Class Bozeman added in the tone of voice of someone who didn't give a shit. Gonzo's replacement had been in the infantry a long time ago, and he'd never worked in a weapons platoon before. "Uh, Lance," he went on. "Do I really have to carry all this crap? This load is like twice what I used to tote back in the day."

He was bitching about the extra ammo and power packs he would be lugging as soon as they unassed their LAV. The third member of a Guns section fire team got to play cargo mule; that had been Nacle's job before Gonzo got WIA, and he'd done it without whining about it. Russell couldn't wait until his buddy was back in action and they could send this FNG somewhere else. Unfortunately the injuries he'd sustained had been too nasty to send him back to the grind, not quite yet.

"Call me Russet, Bozo."

Bozeman clearly didn't care for his new nickname, but even on short acquaintance he'd learned that messing with his team leader wasn't a good idea.

"That's your job, lugging extra mags and pows" Russell went on. "So load them up, don't drop them, and help keep the Alsie fed. Your armor will do most of the lifting for you, as long as we got power packs to keep them running. Which we will 'cause you'll be carrying them. Understood?"

"Understood."

"And listen to Nacle; he knows what he's doing."

The new guy had a couple more years in the service than Nacle, but after a short stint as an 0311 he'd switched to Logistics, which made him a POG at heart. He'd be fine carrying stuff around, but Russell wasn't sure how well he'd do when shit got real. He had a bad feeling that Bozo's real MOS was 1369.

Bozo shrugged but stopped bitching, which was good enough for now. They were setting up on yet another hill; this one overlooked a big patch of forest that the aliens were going to have a hell of time traversing. For a plateau, this valley sure had a lot of hills, Russell though while he made sure their position had a good field of fire and wasn't exposed. In all fairness, though, most of the valley's terrain was flat; they just avoided fighting in those spots because flat terrain was just another name for a kill zone unless you improved it via entrenching tools, digging strips and lots of sweat.

When he was satisfied, Russell glanced up just in time to see it was rainingt aliens again: thousands of contrails filled the sky. Maybe half of them got shot down before they reached the ground, but there'd been a lot of pods in that wave, and some had been big. Shuttles or dropships, able to carry heavy vehicles and plenty of spares. He glanced around, where Second and Third platoons waited for Echo Tango to show up again. They were deploying a lot deeper into the valley, pretty close to Davistown, because even with more Army pukes moving forward, trying to hold the western portion against a multi-divisional force was a little too suicidal even for Devil Dogs. The new plan was to try to sucker the leading Viper units into a series of ambushes leading up to Davistown, which was being turned into a stronghold by the 101st engineer platoon, with lots of local help.

Russell wouldn't have minded fighting inside nicely-prepared positions with lots of boresighted heavy guns in support, but the battalion landing team would continue to 'conduct mobile defense operations,' playing tag with the tangos in other words, which was fun until they caught you. The Army and Guard would get to fight in town. Which was fair enough; their vehicles were a lot slower, so they couldn't run rings around the aliens.

Of course, if the shit hit the fan and the dogfaces got it stuck in, it'd be the Marines' job to extricate them. That was how life in the Suck went. You learned to love it, or at least live with it.

* * *

After the skirmish at Lover's Leap, playing traffic cop for a while suited Morris Jensen just fine. He told Lemon that being bored beat being shot at by a country mile just minutes before their routine job turned into a matter of life and death.

"Yeah," Lemon agreed. "That fight was a bit much." The two old-timers were probably the only members of the squad who knew how lucky they'd been, getting into a close-range firefight with high-tech aliens without losing anybody.

At the moment, he and the rest of the squad were keeping the steady stream of trucks delivering war supplies to Davistown flowing in an orderly fashion. It normally wouldn't be all that difficult, since there was only one highway connecting the town with New Burbank, but the supply units were making use of every country lane, dirt road and game trail wide enough to accommodate their cargo vehicles, and when those secondary roads converged, you started getting traffic jams. And traffic jams required someone to unsnarl them.

"Yeah, too much like old times," Morris said, picking up the conversation where they'd left off after he waved through a mini-convoy of U-hauls that somebody had drafted into service. Transport, whether it was wheeled, GEV or grav-engine, was in short supply. The Army and National Guard were pushing in a division's worth of troops into the valley, with two more digging in at Miller's Crossing. That many troops required a lot of supplies, and it had to be delivered by ground. All air travel had been suspended, courtesy of Viper energy cannon placed on some of the mountains bordering Forge Valley. Anything that poked its head too high up was inviting a laser or graviton blast.

"No casualties, though."

"We got lucky."

The Viper infiltrators at Lover's Leap had been caught at the worst possible time, and someone on higher had been on the ball and hammered the ridge with artillery while the militia kept the aliens fixed in place. A squad of Marine snipers had joined the fray shortly afterwards, setting up and firing their 10mm lasers from three klicks away, and their accurate and lethal shots had killed more tangos in five minutes than Morris' squad had managed in half an hour. By the time the aliens had withdrawn, they'd left some fifty bodies behind, and none of the Volunteers had gotten so much as a scratch, except for Sebastian Wilkes; the dumbass had faceplanted while trying to switch positions and ended up with a concussion despite having his helmet screwed on tight. If those aliens had managed to get organized, they would have eaten his squad for breakfast.

"Hope it's the last time."

"Me too," Morris said, but he wasn't counting on it. He glanced up; the last big landing swarm had arrived a few hours ago, but you occasionally saw a fresh bunch of pods coming down. Earlier that morning, he'd seen an actual enemy starship, and that had scared the ever-living crap out him. It hadn't been very big, maybe a frigate or destroyer, but damn if it didn't look huge up in the sky. It'd opened up on the PDB at point-blank range, and broken off, trailing flames and smoke after return fire tore it a new one. The spectacle before the alien boat vanished back into the stratosphere had been awe-inspiring. It'd hammered in the fact that an entire enemy fleet was orbiting Parthenon-Three. The only reason those ships hadn't turned the whole planet into a close approximation of Hell was that it was against the laws of the Galactic Elders, which Starfarers treated as if coming from the Almighty Himself.

Even that wouldn't save them if Sixth Fleet didn't come back and booted the aliens from the system.

"What's this happy horseshit?" Lemon growled, snapping Morris out of his funk.

A second bunch of U-hauls were stopped on Rural Route 3 while several school buses filled with refugees from the outlying areas went northeast on the Post Road, headed to I-10 and New Burbank. It was slow going; the buses were old, in poor repair, and overloaded, so they were rolling on at a bit over twenty miles an hour. But what had prompted Lemon's comment was a ground-effect fifteen-ton truck, painted Guard olive-green; the lone military vehicle had gone off-road and was speeding along RR-3, hovering over the recently-harvested fields in a way ordinary wheeled transport could never hope to do without getting stuck. That was well enough, but whoever was in the driver's seat would still have to wait until the buses had gone past the intersection.

The hover-truck came to a reluctant stop when Morris planted himself in its way with an upraised hand. The driver raised him on his imp a moment later.

"This is priority cargo, Staff Sergeant."

"Just need to wait a minute, son. Soon as the buses make it through, you can go right ahead."

"No need, Sergeant. I got this."

It took Morris a second to figure out what the Guard driver meant, and by then it was too late. His shouted warning was lost in the roar of the truck's fan nacelles as the Guardsman gunned his engines for all they were worth, raising his vehicle fifteen feet off the ground and allowing him to go over the obstructing slow-moving buses.

In most other places, that would have just been a bad idea. The asshole kid managed to veer to Morris and Lemon's left, sparing them from the torrent of pressurized air that would have crushed them to the ground, but he was still risking damage to the buses and their passengers. The driver was counting on crossing the road quickly enough to avoid it, but that was how accidents happened.

The other, more important problem, was that this particular crossroads was on a slight rise, only barely masked from enemy fire by a nearby hill. The fifteen-foot climb put the truck clear over the top of the terrain obstacles that kept the road in defilade and relatively safe from direct fire.

Even so, what happened next took a lot of bad luck. Bad luck that a Viper gunner scanning the area through the sights of a hi-power laser cannon spotted the sudden motion from six or seven miles away. Worse luck that the ET made a snapshot during the two-second window before the truck dipped down out of sight. Morris' father had been fond of saying 'Bad luck is the universe's way to let you know your limitations.' The Guard kid never got to find out just how unlucky he'd been. He had just cleared the Post Road, managing not to do more than scratch the paintwork on one of the buses, and begun to descend when his truck got hit.

Morris was still shouting after him when a blinding flash of pure white washed over him.

He found himself lying on his back with no idea how he'd gotten there. His ears were ringing but he thought he could hear the roaring-crackling sound of a big fire. There was a salty-metallic taste in his mouth. Everything hurt. The smell of burning things got through his helmet's filters: diesel fuel and electrical fires and something else, something that he feared was the stench of seared human flesh.

When he opened his eyes, he saw thick columns of greasy black smoke drifting in the wind. He ran a quick diagnostics check before moving; his headset was still working properly, and he'd kept up on his imp's MedAlert software. A few seconds later, he got the results: two cracked rib that were going to hurt like a mother as soon as he tried to get up, a sprained ankle, and a bad case of whiplash. His nano-meds were already flooding his bloodstream with painkillers; he'd be able to move and even fight, but he was going to really feel it in the morning.

Someone was screaming not too far away. Time to get off his ass and help.

Struggling to his feet hurt as much as he'd expected, painkillers or not. Seeing the true extent of the disaster was worse than any pain.

The Guard driver had been telling the truth. His fifteen-tonner had been carrying something important. Artillery shells, maybe. Most explosive ordnance was designed not to go off until you wanted it to go off, but a hi-power laser could make all kinds of stuff go boom. The ensuing explosion had occurred a little under five meters above the road. One of the buses had been between Morris and the detonation, which had spared him from the worst of it.

Three passenger vehicles were off the road, one lying on its side where either the explosion or a sudden swerve had knocked it down; the other's nose was crumpled around a tree its driver had rammed when he panicked. The bus that had saved Morris' life had flipped over and was on fire.

The handful of Volunteers that had been directing traffic were all down, but nobody was seriously hurt, at least according to their status carats. Morris ignored them while he limped towards the burning bus. The wounded and dying civilians inside needed his help.

Trying to run on a sprained ankle just didn't work. Climbing over the roof of the overturned vehicle, now effectively a vertical wall but the only way to get to the passengers, was no picnic either. By the time he made it, he was panting under the weight of his battle-rattle.

Flames were erupting from shattered windows. He felt the heat even under this gloves, and the smoke was overpowering his air filters. He peered through an unbroken window, and thought he saw movement there, although it could just as easily have been more flames. It was hard to see; thermal sights were useless.

"Gator, get the fuck outta there! It's gonna blow!" Lemon shouted at him through his imp at max volume, the only reason Morris could hear the words over the crackling fire. He kept looking around, desperately trying to find someone, anybody to save. There'd been children in that bus, children and oldsters too poor to afford rejuv treatments or who'd turned them down for religious reasons. Noncombatants. The people he was supposed to protect.

"Gator!"

He crawled over the burning bus, ignoring the way the skin under his knees began to blister. Was someone trying to climb out? By the time he got to that window, only flames waited for him. He thought he heard pounding coming from below, but he wasn't sure.

Somebody grabbed Morris from behind and bodily flung him off the bus. The impact made his cracked ribs flare up in pure agony and he blacked out for a bit. He dimly felt himself being dragged on the ground while someone cursed up a storm. Lemon.

The explosion when the bus's gasoline tank ignited was muted in comparison to the cargo truck's immolation, but he heard it clearly. He tried to get up despite the pain, but Lemon held him down, obscuring the view from the road. They both knew that if he saw the burning bus he would rush back towards it.

"Let it be, man," Lemon said. "It's over. Let it be."

"Fuck you," Morris growled. In his mind, he saw Mariah in that bus. He knew she was already safe in New Burbank, but those children in there had been someone's Mariah.

"Nothing you coulda done, Gator."

The fire continued to crackle and pop. There wasn't screaming or any other human sounds coming from it.

He'd never felt so old.

Sixth Fleet, Parthenon System, 165 AFC

"PDB Twelve is down, ma'am."

The report was five minutes old. At the rate bad news were coming in, Parthenon-Three was probably down to twenty defensive bases instead of twenty-one. The population centers closest to the destroyed PDBs had lost their coverage and had been interdicted and put to the torch. New Caledonia, Lebanon and Balboa: three sleepy colonial towns, mostly involved in farming and light industry, with a population of under a hundred thousand apiece before refugees seeking safety had doubled their numbers. Half a million civilians were now burning to death inside the Viper force domes that had encircled them. A few thousand had managed to escape when the last surviving remnants of the 87th MEU managed to breach one of the domes long enough to allow a lucky few to leave the perimeter, but now both Marines and refugees were being hunted down by the Viper ground forces that had destroyed the local defenses. They weren't likely to survive very long.

Another two hundred thousand civilians had been killed by orbital bombardment or ground attacks. The Vipers didn't dare use their missile swarms or heavy energy salvos on the planet's surface, but even the sporadic fire allowed under Starfarer conventions would occasionally immolate a building or an entire city block. Those murders would pale in significance as soon as more death domes came online and proceeded to commit genocide in an environmentally-conscious manner.

The aliens were playing it smart, not risking their capital ships but instead sending destroyers and frigates to support the planetary assault ships while they deployed more troops. The vat-grown semi-sentient clones didn't take very long to grow, program and send out to fight; the main constraint on the attack force was the number of landing pods it could deploy, which appeared to be more than enough to do the job. The enemy armada had made another resupply run a couple of days ago and come back with full bunkers and magazines. Sixth Fleet hadn't even tried to interfere. Her orders didn't allow her any discretion in that matter and she understood why. Another hundred-thousand-plus missile volley would inflict irreparable damage on her formation. Sooner or later, though, the Vipers would come to her.

Probably after the planet was depopulated.

The thought filled Sondra Givens with rage. Civilians had never been massacred on her watch. That was only supposed to happen over her dead body. The few times when her ship or fleet had arrived too late to prevent such mass killings had been bad enough. To hold a position nearby while human cities burned was a new experience. New, and quickly becoming intolerable.

"Warp emergence anticipated, ma'am," Space Watch Specialist Morelos said. "Fifty-three minutes from now. Contact is a single vessel, tentatively idenfitied as a courier."

Maybe the incoming boat would announce that the long-promised reinforcements were finally on their way. Admiral Givens didn't feel very optimistic, though. The possibility that she would be ordered to withdraw and abandon Parthenon – and dozens of worlds further down its linked warp chains – loomed large in her mind. Those fifty minutes went by slowly, the waiting interrupted only by further bad news. No more PDBs fell, but they were all taking damage and the Vipers were landing more troops, sending them down as quickly as they were force-grown to adulthood. Their losses were gruesome but the aliens saw assault troops as no less fungible and expendable than power packs.

"Emergence detected. Contact identified as courier ship."

The tiny corvette, its class demoted to mail-carrying duties many decades ago, appeared within Sixth Fleet's formation. Its burst transmission uploaded several encrypted missives along with the regular mail, everything from personal messages for crewmembers to the *Nebraska Times'* weekly crossword puzzle and newest YouMake uploads.

"I'm sure it'll be brimming with good news," she said glibly. "Promotions all around, maybe even news that this whole thing was a big misunderstanding and we're at peace with the whole universe."

Her comment elicited a few chuckles in the TFCC. Gallows humor was the only source of amusement left.

She mentally opened the Fleet communiques, dreading what they would contain but making sure she looked detached, even bored as she did. Sobbing uncontrollably and tearing out chunks of her hair would be bad for morale.

The news was bad enough she wished she could do both those things. The President and the JCS had decided to send a freaking Carrier Strike Group her way, brand-new – *experimental* – weapon systems whose existence she was hearing of for the first time. There'd been rumors about some wild-eyed project along those lines for quite some time, but nobody had thought it was anywhere near completion.

Givens read the fighters' technical specs and mentally added a metric ton of salt to the incredible claims. They sounded much too good to be true. She'd use them, of course. Even if the little fighter craft proved to be only a nuisance, the strike group's modified assault ships and their destroyer escorts would add to her point defenses, and she needed every last bit of those. She noted they'd even butchered a battlecruiser to serve as the group flagship. What a waste.

The rest of the reinforcements in the force designated as Task Force 43 were conventional. An obsolete battleship, the last of the *Planet*-class vessels, which was larger than one of her battlecruisers but had less firepower, armor and shields. Eight light cruisers detached from a so-far peaceful sector, not ideal ships for the massive slugfest to come, but at least their crews were experienced and used to working together. About a dozen light ships, newly-commissioned frigates and destroyers, well-armed and fitted, but crewed by a mixture of reassigned veterans and green spacers that hadn't had a lot of time to learn the idiosyncrasies of their vessels. A quick review of their stats showed their performance was barely adequate, and would likely be even worse when energy beams started flying in earnest.

All in all, though, she'd have traded the carriers for the same tonnage of destroyers and frigates, or even assault ships. Boarding actions were forlorn hopes nowadays, but if most of her Marines hadn't been on P-3, she'd have used them against those missile cruisers, just in case the Vipers had tried to save space by reducing the security complements on their ships. Unfortunately, she didn't have enough warp-rated troops for even one boarding party, let alone the dozens needed to make a difference.

The relief force was twenty-four hours away. One more day she'd spend watching a planet die, and hoping there would be something worth saving when she finally took action.

Fifteen

Parthenon-Three, 165 AFC

"Look at them kitties," Bozo said in near-awe.

"I see them. Slick, aren't they?"

Russell was less impressed with the video feed from the drones orbiting the forward edge of the battle area but Bozeman had never seen the Hellcats in action before. The four-legged war machines hadn't been around when the new guy in the fire team had been a grunt. They'd only been deployed a couple years ago, and most units still hadn't gotten them. The 101st's kitty platoons had arrived after the BLT had been reconstituted last year. After training with them for several months, Russell thought they were neat, but all in all he'd rather be a ground pounder.

They sure could run fast, though.

The thirteen surviving 'cats in Fourth Platoon were conducting a fighting retreat, half of them holding the line while the other half moved to the next fallback position and provided cover for the next dash back. The rear guard greeted the pursuing Vipers with a storm of 15mm rounds and mini-missiles. The snake-spiders dived for cover and returned the favor with their lasers and rocket launchers. For a few furious seconds, a lot of terrain got rearranged without any casualties for either side. Russell knew that happy state of affairs wouldn't last for long.

"Any second now," he muttered; you learned to time the enemy's reactions after being on the receiving end enough times. "Kitties better start moving."

They did. The front line abandoned their positions and bugged out just before the Vipers peppered the area with a short barrage of 89mm mortar bombs. The tangos were still short of real artillery but the third landing force had brought plenty of mortars with them, and they were nasty mothers. The little puffs of smoke and flashes of light going off at thirty feet over their targets looked harmless enough from two klicks away, but Russell had recently learned how nasty the rain of shaped-charge plasma penetrators and hypersonic shrapnel really was at close range. If the Hellcats had waited too long, they would have taken losses, heavy force fields and armor notwithstanding.

You had to know when to walk away, and when to run, as the old song went. True in war, love, business and gambling. In life, in other words.

The Eets wasted no time making a forward rush under the cover of their mobile area shields, but the second half of Fourth Platoon was set up and waiting for them. A coordinated volley took out their field genny; and sent a few luckless Vipers to Hell. A moment later, Charlie's own mortars added to the kill count. The surviving aliens went to ground once again. Russell was willing bet they wouldn't be so eager to chase the 'cats next time.

It would have been great if one of the 101st's tanks had been around to help out, but the three Normies still running were some ten klicks away and had problems of their own. There were never enough tanks to go around. The Corps fielded a whole three Marine armored brigades, and Russell had never been deployed with any of them. He had no idea what the brass ever did with them. Maybe parade them around New Parris so they could tell themselves what tough sumbitches they all were. An additional seven or eight hundred tanks were scattered in platoon- and company-sized bits among assorted units, and that was it. Which meant Charlie had no armor support at the moment.

"Fuck. Their armor's rolling in," Bozo said.

The enemy had brought its own tanks to play.

Russell switched his sensor feed to take a wider look and spotted them. Four of the little Turtles, which had turned out to be a joke, and two Dragons, which were anything but.

The gliding metal mountain coming their way weighed in at some three hundred tons, a tetrahedron roughly thirty feet tall. Its bulk and huge profile made it a dream target. Except said dream target had battleship force fields and armor plating. Only a Normie's main gun could hope to put a hole on that monster with a single shot. The Dragon also had a dozen weapon systems distributed among weapon pods on each of its three sides, including a souped-up version of a firefly that could destroy dozens of shells or missiles per burst and three 333mm grav-cannon, each of which would punch right through a Schwarzkopf's glacis plate. Plus a mortar battery's worth of indirect-fire tubes per side. The Vipers had landed six of those monsters with their last wave. One had gotten caught by a full regimental artillery barrage the day before; it was still burning merrily some fifty klicks west, the thick smoke rising from its funeral pyre visible in the distance. That left five unaccounted for. And they'd found one of them.

"Designating priority target," Lieutenant Hansen said over Third Platoon's channel. Third Platoon's new CO sounded cool as a cucumber, which helped a bit. The old El-Tee, O'Malley, would have been pissing his pants and probably arguing with higher about conducting a retrograde maneuver just about now. "We've got to hit that thing with everything we've got. Fire on my command."

Everyone acknowledged. Specific weapon and targeting instructions followed. It looked like three of the four platoons in the company were going to throw everything at the Dragon, up to and including the kitchen sink, bad language and evil thoughts. The good news is that no enemy area field generators seemed to have survived to tag along. The bad news was that the Dragon carried his own area shield projector as well as close-in *and* internal shields. Digging their way into its mechanical guts was going to be a job of work.

The alien super-tank wasn't just prancing around in the open, either. It was gliding at a steady sixty miles an hour, taking a few potshots at the retreating Hellcats while it used dips in elevation and other terrain features to reduce its profile. It didn't have a turret; its guns were spaced evenly among its three sides, each weapon pod covering a field of fire a hundred and twenty degrees wide. One of its secondaries opened up on a Hellcat that had ducked behind a boulder, and a stream of railgun slugs chewed through the granite like a monsoon hitting a spun sugar confection. The 'cat ran for its life, barely outrunning the long burst and finding safety behind a hill.

Russell turned off the drone feed; the Dragon had its own swatters and was knocking out the little robotic cameras by the cartload, so the view was beginning to deteriorate. He focused on his sight picture and assigned target. Five rounds rapid of 20mm armor-piercing might scratch the super-tank's paint job, but the purpose of his shots was to drain a little bit of power from the force fields protecting the beast's armored skin. He waited for the orders to fire.

Artillery came first, a time-on-target barrage. The ADA systems on the super-tank and its Turtle escorts destroyed many of the shells, but plenty others broke through the area force field and struck both the Dragon and its escorts with multiple plasma penetrators. All four lightly-protected tankettes went up in flames; the behemoth's own shields flickered but held.

His aiming carat blinked green and he fired his five-round stonk as fast as he could cycle the launcher's action. His shots were lost amidst a couple hundred guns of assorted varieties. A myriad beam and physical impacts turned the normally near-invisible outline of super-tank's force field into a colorful bubble and wreathed it in flames before it collapsed.

Nacle opened up with his Alsie a moment later as a second set of gunners took advantage of the shield's failure, striking the Dragon's hull just as another time-on-target artillery volley hit, every shell going off at the same time. Self-forging armor-piercers and plasma penetrators smashed into the ambulatory three-sided pyramid. A dozen molten spears hammered its top structure and made it ring so loudly Russell could hear the impacts over the other sounds of battle.

The Viper death-machine continued advancing and returned fire before anybody could asses what damage the Marines had inflicted on it.

A heavy railgun position six klicks back was devoured by a graviton blast that shaved off the top of the hill where it'd been emplaced. The poor Army bastards manning that weapon never knew what hit them. A Hellcat that had lingered too long to empty its missile load took a direct hit from another main gun and simply ceased to exist, swallowed by the twisting beam of compressed space-time. A sheaf of mortars bombs went off over Charlie Co's firing positions; its area force fields held, for the time being at least.

Every LAV available, twelve vehicles total, raised their hulls just enough for their main guns to clear cover and opened up. Russell and everyone with a ready weapon were instructed to fire at the same time.

The brutal exchange that followed was like a high-tech version of a knife fight: the loser might end up in the morgue, but the winner would be lucky to end up in the emergency room. Or maybe it was like a beamer duel at five yards: nobody walked away from one of those.

Something made the ground heave up under Russell's feet. A moment later the rocky hill he'd been firing from settled down a good six or seven inches lower than it'd been a moment before. A grav-cannon hit, Russell figured. The Viper gunner had aimed low and killed a chunk of hill. A slightly higher angle would have ended with him and the whole squad getting spaghettified along the beam's path. The thought was lost amidst the frenzy of shooting and reloading and shooting again. Portions of the Dragon's armor were deforming under the rain of gravitons, plasma, hypervelocity rockets and a dozen other munition or energy types; molten craters formed as sections of its ultra-dense alloy splashed away, revealing cracks in the crystalline matrix of its hull's second layer. The LAVs' graviton guns were beginning to blast their way in, but only by exposing themselves.

The Dragon shifted aim. Only two of its main guns were able to bear, but each of them scored a hit. An assault vehicle's turret disappeared in a flash of light; another LAV was struck by a glancing shot that knocked out its shields and blotted out one of its (luckily empty) missile launchers. The outpour of fire slackened off. Some gunners were ducking for cover and refusing to follow their aiming directives; others had died at their posts. Either way, they weren't shooting anymore.

Fucker wouldn't die. It just wouldn't…

The end was anticlimactic. The Dragon seemed to shudder, and one of its three weapon pods burst open from the inside; a power pack or some explosive ordnance must have gone off, Russell guessed. The super-tank's three-hundred-ton hulk hit the ground like a dropped anvil and stopped fighting or moving. The Americans kept shooting at the lifeless pyramid for several seconds until the barked orders to check fire finally sunk in.

Russell sipped some electrolyte-rich flavored water from the integral straw in his helmet. He wanted to raise his visor but there were were too many fires raging nearby, spewing all kinds of toxic chemicals into the atmosphere. Better let the filters do their jobs.

"Can't believe we killed it," Nacle said. The barrel of his ALS-43 was hot enough to make the air shimmer around it.

"Can't believe it didn't kill us first," Russell said. *All of us, that is*, he corrected himself mentally. There were plenty of black status carats among the three platoons that had engaged the monster and the Army elements that had joined in the fun. And most of the Viper infantry was still in play; they weren't coming out of their hidey-holes, not after their big daddy had bought it, but sooner or later an AI or a vehicle pilot with normal brains would assume command and herd them forward.

The order to fall back and leave this section of the valley came in before the tangos did anything. Which meant the enemy had pushed through somewhere else and was threatening one of their flanks.

The Marines were getting steamrolled. Slowly, and it was costing the aliens plenty, but all that mattered was the fact they no longer could hold their ground against the enemy.

* * *

"Danger close!"

Ducking for cover inside a LAV was a mostly futile gesture;

the best you could do was make sure you were strapped down tightly enough you didn't bounce inside the armored confines of the compartment like dice in a bucket. Fromm still lowered his head when he heard the warning. A moment later, the shockwave from multiple fuel-air explosives reached the speeding vehicles of Charlie Company.

The massive blasts were aimed at the leading edge of the Viper advance, their spread designed to allow the Marine rear guard to break contact as it fled east. Some of the explosions were close enough to knock out one of Charlie's area force fields and stagger Fromm's command vehicle. The drone feed showed that several Hellcats had been bowled over as well. They all managed to land on their feet and keep running, however. That was a relief, because stopping to pick up anybody forced to ditch out of their suit was likely suicide for everyone concerned.

The Vipers had lost most of their heavy armor during their push towards Davistown, but at least two of their Dragons remained, versus a single surviving Marine MBT-5 and a company of antiquated Army Buford tanks that had been rushed forward to help out. Both sides were losing their heavies at a horrendous rate.

About the only good news so far was that the local enemy force's heavy artillery had been mostly destroyed inside their cargo dropships. That stroke of bad luck forced the Vipers to rely mostly on direct-fire weapons and their mortars; the advantage in artillery was probably the only reason the ETs were still bottled up in the valley.

Other places hadn't been so lucky. Eight Planetary Defense Bases were down, along with three entire MEUs – some two thousand Marines were confirmed KIA – plus tens of thousands militia and Army personnel. Civilians losses had passed the million mark. The primary installations still remained, however, including PDB-18. If it was overrun, that would be pretty much it. The Vipers would be able to fly over most of Parthenon-Three's eastern hemisphere, shifting troops at will and overwhelming the other half of the planet. At that point, even if Sixth Fleet came back and expelled the aliens, the system would be nearly useless as a staging base. You needed cities, factories and the people to man them to provide support for a fleet, not a collection of lifeless craters filled with molten slag.

The total wipeout of the 73rd, 81st and 87th MEUs loomed large in Fromm's mind. No battalion-sized Marine unit had ever been exterminated before, even during the darkest days of the First Intergalactic War, when the Corps had conducted planetary assaults with troops largely outfitted with pre-Contact weapons and equipment. This battle would go down in historical annals alongside Frozen Chosin and Guadalcanal. He was beginning to fear it might end up listed alongside Little Bighorn as well.

Battalion outlined new orders for Charlie Company as the last echoes of the massive artillery barrage faded in the distance. Meet with Army mobile elements on the southern edge of Forge Valley; refit and resupply, then threaten the enemy's flank as it advanced towards its final objective. If necessary, the troops could retreat through Miller's Stream, following the river out of the valley. Such a retreat could only be authorized by the battalion commander, and Fromm had a feeling Brighton wouldn't issue any such orders. This was a stand or die – or stand *and* die – situation. A Viper breakthrough at Miller's Crossing would doom PDB-18 and tip the balance beyond recovery. Fromm would be expected to spend every last man and round under his command trying to slow down the attack.

Fromm went over his remaining assets. He had about a dozen Hellcats left, along with just enough LAVs for the seventy or so effectives left in the company: the rest were all casualties, either too badly injured to fight or killed in action. His troops had managed to recover most of the latter's bodies, but too many of them had left their bones somewhere in this damned valley. He shook his head, fighting sorrow and exhaustion. There was no time for either.

The Army units he'd be joining forces with were a logistics platoon with plenty of spare ammo, and a motorized weapons company. Fromm went over their TOE: four assault platoons, each fielding four High Mobility Multi-Purpose Ground-Effect Vehicles, better known as 'Hunters.' Hunters had less than a third the force field strength and one fifth the armor of his LAVs, but their 25mm railguns and HAW missile launchers provided almost as much firepower. Mobility-wise, the hovercraft could keep up with the Marine vehicles over level terrain, but couldn't climb over large obstacles or hover above ten yards off the ground, not that the ability to fly was all that useful in the face of Starfarer weapons that could engage anything peeking over the horizon from ungodly distances.

On paper, the weapons company would more than double Fromm's firepower. A quick check showed the company commander was a retired Marine who'd mustered out as an O-2 and had made captain in the Army some six months ago, so at least there'd be no arguments as to who was in command. There was a smattering of former Marine NCOs in the unit, but other than that the Army formation was a typical mix of mostly non-warp-rated locals doing their obligatory service and a core of long-term servicemen. Given the lack of hostile natives or even dangerous fauna on Parthenon-Three, all the combat experience of those troops would be virtual, except for a few of the former Marines. A very few: four non-coms had actually fought in earnest. None of the officers had. Going up against hardened Starfarer troops in a battle of maneuver would be one hell of a way to pop their cherry.

All in a day's work, Fromm thought as he raised US Army Captain Bradford Kruger, who was about to get his first taste of combat.

* * *

Four little Indians had become three, then two, and finally, after Lieutenant Morrell and *Butcher and Bolt* bought it, just one. *Fimbul Winter* stood alone against the barbarian hordes at the gate. Well, not completely alone, but Staff Sergeant Konrad Zimmer and his crew sure felt pretty damn lonely.

Nobody was singing. They were all too tired and wrung-out for that.

"Gunnery Pack One is up to fifty percent," Mira said, startling Zimmer from his half-dozing state. He blinked stupidly at her for a moment. "We've got twenty-five war shots available, Zim."

"Okay, thanks." That meant the *Winter* could stop hiding from the Vipers and come out to play again. The retreat towards Miller's Crossing was threatening to become a rout. A lot of the Guard units were being a mite too enthusiastic about their change of location, and some of the Army pukes that were supposed to hold the rear weren't holding shit. Not everybody, granted. The tank company that was currently slugging it out with the aliens while their tank recharged its power pack was a case in point. Captain Ryan was one tough bastard, and he was fighting his under-gunned and thin-skinned Bufords for all they were worth. The seventy-ton hover-tanks were only slightly more survivable than a LAV and their 90mm lasers couldn't score one-shot kills on the Turtles or even a field genny, but those nine – down from their original fourteen – tanks, some odds-and-ends and *Fimbul Winter* were the only things standing between two retreating American divisions, or what was left of them, and an alien division or maybe an entire corps.

The Vipers that had wiped out PDB-12 had force-marched the three hundred miles separating them from Forge Valley in an impressive three days and reinforced the third wave of landing pods and dropships, which were making it down with relative impunity now that only two PDBs could engage them on their final descent. It all added up to a really bad day in a really bad week.

Zimmer shook his head. The important thing was, they'd reloaded half a power pack and were ready to fight. Time to observe and orient. The *Winter* was nominally under the command of Captain Ryan, but the Army tank commander had left him alone for the most part. As long as he didn't seem to be malingering, he was free to do what he wanted. And he wanted to get a piece of Echo Tango.

The current battle was being fought along I-10, which this far west was a graded gravel road two lanes wide cutting through a wooded plain except where it sneaked between medium-sized hills. The Army's Alpha Company, 11th Cavalry Regiment was blocking the road, alongside a Marine platoon and a reinforced company of National Guard infantry scrapped together from three different brigades. The combined armor force had tricked a battalion of Viper infantry into yet another ambush, during which the *Fimbul Winter* had shot out its full battle load and had had to retreat to recharge while the Bufords chased the decimated survivors back – and run into one of the two Dragons left in the valley. Three dead tanks and a hasty retreat later, the American forces were waiting for the inevitable alien follow-up attack. It looked like the ETs were rallying around their big tank and a single force field generator. A few drone glimpses indicated the force massing behind some hills to the west was at least as big as the one they'd beaten off, not counting the alien super-tank. And the good guys weren't getting much artillery support; there'd been a breakthrough in the south and all available indirect fire assets were being diverted to contain it.

Ryan's plan was to take out the Dragon before falling back towards Davistown, where the combined US forces were consolidating in a final bid to deny the valley to the invaders. *Fimbul Winter* would play a decisive role in the operation.

"Good," Mira Rodriguez said when he'd relayed their marching orders. "I want to paint one of those fuckers on our kill gallery."

They'd already stenciled eight Turtles and two partial Dragons on the *Winter*'s hull, but they hadn't gotten a full kill on one of the super-tanks. Lieutenant Morrel's *B & B* had fired the decisive shots and that's where the full icon drawings had been, until a Viper mobile gun had returned the favor. It'd been the damaged spot; they'd put a patch on it, but a slight discoloration had shown the alien where to shoot, and the patch hadn't been as strong as undamaged armor. The *Winter* had immolated the ET gun crew a moment later, but revenge wouldn't bring the dead back.

"Target is in range," Zimmer said. They were turret-down at the moment, but a few crunchies were keeping an eye on the approaching enemy forces. Their laser-transmitted video showed him the Dragon, flanked by infantry. An area field generator was trailing the massive armored vehicle, but a squad of engineers had prepared for it. "It's a go."

The engineers opened up the festivities with a bang.

Mines were great defensive weapons, but Starfarer tech had made them largely useless via systems that could defeat most pressure, sensor and comm-activated devices. The daisy-chained devices buried under the gravel road relied on pre-Contact hand-mixed explosives, wrapped in camo blankets and carefully buried and concealed. Two sets of fiber-optic cables leading to the explosive experts' positions would be use to detonate the shaped charge. A lot of work had been involved, although the mines didn't have enough power to penetrate the Dragon's force field.

The field genny following the super-tank wasn't as well-protected, however, which made it the target of choice.

Five explosions went off once the floating platform reached the designated point. Only one of the charges was close enough to inflict damage, but that did the job. The genny's compromised power plant transformed it into an even bigger bomb, which devoured a couple of luckless Viper companies in its blast radius.

Army and Marine infantry volley-fired two dozen anti-armor missiles as several LAVs and the *Winter* rose up from behind cover and took the Dragon under fire. Its shield, already partially drained by the massive explosion behind it, failed in a spectacular shower of sparks.

"Hit!" Mira announced as she cycled the gun's capacitor for a follow-up shot. The 250mm grav-cannon could normally fire twelve shots per minute, but if you goosed its controls and didn't mind putting a little stress on the barrel and firing system – increasing the risk of catastrophic failure sometime down the line – you could put a second shot on target in under two seconds. She fired again while the echoes of the first impact on the Dragon's armor were still reverberating over the hills like a nearby thunderstorm.

"Miss! Dude, stop jumping around!"

"Dude, there's a glowing crater where we just were," Jessie said. "I stop dancing, we die."

"Shut up and do your jobs," Zimmer told them; his sense of humor had evaporated not too long after the *Butcher and Bolt* did. They shut up.

The gunner had been too focused to make her shot to notice the Dragon was shooting back, but Zimmer had watched the twisting singularity beam as it missed his tank by less than a foot, close enough to make its shields flare up and lose ten percent of their power. The *Fimbul Winter* went turret-down and shifted positions; Zimmer kept an eye on the fighting while tapping into other units' sensors.

Three Bufords had burned a hole in one of the Dragon's sides by switching on continuous beam and staying still to remain on target, turning the 90mm guns into giant blowtorches. That had been ballsy, and had cost them: two of the tanks had been shredded, one by a main gun blast that'd left behind nothing recognizable as a vehicle, the other by a railgun burst that didn't do much visible damage. The Buford simply stopped moving; a thin column of smoke rose from its turret, which meant one or more of the railgun rounds had gotten through and bounced all over the interior, pureeing everyone inside. The insides of that tank had been turned into what the heartless called a 'hose and bucket job.' Zimmer didn't know which of those ways to go was worse.

"Hit! Got you, motherfucker!" Mira shouted.

"Dragon Slayer! Good going, Valkyrie!"

The shot had penetrated right above the alien tank's main gun pod. The Dragon stopped moving and shooting even as more American soldiers and vehicles engaged its still form.

"Jessie, back us up a bit," Zimmer said. He had a bad feeling about this, for all that they were nearly two klicks away from the target.

"Going hull-down, aye."

"Make that turret-d…"

The Dragon blew up in an apocalyptic, multihued light explosion that indicated a catastrophic gluon plant failure like the one that had consumed the mine-destroyed field genny. The difference between the two power plants was at least an order of magnitude, however. The conflagration killed everyone caught in the open for a good mile in every direction. One LAV had its turret ripped clean off and a Buford was tossed into the air like a child's toy, smashing into a hillside with a sickening sound like a giant beer can being crushed. Metal shrapnel moving faster than a railgun round slashed at everything around the dying super-tank. Viper and human alike were scythed down. A heavy fragment struck the *Fimbul Winter* and made it ring like a giant gong.

"Frontal and side shields are down!" Jessie cried out. They hadn't moved fast enough.

The force fields weren't just down, they were out. Overloaded and drained; the diagnostic system estimated it would take ten minutes to come back online. Jessie maneuvered the tank behind some cover. Until the shields regenerated they were hideously exposed. The dash for safety inadvertently put them in view of an enemy firing position five miles away. The Viper gunners tracked the vehicle and lined up a perfect shot.

A hypervelocity missile quartet caught the *Fimbul Winter* on the side.

The last tank of the 101st MEU shuddered under the impacts; an instant later it dropped to the ground and fell still, thin pillars of smoke rising from the two spots where its hull had been pierced.

A Marine on a nearby hill saw the sight of the unmoving tank and shook his head.

"That's a hose and bucket job," he said. "God have mercy on their souls."

Sixteen

Romulus, Wolf 1061 System, 165 AFC

The shipyards around Romulus were as busy as Lisbeth Zhang had ever seen them.

The planet (formerly known as Wolf 1061c) was Earth's oldest colony, a rocky 'super-Earth' with a marginally-useful atmosphere, a Class Two biosphere whose largest life forms had been shockingly similar to Earth's pre-Cambrian trilobites, and a local gravity slightly below 1.5 G-standard. Its close location to Sol System (a mere twenty-minute warp transition away) had made it the focus of intensive colonization and terraforming efforts early on. The system now held three hundred million people, mostly clustered in Romulus and the system's asteroid belt, making it the second-largest extra-terrestrial population center in the US, as well as its fifty-ninth state. Its economy was based on ship-building, both civilian and military, and as a major trading point, with six warp-lines leading to other American star systems.

At the moment, just about everyone who could operate a fabber, or swing a hammer for that matter, was working on warships, either building them from scratch or refitting them. Lisbeth could see the outlines of the *Zeus*, the largest American dreadnought ever built, an impressive-looking ship that could actually hold her own in a slugfest with enemy vessels in her weight class even without warp shields. It still wasn't ready, however, and would not be accompanying CSG-1 and the rest of Task Force 43 as it headed towards Parthenon System. The ragtag formation had taken longer than expected to assemble and prepare for combat. Some yard remfies had been loath to divert their construction efforts into outfitting existing ships, and they'd dragged their feet until the dreaded GAO Inspector General herself had made an appearance. Shortly thereafter, two admirals and a dozen civilian executives had lost their jobs (two of them had been arrested) and things had moved a lot faster.

They were due to leave in four hours. Fifty more minutes in warp space, and the fighters would endure their baptism by fire.

Lisbeth felt Fernando's presence behind her as he entered the *Nimitz*'s largely-deserted viewing room. She hadn't heard him, but she knew who it was, just as she knew where all sixty-three fighter pilots aboard the carrier were, as well as the ten warp navigators in the crew and a couple of older naval chiefs who'd done the warp-dance enough times for their psyches to become accessible to her and others like her.

She didn't know what to call her kind. Something with the word 'warp' in it, of course. Clearly navigators had undergone a similar transformation a good while ago, but they'd been very good at not advertising their otherness, and the brass hadn't seemed too inclined to pry. She hoped things would work out the same for the… What? Warp Adepts, maybe.

"Better than Warp Demons," Fernando said, replying to her unspoken thought out loud.

"Hey."

"Hey yourself."

"Looks like we'll get there in the proverbial nick of time."

"Hopefully." The reports from the last courier ship hadn't been comforting. Parthenon-Three's PDBs were being taken down one by one; the planet would be rendered defenseless and depopulated in no more than three, maybe four days. She'd heard that Admiral Givens had threatened to launch an attack without the promised reinforcements, and had only relented when the new timetable had been confirmed. They would arrive in Parthenon and go to war within minutes of their emergence. There was no time to lose.

"We should get some rest," Fernando said.

"Too wired to sleep."

She'd also found herself needing less sleep of late, without suffering any adverse side effects. At least, none that affected her performance, and that was all that mattered at the moment.

"No sleep for me," she said. "But this could be the last time we are together."

"In this reality, at least. But yes, let's make it count."

They headed towards their quarters, hand in hand.

Parthenon-Three, 165 AFC

Davistown was burning.

Morris Jensen absently noticed the general store's collapse in a cloud of smoke while he scanned Main Street for targets. The Marines were retreating by echelon, half of them moving while the other half covered them. The Vipers were still too far for Morris to engage; for the time being he and the rest of the platoon were simple spectators. And the show sucked.

Remembrance Park was on top of a shallow hill overlooking Davistown, lined with Earth trees and decorated with stone and metal plaques listing the town's dead sons and daughters, the honored fallen of a dozen conflicts from the past seventy years.

Several of the monuments had been blasted into rubble. The Viper's heavy weapons were hitting their positions with enough energy ordnance to punch through the area shields every other minute or so. An Army fire team had been on the receiving end of a graviton blast. The lone survivor had lost an arm and leg; everyone else had been turned into something that looked like a modern art sculpture made of metal, plastic and flesh.

Above and behind Morris' position, a 70mm mortar team emptied its five-shot clip in rapid succession; the light weapon lacked the authority of the Marines' hundred-mike-mikes but they would kill aliens well enough. Somewhere near the town, a gap in the enemy field coverage had provided a target of opportunity: plasma explosions went off over the heads of a handful of aliens caught in the open. A few ETs went down. Not enough. Never enough.

Morris wanted to hope they could halt the Vipers here, but he couldn't delude himself. Might as well hope for Santa and the Easter Bunny to show up, wielding light sabers and kryptonite. You couldn't feel any hope when you had access to a battle map and could see what the situation was.

The enemy forces were steadily pushing forward, undeterred despite taking over triple the casualties they inflicted. Only the presence of Copperhead Rapids to the south and the sheer walls of Mount Kenner to the north kept the enemy from outflanking a lone platoon of the 101st and a few Army units supporting it. Like all towns on Parthenon-Three, Davistown had been planned with defense in mind, and the aliens had been forced to make head-on attacks against prepared positions to gain their objectives. But you could crack the toughest nut if you didn't mind paying the cost.

Morris switched screens to check the casualty rosters. There were too many yellow, red and black icons there. Hundreds, thousands. Now that there was no room to maneuver, the casualty exchange rate was a lot less one-sided, and the enemy had troops to spare.

Two more Army divisions were digging in at the other end of the valley, blocking the direct path to the Planetary Defense Base. The Marines were buying them time to deploy with their lives; one company was somewhere to the south, conducting hit-and-run attacks on the flanks of the advance, but it hadn't made a difference. The original defense plans had assumed it would take a month for the Vipers to reach the end of the valley. The aliens had made it in a week, thanks to the loss of PDB-12 and the fact they had brought more troops than anyone had thought possible. Aliens didn't have enough warp-rated people to transport entire armies, but that didn't matter if you brought millions of fertilized embryos, accepting the deaths of nine-tenths of them during transport, and fast-grew the survivors in-system.

A quartet of Marine LAVs darted towards the hill, their turrets firing to their rear. Morris spotted the four-legged shapes of half a dozen Hellcats running between the armored personnel carriers. And further back, he saw the looming pyramidal shape of a Viper land battleship. More than enough to crush all resistance if they couldn't take it down quickly.

The combined fury of several Marine and Army artillery batteries engaged the Dragon, unleashing sheaves of shield-piercing missiles in staggered waves. Air-defense lasers caught half of them in mid-flight, but the rest slammed into its force fields and, eventually, armor. The giant vehicle disappeared behind multiple explosions. When the smoke drifted off, its pyramidal shape was missing several large chunks, and the massive fighting vehicle had stopped moving or fighting. Call that a hard kill, and that was the last super-heavy tank the Vipers had brought to the game.

They still had plenty of mobile guns and missile launchers, though. They raked Remembrance hill with dozens of heavy weapons, from hypervelocity missiles to grav guns. The hill began to come apart, some impacts carving out divots of earth and stone wide enough to fit an assault shuttle. The ground shook under Morris' feet as he fired at the lead Viper infantrymen, moving with the abrupt motions of striking reptiles as they entered Main Street. They'd brought an area force field, but each shot that hit the invisible force bubble would weaken it and hopefully allow a heavy gun or missile to do some actual damage. The LAVs and Hellcats were adding their fire as well.

Not a single building stood in the town's Green. The churches and City Hall were smoking craters or flaming husks. No humans remained there.

The Vipers kept coming.

"I think it's time to bug out, Gator," Nikolic said.

"They'll tell us when it's time to go," Morris said while he sent five plasma grenades downrange. Half a dozen Vipers who'd gotten ahead of their shields went down; only four got up again and scurried for cover. Counter-fire made the miliatmen duck into their fighting holes and keep their heads down for a bit.

"What's the point in running when all you'll get is a field court martial and a bullet in the head? Or end up in the city and get burned to a crisp?"

"I suppose no point at all," Lemon admitted. "Unless we head out into the wild. Hunker down somewhere, wait out the war."

"If the Vipers win, they'll hunt us down. If we win, the Army'll find out we deserted and it's back to the whole court martial thing. You were a Marine, Lemon. What the fuck's wrong with you?"

"Dunno." Nikolic was quiet for a second. Enemy shots were going overhead, but neither man paid attention to them. "I was never yellow, back then. They didn't call me Lemon 'cause I was yellow."

"I know," Morris said, hoping Nikolic would shut up. Hell of a conversation to have with the enemy less than a klick away and rolling closer by the second.

"I'm just tired, Gator. Never been this tired before."

"I know. Just keep it together, all right?"

"Yeah."

Lemon started shooting again, pausing only to switch mags. Morris erased the private channel conversation. That kind of record was never really erased, not unless you knew more tricks than he did, but it would take a lot of court orders to unearth it. Hopefully none of Lemon's idle talk would see the light of day. By rights he should report Nikolic for plotting to desert, but he wasn't about to rat on his friend. Not for a momentary lapse, at least.

Something made the air shake a few feet over his head. The trench force field glowed for a second before it shut down. Morris was showered with debris from behind. He looked back and saw that a couple of the few remaining trees had been turned into kindling by the near miss. A hundred inches lower and he and Gator and everyone in between would have become ground chuck.

As Morris rushed to replace the portable genny's power pack, he reflected that Lemon's defeatism mattered about as much as last season's Little League scores. Cowards and heroes, the just and the unjust, they were all probably going to die horribly before the day was over.

Sixth Fleet, Parthenon System, 165 AFC

"Warp emergence in fifty-three minutes. Contacts identified as Task Force 43."

"About goddam time," Admiral Givens said.

She had spent much of her time reading the just-declassified briefings on the new ship classes and trying to figure out what to do with them. Since enemy sensors would identify all of them except the *Nimitz* as Marine Assault Ships, her plan was to place them among those vessels, which were arranged to provide point defense, the only thing they were good for, now that their troop holds were empty. The Vipers tended to ignore the troop transports as long as there were higher-value targets around. Hopefully the carrier vessels would be similarly dismissed. The *Nimitz* would also be mixed in among the transports; her lack of offensive capabilities would probably make her another low-priority target.

Rear Admiral Burke, the commander of the first-ever space carrier fleet, had drafted a detailed set of proposals on how to use his ships and fighters. She remembered the man as a solid officer, a pre-Contact Wet Navy man who had made the transition to space relatively well, although his career had stalled after being passed over by newer generations of spacer-born commanders. If he thought there was something to this *Star Wars* nonsense, Givens would give him plenty of leeway and concentrate on the ships she was used to, the ones that would trade broadsides with the enemy at ninety thousand miles, the way it'd been done for millions of years.

Of course, the chances of a positive outcome for Sixth Fleet in a conventional battle were less than twenty percent. Only if they did everything just right and the Vipers made every possible mistake could she hope to eke out something that could be called a victory, and even then there wouldn't be enough hale ships to call her formation a fleet. Maybe Burke's wonder carriers would save the day, but she doubted that.

Not that there was any choice but to meet the enemy in battle.

* * *

All off-duty personnel usually went under sedation for warp jumps lasting more than thirty minutes, but none of the pilots of Carrier Space Wing One bothered. Warp transit no longer disturbed them.

Lisbeth Zhang watched a flow of impossible geometries with something other than her eyes as the *USS Nimitz* navigated through them. Somewhere 'ahead' lay their destination, if such terms had any meaning in a place where distance didn't exist, a place that couldn't be sensed or even conceived by a normal human mind. In some ways, warp transit was a form of time travel. They currently existed in the moment before universal expansion began, when all points were superimposed and all matter and energy in the universe were more closely-knit together than the deepest core of an atom. But even that was nothing but a crude metaphor, because time inside warp was as irrelevant as space. Neither physicists nor mystics had the vocabulary to describe it, let alone comprehend it.

She shared her insights with her fellow pilots and received their feedback like a warm wave of thought and emotion. The other conscious humans inside the ship felt vague echoes from that communication, especially the carrier's navigators, who were also communing with warp space, although at a lower level than fighter pilots. Most of them mistook the overhead thoughts as normal warp-induced hallucinations. Once again, she wondered what she and the others had become. Their neural pathways had been rewritten and changed irrevocably: after the pilots' last physicals, the higher ups had been downright terrified; scuttlebutt was that they'd almost shut down the program before the fighters had proven their worth during practice runs. They couldn't afford to toss aside a weapon that might turn the tide, however, so they'd buried the truth under a sea of euphemisms.

Bad odds.

There was a chorus of agreement, tempered with bravado and punctuated with oorahs and a smattering of hooyas from the former Navy personnel in the Space Wing. She sent out an oorah of her own. Between her stint as a ground-pounder and the past year's ordeals, she was a Marine now. And Marines laughed at bad odds.

Emergence.

Reality felt cold and full of sharp edges. Even the air she breathed had an acrid aftertaste. The sense of communion with her fellow pilots died down but didn't disappear. Every time she went into warp with them, it grew a little stronger.

"Wing meeting scheduled for 0530 hours," her imp reminded her. Fifteen minutes from now. A final briefing before they went to war.

She was ready. Eager even.

They all were.

Parthenon-Three, 165 AFC

Yet another ambush worked like a charm.

The Viper infantry chasing Fromm's troops outran its support vehicles and blundered into overlapping fusillades from two concealed platoons on their flanks. Fromm ordered an about-face; a dozen combat vehicles reversed course and shredded the disorganized and demoralized Vipers with direct fire, scattering them. A squad of Hellcats emerged from hiding and ran down the survivors, mowing down any groups that tried to rally or stand their ground.

The vat-grown assault troops had literally been born yesterday, or at most a couple days before that, and their implanted neural programming wasn't enough to instill anything but a crude understanding of tactics. Their computerized commanders only held a limited repertoire of decision trees in their data banks, and they couldn't anticipate every possible eventuality. In this case, they'd decided that maintaining contact with the mobile force tormenting their southern flank was more important than waiting for support vehicles to catch up with the pursuers. The result had been entirely foreseeable: several enemy companies had been savaged without inflicting any losses on the Americans.

On the other hand, the Vipers had troops to spare, and two regiments were following the doomed vanguard, pouring through every possible pathway. Water doesn't have to be smart to fill all available crevices, and the aliens only needed to be smart enough to keep coming until they managed to pin down and destroy Fromm's units.

His mortar section put a hundred-plus bomblets between the aliens and his dismounted troops, allowing them to get back into their vehicles and retreat. It would have been nice to have some real artillery to hammer the aliens, but all the available tubes were at Miller's Crossing, trying to stop the main attack. Fromm's forces had relieved some of the pressure on the defenders in the north, and he hoped that this last counterattack would convince the Vipers to send even more troops after him. One could argue they weren't doing much good at all, that the aliens had enough troops to conduct a full-scale assault on the eastern gap while retaining enough surplus forces to chase down his two-company force. On the other hand, he was tying up more aliens here than he would from inside a trench line in the northeast end of the valley.

After breaking contact, Fromm sent his drones forward to keep an eye on the enemy, mindful he only had a few of them left. The flying 'bots stayed out of swatter range and managed to survive the few fireflies still in play to keep him appraised of the situation. If the Vipers stopped chasing him, he would go back and hit them again. It'd be risky, and even the dumb AIs coordinating the enemy might manage to mousetrap his force. But that was part of the job.

The drones orbited the hilly terrain on the southern edge of the

Valley. The two enemy regiments were being reinforced by what appeared to be an entire brigade, more than enough troops to block every route north. Fromm didn't see many mobile force fields and only a company of Turtle light armor in support. His forces had the edge in mobility and local firepower, and he'd apparently provoked the aliens into committing troops they might need for their primary assault. The half a division the Vipers were sending off to chase him had been removed from the main event as surely as if he'd shot them all dead.

Shooting them all dead would be even better, of course. Pity he was too outnumbered and outgunned to do that.

No matter. The enemy had taken the bait, and he was going to make them bleed every inch of way.

* * *

"Shit, those are Turtles," Russell said, watching the view from their LAV's sensors. The little alien tanks had crested a hill and were on the platoon's left flank. The Land Assault Vehicles turned their turrets towards them and engaged the unexpected targets at twelve hundred yards. Problem was, the Turtles were shooting, too.

"Those clown cars can't hit shit, Russet," Dragunov replied. "Keep your…"

That was when they got hit.

He'd been through it too many times already, but you never got used to waking up after getting fucked up by enemy incoming. Russell could see out of a huge hole where the LAV's turret used to be. A bunch of missile contrails flew overhead. His whole body felt numb; the last time he'd felt like that, about thirty percent of his body mass had been gone. He was scared to run his diagnostics app.

Someone was moaning nearby; that got him moving.

Russell sat up while he queried his imp. His bio status was nominal for a change, just a few bruises when the LAV plowed into the ground at a good eighty mph. He checked the fire team next while he turned towards Bozo, whose carat was yellow fading into red.

Nacle's status icon was black. Russell forced himself to ignore that. Black was beyond help. Yellow-red wasn't.

The LAV had eaten a burst of high-caliber railgun rounds, dense metal traveling at hypersonic speeds, five or six rounds hitting within a fraction of a second from each other. At least one of those had hit the main engine; the rest had blown off the turret and the poor bastard manning it. Sheer luck that none of the rounds had gone bouncing around the compartment; that would have killed everyone. As it was, a third of the squad was down. Lots of red and black carats.

Bozo had been sitting quietly for a change when a fragment had ripped off his left arm at the shoulder. Even his nano-meds weren't enough to staunch the flow of blood from the wound; he was going fast. Russell fumbled around his belt and came up with a first-aid 'glue gun.' He sprayed a thick coat of coagulant gel over the spurting hole. Bozo whimpered and passed out, and for a moment Russell thought he'd lost him, but the carat stayed red; out of commission, but alive.

Time to check on the others. The LAV's driver was dead; two railgun rounds had gone through him like a chainsaw. Staff Sergeant Dragunov had bought it too; a fragment had blasted a hole in his helmet big enough to put a fist through. Two other guys from the squad were down for the count but stable. And Nacle was gone from the waist up; Russell only knew it was him after identifying everyone else inside the LAV. That left six guys who'd gotten knocked around but still functional.

The deaths were just data points right now. They had a mission, and he was the highest-ranked fucker left standing.

First, figure out what was going on. A dead LAV was a big target, but they weren't taking fire at the moment, so maybe they were out of sight for now. Sooner or later, they were going to have to get the fuck out; a stopped vehicle was a bullet magnet. Russell peeked outside via his imp. The combined take of any drones still alive and observation posts back at their rally point gave him a clear picture of what was going on outside the smoking ruins of the vehicle. The view plain sucked.

The LAV had fallen into a ravine between two hills, which was about the luckiest thing that could have happened under the circumstances. They were out of line of sight from the battle, which was raging a good half a klick from their current position. The company and the Army dog-faces had pushed the Vipers back and were making sure the survivors didn't get any bright ideas. The Turtles that had fucked them up were gone. The only alien mini-tank Russell could see was engulfed in fire. The enemy had scattered but was regrouping. The American counterattack had taken a big chomp out of ET, but they were going to have to pull back or risk getting enveloped. Two companies just couldn't cover enough frontage even on these narrow gaps, and more Vipers were coming.

"Get the wounded out," he told the squad's survivors. "We've got a ride coming."

An Army ambulance was heading their way, moving as low as its ground-effect engine allowed, and darting from cover to cover. Russell approved; there were no rules against shooting at medevac vehicles. By the time the ambulance arrived and they'd loaded up the wounded, Charlie and the Army pukes were heading back the way they'd come, leaving a trail of dead Eets on their way. They'd poked the aliens, and now they were getting poked back. Russell knew there were a couple of ambushes waiting for the ETs if they kept following them.

Problem was, it looked like the Vipers were sending enough troops their way to absorb the losses and keep coming.

Seventeen

Parthenon-Three, 165 AFC

The Tangos were breaking through.

Morris had been in enough fights to have a feel for when things were going to hell. The mad scramble down I-10 after the loss (and destruction) of Davistown had been the next best thing to a rout. He remembered the ride on the back of an open cargo truck only as a series of flashes: broken-down vehicles scattered on both sides of the road, where they'd been towed or pushed out of the way. Dead cattle lying on an open field. A family of six making their way on foot, baggage slung over their heads, waving desperately at the vehicles that passed them by without stopping. A trio of Buford tanks going towards the fighting; those poor bastards were probably goners by now.

He and the rest of the Volunteers had gotten three hours to rest and then they'd been put back on the line. Ten minutes after they'd assembled at their fighting positions, the Vipers had come a-knocking.

The ETs didn't have much artillery in play, but what they had was pounding on their lines, and enough leakers were getting through the shields to produce a steady trickle of casualties. And a lot of the troops in the fighting positions next to Morris weren't doing much fighting.

Morris had replaced his Iwo with an ALS-43 its previous owner no longer had any use for, and was laying down a steady stream of armor-piercing and explosive rounds on the Vipers crowding the slope below his entrenchment, some less than a five hundred yards away. A battery of four-barreled anti-tank lasers not too far behind him was also in the game, and most of the Volunteers' platoon as well, even Lemon, who was making up for his skedaddling talk by fighting like hell. Units whose experienced NCOs were kicking people's asses into shape were doing okay. But too many positions were only generating sporadic fire, effectively unaimed, grunts lifting their guns over their heads and aiming through their imps without exposing themselves. Which was fine if you were using a beam weapon, but Iwos generated recoil, and if the guns weren't properly braced against your shoulder their shots would scatter all over creation.

Too many weekend soldiers had joined the Guard and the

militias only for the tax breaks and treated training like a joke, because they'd been certain that a core planet was never going to be invaded, not as long as there was a Navy to keep the aliens away. Granted, Morris had moved to Parthenon believing the exact same thing, but even so he'd made an effort to be ready for the worst, because life had a way to turn your expectations into a bitter joke. Too many hadn't, and they were paying for their lack of imagination with everyone's lives.

"Damnit," he muttered as he switched targets and hit an advancing bunch of Vipers on its flank. Two or three of them went down for good and the rest scrambled for cover like so many cockroaches. He used his imp to identify the platoon of slackers manning that stretch of the line, and broke into its command channel. "Listen, assholes!" he shouted at them. "You stand up and start pouring it on, or I'm going to walk up and *machinegun* your asses into hamburger! Do you fucking copy?"

"Who the fuck is this?" someone shouted back. It was a lieutenant – a fucking *Marine lieutenant* –huddled in the trench along with a bunch of Army troops, all rear echelon assholes that had somehow been thrown into the line. Someone must have thought a Devil Dog officer would be just the thing to motivate those troops, but this happy asshole – he ID'd him as one Randolph O'Malley – was hunkered down with them, not even firing his weapon. Morris had masked his call sign, a trick that would only work as long as an O-3 or higher didn't get involved, but in a few minutes none of this would matter. Except he would be damned if he was going to let those cowards hide in their hole like scared children while there were aliens to kill.

"I repeat, identify yourself," the chickenshit El-Tee said.

He roared back at him in his sergeant's voice: "I'm the guy who's gonna kill every last one of you! I got a platoon of Marines doing morale sweeps. If we don't see you going up and at 'em in ten seconds, we're gonna light you up and use your bleeding corpses as footrests! Do you fucking copy?"

That got them moving. More bullets and grenades started coming from that section, some of it actually hitting the enemy.

It wasn't much, but every bit helped.

* * *

"Our position is becoming untenable," Captain Kruger said.

Fromm could hear growing panic and shock in the officer's voice. It started when two Hunters had been caught by the same

Turtle platoon that had destroyed one of Fromm's LAVs along with the Army vehicles. It wasn't easy to lose men and women under your command, and the first time was also the hardest. Kruger wasn't afraid for himself; his command car had been on the lead of the counterattack that wiped out the Viper armor and pushed their infantry back. But he cared for his troops, and didn't want to sacrifice them.

Even if Kruger was right, however, there was nowhere to run. Their planned escape route along the river had been cut off. Fromm's LAVs could fly over the mountains, if they didn't mind becoming a target for every Viper heavy gun in range, not to mention abandoning the Hellcats. The Army ground-effect vehicles didn't even have that option. They might try running via a few mountain trails that would eventually become too narrow to accommodate their vehicles, or take their chances on foot. Neither was a good option when dealing with enemies who could outrun them in broken terrain. Alternatively, the combined force could attempt to break through the encircling troops and try to flee towards Miller's Crossing. They'd just have to fight a few divisions of aliens standing in their way. Staying where they were and fighting a battle of maneuver was probably the most survivable course of action.

"I disagree, Captain," he told the Army commander. "We will proceed with the plan. An enemy battalion has fallen out of contact with the rest of the opforce; we will engage and destroy it. Carry on."

Kruger didn't protest any further. Just was well.

They were taking heavy losses, but they were doing their job. The Vipers attacking Forge Valley's eastern mouth had lost all of their armor. The tank company Fromm's people had destroyed might have played a decisive role in the northeast; now they were just more scattered debris among the mountains. It'd been worth losing a squad from Third Platoon, even though most of the dead and maimed were men he'd come to know personally during the Battle of Kirosha. Those Marines had survived a brutal fight in Jasper-Five only to fall in yet another planet, light years away from their homes. Fromm knew those losses would come back to haunt him, assuming he survived the day, but he was too busy to mourn now.

As the combined task force maneuvered to take out the lost Viper battalion, he took a moment to check on the larger battle going on to the northeast. That had turned into a simple slugging match, alien light infantry wasting itself in head-on assaults against prepared positions. That kind of suicide attack only worked with overwhelming numbers, but it was beginning to bear fruit. Two times, the enemy had reached the final protective lines of the blocking force and nearly overrun them before being slaughtered by the combined fire of every unit in range. The second time, a Guard company had broken ranks and tried to flee to the rear, until 'friendly' artillery fire had herded it back to its fighting positions. Colonel Brighton hadn't been bluffing about that. There probably were a number of one-star Generals screaming about it just about now. General Hamill, who commanded the Marine ground forces, would tell them to pound sand; he'd already fired two of the Army's top brass, with the endorsement of Admiral Givens, who was in overall command of Parthenon System's defenses.

Sooner or later, the line would break, as it had done around too many PDBs already. When that happened, Fromm's command might survive a bit longer than the rest of the 101st, but only for as long as the Vipers pulled back from the ruins of PDB-18 and New Burbank and hunted him down for good.

He couldn't worry about that, either. He had aliens to kill.

Sixth Fleet, Parthenon System, 165 AFC

Lisbeth Zhang went over the checklist a final time as she waited for clearance to launch.

Sixth Fleet had jumped a few seconds ago, emerging in the vicinity of Parthenon-Three and engaging the alien armada. It was time for Project Lexington show the universe what it was worth.

"Lamia, you are cleared for launch."

That would be the last time she'd hear from the *Nimitz*'s flight controllers until she came back from the sortie. You couldn't stay in touch with the mothership, not when the enemy could zero in on graviton transmissions and use them to target your crate. The same applied to the rest of Flight B, Strike Fighter Squadron Ten (a.k.a. the Dragon Fangs). She'd be all alone out there. At least, she would be according to the known laws of physics.

Transition.

Her designated target was an enemy dreadnought. All the fighters were going for capital ships, hopefully before they could launch their entire missile load. That many vampires under the control of sapient operators rather than dumb computer systems would probably wipe out half of Sixth Fleet before the first energy weapon was fired. She and the other five War Eagles in Flight B were going to emerge five thousand miles behind the target –

beyond point-blank range in space combat – and take it under fire.

She spent the few subjective seconds of the trip in blessed, silent darkness. Her fellow pilots were close by, and their presence comforted her.

Emergence.

The six-fighters of Flight B were thousands of miles from each other, but Lisbeth knew where each of them were, as surely as her visual sensors revealed the dreadnought that was their target.

The Vipers went for sinuous, curving shapes in their warships; there wasn't a sharp angle to be seen in the three-mile long capital vessel. The dreadnought looked almost like a balloon animal, its comical lines belied by its sheer size and the technical specs flashing on her imp's tactical display. The six fighters had emerged behind the alien ship's main thrusters, where artificially-generated gravity waves pushing against the fabric of space-time reduced the effectiveness of its sensor systems. That worked both ways, of course, but the fighters were relying on passive sensors, mostly infrared, and capital ships ran blindingly hot against the dull background of space.

She aimed at the pre-designated spot, one of the massive engines on the upper quadrant, and fired. The massive cannon was theoretically recoilless, but the fighter did not have the shielding a normal battleship mount would have, and residual gravity emanations made the whole craft vibrate slightly with each shot. Her firing computer corrected for the disturbance as she sent another blast of fundamental force towards the target, and another.

The entire flight did. They each had five shots before their main gun's capacitor ran dry; they emptied them in under ten seconds.

Pinpoint accuracy in space combat was not possible, given the distances and speeds involved. A ship's main gun had a Circular Error Probable of two hundred meters at half a light year away, and slightly over ten meters at the current, impossibly close range. The estimated hit probability for each fighter was in the order of twenty percent.

All six fighters hit the same two-meter spot on the Viper dreadnought with their first volley. The rear quadrant shields could not withstand two simultaneous blows, let alone five. Neither could the armor behind them; the impossibly-close barrage vaporized it. The following four volleys hit within twenty meters of each other. The combined blasts stabbed deep into the bowels of the ship, tearing engines apart and cracking the heavy-metal cores of massive gluon power plants. Ravening strange matter particles were released from their containment bottles, free to roam and generate physical reactions that transformed large amounts of matter into energy.

As soon as their fifth and final shots were fired, Flight B fled into warp. Their last sensor readings showed a massive thermal bloom on the rear of the Viper dreadnought.

From inside warp space, Lisbeth felt the death screams of fifteen thousand Nasstah. The dreadnought had been obliterated, something they'd never imagined possible after a single pass. But that was of minor importance next to the feeling that those deaths had somehow reached into warp space – and touched something there.

Flight B reappeared in normal space some hundreds of miles away from their carrier vessel. It took some maneuvering to get close enough to the carrier for its grav-grapples to bring them in, using a modified version of the systems that handled shuttle landings. The return trip ended with a familiar jolt as they were conveyed deeper into the ship, back to the catapult platforms that had launched them. Lisbeth's first combat sortie was over.

"That's a kill, Flight B," the space traffic controller said, almost shouting in shocked enthusiasm. "Confirmed kill, scratch one dreadnought. Flight A inflicted severe damage on its target. Flight C downed another Sierra. You have destroyed two dreadnoughts and severely damaged a third on this sortie. It's... it's fucking incredible."

Lisbeth shuddered in her seat while the flight crew rushed forward to replace her main gun's power pack. In five minutes or so, she'd be ready to go out there again. She should be elated after she'd helped destroy a capital ship. Or maybe amazed: nobody expected they would inflict catastrophic damage on a heavily-shielded and armored dreadnought with a few shots, even at close range. The only reason they'd pulled it off was the psychic link she and her fellow pilots shared. That realization should have filled her with awe.

Instead, she felt drained, and strangely enough, afraid.

Something had happened in warp space. Something bad.

* * *

"Dear God Almighty," Admiral Givens whispered. The tactical holotank display combined the input from hundreds of sensor systems and had been confirmed by multiple sources, but she still couldn't believe what she was seeing.

Three Viper dreadnoughts and five battleships had been destroyed outright, and all the rest were heavily damaged; the enemy armada's flagship was drifting at a mere two kilometers per second, essentially dead in the water. The fighters had ravaged the alien ships of the line, turning the stately maneuvers of the enemy fleet into a shambles as it tried to deal with the unexpected threat. The tiny warp emergences hadn't even registered in the aliens' sensor systems until after they'd fired their load and escaped. A hundred and eighty fighters were preparing for their second sortie; they'd suffered no casualties and destroyed more tonnage than Givens' entire force had in all its previous engagements at Parthenon combined.

She wished she could enjoy the unexpected success of the new weapon systems, but her ships had problems of their own.

While the fighters performed miracles, Sixth Fleet had been dealing with another Sun-Blotter, eighty thousand missiles headed their way. The enemy hadn't been able to perform a full launch before the fighters struck, but even half a mass salvo was a lot to handle. The swarm of vampires was thirty seconds away, and a lot of them were going to get through.

"For what we're about to receive, may the Lord make us truly thankful," she muttered. Her old mentor, Admiral Carruthers, had been fond of that sarcastic prayer.

Eight thousand American missiles flew towards the eleven thousand survivors while standard point defenses redoubled their frantic efforts. The ensuing fireworks were actually impressive even with standard visual sensors, a rarity in space combat. Thousands of flashes in the dark blinked malignantly on the main view screen; the tactical holotank ran the counter of survivors. Two thousand and seventy-six missiles emerged from the massive conflagration and entered the final energy weapon gauntlet. Twelve hundred and ninety-one reached Sixth Fleet.

The *Halsey* shuddered more violently than in previous engagements; the shaking was enough to knock an ensign off her seat. The foolish child hadn't strapped herself in. Givens almost chided the crewmember for her carelessness, but shrugged instead and concentrated on the damage reports. The American dreadnought had taken four direct hits. No fatalities and only eleven light casualties among her crew, but one of her main gun turrets was out of commission, reducing her firepower by twenty percent. The last surviving President-class light cruiser in the galaxy, the *USS Chester A. Arthur*, was struck a dozen times, suffering catastrophic levels of damage; her surviving crew was taking to the escape pods. Two destroyers and one frigate had been destroyed outright, and several other ships had been heavily damaged. Bad losses to be sure, but nothing like what would have happened if the warp fighters hadn't disrupted the missile launches and the manual controllers aboard the now-dead and crippled dreadnoughts.

The Vipers had shot their bolt, and Sixth Fleet still stood. Even better, the enemy's battle line had been brutalized, and hers had just begun to fight.

"Our turn," she said. Then, in her command voice:

"Fire at will!"

Parthenon-Three, 165 AFC

The area force field burned out with a final cyan flash. A moment later, a second missile volley slammed into the fighting holes where soldiers and Marines were making their last stand.

Multiple impacts hammered into the smaller and weaker portable shields protecting the dug-in infantrymen. Some held, but those that didn't allowed an entire trench section to be washed over by plasma explosions that broiled alive everyone inside. Seven personnel carats went from green to black in the space of a second.

"We have to fall back!" Captain Kruger said over the commander channel.

"Hold in place," Fromm ordered curtly. "Send your reserves forward and plug the gap as soon as the area force field is back online. I'm sending you reinforcements. Repeat, hold in place."

"Hold in place, roger." The Army captain's voice had a distant quality; the man was in shock and relying on his training to get through it. Robot-like obedience was better than panic, but Fromm shouldn't expect much from the officer; the continuing losses had essentially broken him. That was the only explanation for the pointless plea to retreat.

They were surrounded. There was nowhere to go.

Destroying the trapped Viper battalion had been surprisingly easy. Its controlling computers had been destroyed at some point; nobody had been in charge of the hapless vat-grown troopers. Caught in a narrow cul-de-sac and too tightly-packed to deploy, the aliens hadn't been able to defend themselves from point-blank LAV and Hunter fire that wiped out the entire unit while Second Platoon's dismounted Marines kept a relief force from reaching the killing ground in time to do anything except dispose of their dead.

The maneuvers required to escape in the aftermath had cost them their last few drones, however. Without the ability to keep an eye on the enemy, it was only a matter of time before they stumbled into more trouble than they could handle. Fourth Platoon's Hellcats had run into what they mistakenly thought was a Viper company. In the ensuing firefight, they discovered the hard way they were tangling with a reinforced battalion, and while trying to extricate the mobile infantrymen, the entire formation had found itself cornered. Only about a squad's worth of Hellcats were still functional; half a dozen pilots had been forced to abandon their damaged battlesuits and become lightly-armed infantrymen.

His two companies, now down to about four platoons of effectives, had managed to gain the heights of a hill, one flank anchored by Copperhead Rapids, the other protected by a sheer cliff. There was a ravine leading out of the hill, but it led to an open area that would be harder to hold against an attack, and which would likely end up invested by other Viper forces. Breaking contact without taking massive casualties would require artillery assets he didn't have. In the course of the running battle, they'd been forced to abandon most of the support platoon's vehicles; those rear echelon troops were holding their pistols and carbines and readying themselves to fill the fighting positions being vacated by the wounded and dead.

The Viper battle computers would soon divert enough forces to overrun the American position. The enemy couldn't make their numbers count at first, but after a while they organized their rocketeers into groups. Their coordinated volleys from beyond small-arms fire were overwhelming their shields and their few anti-air defense assets. The steady bombardment was slowly but surely grinding them down.

Fromm sent out Lieutenant Hansen and the dismounted Hellcat drivers he'd kept in reserve to bolster the Army's position. That left him with a handful of walking wounded, a couple of squads of truck drivers and loaders, and the company communication specialists as his last uncommitted forces. The temptation to grab a rifle and rush into the fight was strong, but he knew that he would only be allowed that luxury when the battle was well and truly lost.

They'd found their death ground. The only option left was to fight.

Sixth Fleet, Parthenon System, 165 AFC

It's chasing us, Lisbeth thought. *It's getting closer.*

As a child, she'd sometimes had nightmares about being pursued by something so terrible she didn't dare to look back. Whatever was happening inside warp space was worse. Whatever she and her fellow pilots had woken up was becoming more active and aware with every sortie they launched. She didn't know what would happen if it caught them, and she didn't intend to find out.

Her War Eagle emerged five thousand miles from a missile cruiser, moving at an angle that was increasing the distance between her and the target by thousands of meters per second. She adjusted course and opened fire, noticing the ship's point defense was shooting back. Her warp shield absorbed most of the incoming, but a few near misses reduced her force fields by thirty percent in the time it took her to fire a single shot into the target and flee back into warp.

She almost hesitated before jumping, even though to stay in normal space was certain death. Flight B had lost one fighter already: Goober had lingered a moment too long, and a Viper frigate had scored a hit from twenty thousand klicks. It hadn't taken long for the aliens to realize what was happening, and to re-task light vessels to scan for small warp emergences and target them with their main guns. They no longer could afford to fire their full ordnance load between jumps. It was shoot and scoot time, and even then they were taking losses.

Transition.

A feeling of pure dread washed over her. She and the other pilots were sharing warp space with something else. The presence chasing her was getting closer. In the few seconds she spent there, she became certain it was gaining on her, even though a chase should be impossible in a place where neither time nor space mattered.

Too many jumps. Every time a living mind entered warp, it broadcast some sort of signal. Do it enough times, and it would be detected and traced to its point of origin. By who or what, she didn't know. The real warp demons, maybe. Or the thing she'd seen in that Marine's eyes, back during training.

Emergence.

She reappeared on the other side of the enemy cruiser, a mere handful of miles away, close enough she could have seen the vessel clearly with the old Mark One Eyeball if she had a window to look out from. She took two shots while a point-defense laser fired ineffectually into her warp shield, and jumped just before a massive explosion devoured the Viper vessel and nearly enveloped her fighter.

"You do not belong here," Goober told her. The dead pilot was sitting next to her, even though there wasn't enough room in the cockpit for another person. None of what she was seeing was real, of course; the images were just a story her mind created to make sense of surroundings that didn't conform to any natural law.

"Who are you?" Lisbeth asked the apparition.

Goober grinned. His face began to change, to run down like melting wax, revealing something glistening, dark and hungry.

Emergence.

She was back in the vicinity of the *Nimitz*, the terror of the last few moments beginning to fade away like a half-forgotten dream. Just another warp-induced nightmare, she told herself. Just because psychic powers were real didn't mean other things were, things like monsters and demons.

Going through docking procedures in the middle of a battle distracted her enough to stop thinking about it. The important thing was the fact she'd gotten another confirmed kill, this one all of her own. They were directing individual fighters after cruisers and destroyers now, because there were no other higher-value targets left: the Viper dreadnoughts and battleships were all down. The battle had been as one-sided as pitting a 21st-century aircraft carrier group against a World War One fleet would have been.

That was her last sortie. The strike group had done enough, and its casualties were mounting unnecessarily. The ordinary vessels of Sixth Fleet now outnumbered and outgunned the survivors, and they were mercilessly cutting them down. The hopeless battle had turned into an enemy rout.

A few bad daydreams were a small price to pay for victory, she decided.

Parthenon-Three, 165 AFC

Bringing the ALS-43, his Iwo and ammo for both on the long hike to the top of a hill hike was a pain in the ass, but Russell didn't want to part with any of his firepower. He was the last member of his fire team left on his feet, and he was going to make the tangos pay.

"Move it, shitheads!" Gunny Wendell growled. The non-com was in command of what was left of Third Platoon after the new El-Tee had his LAV shot to shit. Lieutenant Hansen wasn't dead, but he was down for the count. Not that it mattered; there were a whole twelve Marines able to fight in the weapons platoon.

Everybody was loaded beyond capacity, but they kept up the

pace. The assaultmen were the worst; each of them was lugging five full reloads for their Light Missile Launchers on their backs. The remnants of the Guns squad were also carrying two portable field generators, which would come in handy since they were moving beyond the area shields protecting the main force.

By the time they made it to the top of the ridge, Russell's power supply was down to twenty-five percent. On the other hand, he had a great view of the battle below.

The Vipers were moving forward in dribs and drabs under the cover of massed laser and missile fire; Russell's sensors turned the light beams into a beautiful lightshow. The scurrying ant-sized figures looked like scaly tarantulas. Plasma bullets from the Marines and Army dog-faces firing on the ETs flashed like fireflies when they hit their shields. The effect when they finally took down an alien grunt wasn't very spectacular: the tango would just stop moving, or would sometimes break into two pieces. It all looked pretty tame from the top of the mountain, unless you knew what it was like down there, all swirling panic, deafening sound and sudden death. It sucked to be down there.

And it was about to suck even more. For the Eets, at least, although there was plenty of suck to go around.

Setting up the ALS-43 took a few seconds. Russell was ready long before the assaultmen were, but he held his fire. The first volley had to count. The Vipers' sensors should have picked them up, but there was so much shit flying around that the Marine flanking force had managed to climb a small mountain without drawing anybody's attention. It helped that most of the alien grunts were dumb as rocks, of course, and that a lot of their computer minders and their few normal-brained war leaders had been sent to Jesus, leaving the few survivors in charge of a lot more troopers than they were able to handle. All of which had allowed a squad of heavily-armed Devil Dogs to outflank a battalion-sized force. Pretty neat, until they made themselves known. He didn't think they'd brought enough guns to take out a whole battalion.

"Everybody ready?" the Gunny asked. Everybody sent back an acknowledgement. "Let them have it!"

Twelve Marines poured it on, their coordinated volleys tearing holes in the area force fields and hitting the field generators themselves. The last two gennies went up in smoke, killing dozens of enemies and leaving hundreds more protected only by their personal shields and the grace of God. And God wasn't in a gracious mood just about now.

The two surviving hundred-mike-mike mortars in the rear had been waiting for this. The quick-firing tubes emptied their fifty-bomb magazines in five seconds, targeting the unprotected areas with a combination of plasma and fragmentary bombs, with their last two thermobaric charges for a chaser. The pass disappeared in glowing mass of hellfire. Russell and his fellow Marines checked fire; their sensors couldn't find targets, and dropping grenades or missiles would only waste ammo without doing much more than add insult to injury.

When the smoke cleared, most of the stick figures were gone. A third field genny in the rear was also out. After that, it was a massacre. A few Vipers tried to return fire, but the Weapons Platoon was in a perfect position to spot and engage them before they could hit anything important; the remaining survivors ran until they slammed into their follow-up forces, stalling the entire advance.

I guess we did *bring enough guns for a whole battalion,* Russell thought. *How about that.*

That had gone was well as it could have, but from that height Russell could see the rest of the Vipers surrounding their position, well over three thousand in number, which was plenty enough to go through them. His heart sank. They'd killed maybe two thousand aliens during the last two attacks, and it wasn't going to matter. The mortars had shot off all their special munitions in that final volley and the weapons squads on the ridge had burned through two-thirds of their ammo. That was it. They were done.

"Listen, maggots. Check your new aiming vectors," Gunny Wendell said, acting as if they weren't all dead men walking. "When they enter the pass, we will engage their generators, just like before. Two LAVs are going to move forward and plug the gap down below, so watch out for them. Any blue-on-blue hits and I'll fucking blue and tattoo your asses."

That all sounded great, if one didn't know that those LAVs were the last ones left in working order, and that they would last all of five minutes before Viper rockets hammered through their defenses and turned them into scrap. Or that the weapons platoon just didn't have the firepower to take out another field genny. They'd blown their load and it was all over but the shouting.

Russell still sent a dutiful acknowledgement. If you had to go, might as well go with your hands around the other bastard's throat, figuratively speaking. He spent a few seconds wishing he'd found out the name of the witch; sending her a goodbye email would have been nice, even if chances were the transmission would never be received or passed on.

The Vipers took a while to deal with the influx of survivors from the shattered attack. Some of the runners didn't stop until they were shot down, which finally convinced the rest to rally. All their obedience got them was the dubious honor of being in the front lines of the new assault. Russell could almost sympathize with them. Life as a grunt sucked, whether you had skin or scales.

The reorganized aliens began to push forward. They didn't have any artillery or even mortars anymore, but Russell could see plenty of rocket launchers among them. More than enough to do the job. This wouldn't take long.

"Wait for it," the Gunny ordered. "Wait for..."

A FLASH message stepped on the transmission. ENEMY SPACE FORCES NEUTRALIZED. FRIENDLY AIR SUPPORT INCOMING. REPEAT. FRIENDLY AIR SUPPORT INCOMING. DO NOT ENGAGE AIRBORNE ASSETS.

Airborne? Shuttles could do assault runs, but the Vipers' rocket launchers were perfectly capable of going surface-to-air, not to mention all the heavy energy weapons scattered around the valley, which could range all the way into space. A shuttle attack would get slaughtered without accomplishing anything. What the fuck were they talking about?

A few moments later, he had his answer.

The weird-looking vehicles materialized from the twisted-space shimmer of a warp jump. A dozen of them appeared over the sky and opened fire with something bigger than a Stormin' Norman's main gun and a bunch of smaller energy weapons, tearing into the largest Viper concentrations around their position. The attack lasted maybe two seconds all told before the flying cannons disappeared back into warp, but that was enough. That single volley obliterated all enemy force fields and consumed half the ground forces around them.

Maybe a regiment's worth was able to run away.

Russell didn't know what those things were, but he cheered them at the top of his lungs. They all did.

Eigtheen

Parthenon-Three, 165 AFC

"Carrier Strike Group One," Morris Jensen muttered, tasting each word like one would a new, exotic dish.

"Whatever the hell they are, the sure came in handy," Lemon said as they enjoyed the rocky ride inside the wheeled truck taking them to New Burbank. The converted cabin had bleachers attached to its sides and a few straps to keep the twenty grunts inside from bouncing from the walls, but that was about all the comfort they provided. Despite that, about half of the Volunteers inside were fast asleep. It'd been that kind of day.

"Blew the Vipers clear off the system," Lemon went on. He'd gotten the straight dope from his buddy the former Chief, who'd survived the battle and gotten back in touch with him. The aliens had lost all their capital ships and all but a handful of cruisers, something like seventy percent of the tonnage they'd started out with when they invaded. Sixth Fleet had chased the survivors all the way into Heinlein, where a few thousand Americans still lived; it turned out the aliens had brought all the troops they'd been using there to Parthenon, figuring on coming back later and finishing the job. Now they'd been booted out of there as well. And those space fighters had been the reason why. Good old American know-how had won the day once more.

"Wonder if I'll be able to collect any insurance," Nikolic wondered out loud. When he wasn't playing around in the militia, he owned and ran a hardware and small-fabber store in town. The fabbers had been requisitioned and carted away before the battle, and he'd hopefully get them back in the same condition they'd been in; the rest of his business had gone up in smoke.

"If not, there's always grants and emergency loans."

Morris' farm had been in the path of the Viper advance; he hadn't bothered checking on what they'd done to it. There would be plenty of time for that later.

The truck ride became smoother as they reached the city proper, which had been hardly touched by the battle. A few missiles and beams had made it through and there'd been casualties, of course: over three thousand dead and twice as many injured, but a quick peek through the ubiquitous public cameras on every city corner showed most of New Burbank stood untouched. Lucky bastards.

They spent the last fifteen minutes of the ride through town in companionable silence. Morris almost nodded off, but he was afraid of falling asleep. The dreams had been bad, especially the ones where he was back on top of the burning bus. It was going to be a while before sleep came easy to him, if ever. But there was something he knew would make him feel better.

Finally, the truck stopped and someone banged on the outside, letting them know it was time to get off. The tattered remains of Second Platoon, F Company, Volunteers Regiment, stepped out into the morning light. A small group of cheering civilians waited for him. Friends and family from Davistown. Someone had made a banner: GOD BLESS YOU. WE LOVE YOU.

As soon as Morris was out, a small figure disentangled herself from the neighbors who'd been watching over her and came running towards him. He knelt down just in time for Mariah to barrel into him like a soft, towheaded missile.

"Grampa!"

"Here I am, pumpkin. Here I am."

It'd been worth it, all of it.

* * *

"Corporal Edison! Front and center!"

Russell froze in mid-stride and suppressed a curse. He'd been headed towards New Burbank's red-light district, three months' pay burning a virtual hole in his pocket. Ninety-six hours of liberty beckoned, and he'd already burned two of those visiting Gonzo in the hospital. It'd been rough; Gonzo had taken the news about Nacle very hard. Russell was just beginning to process the loss, and it'd be a good while before the whole thing ran its course. He'd been through it enough times, burying his buddies, and he knew how the aftermath worked, not that it was always the same. His gut feeling was that this one was going to be worse than most. And getting drunk and laid would help; a little bit, but it would help.

He turned around and stood at attention, facing the Navy officer who'd stopped him in his tracks. The female Navy officer. At first he didn't recognize her. Her face was the same, though, even with the unfamiliar military hairstyle and white officer's hat. His mouth twisted in a nervous half-smile.

"Congratulations on your promotion," Lieutenant Commander Deborah Genovisi said. Her smile was anything but nervous; the last time she'd seen that grin, that and her long hair had been all she'd been wearing.

"It ain't official yet, ma'am," the soon-to-be-minted non-com said; he'd get his extra stripe when he was back from liberty. It didn't matter much either way. He'd been a corporal before, and chances were he'd end up busted back to lance coolie soon enough. That was how he rolled. "Pleased to finally learn your name, ma'am."

"At ease, Corporal. We're both off-duty."

"Of course," he said, forcing himself not to add 'ma'am' at the end.

"As you can see, I've been reactivated. Looks I may be trying my luck aboard one of those new warp fighters, now that the Navy has decided it wants in on the action. We couldn't let you Marines have all the fun, could we?"

"I guess not." Hearing those flying guns that had saved Russell's bacon were property of the Corps had been a very pleasant surprise. He'd been looking forward to rubbing the fact in the noses of any bubblehead he ran into, from here to eternity. Except the Navy would probably steal the whole thing. It wouldn't be the first time the Marines got screwed.

"I have quarters not too far away, if you wouldn't mind a night cap and some company." Her voice softened. "I think we both could use it."

Fraternizing with an officer was a bad idea, even one outside his chain of command, but Russell had never been afraid of bad ideas. That was how he rolled. And maybe it was only fair for a Marine to do a little Navy-screwing of his own.

His smile grew wider.

* * *

"That's the last of them," Lieutenant Hansen said, highlighting the spots on P-3's map where the final mop-up operations had just wrapped up. He was still in the casualty list, but he could handle doing the paperwork entailed in the aftermath of the battle. "All alien forces on the planet are accounted for."

He was mostly right. All major Viper concentrations on Parthenon-Three had been exterminated, but scattered individuals still remained, hiding out in squad-sized groups or even individuals. Hunting down those remnants would take weeks, or the month or so before the aliens' consumables ran out and they died of natural causes. Vipers could find no nourishment in human friendly worlds, or breathe their atmosphere for that matter.

Fromm figured the militia, Guard and Army units tasked for that purpose wouldn't wait for starvation or asphyxia to do the job, though. They had acquired a taste for Viper blood.

The aliens had come to exterminate humanity, and were quickly learning such behaviors could be easily reciprocated. One would think the fate of the Snakes and the Gremlins would have sufficed to teach that lesson to every Starfarer in the known galaxy.

If the US won the war... The three enemy empires comprised slightly over fifteen percent of all known sophonts in the galaxy. If it was a fight to the death, humanity would be wading in oceans of blood.

Fromm went over the casualty lists one more time. They'd lost a few more people during the march back to friendly lines. An enemy without the option to surrender died hard. Mercy under the circumstances was suicidal, though. It'd still been hard, firing upon helpless enemies who'd exhausted their ammo and were no more dangerous than wild animals.

He shrugged. You could repent and mend your ways later, or your children and grandchildren might, as long as you survived. If he had any tears to shed, they were for the men and women who'd lost their lives stopping the invasion force. His company had been worse than decimated: even after all the wounded were fit to return to duty, he was going to have to rebuild the unit almost from scratch. There would be plenty of manpower available now that full mobilization was underway, but turning those individuals into a fighting force would take a good deal of work.

The 101st MEU and the rest of Expeditionary Strike Group Fourteen would be heading back to New Parris for rest and refit. Fromm didn't think he would have as much time as he had after the actions at Jasper-Five. His guess was that the US would take the war to the Vipers and Lampreys now that their fleets had been savaged and humanity had a new weapon to make up for its numerical inferiority. Going into the offensive had its own risks, of course. Fromm remembered the field exercise against Viper defense forces, which weren't comprised of half-sentient clone soldiers but smart, dedicated and well-equipped professionals. Those troops would be defending their homes, and wouldn't go down easily.

The war would go on.

The thought filled him with dread, intermixed with a sense of eagerness that made him hate himself.

Trade Nexus Eleven, 165 AFC

Guillermo Hamilton was watching the latest news report from a passing American vessel, enjoying it in its full holographic glory, when Heather McClintock all but ran into the office.

"There you are," he said. "Have you seen the footage from the Battle of Parthenon? It's..." The look in her face finally sunk in. "What's wrong?"

She was already transmitting a set of instructions to all the systems in the alleged trading post. Hamilton's eyes widened in shock when he saw the self-destruct codes flash before his eyes. "The fuck is going on?"

"Hope you had your bug-out bag packed up," she said. "We've got to get out of here in the next hour, or we're in deep shit."

"What are you talking about?" he asked after her while she ran upstairs towards her bedroom. He'd tried to invite himself in there a couple of times and been politely rebuffed. Now, he followed her in. It was much as he expected; the only decoration in sight was a holo of some guy in a Marine officer's uniform. The 3-D image flickered as Heather threw it into a duffle bag that was mostly packed already. Having a bug-out bag was a standard procedure.

"My criminal contacts paid off again," Heather told him. "The Boothan Clan owns a handful of security officers in the Nexus. A set of sealed orders came in via courier this morning, addressed to the Vehelian Guard Commandant. One of the corrupt cops hacked into the system and took a gander, just in case it was something important. It was. Paying for it cost me a good bit of coin, but it was more than worth it."

"So?"

"All humans in TN-11 are to be detained and handed over to the Imperium. The Ovals are waiting for a regiment of Spaceborne Infantry from their sector fleet to arrive before they start rounding us up; they are due in an hour. Figure another hour to deploy and coordinate with local security forces, and then they'll start picking us up. We need to be off this station before that."

"Dear God. That means..."

"War. War is what it means. The Ovals are joining the Alliance. Or, at best, they've caved to the Alliance's demands and are just going to step aside and let us get slaughtered. At least they want to keep us alive, for now. They're following the Imperium's lead."

"That's plenty bad. Are you sure?"

"I hacked into the Nexus' space traffic control system to look for confirmation. Two Oval planetary assault ships are inbound, ETA sixty-four minutes. Guess how many troops they can carry."

"A regiment."

Heather nodded, throwing a couple of additional items into the bag. She removed a handful of beamer power backs from a side compartment and stuffed them into several pockets of her jumpsuit before giving him a sidelong glance. "Better get packing."

He did. "The official bug-out plan isn't going to work," he pointed out while he opened a closet in his bedroom and pulled out his emergency bag. That procedure required at least twenty-four hours' advance warning, not two.

"I know. Nobody expected the Ovals would switch sides, let alone this suddenly. Luckily, I'm used to improvising on short notice. An American-flagged freighter, the *Maffeo Polo*, is currently docked on Level Sixteen and is due to leave in fifty minutes."

"They aren't going to let us go!" Guillermo protested. His bag was mostly prepacked, out of habit more than anything else, but it lacked a few personal things he had to jam into it in a hurry. From the way Heather was looking at him, he'd better hurry or she'd leave him behind. "They'll just refuse to clear it for departure."

"Well, yes," she said. "My plan is to not give them any choice in the matter. I've been on my imp ever since I got the news, working with the US Consul to facilitate our exit strategy."

Guillermo didn't know what she was talking about, and he was afraid to ask.

"Don't worry, Gill. I've got this."

They were on their way out a moment later, not sparing a second glance at their home for most of the past year.

"The Consulate is quietly evacuating and destroying all files," she went on as they briskly walked down the crowded promenade leading to a transit tube. The colorful gathering of aliens now seemed vaguely threatening to Guillermo. "Consulate personnel will meet you at the *Polo*'s docking bay. They'll tell you what to do." She handed him her bag. "Here, take my stuff with you."

"Where are you going?"

"Like I said, I need to facilitate our exit strategy." She grinned at him, and he felt his blood go cold. "I'm off to do some ground-pounding. Not your kind of scene, Guillermo. So be a good boy and hold my fucking bag, willya?"

He nodded stiffly and kept walking towards the lift while she went off deeper into the massive space station.

* * *

One does not simply walk into the Central Control Center of a Vehelian Trade Nexus.

Heather strolled casually past the Nexus Administration Building, noting that security had been increased. Where normally only a couple of bored-looking guards stood by the double set of sliding doors leading into the building, there was a full squad of Emergency Services troopers in light combat armor standing at attention. Vehelians were taller and wider that humans; the guards looked like gigantic death-robots in their faceless helmets and shiny breast plates, holding their weapons at port arms. She'd seen what their lasers carbines could do, and had no desire to be on the receiving end of one of them.

The guards automatically scanned everyone who entered the block of streets containing the station's administrative offices. Heather's imp had altered her ID codes; she would show up in their scanners as a member of the Vatyr species, humanoids about the right size and shape for her to pass as one, especially under the bulky outfit she was wearing. The same camouflage system hid her weapons from a casual scan.

The Emergency Service guards might dress like soldiers, but they were cops with mil-spec gear. They weren't thinking like soldiers. For one, they were still hooked up to the station's intranet; one of them was actually chatting with his prospective mate while standing at attention and pretending to give a damn. Against real soldiers, what she was about to do would have failed spectacularly. Military comm systems were hardened against intrusion; the police version relied on decent but hardly impervious firewalls, and the CIA electronic warfare devices were top-class, purchased from the Puppies at a 'best friends forever' discount. She was about to find out if the Agency had gotten its money's worth.

Execute, she ordered her imp.

Every ES cop within a three-block radius collapsed limply to the ground, some of them convulsing feebly, the rest still like the dead.

"Go, go, go!" she cried out as she rushed past a couple of twitching forms, beamer in hand. The sensory overload program she'd sent via the Emergency Services command channel wouldn't kill the Oval security officers, but it would keep them out of the way for at least thirty minutes. Hopefully that would be enough.

The multispecies workers inside scattered from the sight of an armed intruder in their midst. Only one Oval civvie, looking pretty tough despite wearing a plain office tunic, tried to get in her way. A stun blast scrambled his nervous systems and sent him to the ground. Heather vaulted over him and ran deeper into the complex. Behind her, a platoon of Warp Marines was deploying, their weapons and armor similarly hidden from view until she'd given the 'go' order. They would make sure she wasn't disturbed while she finished the task at hand.

She had to stun a couple more people before she made it to the CCC; several people inside the large control center were also down, being connected to the Emergency Services network she'd turned into a weapon. They included the Guard Commandant; his massive form was slumped over a console, an overturned cup of steaming noodle soup he'd been drinking making a mess on his desk. A glance at the screen showed her the updated ETA of the planetary assault ships: thirty-two minutes. This was going to be close.

A chorus of 'Clears' answered her status query. The Marines had taken blocking positions on both sides of the avenue facing the building. So far all they'd had to do was wave their guns to scare the civvies away. Frantic calls for help were being sent by hundreds of cybernetic implants, but Heather's imp had just finished hacking the communications center's main computer. None of those calls were going to reach anybody.

Once she had secured the comm systems and uploaded a very special piece of Puppy software into the CCC's computer, she placed a call to the next-highest Emergency Services officer in the base, a Captain Jeek, currently at the military docking level, where he was awaiting to take charge of the incoming Spaceborne Infantry troops. She didn't give him a chance to speak.

"Listen carefully, Captain. I have taken over the Trade Nexus' Central Control Center. You will comply with my instructions or I will start shutting off assorted vital systems on select portions of the station. Among my first targets will be the military docking station. Do you understand?"

"You do not dare do this!" the Oval officer blurted. "You would be at war with half of the galaxy!"

"Your polity is in a state of war with the United Stars of America," she said. "That makes this station a legitimate target." While she spoke, her imp was downloading the space station's data records, which among other things confirmed everything her criminal contacts had told her. The Ovals had betrayed the US, the egg-headed bastards. They hadn't gone so far as to declare war, but were basically rolling over and playing dead for the Tripartite Alliance.

"You cannot do this!" She wasn't sure if he meant she couldn't physically do it, but she decided to be literal about it.

By way of response, Heather had all the emergency doors of the military docking level shut closed, sealing Jeek and his bodyguards between two airlocks, one of which she could vent to space with a mental command of her imp.

"Wait!" the good captain shouted. "Wait!"

"Do you understand the situation now, Captain?"

Jeek made an affirmative gesture. The officers' double row of ridges, the only noticeable facial feature among Ovals, were turning purple with rage. "I understand," he said.

"You will proceed as follows," she continued. "All human personnel in the Nexus will leave the station, and your security officers will not hinder their movements in any way. The evacuees will board the starship *Maffeo Polo*, at which point we will exit into warp space. Under the circumstances, we will have to make a warp transition while in close proximity to your station, which will result in some property damage. I would like to say I am sorry for any needless destruction, but I would be lying if I did."

The purple ridges were now a deep magenta, and they were throbbing steadily, a clear sign Jeek was suffering from a massive stress-induced headache. She almost felt sorry for him.

"While the evacuation proceeds, the assault ships due to arrive in the next half an hour are to change course and head away from TN-11 until they move beyond firing range. They will not come any closer until after we are gone. Failure to comply will result in the destruction of this facility. Do you understand?"

'I understand," he repeated. It wasn't like the Ovals to fold so easily, but the sudden change in allegiances had taken the station's personnel by surprise, too. It took some work to switch mental gears and accept that former friendly neutrals had now become enemies. It'd taken Heather almost a minute to make that leap.

"Good," she said. "Maybe next time your superiors will know better than to threaten my country."

* * *

"I really must protest this seizure of private property," said the skipper of the *Maffeo Polo* for the umpteenth time. Heather had only heard the complaint about half a dozen times since she'd made it to the docking bay and waited for the last refugees to enter the ship, and she was already sick of it. She considered using her beamer on the merchant captain – on stun, of course – but decided that would complicate matters.

Fortunately for everyone concerned, the only American vessel in the system was a massive bulk cargo freighter, currently laden with a hundred and fifty thousand tons of fabber feedstocks earmarked for Sol System, eight warp transits away. Even with full holds, the ship had enough space for the six hundred or so humans in TN-11, although the accommodations would be Spartan at best and its life support system was going to be strained by having to provide basic consumables for ten times as many people as it was designed to keep alive.

"Protest all you want," Heather said. "Your ship was about to be seized by the Ovals, rather than borrowed by the US government. Not to mention you and your crew would have been interned and possibly killed."

The captain shut up, letting Heather consider the situation.

This was going to be almost as bad as the Days of Infamy. The Ovals had been major trading partners and there were hundreds of ships and thousands of humans inside their borders. Most of them wouldn't have any warning until they were captured or worse. The financial losses alone were going to badly hurt the country.

At least getting away wouldn't be a problem. New Jakarta was ten warp-hours away from the station. It was GACS space, but the Pan-Asians were on America's side. And given that the Ovals were clinging to at least the pretense of neutrality, their fleet wouldn't follow the *Polo* there. The US would have to decide whether seizing thousands of citizens and billions of dollars in property, not to mention allowing enemy forces to travel through Vehelian space, was enough provocation to declare war on the O-Vehel Commonwealth.

She shrugged. Deciding such things wasn't her job. She'd managed to save a few hundred souls, the best she could do under the circumstances. Her biggest regret was losing contact with Honest Septima, who'd been proving to be a priceless fountain of information about the Imperium.

"That's the last of them," Guillermo said. After he'd recovered from his shock, her fellow spy had helped organize the evacuation. Not bad for a suit.

"Going into warp while docked is going to destroy this entire level," the captain of the *Polo* said. "Tens of millions of GCUs in damage. And it will certainly be construed as an act of war!"

"They shouldn't have started it, then," she told him.

A few minutes later, the *Maffeo Polo* fled the system, tearing a big chunk out of TN-11's docking bay and leaving a mess of escaping atmosphere and electrical fires in its wake. There were no casualties, but the damage was just as bad as the captain had feared. And Heather didn't feel the least bit sorry about it.

The war had taken yet another turn. Warp-induced visions of destruction haunted her for the entire trip.

If you want to hear about new books before anyone else, join our Mailing List. We'll only send you notices about new releases, nothing more, nothing less. We hate spam as much as you do. For more news and information, check out our website: www.cjcarella.com

GLOSSARY

(**Note:** Some of the military/Marine jargon below comes from current and past terms used by the US military; others are made up, on the grounds that new terms would have been developed over the decades since First Contact).

03: Warp Marine Slang for someone with an infantry MOS, as opposed to a POG (see below).

1369: A fake MOS that indicate an individual is unlucky and wont to give oral pleasure to males of the species.

AFC: After First Contact. The new US calendar has Year Zero beginning on the day the Risshah bombed the Earth, killing some four billion people.

ALS-43: Automatic Launch System. Portable heavy weapon that fires a variety of 15mm ammunition, including grenades, armor-piercing and incendiary rounds. Also known as the All-Good or Alsie.

Area Force Field: A heavy force field can generate a sphere hundreds or even thousands of yards in diameter. Vehicle-mounted versions are used to protect advancing troops.

Blaster: Slang magnetically-propelled slug-throwers that usually fire plasma-explosive bullets. Also see Infantry Weapon Mk 3.

Biosphere Classes: The four known forms of life in the galaxy, which appear to descend from four primordial biology groupings that somehow spread throughout known space. Class One. Two and Three Biospheres are carbon-based but each has a distinct biochemical makeup that make them incompatible with each other. Class Four entities are silicon-based and can only survive under environments other classes find uninhabitable.

Bloomie: Thermal-pulse weapon of mass destruction, which generates a distinctive force field-contained 'blooming onion' shape that persists for several hours. Designed to minimize damage to the ecosystem, it generates heat without producing radiation or other effects, and the force fields radiate most of the heat beyond the planet's atmosphere after reducing everything within the area of effect to molten slag.

Bubblehead: slang for Navy spacers, from the shape of the

'astronaut' helmets issued during the early years after First Contact.

CVW: Carrier Space Wing. Operational naval space fighter organization comprising all warp fighter squadrons in a carrier vessel.

Dabrah: Pal, friend. Short for 'dudebro.'

Domass: Stupid, idiot. Contraction of the words 'dumb' and 'ass.'

ET: Extraterrestrial, common vernacular for aliens. Also rendered as Echo Tango, or simply Tango.

Eet, Eets: Slang version of ET; both terms are used interchangeably.

FNG: Fucking New Guy. Term of endearment for new soldiers and spacers.

Foxtrot-November: Unofficial acronym for 'Fucking Noob.' See also FNG.

Full Goldie/Goldilocks Planet: A world with conditions nearly identical to Earth's (95% or higher on all major categories, including oxygen/nitrogen mix, gravity, and average temperatures).

Gack, Gacks: Slang; derogatory term for the Greater Asia Co-Prosperity Sphere and its citizens.

Galactic Imperium: The largest known Starfarer polity, and the only one comprising several member species of roughly equal power.

Greater Asia Co-Prosperity Sphere (GACS): A federation comprising China, India, Russia and an assortment of Asian countries and former Soviet Republics. Other than the United Stars, it's the only human polity with a presence beyond the Solar System. Commonly referred to as the Pan-Asians or the Gacks.

HAW: Heavy Anti-Armor Weapon. Large missile usually mounted on combat vehicles or deployed by company-level anti-armor teams.

Hrauwah: Starfaring species and early US ally. Pseudo-canines with arboreal adaptations, the Hrauwah are social obligate carnivores vaguely resembling a cross between a dog and raccoon. Also see Puppies.

Imp(s): Short for 'implant,' a catchall term for the numerous bionic systems most humans use for communications, first-aid, protection and entertainment. Imp services include: full biomedical monitors, virtual reality displays, mapping and location apps, targeting and sensory arrays, among many others.

Infantry Weapon, Mark Three (IW-3): The standard issue

personal arm of the Marine Corps, a dual-barreled grenade launcher and assault rifle, firing 4mm explosive plasma rounds and 15mm airmobile ordnance grenades.

Iwo, Iwo-gun: Slang term for all Infantry Weapons.

Kirosha: A continent-spanning kingdom on the planet Jasper-Five; the same term is also used to refer to the inhabitants of the kingdom and its capital city.

Lampreys: Slang term for the Lhan Arkh species.

LAV: Land Assault Vehicle, an armored personnel carrier/infantry fighting vehicle, sixty tons in weight, capable of carrying an infantry squad, armed with a 25mm laser or a 30mm grav cannon, as well as four HAW missile launchers. Its gravity drive allows it to fly and maneuver at speeds of up to 300 mph, but its main purpose is to fight at ground level. Crewed by a driver, gunner and loader.

Lhan Arkh/Lhan Arkh Congress: Class One Starfarer species, commonly known as the Lampreys due to their funnel-shaped, tooth-ringed mouths. The Lhan Arkh Congress, a sort of communist oligarchy, is one of the largest polities in the known galaxy.

MBT-5 'Schwarzkopf': Main battle tank of the Marine Corps, a hundred-ton, gravity drive vehicle armed with a 250mm grav gun mounted on a turret, three 15mm ALS-43 guns, an Air-Defense Gatling laser on its cupola, and two 20mm plasma projectors (one coaxial on the turret, the other bow-mounted).

MEU: Marine Expeditionary Unit, consisting of an infantry battalion, and several organic attachments, including a tank platoon. The most common Corps deployment and administrative unit.

MOS: Military Occupational Specialty, a numerical code indicating a soldier's career field.

Obie: Someone performing his Obligatory Service, especially during the first two years.

Obligatory Service Term: A four-year military conscription system all US citizens must participate in. Eligibility starts at age sixteen; one must be enrolled before age twenty. Failure to comply is punishable by a four-year prison term and loss of citizenship status. In addition to basic military training, OST conscripts receive basic education equivalent to the last two years of high school and/or vocational training or college courses.

Nasstah/Nasstah Union: Class One Starfarer species, bearing some morphological and cultural similarities to the Rishtah (a.k.a. Snakes). Their largest polity, the Nasstah Union is openly hostile towards America and humanity in general. Commonly known as the Vipers.

Ovals: Slang term for the Vehelian species.

POG, Pogue: Person Other than a Grunt, used contemptuously for soldiers with non-combat occupational specialties and less frequently to refer to civilians in general.

Portable Force Field: A small area force field, usually configured to project a wall of force or a small bubble, meant to improve entrenchments and other fighting positions; it is too cumbersome to be used on the move. Issued at the squad or platoon level.

Pow, pows: Short for power pack, the high-density batteries used to supply energy to combat armor and some weapon systems. Not to be confused with P.O.W. (prisoner of war).

Puppies: Common term for the Hrauwah species, due to their resemblance to short-haired humanoid canines.

Rat: A derisive term for corporate employees, bureaucrats and city dwellers of all stripes, originating from a popular song from the First Century AFC.

Remfie: Civilian, especially those with little understanding or appreciation of the military. Less-commonly, military personnel operating far behind the lines who show same. Origin: REMF, Rear Echelon Motherfucker.

Risshah/Risshah Nest Collective: A Class One species brought into Starfarer society as a client of the Lhan Arkh Congress. The Nest Collective was largely destroyed in war with the USA, although a few million members survive under Lhan Arkh patronage.

Shellies: Slang term for tank crews.

Snakes: Derogatory term for the Risshah.

Stormin' Norman: Common nickname for the MBT-5 Schwarzkopf tank

Tango: Short for Echo Tango, or ET (see above), used somewhat less frequently than ET or Eet. Also, military vernacular for 'target.'

Textic/Textic-American English: Written form of modern English, notable for the use of shortened words, anagrams and other minimalist techniques to maximize meaning with the minimum number of letters, numbers and characters possible. The spoken version can be found mostly among the lower classes in human cities or enclaves.

United Stars of America: A nation comprising the former United States, Canada and portions of Mexico on Earth, as well as several dozen star systems around the galaxy.

Vehelians/O-Vehel Commonwealth: Class Two Starfarer species that has a mostly commercial relationship with the USA.

Vipers: Slang term for the Nasstah species.

Warp Rating: A living being's ability to endure entering warp space, ranging from 1 – can only endure warp travel while sedated or unconscious, to 4 – can enter warp in a sealed suit and survive. Less than ten percent of most Starfarer species (the average is closer to five percent) are warp-rated. Humans, for reasons not yet understood, are an extraordinary exception, with fifty percent of their population rated at level 1 or higher.

Wyrms: Slang term for members of the Wyrashat species.

Wyrashat Empire: A Starfarer polity dominated by the Class One species of the same name.

Made in the USA
Middletown, DE
31 August 2017